The Moonshawl

A Wraeththu Mythos Novel

The Moonshawl

A Wraeththu Mythos Novel

Storm Constantine

To Caroline
much love

xxx

IMMANION PRESS

Stafford England

The Moonshawl: A Wraeththu Mythos Novel
By Storm Constantine
© 2014

This is a work of fiction. All the characters and events portrayed in this book are fictitious, and any resemblance to real people, or events, is purely coincidental.

http://www.stormconstantine.co.uk

ISBN 978-1-907737-62-6

IP0041

Cover art by Ruby
Cover design and interior layout by Storm Constantine
Edited by Wendy Darling

Set in Palatino Linotype

An Immanion Press Edition
http://www.immanion-press.com
info@immanion-press.com

The Calendar of Wraeththu

January - Snowmoon
February – Frostmoon
March - Windmoon
April - Rainmoon
May - Flowermoon
June - Meadowmoon
July – Ardourmoon
August - Fruitingmoon
September - Harvestmoon
October - Vintagemoon
November - Mistmoon
December – Adkayamoon

Monday – Lunilsday (Lunday – Loon-day)
Tuesday – Miyacalasday (Calasday – Cah-laz-day)
Wednesday – Aloytsday (Loitsday – Low-its-day)
Thursday – Agavesday (Gavesday – Gar-vez-day)
Friday – Aruhanisday (Hanisday – Har-neez-day)
Saturday – Pelfazzarsday (Pelfday – Pelf-day)
Sunday – Aghamasday (Gamasday – Gah-mahz-day)

Contents

Acknowledgements

Thanks to everyone who helped me shape this novel. To Louise Coquio and Paula Wakefield, who were my critics and work-shoppers, and who hauled me over any gaping plot holes, and all those other niggling infelicities that plague the writer at work! To Wendy Darling for her keen editing and all the suggestions she made to strengthen the story. To Lisa Mansell who checked and corrected my Welsh! To Paul Cashman, for proof-reading and picking up those sneaky typos. To Andy Collins for his suggestions concerning the background to the story. And to Tanith Lee for her ongoing inspiration and support.

Introduction

The ancient spirit of Alba Sulh still lives. Perhaps now, released from human negligence, it stretches its soil-damp limbs, rises from protective sleep and sees the land is free again. I believe it to be a contrary spirit, rife with petty evils, random spurts of compassion, and incomprehensible notions. For a while, perhaps coiled around the clutching roots of those trees that remained and were regrowing, it watched, waiting to assess the new sentient beings who had come to live upon its skin; they might be the same as those who'd come before. But now, somehow, did it not have the power to affect those lives in a way it never had?

The spirit has many faces, many moods. It rides the gales above storm-bent forests as a throng of shrieking ghosts. It shivers as pale light in the deepest glades, offering promises with a silver smile. Animals can sense it – even see it. And hara? Hara are closer to it than their human forebears. This is the way we have been made to be, or the way our harlings are evolving. Alba Sulh desires to be wild and magical. It desires to be mysterious and misty, to seethe with phantoms and strange whims. This land was always that, a romantic, idealised archetype in the minds of human dreamers. Now, with only their thoughts and dreams remaining, they too ghosts amid the fields, Alba Sulh *becomes*.

Ysobi har Sulh

Chapter One

I rode to Gwyllion in the early summer time, through the ancient ochre and lilac mountains and then into their deep, lush river valleys, along the old road, where laden canopies of oak and beech and sycamore held hands above my head. The light was green, an intense deep glow of many subtle shades, sometimes almost black, sometimes pure emerald-shot gold. Mossy banks rose on either side of the road, warted with immense green and gold-furred rocks, over which an occasional root might trail, it too dressed in moss.

I was still not entirely well. The hurricanes of recent years still weighed heavily upon me. I was a stranger to myself, somehow reborn, renewed, but also older in my mind, burdened by knowledge, yet reassured in some small measure by wisdom.

Those of you who know my history – don't think I'd been sent from home as punishment or reward for my mistakes. The truth was that a phylarch of the Wyvachi, a sub-tribe of the Sulh, had a yearning to create his own spiritual customs for his hara. He wished for them to be taught in the way that hara in Immanion or Yorvik were taught. Not long after Bloomtide, early spring, a message came from the scholarly city of Kyme for me, whence such commissions often came: *You might be interested in this assignment, Ysobi.*

I debated for a month or so, afraid of change yet craving it. A couple of weeks before Feybraihatide I told Jassenah, my chesnari, about the commission, having already decided I would take it. We were in the kitchen of our small, comfortable house, with the windows open and scented air pouring in. Jassenah, with his thick dark gold hair tied back, ready for work, his expressive face unusually motionless as he listened to me, my inevitable lies. When my words fizzled out, there was a silence between us, as there often was. 'You wish to go?' he asked at last.

'I think I wish to work,' I told him. There was little for me in Jesith now. My former commissions were no more; I was not considered "suitable" to continue in that line of work. Somehar else was now the main hienama of the town. I was regarded as a scholar and, at the behest of our phylarch, Sinnar, had helped form the Lyceum of Jesith. I had become immersed in the land – its legends interested me – so I had been encouraged. Anything to put the past behind us.

'I see,' said Jassenah. 'What does this work entail exactly?'

'Apparently, a study of the landscape, its folklore, and the shaping of a suitable yearly round for the hara of Gwyllion.'

Jassenah eyed me steadily. 'And there is no local har to undertake this native task?'

I held his gaze, wondering why I felt as if I was deceiving him: this part was correct. 'The phylarch asked for a hienama of Kyme. We can only suppose he can afford it.'

'Are you asking me or telling me?' Jassenah enquired.

'I'd like to do it,' I replied. 'It sounds interesting. There could be a book in it.'

Again, a silence.

'The work is academic,' I said. 'And I'd hardly be missed here. I'd like to be doing something worthwhile.'

I was of course trying to escape some kind of parole on my life. In Jesith I was watched and constrained. I had no doubt the hara cared for me – they had welcomed me back after all – but they couldn't trust me in the way they had. I accepted this. I hadn't proved trustworthy.

Jassenah had turned away from me, tidying pots that were already tidy. 'How long for?' he asked. 'How long do you intend to be away?'

'A few months or so. You and Zeph could visit me. The countryside is said to be beautiful up there.'

Jassenah faced me again. 'Can you be honest with me, Ys? Are we really talking about how you need to escape *this* place –

perhaps *us*?'

I paused before answering. 'While we've been talking I realise I want to escape,' I said, 'but not *us*. Jesith makes me claustrophobic. It's like an open prison.' I took a breath, wondering if the next thing I said would be appropriate. 'We could even go together.'

Jassenah snorted. 'Of course I have the time for that!' He shook his head, laughed shakily. 'Ys, if you want to go, go. I'm not your gaoler. I appreciate it's sometimes difficult for you here.' He put his hands on my shoulders. 'But Jesith is my home, it's my life. I love what I do here. I don't want to leave.'

'I wasn't thinking of anything that permanent,' I said.

'I know... It would be good for you to go. I'm being selfish. I can't keep you on a leash.'

'You don't have to. I thought you knew that now.'

He nodded, smiled at me, turned away. He'd never trust me again.

In the late afternoon of a glorious Flowermoon day, I rode my piebald cob, Hercules, into Gwyllion. I'd travelled light, bringing with me only several changes of clothes, three books, and a few basic toiletries. This lightness had made the journey easier for both Hercules and myself. We'd grown even lighter as we travelled. Gwyllion was a small town with a modest population, and even from the start I found the hara innately tribal. Their phylarch was like a king to them. He lived with his family on an estate to the north of the village. Before going to introduce myself to the lord of Wyvachi, I sought out a local inn – there were only two in Gwyllion – and booked a room there. The keephar of The Rooting Boar asked me, naturally, what brought me to their town, and I explained I'd been hired by the phylarch.

The inn was empty at that time of day, so the keephar came to sit with me to satisfy his curiosity about a stranger to his town. He told me his name was Yoslyn.

'Oh, the hienama!' said the keephar. 'We were told of this. It will be good to celebrate the festivals again.'

'You have no hienama?' I asked. A certain discomfort settled over me.

'Not now,' said Yoslyn.

'And there's nohar among you wanted to take that role?'

'Not really. Hara have too much to do around here for that. We want somehar to do it for us, make the blessings, talk to the corn for us... naming days, chesna bonds, all that.'

'Well, I didn't think my work here would...'

Yoslyn interrupted airily, as if I hadn't spoken. 'Tiahaar Wyva told us he'd sent to Kyme for a Nahir Nuri for us. It will be wonderful for the community. Pity you're here too late for the Feybraihatide arojhahn. Many of us want to revive the old customs. Mixing them with the new, of course!'

My imagination obligingly presented me with a grisly visualisation of hara being slaughtered in the fields at Cuttingtide. The phylarch, Wyva, clearly had not presented his requirements to Kyme accurately. Or perhaps that had been deliberate. 'I can train somehar up,' I said, 'to do these things for you when I leave.'

Yoslyn gave me rather a hard look. 'I doubt you'll find anyhar round here keen on that,' he said. 'We're simple hara. We like a simple life, and we've no time for so much learning. It takes a special har to be a hienama. You have to want to be one, for a start.'

I could hardly blame him for these sentiments. 'Well, we'll see,' I said, smiling with what I hoped was suitable brightness. 'I'll talk to tiahaar Wyva and find out what's needed.'

First impressions of a har, unbiased, are always useful, but so is the information you can get from the hara who regard him as lord of their lives. You can tell a lot, for example, from whether he is loved, reviled or scorned, or the words that are not spoken – in fear.

'So tell me of the family,' I said. 'The family of Wyva har Wyvachi.'

The keephar smiled, a good sign. It was a smile of affection, reflecting a certain amount of humour. Perhaps Wyva was not wholly wise. 'There is Wyva, who is phylarch, as you know, his chesnari Rinawne and their harling, Myv. He's a strangeling child, or changeling maybe. Sweet, but distant as a star. He walks his own path, they say.'

I nodded. 'Born this way?'

'They say so.'

Hesitation? Perhaps I wanted it to be there, a mystery to solve.

'The household is not overly large. Wyva is second generation and has two brothers, Cawr and Gen. Wyva and Cawr have taken the bond, but only Wyva has made new hara from the blood. Meadow Mynd is an old house, and was in Wyva's family long before his hostling became har.'

'That's unusual to find,' I said, with a gossipy inflection in my voice. I indicated with the wine bottle in my hand that the keephar should join me in refreshment. He appeared eager to do so.

'The Mynd is a beautiful house,' he said as he filled a cup. 'None would leave it willingly, and none did.' He laughed as he took a drink. 'Wyva is a good har, and fair. He'd see none go hungry.'

'What of his chesnari?'

'Good, too. We have no complaints with any of them.' Again he laughed. 'As long as you don't toss the count stones with Wyva's brother, Gen. He's a renowned cheat!'

'I shall take care not to.'

'We need a hienama,' Yoslyn said firmly. 'The spirits are strong in these fields and forests.'

This remark took me by surprise. 'Can you explain to me what you mean?'

Yoslyn shook his head. 'You'll see. It's not a bad place; it is rich. But the spirits are strong.'

The road to Meadow Mynd was a summer tunnel, a faery path rising to sun-stippled heights, then down to green shadowy hollows. To either side, legions of pines in straight lines marched away from me. These, I supposed, were a legacy of earlier human forestry; the pines had not been harvested for over a century. To the west of me, paths of sunlight carved down the occasional wide avenues between the trees. They looked like processional ways. And then eventually, I saw upon one of these paths a figure on a horse, rendered in silhouette by the afternoon sun. Horse and rider were both so still, some three hundred yards from me. I had no inclination to pause, to call, or to investigate. Neither did I think I'd seen something supernatural, even though I'd perceived a deep purple glow around the horse. I had to keep moving.

Meadow Mynd eventually came into view when the pines thinned out and gave way to older, deciduous trees. Massive oaks spread their history against the skies. I caught the silver glimmer of water through the aching green, and a herd of deer for some time walked beside me, some distance off amid the mossy trunks. They were unafraid and watched me curiously, the does sometimes pausing to stare unashamedly, heads up, ears forward. Perhaps hara from the house fed them, and they associated me with that. As I rode Hercules at a walk up the driveway, I heard the tolling of a bell in the distance. An odd time of day for that, I thought, unless it was to gather hara in from the fields. It was a beautiful, yet melancholy sound that reminded me of days long gone, my lost human childhood.

The house was grey and sprawling, its walls peppered with yellow lichen, its windows small and frowning, but for some on the ground floor, which were like doors. Hara were at work in the gardens – which appeared to be a meld of both ornamental and vegetable, all strangely mixed up together – and paused in their labours to watch me draw near. Above the front door was a wide lintel of stone, supported by two columns adorned with twisted ivy, of both carved stone and living leaf. A harling squatted atop the lintel like some kind of gargoyle. I assumed this to be the son of Wyva and Rinawne and waved to him. The harling regarded me expressionlessly,

17

and then bounded away up the wall behind him like a wild beast, leaping through the old ivy stems. I could see now what Yoslyn meant about him.

A har came out of the house, perhaps having been alerted by a member of staff. I didn't know who of the family I was looking at, or even if it was just a high-ranking employee. He was nearly as tall as me, with a thick mane of loose, curling black hair. His brows were thick, his mouth wide, his eyes a striking blue. He was not conventionally beautiful, but possessed an arresting presence. I could tell at once he was a har used to getting his own way.

'You must be Ysobi har Jesith,' he said to me, inclining his head. He had a strong Erini accent. 'You're welcome here to the Mynd.'

'Thank you, tiahaar...'

'I am Rinawne har Wyvachi. Please, come on in. Our hara will see to your horse.' He jerked his head and a har previously unseen came running from... somewhere. He led Hercules and my baggage away, seemingly before my feet were properly in contact with the ground.

'Good journey?' enquired Rinawne.

'A good time of year to travel, yes,' I replied.

'You must want a meal...'

'No need, tiahaar. I stopped at an inn in town before coming here, booked myself a room.'

Rinawne's eyebrows lifted. 'We have accommodation for you. Private. Not in the house.'

'Oh, that's kind of you.' I had, of course, expected this, but it was best not to make assumptions.

'I'll send somehar to cancel your reservation. Do you have luggage?'

'Only what I have in my horse's saddlebags.'

Rinawne grinned. 'You travel light, then.' He gestured. 'Come in. We'll take refreshment anyway. I always look upon any excuse for it as a gift.'

I laughed. 'Thank you.'

'Wyva will be here soon,' Rinawne said. 'He's out doing something somewhere, perhaps looking at a field or a ditch. Such things concern him.'

Again I laughed, hoping that was meant to be a joke.

Rinawne smiled widely. He conducted me into a living room that smelled strongly of roses. A huge bowl of them adorned a table beneath a window. 'The scent of flowers is like bringing the outside in with you, isn't it?' Rinawne said, brushing a hand over the white petals. As he moved I caught a scent from him, which I can only describe as *green*; something of cut grass, of reedy hollows, of the darkest corners of summer.

'Where I come from – Jesith – is famous for its vineyards,' I said. 'The aroma of the vine, of the grape, is very strong. They even make a perfume of it.'

'I hope you've bought samples of both products with you,' Rinawne said.

I hadn't. 'I regret it didn't occur to me to bring any produce with me.' That is the sort of thing Jass would have thought of, naturally, as would Zeph, our son. I should have thought of it, too. Perhaps Jass had even mentioned it to me, but I'd not heard him. That was not an uncommon happening, as he was fond of telling hara. 'As the industry has grown in our town, so has the variety of produce. My chesnari works for the yard. He's the manager for our phylarch. I'll write to him, have him make up a hamper. I really should have thought of it, as he'll no doubt remind me!'

Rinawne grinned. 'Oh, don't trouble yourself about it. I was being presumptuous, as Wyva often likes to remind *me*!' He grinned. 'Although I do love presents! It seems we both have our weaknesses, tiahaar.' He gestured at one of the sofas, which was upholstered in faded green and cream tapestry. 'Please, sit down.'

I did so and he sat opposite me, leaning back with one arm along the top of the sofa, his legs loosely crossed. 'So you are here to invent a religion for us,' he said, still smiling.

'I wouldn't put it quite that way,' I replied. 'A community benefits from shared spirituality, and it's best if that spirituality can be drawn from the local environment itself. I'm interested in folklore, in history. The land has many tales to tell.'

'To be sure,' Rinawne agreed.

I paused. 'The keephar of The Rooting Boar advised me the spirits around here are very strong. Did he mean anything in particular by that?'

Rinawne inhaled deeply through his nose, perhaps slightly impatient. 'Hara want ghosts, they want mysteries. In your position, I'd do my best to give them.' He grinned. 'As you might be able to tell, I don't follow faithfully the heritage of my home country. I'm not the most spiritual of hara.'

'Not spiritual, and perhaps a sceptic,' I said, smiling also, 'but are there no special... energies to this area? A sceptic might give me a more accurate opinion than a dazzle-eyed believer.'

'Now, here's the thing,' said Rinawne, leaning forward a little. 'I *wouldn't* call myself a sceptic particularly. I've my own tales to tell.' He wrinkled his nose. 'There are... spots that raise my hair here and there. This is an old land, soaked in blood. We hara are sensitive to echoes, aren't we?'

'Yes,' I said simply.

Rinawne suddenly became alert, twisted his body to look out of the window behind us. 'Ah, here is Wyva,' he said. 'I'll go and organise us some tea.'

And so he left me, before his consort and lord of this domain came into the room: Wyva har Wyvachi. The phylarch looked at the air in the doorway as if he perceived a shadow passing by, then he turned to me, smiled. 'You must be Ysobi. Thank you for coming here.'

'My pleasure,' I replied, getting to my feet.

Wyva waved a hand at me. 'No need for that. Please, sit.'

I did so. Wyva was a slim har of medium height, with rich brown hair that hung down his back, a swathe of it drawn away from his face into a band decorated with feathers and what appeared to be a rabbit's foot. His face was finely sculpted, and suggested a sensitive character. I perceived the smallest of weaknesses in the chin, but it could be overlooked. 'Tiahaar Rinawne told me you have accommodation for me,' I said. 'I'd like to thank you for that, too.'

Wyva's smile widened. 'Well, you'll need somewhere to work, won't you? And I'm sure the place I've chosen will fascinate you. It's called Dŵr Alarch, an old tower, built as a folly some hundreds of years ago. It was renovated late in the human era and used as a holiday home. In winter and early spring you can see it from here, but the trees hide it during other seasons. At night, if you light all the lamps, it can be seen from three counties, or so the story goes.'

'Then I hope it has ghosts,' I said.

Wyva laughed. 'Oh, plenty of them! This land does seem to retain them as much as the lichen on the rocks. There is a wealth of material out there for you to discover.'

'I can already feel it,' I said, and indeed my senses were twitching eagerly, wanting to be immersed in this magical landscape. I felt it wasn't going to be difficult constructing a rich and mystical system for these hara, tuning in to whatever was around me.

Rinawne reappeared, accompanied by a har bearing a tray laden with things to eat and drink. The vanilla aroma of freshly-baked cake filled the room and made me hungry. After we'd set about helping ourselves to these refreshments, Wyva told me of his library. 'The volumes here have been collected by my family for many hundreds of years.'

This was an unusual statement, of course. He was clearly referring to human ancestors as well as harish ones. I simply nodded, my mouth full of cake.

'Among them are quite a few titles concerning local folklore. In fact, an ancestor of mine wrote three of them. You're welcome to frequent the library as often as you wish, as if it were your own. The doors here are never locked. Come and go as you please.'

'That's generous of you.'

Wyva made an airy gesture with one arm. 'It's not a problem. But for the most part, I wouldn't be surprised if you merely wish to walk in the fields and forests. That is perhaps the true library of this landscape.'

I nodded. 'Most certainly, but other... *people's* experiences and thoughts are very interesting. I love folklore and personal accounts. Even if it's just down to wishful thinking or hallucination, it produces rich imagery.'

Wyva laughed. 'You could say that! There are some very colourful stories.'

'I'll show you over to the tower shortly,' said Rinawne. 'We'll need to take supplies. I thought everything should be fresh for you.'

'That's wonderful, thank you.'

'Yes, settle in,' said Wyva, 'then please join us here for dinner later. We can discuss how you wish to proceed. If you need volunteers, we can supply them.'

'Volunteers?' I was puzzled.

'Well, for the majhahns you'll write,' Wyva said. 'Get hara to perform them, get feedback.'

'Oh, yes... I see.' I paused, wondering if now was the right moment to broach what had sprung back to mind, then pressed on. 'The keephar at The Boar seemed to think I was being appointed as your new hienama. Is that in fact what you're looking for, ultimately?'

Wyva laughed. 'I think perhaps that is what hara *hope* for, not necessarily what I had in mind, at least not with you.'

'I agree a community benefits from a spiritual leader,' I said, 'and perhaps I can help train one up for you, but I'm not really in the position to commit myself to staying here in that role.'

'I understand,' Wyva said amiably. 'It wasn't what I asked for. The hara in the town jump to conclusions.'

Rinawne snorted. 'Is that what it is?'

Wyva gave him a sharp glance, said nothing.

'I take it you had one before... a hienama that is?'

I could see Wyva attempted swiftly to cover a silence. 'We

did, yes – Rey – but he left the post. Hara are simply feeling the loss of that, mainly because they enjoy the seasonal celebrations. As you said, I'm sure it wouldn't be difficult to train somehar else to take charge of that.'

I realised then that something had happened here. A shiver went through me, for I was no stranger to communities being affected by "happenings" concerning hienamas.

We could see Dŵr Alarch long before we reached it, so the trees didn't do that good a job at hiding it. The tower was hexagonal, a dark column atop its hill, surrounded by soaring beeches where crows roosted. There were many long, arched windows and it was crowned by a crenellated battlement, over which was a high, domed glass roof. 'The top floor is a nayati of sorts,' Rinawne told me. 'Wyva had that roof put in around fifteen years ago, so that whoever lived here could see the stars.'

'Without going outside,' I added. I was leading Hercules, who kept bumping his nose into my back.

Rinawne chuckled. 'Indeed. It's a good room, however.' Before we entered the tower, Rinawne indicated a stable where Hercules could be housed. 'There is a field below you may use if you want him to roam free.'

Rinawne now led me to the foot of the tower and removed an enormous black iron key from his coat pocket. Before applying it to the lock, he held it out for me to see. 'Isn't this marvellous? It should open a door to secrets.'

'Perhaps it does,' I said lightly.

Again, Rinawne laughed and opened the door. 'As long as the secrets aren't mice and damp, I'll be happy.' He led the way inside.

The entrance hall, if it could be called that, was tiny. A door led off to a hidden series of rooms, which Rinawne told me comprised a laundry, a second toilet, a generator and the heating arrangements. 'Most ghosts can be traced to the wheezing of the boiler,' he said. 'Any trouble with it, and we'll send somehar from the house. We have a har who is a boiler whisperer; he gets it to obey.' Rinawne indicated the stone stairway that curled around the inner wall. 'First floor is the kitchen. Shall we inspect?'

We'd brought with us panniers of supplies and together hauled them upstairs. The steps were steep. There was a rope affixed to the wall to aid the climb and the air was chill, even though the day outside was not. The cold seeped from the very walls. Yet the long windows around every corner dispelled any tendency to gloom the stairwell might otherwise have held.

I'd been expecting rather austere accommodation, but was pleasantly surprised when Rinawne opened the heavy wooden door upon the first room. A breath of warm air came out, scented with honeysuckle, which must emanate from a shallow brass bowl of dried flowers on the dresser. The rather dank, chill atmosphere of the stairway disappeared entirely. The floor was of tawny polished wood, as were the table and chairs, and the shelves of the large dresser were stacked with crockery. An immense cooking range dominated one part of the room, and three of the long, arched windows looked out upon the landscape. I could see a farm we had not passed, since we'd followed a path through the forest. 'There you will get your milk, cheese and eggs,' Rinawne said, following my gaze. 'And meat if you want it. Choose yourself a chicken and it will be delivered, plucked and gutted, to your door in time for dinner. Have it charged to Wyva's account.' He grinned. 'Let's not unpack your stuff yet. Have a look at the rest of the place, then I'll leave you to settle in.'

He left the room and bounded up the stairs two at time. I followed. The next room was the living room, although Rinawne told me that in his experience people who'd stayed here usually chose the kitchen as the room in which they spent most time. However, this room was beautiful to me. The walls were a dark, muted mulberry colour, and the furniture and ornaments were Oriental in style, also of dark reds and golds. The floor was a mass of thick patterned rugs, and heavy indigo-coloured drapes hung at the long windows. 'This is amazing,' I said, 'more than I expected.'

'Some hara find it a bit much,' Rinawne said, 'a bit heavy. It's not to my taste really.'

'Well, it's entirely to mine,' I said. 'I think I'll be very comfortable here.'

'Let's show you the rest, then.'

The next storey housed the bathroom. This had a floor of black and white tiles and an immense snowy bath that stood upon gilded, elegantly-clawed feet. The washbasin was similarly huge and along the walls brass lion heads held in their jaws an array of thick golden yellow towels. The toilet was more like a throne, as it was surrounded by a wooden alcove. There were carved arms where I might rest my own. 'Whoever built and furnished this place liked luxury,' I said, running my hand over the carvings above the toilet; two gargoyles and a griffon posed to gaze down upon whoever sat there.

'Luxury or excess,' Rinawne said. 'Most of the place is the same as it's been for a very long time. Wyva keeps it cared for.'

'It must have meant something to his... family, then.'

Rinawne nodded. 'Heritage hasn't gone away in this part of the world. You don't find it often, but Wyva's family don't see themselves as that far apart from their earlier human ancestors. They merely underwent a *change*, then everything carried on as before. Well, nearly everything. Come, let's look at the main bedroom.'

As I turned to leave, a shiver went through me and I looked back quickly. An image went through my head of clocks, immense clocks. I saw a brief flash before my mind's eye of this room and it was not a bathroom. The floor was still of black and white tiles, but it was mostly empty. I was aware of presences I could not see, or rather could not focus upon. 'This wasn't always just a bathroom,' I blurted out.

Rinawne came back to me as he'd already gone partway up the stairs to the next floor. 'What do you mean?'

I laughed, somewhat shakily. 'Forgive me, I just had an

impression, that's all. I have a feeling this room was used... in some way... for ritual.'

'Really?' Rinawne didn't sound convinced. 'Well, I suppose you must pick things like that up, although I'd always believed this place to be only a folly, in every sense. But then it is very old.'

'It was probably nothing,' I said, mustering what I hoped was a plausible smile. 'The bedroom, then?'

'You'll love it,' Rinawne said.

And I did. Unlike the living room, it was a light and airy space, with a wide divan covered in a gold quilt, beneath which were sheets of a delicate silvery grey. The walls were also of this dove-like colour and rolled with faint traceries of gold, so that it was like some kind of rich marble. A frieze of stylised swans ran around the top of the room. The rugs beneath my feet, laid over a golden wooden floor, were thick white fleeces. 'Sumptuous,' I said, inadequately.

'This is my favourite room,' Rinawne said, running the fingers of one hand lightly over the wall by the door. 'I like light and air, and believe me a great deal of the Mynd was dark and gloom when I first came here. The house sort of *squats*, I think. Its ceilings are low, so you have to curb its liking for dreariness. I was allowed to make a few changes only to certain rooms.'

I nodded, at first unsure of what to say to that. 'Old places can be gloomy.' I wondered then how Rinawne and Wyva had met, what circumstances had thrown them together. I had not so far detected any great passion between them, and yet they did have a son, so at one time things must have been different.

'I won't show you to the top room,' Rinawne said, somewhat mischievously. 'I'll let you find that for yourself. There's a spare bedroom beneath it, in case you should ever have guests, but it's fairly plain to look at in comparison to the rest of the chambers.'

'What does the name mean, Dŵr Alarch?'

'The Swan Tower,' Rinawne replied. 'I believe it's always

been called that.' He smiled. 'Come to the house around 6.30,
and meet everyhar. *That* will be an experience for you!'

'That daunting?'

Rinawne shook his head, grinning. 'No, they are an
interesting bunch, a host of stories all bundled together. You'll
enjoy it. I expect Wyva will ask some of the town assembly hara
along as well. They'll be curious about you.'

I ducked my head. 'I'll look forward to it.'

'Until later, then.' Rinawne swept a bow to me. 'Enjoy
exploring.'

And with that, he was gone, as suddenly as a phantom, but
for the light patter of his feet upon the cold stairway, and I was
alone in the silence of my new home.

Before investigating the top room – and I was aware of
relishing the delay – I decided to make myself some tea and
unpack my belongings and supplies. As I descended the spiral
stairs I was aware of the hum of the place, its non-silence that
had no sound. I had no doubt that it was sentient, watching me.
A spirit of place was gauging whether I'd fit in.

Rinawne had been lavish with the supplies and I quickly
filled the cupboards and cold store with produce. I put my
belongings in the bedroom, the clothes, the three books, and
my meagre toiletries in the bathroom. I felt these few items
were all I possessed, that I'd left nothing behind. I'd lost my
interest in *things* some years before. A lot of the time my life felt
like I was acting, waiting for the play to finish, somewhat tired
with it. Perhaps this landscape would revive me, intrigue me
with its mysteries. Perhaps I would learn to trust again, not
least in myself.

I made my tea and poured a second cup for the spirit of the
tower. I was not yet sure completely where its heart lay, but
decided to put my offering in the living room. However, as I
stepped beyond the kitchen door into the cold breath of the
stairwell, the basement called to me strongly, so I went down
there instead. The door was stiff in its frame and required my
shoulder to open it. Inside, the air smelled strangely hot, and of

metal. There was a monstrous boiler in there, a fairly compact muttering generator, and a series of ancient wide and shallow sinks; presumably, the laundry area Rinawne had referred to. There was a small toilet room with more antique fittings, and a narrow window misted over with spider webs and caked dust, above a window sill drifted with dead flies. Clearly, care of the tower did not extend greatly into this lower area. Still, it was here the tower wanted me to leave the tea, so I did, on a wide wooden table near the sinks. I bowed to the room. 'Let us be of service to one another,' I said, and went back upstairs.

I sat for thirty minutes or so, half drowsing, gazing out over the landscape through the long windows of the kitchen. Whatever phantoms might lurk within the stones of this place, the atmosphere was benign, comfortable. A dog was barking down at the farm, in a curious gulping, endless way. I did not like the sound of that; it was mean and hostile. Mostly likely a guardian creature to be avoided.

Then it was time to visit the topmost room, find out if it would welcome me. Out into the gelid stairway again, fancying my breath actually misted the air, although I'm sure it could not really have done, and on up the twisting stone gullet to the top of the tower. When I opened the door to the highest room, a waft of old incense drifted out, reminding me strongly of my original home in Jesith, the resins I used to burn there. The floor was again pale wood, polished to a satin sheen, and covered mostly by a thick crimson carpet that was patterned with black geometric designs. There were several altars or shrines around the walls, all of them empty, as were the two bookcases that lay between them. The windows here had no drapes, but there were blinds that could be lowered over them. I gazed up at the glass dome above and saw this too could be robed. The blinds that cleverly moulded themselves to its shape were cobalt blue and decorated with white stars, some of which were quartz sewn into the stiffened fabric. Stars, real or not, were available at all times here.

Of all the rooms in the tower, here was where the resident

could make his mark. The other spaces were filled with furniture and decorations of Wyva's choice, but here, apart from the carpet, the blinds and the very basics of furnishings, it was waiting for a personality to imprint itself. My few books would do little to fill the empty shelves, and I'd brought no ritual paraphernalia with me, but I would enjoy foraging in the forests and fields around me for items to adorn the vacant shrines. Perhaps Wyva wouldn't mind me borrowing books for these forlorn shelves.

For a moment, I was taken back to my old home; how I'd loved it. I remembered the pleasure of teaching, and not simply the obvious parts of it that later I was condemned for. Perhaps some vile spirit had lived in me once, but it was hard to remember. That was like looking back at a different life, a dream. I hadn't meant to be vile, certainly, but I knew I'd been cruel. What had driven me to that? It had driven me almost to my own death, a taint maybe of human life, a shred of sickness inside, shrieking and throwing itself against the walls like a maddened creature locked in a dark space. It was dead. It had to be dead. Now.

Standing there, in the opulent glow of that room in waiting, with the mellow sunlight of late afternoon making narrow paths of light through the trees, I felt I had somehow come home again. I was scornful of the past and everyhar in it. Here, I might live once more. Here, I might be respected and loved as a trusted friend. In Jesith, even my son had been taken from me by my history. When he looked at me, it was through the eyes of the stories he'd heard, half wary, half pitying, but with very little love.

Again, as in the nether regions of the tower, I bowed to the room and said aloud, 'Let us be of service to one another.'

Chapter Two

Before I went back to Meadow Mynd, I investigated the small collection of buildings that clustered some distance from the foot of the tower. There were two stables, one of course containing Hercules, and several sheds where coal or wood might be stored. There was a run for chickens; eggs on my doorstep would be agreeable. I'd ask about procuring a few birds of my own.

The forest spread below me; an archetypal magical landscape. So many rich hues. Perhaps I would paint it. And then, from the murmuring depths, came a thin skein of song, utterly beautiful. I would have liked it to be the voice of some magical being, but it was most likely that of a har walking home through the trees. Who wouldn't be inspired to sing in such a place as this? I couldn't make out the words, and the song wasn't melancholy, but there was a sweet wistfulness to it, like the memory of pain, when it no longer hurts but is faintly remembered. Tears came to my eyes but did not fall. I listened to the wondrous song, gazing through a fabulous watery glimmer that rendered the scene around me into a hazy mist of colours. Perfect.

I decided to walk to the Mynd rather than ride, so as to immerse myself more in the landscape. Approaching the house along the path through the trees was like walking towards the start of a fairy tale. The sun had made bronze of the light and already a lamp of welcome gleamed above the porch. Lights were many in the lower windows, while the occasional dim glow from higher casements suggested further tales to me: the strange harling Myv in his room, reluctant to come downstairs, perhaps with a harried carehar pleading with him to behave, suppressing the urge to slap and drag. Perhaps another room concealed a brooding relative, or a pair of lovers, one of whom is chesna with another har waiting in the room below. Perhaps there was a dim-lit room that had no har in it at all but for memories, a sigh, a shadow across the window.

Smiling at these fancies, I went to the front door and found, as Wyva had earlier indicated, that it stood wide open. Surely they would close it at night? I ventured inside, glancing into the drawing room on my right where Rinawne had taken me earlier. Dimly lit, it was empty of living presences. I noticed now what Rinawne had mentioned; how low the ceilings were. In large old houses of earlier human eras, the tendency had been for space and height, perhaps as a mark of affluence. Here, the house seemed to hug itself, with its narrow passages and dark corners, although I could appreciate how it could create a more homely and informal atmosphere than somewhere grand and spacious.

A grey, rough-coated hound came into the stone-floored hall ahead of me, from somewhere deeper in the shadows of the house. He or she regarded me curiously for some moments before padding off. I thought I might as well follow the animal, and indeed it led me into a room where four hara were gathered. One of them was Wyva. The dog went up to him and pressed its head against his thigh. He caressed the creature, at the same time noticing me at the threshold. 'Tiahaar Ysobi, welcome,' he said. 'Please, come in.'

All the hara turned to look at me. Two were clearly close relatives of Wyva's, perhaps brothers, or even his hostling or father. It is difficult to tell a har's age from his face. Only when they speak can the years be sensed. The other was young, awkward and blond-haired, and had blunter features than his companions. While the three older hara stood together, drinking wine, this younger one was hunched on a chair before the fireplace, hands thrust between his knees, his lower legs splayed. He must be at least five years past feybraiha, I decided, yet still itchy in his skin.

I inclined my head to the company and came forward. They

all greeted me affably enough.

'This isn't everyhar,' Wyva said, 'and you might meet more of us later, but for now I'd like to present to you my brothers, Gen and Cawr.' Wyva handed to me a glass of red wine, which I took.

'Welcome,' said the har named as Cawr. He was more robust-looking than Wyva, fuller of face, whereas Gen, his sibling, looked to be all the cheat that Yoslyn had hinted at. His face was narrow, his eyes a little slanted, his smile that of a satyr. Yet for all that, the good-natured spark in his eyes did not suggest a har of evil character, simply a tricky one.

'I've been settling into my tower,' I said. 'An amazing place.'

Wyva smiled warmly. 'Glad you like it, but I guessed you would from the moment I met you. I love the old place, and make sure it's coddled and loved.'

'I can see that,' I said.

'You've been long awaited,' said Gen, grinning. 'I don't know how much time you've set aside for research and writing, but brace yourself for an inundation of requests for chesnabonds, harling naming and festivals for every possible excuse. I hope you're good at stretching time.'

'I took a course in it at Kyme,' I said.

Gen laughed. 'Being able to duplicate yourself might also be of use.'

'My skills in that are rusty.'

Wyva appeared a trifle uncomfortable with this mildly flirty exchange. 'Everyhar knows why Tiahaar Ysobi is here with us,' he said stiffly. 'Anything else we receive from him is a bonus.'

'I'm sure,' Gen said, taking a drink of his wine. His eyes never left my own. I would have to take care with this one.

Before anything else could be said, Rinawne appeared at the doorway, in what can only be described as a 'grand entrance'. His thick curling hair was starred with small white flowers, his costume of tunic and trousers fashioned from flowing cream fabric. His eyes seemed to blaze from his wide pale face. And at his side was the changeling creature, Myv. He did not appear shy or even sullen, only rather *not there*.

'Greetings, harakin,' drawled Rinawne. He raised a hand to them.

I watched for signs of dislike in the Wyva-clan, or discomfort, but there appeared to be none. They greeted Rinawne pleasantly and easily enough. I did notice, though, their eyes skim over the harling, as if they didn't want to dwell on him too long. Nohar greeted him and he said nothing.

'You must be Myv,' I said to him.

He looked at me with disinterest, but was trained enough to say, 'Hello.'

The harling had a look of Rinawne about him, the wider, high-cheekboned face, the thick dark tumbling hair. 'Easy to see your hostling in you,' I said.

The harling grimaced. 'No, he's not in me. No.'

Rinawne laughed lightly. 'Wyva is his hostling, tiahaar.'

I reddened at the mistake. Because Rinawne was dressed in flowing garments and had a flamboyant air, I'd judged him to be soume-prevalent and therefore typical hostling material. I should have known better, and was glad my chesnari and son had not been here to witness it, since it was the kind of thing they loved to scold me about. 'Forgive me,' I said, bowing my head. Fortunately, it appeared the Wyvachi siblings had recommenced their conversation and had not noticed my gaffe. The young har set apart, however, was grinning at me. Myv went over to him and squeezed beside him on the chair.

'Don't worry,' Rinawne said. 'You're not the first to come to that conclusion, nor will be the last. Myv spends most of his time with me, so the bond does appear at first glance to be like that of hostling and harling.'

I was grateful for his graciousness. 'I've fallen in love with the tower,' I said. 'The ritual room is marvellous. It makes me eager to start work here.'

'I can take you to a few interesting local sites tomorrow, if you like,' Rinawne said. 'Tell you a few stories along the way, get you started.' He smiled.

'Thank you.' I had planned to roam around alone, but the prospect of hearing tales appealed to me.

Several more hara joined our company. Introductions were made, but the names didn't remain in my memory that night. Modryn, the chesnari of Cawr arrived, but no more harlings. Two hara from the town made an appearance, to whom I was introduced. They were members of the Gwyllion Assembly, a town council. One of these hara was Selyf, a tall scholarly-looking individual, who was the keephar of an inn named The Crowned Stag. 'I hope we will see you there,' he said. The other was a farmer named Tryskyr who, second to Wyva, owned the most land in the area.

After around half an hour spent in formal conversation, none of which I found particularly interesting, a househar announced that dinner was ready and the company surged towards the dining room further into the house. Here, a coven of candles burned in ornate candelabra placed upon the table, augmented by the glow of a round moon that flew in through the uncurtained windows and alighted upon every surface like a silver bird. I was aware of a strange sense of imminence as I took my seat next to Wyva, who sat at the head of the table. Rinawne commanded the other end of the board, with Myv beside him, fidgeting.

'No suggestion the Whitemanes were going to send somehar here to meet tiahaar Ysobi?' Cawr said to Wyva, in a sarcastic tone. A househar glided ghostlike around the table dispensing soup from a silver cauldron held by a silent harling at his side.

Wyva grunted, pulled a sour face briefly. 'I'd expect to see the sky turn upside down before that.'

'You never know,' Gen said. 'They have their whims. At the very least, you'd expect them to be curious. They weren't that averse to Rey, despite his close connection to us.'

Wyva made a noise of irritation. 'Nohar knows what motivates or interests them, really.'

'The Whitemanes are local oddities,' Rinawne explained to

me. 'Many of the hara around here believe them to be half-breeds, half fey. I suspect simply a strange inception, way back in their past that has spread an unearthly taint throughout their kind.'

'They like to think they own the most land in the area,' Tryskyr added. 'While Wyva is the har in charge of Gwyllion and its environs, the Whitemanes are... something else. They don't seek power exactly, but they do have influence.'

'They're an old family,' Wyva said. 'Their roots go back as far as ours, but... they have a strange way with them. I doubt you'll come into contact with them much, Ysobi.'

'They are being made to sound more interesting than they are,' Gen put in. He poured wine into his glass, reached over to fill mine. I wondered whether a housellar was supposed to do that, and whether Gen was impatient, couldn't wait, wanted a drink. 'The Whitemanes are eccentrics, as are many of the families in these parts, in one way or another. History has bequeathed us a strange legacy. We are far different from the humans who came before us, yet in some ways not that changed. We have our alliances *and* our feuds.'

'There are some who question the original imperative hara had to cast off human heritage entirely,' I said carefully. 'While others still insist it was essential. You'll find many discussions about it around academic tables from Kyme to Immanion.'

'You must've been to both those cities,' Rinawne said, and as I glanced at him, I saw in his eyes a veiled warning not to pursue the line of conversation that had been started.

'Yes, I have,' I said. 'Kyme is far smaller than Immanion, of course, but to me more intriguing. Immanion is glorious, as you might expect, like a fabulous and sensuous dehar bathing in the crystal ocean.'

'That sounds more like my kind of place,' Rinawne said, smiling. 'Warmth, sea, opulence, rather than sneaky little corners and dark little streets full of beady-eyed hara clutching dusty books.'

'Ah, you've been to Kyme, then,' I said, and everyhar

around the table laughed, Rinawne louder than all of them.

There were other morsels served to me that night, along with the exquisite dishes; the small titbits that comprise the truth of a har's nature. These things are naturally revealed slowly. Even when you meet a har who seems to want to pour his life story over you like glue at the first meeting, that is not the truth. The truth is precious, guarded, and is hoarded long before being presented to you to taste. Some truths fall from a har's back like feathers from wings he doesn't know he has. You pick them up in his wake, gaze at them, see the stories there.

I came from that meal feeling I knew at least something about the collective nature of Wyva's tribe. They were affable, fairly simple in outlook, undeniably old-fashioned in some of their adherence to archaic human customs. They seemed on the whole fair-minded, and most of Gen's trickiness was an act. I sensed that a nervousness lurked beneath his surface bravado. Wyva projected mildness, but I sensed steel within him. He would not tolerate what he perceived to be wrongdoing. The mildness would fall from him then. Perhaps he could be terrifying. Cawr struck me as somewhat pettifogging, too attached to meaningless detail. I hadn't been surprised to learn he was responsible for the estate's accounts; he was perfect for that task. But Cawr had also a great generosity of spirit that was almost palpable. He was far kinder than his brothers. Cawr's chesnari, Modryn, was a contained creature who didn't add much to the conversation that night. He did tell me, however, that he ran the local school. 'Kyme has been good to us,' he said. 'They sent me a cartload of books when I asked for assistance.' He smiled at Cawr. 'And *he* is another benefit of my coming here.' Cawr smiled widely in return. Clearly, they were very happy with one another. Rinawne was, perhaps deliberately on his part, still something of a mystery. Was he bored, restless, resigned, content, mischievous, cruel, sweet, mystical, pragmatic? Perhaps all of these things. I could tell the harling irritated him sometimes, but he never showed it overtly.

Nohar else around the table took notice of Myv but for the younger, rather awkward har who seemed like an outsider. His name, I learned, was Porter har Goudy, which I found delightful. It was like the name of a character from an ancient story, somehar who should live in a leaning, turreted house in a place like Kyme. He was simply introduced to me by his name, not by his connection to the family. This was not offered and I sensed I should not ask. Yet. Porter whispered with Myv. They seemed to be playing incomprehensible, secret games with each other. When Porter spoke to him, Myv turned his head at once, looked the other har right in the eye. Rinawne, I sensed, was grateful for this rapport.

I didn't pay that much attention to the two hara from the Assembly, not because they were unremarkable particularly, but because there was much else to occupy my thoughts. They were more interested in seeking Wyva's favour than talking to me, in any case.

After dinner, the company moved to the drawing room, where Rinawne had entertained me earlier in the day. Here, a huge fire frolicked in the wide hearth, and a selection of drinks was laid out waiting for us. Around midnight, Rinawne made a discreet signal, and everyhar in the room knew at once it was time for our party to break up. I felt slightly fuzzy-headed, because all the local wines and liqueurs Wyva had insisted I try had been strong.

'You must not stagger through the forest alone,' Rinawne announced to me. 'And since our other guests take a different road, Porter can guide you.'

I expected some small protest from Porter, if only a grunt or a sullen expression, but he merely nodded and said, 'I'll fetch a lamp.'

While the har was doing this, Wyva said to me, 'I hope you enjoyed this evening, tiahaar.'

'Very much,' I answered, truthfully. 'Both the food and the company were excellent.'

This flattery pleased Wyva, which was useful to know.

Porter returned with his lamp, and also my coat, which I'd left in the hallway. After saying my goodbyes, I followed the young har out into the night. The moon had fallen somewhat by now, but the night was full of song. Birds, beasts, insects; all added their voices to the hymn to nature. Even the trees creaked and rustled their own accompaniments. Porter, while not sullen, did not seem a har given to light conversation, but even so, I felt I should start some. Where else but with some information about him? 'You're a relative of Wyva's?' I asked.

'Not so much,' he replied. 'They took me in.'

'Ah, you lost your family?'

He expelled a short laugh. 'In a fashion.' I did not perceive bitterness in his words, merely a lack of interest. 'I know what it's like in other places,' he said. 'Not all hara have families like they do round here, like tribes of their own.'

'Mmm, it does seem to prevail in rural environments,' I said, feeling the dust of Kyme needed brushing from my tongue.

'But I like the countryside,' Porter continued. 'Don't think I could be doing with city life.' He had clearly, at one point, considered running away, I thought. Perhaps had even tried it, and disliked what he had found, and had returned.

'There is a very old story about a town mouse and a country mouse,' I said. 'Did you ever hear it?'

Porter laughed. 'Rinawne knows that story,' he said. 'Yes, I heard it.'

'Stop,' I said, putting a hand on one of Porter's arms. 'What's that?'

We both stood still, me hardly breathing.

'What is it, tiahaar?' Porter asked softly. 'What am I looking for?' He was gazing around himself, his frown made deep by the light of the lamp.

'Looking? Nothing. I heard... I'm not sure what it was. A voice, maybe calling, maybe singing... not sure.'

'Learn this soon, tiahaar,' Porter said. 'Every creature of the forest has a weird sound to make, and hara who don't live here think mad things about it. A fox screams blue murder. An owl has a ghost's lament. The creaky trees are like coffins opening. Learn the sounds well.'

'Why, might there come a time when I might need to know the difference between that and a real murder, a real ghost, a real coffin opening?'

There was a short silence, during which Porter regarded me contemplatively. 'You're supposed to be a holy har,' he said, with the slightest inflection on 'supposed'. 'You must know there is more than one real.'

'Yes, I know that,' I said. 'Thank you, Porter. I shall learn the sounds.'

He brought me to the foot of my tower, which stood dark and ominous against the night. He waited as I fumbled with the immense key, and held the light above the lock so I might see better. I realised I would have to learn about the lock too, so that I might open it, if I should ever need to, in a hurry. But perhaps I should be like Wyva and leave my abode unlocked. Would it be safe? From the farm came the cry of hounds, not one now but what sounded like dozens. Their voices rose and fell in long ululating moans. Tomorrow, I must go down there and see about ordering produce.

Porter stood at the threshold until I had turned on the lights in the stairwell. 'Thank you for your company,' I said, and with these words he seemed satisfied, nodded his head to me and went back into the dark of the trees.

Once alone, tiredness fell over me like a mist. I discarded my clothes quickly and sought the comfort of my wide bed, leaving a night-light burning in a shallow dish beside me. Shadows swayed upon the gold-flecked walls, and the swans high on the walls flew about me in their endless flight, but I felt no malice near, no strangeness, perhaps only a benign watchfulness, like a har in a chair nearby, ready to watch over me as I slept.

Chapter Three

The morning dripped like pale honey through the veils of my bedroom curtains. For some minutes I lay half awake in this golden hue, drowsy, feeling as if a cherished hand had touched my cheek to wake me. I raised my arms above my head on the pillows, gazed at the ceiling. Patterns moved there, like water; there must be water below, outside. How odd their shine should find their way into my high bedroom.

Eventually, I raised myself and threw on a robe, belting it as I descended the cold stone steps beyond my room. But not even the unforgiving stairwell felt sinister today. I could sense the land stretching and awakening around me, beyond the stone. Tantalising perfumes skimmed like dragonflies beneath my nose; the scents of the season.

In my kitchen, I prepared myself a plate of scrambled eggs, cooked in rich, yellow butter. Rinawne had also supplied bread, wrapped in linen, which had been baked in the kitchen of the Mynd. From this loaf I cut two thick slices and also slathered them with the butter. Then I made tea, dark and strong. Perfect.

While I ate, I gazed out of the window opposite me. I could see beyond the green-hazy trees the low-slung buildings of the farm. The only tall one was the barn. A couple of figures were moving around, engrossed in their morning duties. Later I would call on them.

I had left my notebook on the table, along with a pencil, and now wrote upon the first page:

Cuttingtide rite. Begin with awakening. The sounds and scent. Dehar of the green. A song.

Then I ate some more of my breakfast.

I didn't know precisely when Rinawne intended to call for me, but by the time I'd finished eating and had dressed, I wanted to visit the farm. I resolved to leave a note for Rinawne. This I pinned to the door, with one of the sharp little black tacks I found in a jar in a kitchen cupboard: *'Seeing about the regular slaughter of chickens below. Will be back shortly or meet you there. Ysobi.'*

Already I felt absorbed by this landscape. Pinning up my note was like leaving a message for a friend I'd known for a long time.

While a wider path wound around the hill up to the tower, there was also a straight track down to the farm. This was steep, little more than a gully, mulchy with last autumn's leaves. Green shoots were pushing through the earth all around me. Another image flashed across my mind, and I got out my notebook. *Dehar rising from the earth, growing like a plant.*

Once the path evened out, it widened, leading to the main yard of the farm. I was surprised by the shabbiness of the place, somehow expecting every archetypal feature of this land to be shining and perfect, a dream of what it should be.

As I drew nearer, a noisy ruckus broke out, of what sounded now like four dozen hounds or more. Some were yapping, some uttering unearthly howls. I also heard the occasional threatening growl, but the dogs were out of sight. In response to this alarm, a har emerged from the farmhouse, the back door of which was open. He was a strange-looking specimen, thin and tall, with lank, light brown hair hanging past his shoulders. He was dressed in a woollen tunic and baggy trousers tucked into boots, and over this he wore a grubby knee-length apron, once white, now grey and also stained suspiciously across the chest and skirt with rusty patches. He was drying his hands on a surprisingly clean white towel.

'Yes?' he demanded. At the sound of his voice, the dogs fell quiet.

I inclined my head. 'Good morning, tiahaar. I am Ysobi har Jesith, and I'm staying at the tower...' I turned and gestured

41

back up the hill.

The har followed the line of my arm as if he'd never noticed the tower before. 'What of it?'

'Tiahaar Rinawne suggested I speak to you about ordering a regular supply of dairy produce and meat. I understand it's acceptable for this to be charged to tiahaar Wyva's account.' I groaned inwardly. Why when I tried to put hara at ease did such stuffy, formal phrases drop from my lips.

The har narrowed his eyes at me, the ghost of a smile haunting his lips. 'You're that hienama,' he said.

'Yes.' I shut my mouth before another pompous set of words escaped.

'Blue or white cheese?

'Both would be... I like both.'

'Milk with the cream on? Pint a day?'

'Yes, and a chicken a week would be fine. And a dozen eggs. Cheese once a week should do also.'

The har nodded. 'Well, it's not far to walk and ask if you need more, is it?'

'No, very close.'

'You want veg – potatoes, carrots?'

'I have some supplies. I'll come and ask.'

'Fine. You'd better sign a slip, then. Don't want Wyva thinking I'm robbing him.'

'Absolutely not.'

'I'll start deliveries tomorrow.'

'Perfect.'

The har disappeared into the house and came out again shortly afterwards carrying a receipt book. Here the details of my order were inscribed, in a hand far neater than mine. I appended my signature.

Once this ritual was done, the har stood with hands on hips staring at me, as if astounded I was still standing there.

'Good day to you, then,' I said, and retreated.

As I climbed back up the hill, I saw that Rinawne had arrived and was reading my note.

Rinawne proposed he took me for a walk along the River Moonshawl, through the Shawl Field and to Moonshawl Pool.

'So there is a story there,' I said, 'a shawl, a pool and the moon.'

'It's quite a recent one as folklore stories go,' Rinawne replied. 'Come, I'll talk as we walk.'

He had brought with him a small stout pony, onto whose back was strapped a picnic basket. The pony wore a straw hat, from which his ears poked out.

We walked down from the tower in the opposite direction to the farm, through a veil of forest, and out into the fields of the Wyvachi estate. We crossed a hay field, where the grass was knee high, and here Rinawne began his tale.

'I say recent, but what I mean by that is that this is a tale of the era of hara, not an old human story. But even so, it happened long ago, when Wraeththu were establishing themselves as phyles and tribes within this land.' Rinawne indicated we should climb a stile ahead. When we jumped down on the other side, he said, 'This is the Shawl Field, called in the old tongue Maes Siôl and there ahead is the River Moonshawl, Afon Siôl Lleuad.'

The field was like any other, and the river flowed slow and wide. Insects flew around us and I saw a flotilla of ducks paddling their way by. There were no sinister aspects to the scene. Perhaps I was wrong to expect them; not all stories end tragically.

Rinawne led me to the riverside, and here we sat down on the edge of a small bank, of around a foot's height above the water. The pony began to graze and Rinawne took off his boots and socks to dangle his feet in the lazy flow. 'The story concerns the first harling ever created in this area,' he said. 'When he broke out of his pearl, his hostling picked him up at once and went with him into the forest.' He paused. 'It was night time.'

'Do these hara have names?' I asked.

'The harling was called Lunar, the father was called Grass

43

and the hostling was called Oak.'

I laughed. 'You just made those up.'

Rinawne shrugged, grinned. 'Do you want the story or not?'

I gestured with one hand. 'Please, carry on.'

'Grass went to a glade in the centre of the forest that was known as sacred – or haunted – depending on your point of view. There was a pool in this place where often the moon was said to admire her reflection. Here, Grass made ritual and summoned an ancient entity born of the trees, of the light of the moon, its reflection in the pool and its sparkle upon the river water. Grass asked this creature to protect his son, and the entity agreed to this, for it was pleased with the offerings Grass had made to it.'

'Does the entity have a name?'

'*You* can make that one up,' Rinawne said, rolling his eyes. 'Anyway, the spirit told Grass he must do four things before the sun rose. He must dangle his harling over the pool so that his reflection would be captured there. He must climb the highest tree of the forest and hold up his son to the light of the moon. He must swim in the deepest part of the river and immerse his son wholly within it, and he must come out of the river in a certain field, and here weave a crown of grasses for the harling. When these actions were complete, so the harling would be offered protection and none could harm him in this life. And Grass must also name the harling then: Lunar.'

'That's odd – four tasks. In tales of this type, there are usually three, or perhaps even five or seven – never an even number.'

Rinawne shrugged. 'It was how I heard it.'

'Which tree was it in the forest, do you know?' I asked. I'd got out my notebook.

Rinawne put his head to one side. 'I have no idea. Why?'

'Well, if I'm to create rites for the wheel of the year, it might be useful to know.'

'I'm sure it doesn't matter which tree it was,' Rinawne said. 'I never said the story was based on fact.'

'Is the tale known widely around these parts?'

Rinawne gave me a strange look. 'Yes. Why?'

'Then it's probably important which tree it is. Don't worry. I'll ask around.'

'Well, here is your deepest part of the river,' Rinawne said, gesturing at the water. 'Hara already bathe here on Midsummer Eve and they build a bonfire in this field.'

'Then the basics are established,' I said. 'Just needs weaving into the whole picture.'

Rinawne appeared uncomfortable. 'Mmm, I don't know. I'm telling you the story because I thought you'd like it, not because I thought it should be in your new system. Are you going to write down and use every little thing I say to you?'

I grinned at him. 'No. I might end up with enough material for several wheels of the year! I'm just taking notes, mulling things over.'

Rinawne shrugged. 'Well, it's of no consequence to me. But check things with Wyva first. Hara can be edgy about old stories around here. Anyway, do you want the end of this tale?'

'Of course.'

Rinawne leaned back on stiff arms, gazed at the sky. 'Grass did all these things he'd been bid to do, and the harling never whimpered once, even when he was held up above the tallest tree and dunked into the cold water. When Grass emerged from the river, the spirit was waiting for him.' Now Rinawne turned to me and acted out his story with expressive hands. 'It took from the harling the cold droplets of water on his body, and drew from his eyes the shine of the moon, and took from his head the crown of grasses. These it wove quickly into a glowing shawl that held moonlight within it and all the secrets of the forest and the water.' Rinawne held the imaginary harling up to the sky. 'Grass took this gift and wrapped it around his son, who he then named Lunar. The harling stretched and sighed and fell asleep amid the soft folds. The spirit told Grass that he and his chesnari must wrap Lunar in this shawl on the nights of the full moon until he reached his feybraiha. Then the shawl must be put away in a secure place until the next harling was born to their family, when it could be used again.' Rinawne's arms fell, his imaginary creatures put away.

'And did it work?'

'Well, we must assume so, since that family had previously had a curse put upon it to damn their harlings, and they are still thriving. Myv is the living proof.'

'A Wyvachi myth! And the shawl?'

Rinawne grinned secretively and made his voice low, mysterious. 'Myv sleeps with an old woven silk blanket on his bed on the nights of the full moon.' He made a slow, dramatic gesture with one arm. Such an actor! Then he laughed, rubbed his nose. 'I can't say it's the original shawl, but the Wyvachi won't abandon the tradition.'

'I should think not! Would you risk it, then?'

Rinawne shrugged. 'It's not for me to say. Families have their customs.'

I pondered for a moment. 'But in that case, Wyva must've had the shawl on his bed. What about his brothers? How did they share it?'

Rinawne gave me a shrewd glance. 'Ysobi, Wyva and his brothers are not the same age. Nowhere near.'

'Of course... That must be how they work it.' I laughed. 'Planned pearls.'

Rinawne patted the air, brushing away gnats from his face. 'Something like that. But the fact is, it's a delicate shawl that's well past its best. There will come a time when it can no longer be used anyway.'

'Then the family should call upon the spirit to make a new one, perhaps?'

Rinawne stared at me, smirking, for a moment, then laughed. 'The great scholar, Ysobi. Falls for the story completely.'

'Did you invent it, then?'

'No, Wyva told me about it when we had Myv. He had to

explain about the shawl then, of course, albeit making the story as dull as possible!'

'I hardly know the har, but he doesn't strike me as superstitious.'

Rinawne pulled a sour face. 'He isn't, normally. I suppose the tradition started because the Wyvachi felt they had to do something to... well, the legacy of the first days lies within us all, in one way or another.'

'What do you mean?'

'I mean sometimes hara create rites to forget the distant past. You must know as well as any har what the early days of Wraeththu were like.' Without pause, he got to his feet. 'Are you hungry?'

'A little.'

Rinawne went to fetch the picnic basket from the pony, and as I waited for him I thought about Myv's strangeness. I didn't believe the Wyvachi ancestor had conjured up a spirit who'd woven a magical shawl, but I did believe a shawl had been created under ritual conditions to protect the harlings of the tribe. And what of the curse Rinawne had mentioned, the vague allusions to hidden tales of the past?

Rinawne spread out a white linen cloth upon the grass, and here arranged the refreshments he had brought. I decided to do some more poking around.

'So, what's the story of Porter har Goudy?' I asked. 'Such an intriguing name, I'm sure his history must be interesting.'

Rinawne bit into a sandwich and chewed for a while before answering. 'He's part of our family. What do you want to know about him?'

Now I simply felt interfering, and shrugged uncomfortably. 'Well, he doesn't appear to belong to anyhar in particular, and is clearly second generation, if not third. I was just... curious.'

Rinawne put down his sandwich, half eaten, and lay back on the grass. 'Oh, he's not related in blood, if that's what you mean. He's the son of our previous hienama, Rey har Goudy.'

That took me aback. 'Oh... *now* tell me there isn't a story.' I risked a smile, wondering if Rinawne objected to my questions.

He exhaled through his nose, considering for a moment. 'Let's just say...' He turned to me, leaning his head upon his hand. 'Rey was – *is*, he's not *dead* – a singular har. He was fey, more fey than the Whitemanes. He fell in love with the land so much he fell right into it. Or maybe it was something to do with who Porter's father was. He never told us, but I knew he had liaisons with a lot of hara in Gwyllion. Secretive about it. Anyway, he decided to leave harish society, walk his own lone path. So he left Porter with us, and we sought a new hienama from Kyme.'

'Seems... heartless. Leaving a harling behind. That's leaving more than life, in a way.'

'He's his own har,' Rinawne said. 'You'd understand if you'd met him.'

'Did he perhaps *resent* his son in some way?'

Rinawne shook his head. 'Oh no, nothing like that. He cared for Porter so much he left him with us. It wouldn't have been good for the harling to be carted off into the wilderness to live on sticks and berries. He'll see his hostling again one day, but for now he loves his life here. He's happy with us, part of the family.'

I nodded. 'I can't dispute that.' I looked Rinawne full in the eye. 'I am *not* your new hienama from Kyme.'

'We know that.'

A thought came to me and I had to voice it. 'Rinawne... I've been asked to create a spiritual system for this community, but you had Rey... Surely he had majhahns he used and that hara knew? Are these to be rejected now? And even before his time here I assume the hara here celebrated the seasonal festivals in some way. It seems odd that nothing has been recorded or memorised, or used again.'

Rinawne considered me for a few moments. 'Wyva wants something new,' he said. 'You see, Rey...' He screwed up his nose. 'Well, he wasn't a one for fanciful words and all that. His idea of a ritual was sitting in a wood and thinking about it.'

'I see. And that's what hara did?'

Rinawne made a dismissive gesture. 'Oh, it was a bit more than that but not much. We had our little seasonal thinking session, then a feast, or rather a party. Wyva wants more than that, such as he's heard other phyles have. I think secretly he wants hara in the surrounding counties to be saying to one another, "oh, it's the Gwyllion Natalia rite next week. Are you going to it?" Understand what I mean?'

'He wants theatre?' I smiled.

'I suppose you could call it that. Something more... ceremonial.'

'I understand. Such events draw a community together. I'll bear in mind what you've told me.'

Rinawne sat up. 'Good! Now let's enjoy this elegant repast, which was so meticulously prepared by me, then go visit the Moonshawl Pool. Perhaps we can find your tallest tree.'

As soon as the glade opened up before us, I could tell that Moonshawl Pool – or Pwll Siôl Lleuad, as Rinawne told me it was known in the old language – was an ancient sacred place, and perhaps was still regarded as such among the local hara and used for rites. The damp grass was vivid with new growth beneath our feet; Rinawne's pony was eager to tear at it, devour it.

Rinawne led me to the edge of the clear water. I could see that the pool was maintained by a spring and that a quick stream gulped away from it, perhaps to join with the river. Opposite me was an immense mossy rock, from which it seemed ideal for harlings to jump into the water. Sunlight came down in rods through the unfurling leaf canopy above, but even so the glade was partially in shadow.

'Eldritch place, isn't it?' Rinawne said carelessly. 'You should drink the water. It's supposed to be lucky.' He knelt down and scooped a handful to his mouth.

I knelt beside him. 'I'd like to meditate here for a few minutes, if that's all right.'

'Of course. Do your hienemarly thing.' Rinawne grinned. 'There are usually mushrooms in the hedgerow to the next field. I'll go gathering while you ponder the mysteries of life.'

Not until Rinawne had left me, his departure accompanied by a theatrical wave of his hand, did I stoop to drink the water. It was as cold as winter, and so pure as to be almost without taste. There was a faint sparkle to it that fizzed in my throat.

'May the guardians of this site reveal to me it secrets,' I said aloud, and then composed myself upon the grass, sitting cross-legged with my hands upon my thighs, palms uppermost and open.

I tried to concentrate on the story Rinawne had told me, visualising the har he had named Grass coming through the trees to the pool, his harling in his arms. The image wouldn't stick in my mind, and on the brief occasions it did, I felt Grass was always looking behind him, as if pursued. I sensed urgency. But another image wanted to impose itself across that of Grass, and it was so strong, eventually I let it have its head.

In the mind picture, I was unsure whether it was day or night time. I caught brief glimpses of something pale through the trees, drawing haphazardly closer to the pool. Within the visualisation I got to my feet, cautiously approached whatever was weaving towards me. I saw a pale figure, its arms held out in front of it, touching the trunks of the trees, as if blind, and trying to feel its way forward. It wore a tattered white robe, and very long white hair fell over its face, obscuring its features completely, but it was not the white of human old age, more like the platinum white found rarely in hara. This must be a har. He was stumbling, disorientated, and now I could hear he was moaning softly, monotonously.

'Tiahaar,' I said softly, and the har paused. Then he began to grope his way in my direction.

'Help... I need...' The words were broken, ragged with the most awful despair, and shook me from my visualisation.

Opening my eyes, for a moment I too was utterly disorientated, unsure even of where I was, but then the sound of breaking undergrowth brought me to my feet. This was no visualisation. A har dressed in white – a torn robe, filthy to the knees – and with long white hair hanging over his face was trying to reach me. Pitifully, he patted the trees around him, turning in a circle, his robe catching on shrub branches, tearing further. All the while he uttered that relentless, frightened moan.

'Tiahaar!' I ran towards him. 'Stay where you are. I'll come to you.'

As I reached him, the har fell heavily into my arms, and I staggered backwards beneath the burden. His hands clutched my arms, the fingers digging into my flesh, then withdrawing, then digging in again. He smelled... of *sickness*. 'Wraeththu,' he gasped, 'help me, help me...'

And then... Then there was nothing in my arms, no sense, no physical memory even, of the weight against me. Nothing.

'So this is your secret,' I murmured shakily to the glade.

Around me was silence, no birds singing, no rustle of life in the bushes. Not even the soft gurgle of the water as it flowed away to brighter realms.

I sat down heavily where I stood, put my head in my hands, experiencing a strong desire to weep, yet no tears came. Something horrific had happened here once. There could be no mistake. It had left its mark, its imprint, and it was so strong it could feel like the physical weight of a har in my arms.

Ten minutes of deep breathing restored me almost to normality, yet I could still feel quivering anxiety within me, the gift of whatever apparition it was I'd seen.

I heard the sound of a har whistling and guessed this was Rinawne returning to me. For some reason, I knew I wouldn't tell him what had happened; it was as if the har of my vision had begged me to silence.

'You look like you've seen a ghost,' Rinawne remarked cheerfully as he emerged from the trees.

I smiled, gestured with both arms. 'Well, I went... quite *deep* into the landscape.'

Rinawne rolled his eyes. 'By Aru, don't end up like Rey and not come out again!' He sat down beside me. 'No mushrooms to pick today, sadly. Shall we go back to the Mynd? You can stay for dinner again if you like. And I can show you the whole house. Would you like that?'

I sensed he was speaking to me as if I were... well, perhaps slightly ill. Did I look that bad? I tried to pull myself together, put aside what I'd experienced.

'I'd love to see the house. Not sure about dinner, though. I need to write up some notes, so I don't forget things.'

Rinawne slapped my shoulder. 'Oh, plenty of time for that. You can sit in the library for a while to do your writing. The day is young. Come on!' He dragged me to my feet.

Rinawne had some domestic tasks to attend to, so left me alone in the library of Meadow Mynd. Although I'd intended to write up some ideas and impressions of the morning, I was instead drawn to explore the packed shelves around me. There were many dull books that looked as if they'd never been read and had been put there simply to fill space. But there was plenty to interest me too – namely a row of titles on folklore and local mysteries. These were very old books, from the human era. As I examined them, some well-thumbed and fragile, my mind kept flashing back to my experience by the pool; who *was* that har? What had happened to him? I could still hear his horrible moaning, and the hoarse words he'd spoken. *Help me...* But how? I felt reluctant to talk about the episode with any of the Wyvachi, mostly because it was likely the har I'd seen was, or had been, connected with them in some way, and perhaps not in a good way. I wondered, for a moment, whether it could have been the mysterious, vanished hienama, Rey. But as far as I knew, Rey was alive, and the har I'd seen had disappeared before me like a ghost. Would this mystery be a distraction from my work? What I'd experienced during – and after – my meditation was not in any manner useful for the job I'd been sent to do. Still, there was the moonshawl to consider. Was this a taboo subject or not?

As if in answer to my silent question, Wyva sauntered into the room. I sensed he'd been told I was here and was looking for me. 'Ah, you've found the treasure trove of the house,' he said. 'Its heart.'

I turned and smiled at him. 'I hope you don't mind me nosing around. Rinawne left me here while he had some jobs to do.'

Wyva made an expansive gesture with both arms. 'You're welcome to treat our home as your own. You don't have to ask to look at the books.'

I considered for a few moments before asking a question. 'I've heard a local legend about the moonshawl,' I said. 'Is there anything about it in the library?' Some instinct made me omit Rinawne's part in my discovery.

Wyva gave me a strange look; wary, slightly disapproving. 'I don't believe there is. What did you want to know and why?'

I closed the book I was perusing, wishing now I hadn't broached the subject. Wyva was all prickles before me. 'Well... I wondered whether it could be included somehow in the yearly round – the pool, the river, the meadow. I was wondering if the tree still stood.'

Wyva continued to stare at me. 'I'm not sure that legend is... *appropriate* for what we want,' he said. 'It comes from a difficult time in harish history, surely not one to be enshrined in spiritual practice.'

I should never have spoken. My instincts had known it was a sensitive topic because I'd not mentioned Rinawne had told me the story. Clearly, Rinawne's mouth ran away with him; he'd forgotten who he was speaking to when he'd told me the tale. But, in retrospect, the signs had been there he'd slightly regretted telling it to me. It was now abundantly plain to me that under no circumstances would Wyva *ever* allow that story to be used in my work. This was a shame, I felt, since hara already celebrated in the Maes Siôl at Midsummer. 'I'm just mulling over a lot of ideas, jotting down notes,' I said. 'I don't know the full story but won't use it if you feel it's not right to do so. There are plenty of other stories I can adapt.'

'Yes, that would be best.' Wyva softened, gripped my right shoulder briefly. 'Just tell me what you plan to use, so I can advise you over what's appropriate. It might sound silly but some of the stories from the dawn of Wraeththu are considered almost... *unlucky* by hara around here. You weren't to know.'

'Is there anything else I should avoid?'

'Not that I can think of, but please check with me before doing a lot of work with particular legends to save yourself wasting time. It's probably best to stick to the older material, and update that with a harish slant.'

'I'll do that.' I put down the book I was holding, aware my heart was beating fast and that I felt slightly angry.

Wyva put his head to one side. 'I don't want to make your work difficult. I know how all this must sound.'

I managed a smile. 'It's quite all right, and best we establish the boundaries before I waste any time, as you said.'

'Will you stay for dinner again this evening?'

I nodded. 'Yes, that's kind of you. Saves me cooking!' I realised that to refuse might have seemed churlish, yet I couldn't dispel the feeling of irritation, of being somehow *thwarted*. First there was the unspoken assumption I was expected to perform hienama duties, and now this – being somewhat shackled in what material I was permitted to use. Still, no job of this kind would ever be straightforward. I must simply toe the line, respect hara's feelings, and make my work easier.

Some moments after this – and it felt like a rescue in the rather taut atmosphere – Rinawne appeared at the library door. 'I'm all done,' he announced. 'Your tour guide awaits you.'

I bowed my head. 'Thank you, tiahaar. I'm ready to be amazed!'

Both Rinawne and Wyva laughed; the atmosphere became relaxed.

As I've already mentioned, Meadow Mynd wasn't one of those grand mansions with huge sweeping staircases and airy halls. The rooms were fairly modest in size, and the staircase of dark oak unimposing. The house was full of nooks and crannies, odd little window seats where somehar might curl up to read, narrow corridors leading only to bizarre tiny rooms, such as the one containing an ornate lavatory covered in baroque designs. There was a 'gentleman's Turkish bath room', (a true remnant of olden times), and the ante-room to it was full of riding boots and coats of cracked leather, which looked as if they hadn't been moved for hundreds of years. 'Yes, relics,' Rinawne said rather mordantly, as he noticed me inspecting these articles.

'It's like a museum,' I said.

'Exactly like a museum. Fusty and smelly. If it was up to me, I'd throw out all the junk and air the whole place, but it's not up to me. I have a couple of rooms I was allowed to redecorate when I came here, to be more to my taste, but it was made clear that would be all I was allowed.'

'Do the Wyvachi... *revere* objects like these?' I asked carefully.

'It's not that. They just won't throw anything away. Perhaps one of these pairs of rotting boots belonged to great great great Uncle Bertie. Who knows, he might come back for them?' Rinawne grinned.

'And are there ghosts here?'

'To be sure – if you're open to them. I'm not. I banish them from my thresholds. I prefer to live in the present moment. You're always asking about ghosts, aren't you?' He gave me rather an arch look.

Beyond the boot room the domestic quarters began: kitchens, pantries, laundries and so on. It didn't surprise me to find most of the appointments in these rooms to be antiques.

'I quite approve of *this* old stuff,' Rinawne said, affectionately touching one of the copper saucepans hanging from a rail above the cooking range. 'In kitchens, things can be old, because they know the food better and how to make it delicious. Just doesn't feel right to me elsewhere. I like these rooms.'

In a smaller kitchen beyond the main one, we came across three of the Mynd staff, who were sitting round a circular table, plucking feathers from what appeared to be game birds and gossiping together. They greeted Rinawne warmly, while awarding me wary glances.

'Dinner,' Rinawne explained, gesturing at the birds. 'No doubt Wyva wrung their necks only an hour ago.'

'Fresh,' agreed one of the kitchen hara. The tiniest feathers floated in the air and there was a smell of blood.

Rinawne strolled around the table, put his hands on the shoulders of the har who'd spoken. 'This is our head cook, Dillory, and these *scullions* here with him are Barly and Fush. Yes, Fush. Ridiculous name.'

The young har in question grimaced at Rinawne, but was clearly not offended.

'Anyway, we are off and onwards,' Rinawne said to his staff. 'Keep up your excellent work.'

He sailed out of the room and I followed.

From there, we meandered back into the warren of the main house, with its odd little rooms. The library was the largest of them; the drawing room and dining room were next in size. There was a hexagonal conservatory tacked on to the east wing of the house like a quartz growth. There were sitting rooms with clocks where at one time female ancestors might have sat with their embroidery or to read. Sunlight came dimly through the mullioned windows, fighting with heavy drapes that lolled around the frames. As well as the dining room there was a breakfast room facing east to bask in the morning sun. Here, the round table was already set for the next day's breakfast. I wondered if, in fact, anyhar ate in there.

Perhaps Rinawne divined my thoughts. 'Wyva always has his breakfast here. Sometimes I join him. Sometimes the rest of them do.'

I smiled at him. 'I did wonder. So much of this house seems like a display of the past, to be looked at, not touched.'

Rinawne wandered to the window, looked out upon a lawn that swept away to tall evergreens, including a monkey-puzzle tree. The other species were unknown to me, obviously brought from far countries in the distant past. 'This is perhaps the most haunted room in the house,' Rinawne said. His voice was almost wistful.

'Oh? Will you tell me the story?'

He turned to me, shook his head. 'I don't know its history. All I know is that something haunts this room. I'm quite sure it doesn't appear to Wyva, because he comes here every day.'

'And you think he wouldn't if he... *saw things?*'

Rinawne shrugged. 'Well I wouldn't want some sulky ghost gawping at me while I was eating, would you?'

'Have *you* seen it?'

He laughed. 'Oh, the thing tried it on with me at the first, but I wasn't having any of it. Nothing can haunt me. I sent it packing from my mind. I learned to do that from an early age.'

'What did you see?'

He shrugged. 'Just a vague shape in the curtains, a hand reaching out. I spat at it and it went.'

'That must have surprised Wyva.'

'Nohar said a word. The whole family was here that day too because I was new.'

'Perhaps they were testing you.'

Again, Rinawne laughed. 'Now your imagination is running away with you. They must be used to what is in this room, and each of them deals with it in a different way. I just used my way and that was that.'

Rinawne was a frustrating creature. He led me on into mysterious avenues and then pulled me out again before anything could truly manifest. *That* was his way. Intrigue, then debunk. I thought of a skittish young har brought to this house to forge some alliance through chesna-bond with the Wyvachi. Unknown, somewhat wild, unpredictable, he is taken to the haunted room. Clearly, he sees something and spits at it. And the family say nothing, don't react? It made no sense to me, and I had no idea how much of that story was true. Perhaps none of it. Somewhat annoyed, my feelings shouldered aside my common sense and a remark came out. 'You got me into trouble today.'

Rinawne frowned quizzically. 'I did? How?'

'When Wyva came into the library I mentioned the moonshawl story and that I was considering incorporating parts of it into the yearly round.'

Rinawne uttered a derisory sound. 'Oh dear. I did try to... well, *warn* you. He didn't welcome the suggestion, I take it?'

'I was told in no uncertain terms to abandon that thread of work. Why is he so sensitive about it? It's not a gruesome story, nor does it show the family in a bad light. I'm surprised he doesn't want it included.'

'The Wyvachi are *very* sensitive about the past,' Rinawne said. 'Like a lot of tribes they have cupboards bulging with skeletons from the early days. I bet your own tribe is no different. It's just that most tribes have forgotten such things now, have let them fade, as they should. You won't find that round here. The past still lives for hara in these lands. In my opinion, your job should be to shift them forward from that, so I agree with Wyva in this case. I'm really sorry. I only told you that story because I thought you'd like to hear it. I just don't think sometimes.'

'But hara already use the legend in their celebrations,' I said, unwilling to let the subject drop. 'You told me so.'

He frowned. 'This is part of the problem. The Whitemanes use that field, not Wyvachi hara. It's common land, but Wyva isn't happy about it.'

'And you omitted to mention that?' I sighed. 'What *is* it about the Whitemanes? How can I do this job if information is withheld from me and I go blundering into areas that cause offence? It would *help* to know.'

Rinawne put his head to one side, inspected me for some

moments. 'Don't get angry, Ysobi har Jesith. Was but a small mistake. Ask Wyva about the Whitemanes. I don't trust what might come out of my mouth.'

'So what you're telling me is that the job I've been commissioned to do is not for everyhar in Gwyllion, and what I devise might clash with what other hara are doing?'

'Speak with Wyva about it,' Rinawne said. 'He's the one who wants this.'

I was beginning to understand more clearly now why he did.

I didn't want to stay for dinner and yearned for time alone, but there was no polite way out of it for today. After the breakfast room, Rinawne showed me no more of the house – the fascinating top story with attics, for example – and conducted me back to the library. I sensed a wall of frost between us, not a serious one, nor an unbreakable one, but there nevertheless.

The day had so far disappointed me in several ways. I resolved to concentrate on my work, write up some fairly soft and hackneyed yearly round for the hara in the village, and be on my way. But to where? For the first time, the thought struck me: I'd been in Gwyllion for less than two days but already it felt more like home to me than Jesith.

I asked to return to the library to work, and Rinawne said he would fetch me at dinnertime. Once seated at the glossy old table that dominated one half of the room, I got out my notebook and wrote up the incidents of the day. None of them would be of any use for my work, but I wanted to remember the details clearly.

I remembered Rinawne telling me in his story of the breakfast room ghost how he had seen an arm reaching out to him. This reminded me of the seemingly blind ghost at the Pwll Siôl Lleuad . Were the two connected? Rinawne had described the ghost as 'sulky', yet what I'd seen at the pool was a terrified har who asked for help, who had uttered the word 'Wraeththu' as if hara were either little known to him or he felt separate from them, even though I was certain he was har himself. Did that perhaps indicate some incident in the Wyvachi past where a newly-incepted har had perished in this house or its estate under traumatic circumstances? The ghost was not asking help of the Wyvachi, but of me. These ideas swam around my head. I wondered whether I was jumping to conclusions, or simply fashioning a fictional tale to my liking. At that stage, it was impossible to tell.

As the light began to fade in the room and the gardens beyond the windows sank into twilight, I considered the Whitemanes also. The Wyvachi clearly had no liking for this other family, who perhaps considered themselves a separate tribe. But that didn't make the Whitemanes horrible hara; it merely spoke of a rift or a clash of interests. I decided I would have to make their acquaintance and see for myself. But tomorrow, I would start my work properly. I would begin with the season we were now in – early summer – and work forward from there. While I was familiarising myself with the landscape, I might as well make use of the season to help me acclimatise.

The younger hara weren't present at dinner; there were only Rinawne and Wyva, Gen and myself. Cawr was out visiting friends with his chesnari. Gen didn't have a chesnari – no surprise to me. He was the archetypal rakehellion brother from an old novel – setting hearts and bodies alight but never there to watch the last burning embers fade to cold.

There was no more talk of local stories, or even my work. Wyva spoke of running the estate, rambled fondly about certain animals he owned, and bickered mildly with Gen who'd forgotten to complete certain mundane tasks for him. Rinawne caught my eye once and winked.

During dessert, Gen asked me if I'd like to visit the village with him the following evening. I saw no reason to decline, although sensed a stiffening in Rinawne's posture at the foot of the table.

'I can take you to some more sites tomorrow,' Rinawne said to me.

I was silent for a moment. Tomorrow's work was already decided upon. I didn't want another day with Rinawne, followed by further difficult to decline invitations to the Mynd. I smiled at him. 'Not tomorrow. I *must* write out my ideas for the first part of my work. Perhaps later in the week?' I didn't want to get into the habit of Rinawne leading me about every day.

Rinawne stared at me with quite a hard expression. 'As you wish.'

'How about Agavesday?'

'Fine.'

Clearly, it wasn't fine.

I glanced at Wyva, wondering what he might think of this exchange and its implications, but he was once again talking with Gen about trivial matters. He was either rather stupid in respect of Rinawne or simply didn't care what his chesnari might get up to. I knew without the shade of a doubt that Rinawne intended at some point to pounce on me. What I was rather confused about was that I didn't find the idea totally repellent.

Later, as I lay on my side in the darkness of my tower bedroom, I thought of my chesnari and son, so far away. Did they miss me, or had my absence healed over so that I was already a wound forgotten? Restlessly, I turned onto my back, my left arm behind my head. I realised that ever since I'd returned from Kyme, Zeph and Jass had been slipping away from me, bit by bit, drawing away in spirit. I hadn't really noticed, but now it seemed obvious. I'd let them keep on drifting, or maybe it was me who'd drifted. I remembered the day of my departure – Jass hurrying around the house preparing to leave for work, making a cursory check of my luggage to ensure I'd packed essentials. Then a brief farewell, his expression tight, but not sad. We hadn't even embraced. Zeph had come into the kitchen as I'd finished drinking my breakfast coffee; long-limbed, lanky Zeph with his bewitching lazy smile – which, incidentally, he rarely turned on me. 'I hope it's good for you in that place,' he'd said, but it was as if he was saying it to any har who might need restoration. 'Well, got to go. Goodbye.' And that had been that.

I remembered the way I'd felt about Jass when I'd first met him, the aches and longings he'd inspired in me. I remembered the utter conviction we should make a harling, and how my stupidity had spoiled his pearl's delivery for Jass. That he'd forgiven me then was miraculous. No wonder his ability to forgive had worn away. Or maybe what happened had eroded his love to a point where it was so thin it was less than a ghost. Zeph was and is *his* son; they are close, a single beating heart. Where Jass goes, Zeph follows. And now, as I thought of these things, another realisation came to me: I'd lost them.

Perhaps it didn't have to remain that way. Perhaps I could change things. The question that had to be answered was whether I wanted this. Even if my relationship with Jass was damaged beyond repair, Zeph was still my son too, and I must not relinquish him so easily.

In the morning, as I was eating breakfast, I wrote two letters – one to Jass, one to Zeph. To Jass I wrote of Wyva and his family, and requested that a hamper of Jesith produce be sent up to them. I spoke of how the landscape was inspiring for my work, and things were going well. I told him of the tower, describing it in detail; this made for a fairly long, chatty letter.

To Zeph I wrote more, of the folklore stories I'd heard and read, of the magic of the land. I told him about Myv and Porter, and how the dogs howled so strangely down at the farm at night. I told him I was often alone, but not lonely; the land and the tower were my company. And if I craved harish company, I could wander up to Meadow Mynd and talk with hara there. I paused and thought for some minutes before adding the final paragraph suggesting he might like to come and visit and that I was sure he'd be welcome. In my heart, I knew that invitation would not be taken up, but at least I'd made it.

Chapter Four

Rain came with the morning, turning the world grey and dull. This would not have been good weather in which to wander about with Rinawne, so we'd probably have had to cancel any planned walk anyway. The air had gone chill, so I stoked up the stove in the kitchen, which soon became warm and enfolding. After breakfast, I took up my letters and went to saddle Hercules. He didn't look very happy, standing beneath a dripping tree at the edge of his field. As I didn't know the area that well yet, I took the widest path that led to the southeast of the farm. This meandered somewhat, but I rode as swiftly as possible to Gwyllion and left my letters at the mail station, where they would be picked up by the next courier travelling south. Then I returned to the tower and stabled Hercules in knee deep straw with sweet hay to nibble at. I determined not to venture forth in the rain again that day, and went inside to work.

The Wheel of the Year has already been well-formed to fit harish beliefs by Flick Har Roselane, so most scholars devising improvised versions begin with his work. It's quite telling that the circular story fits better into an androgynous version than it did in the ancient human version of male and female. Perhaps this was the way it was always meant to be for the sentient beings of this world, and yet the kingdoms of animal and plant remain mostly divided into two genders. I feel that the predominating forces of soume and ouana – or, crudely, female and male – should not be overlooked or ignored, because these forces do have different 'flavours' and strengths, and represent specific things. Hara incorporate both these aspects but utter balance is difficult, if not undesirable, to achieve. At certain times, soume or ouana might dominate – and I don't mean in a literal sexual sense. I believe we exist upon a varying scale with ouana at one end of it, and soume at the other. It is rare our being will rest blithely in the centre of that scale. So, to me, celebrating these aspects in their pure form, as well as their variations, should be part of spiritual practice. To deny this reality seems to deny the true nature of our being.

I thought about myself at that moment, snug in a cosy environment, writing up my thoughts. My soume aspect welcomed the comfort and, I felt, was eager to bring colour and imagination to the work. The ouana part was the scholar, wanting to be sure of his facts and not go skipping off down fanciful roads. Both were needed, and in some parts of my new system, perhaps one aspect would be foremost at certain seasons. Natalia, in mid-winter, would be wholly soume because of its connection with the birthing of pearls.

Feybraihatide, at the eve of Flowermoon, had passed, so even though that month still reigned, I began work upon Cuttingtide, which falls in the last third of Meadowmoon. I felt a frisson of excitement course through me as I thought of this. The words were somehow apt. Meadowmoon for the meadow, the moonshawl, and cutting... somehow that seemed relevant too. Cuttingtide, being associated with the death of the dehar Morterrius, is perhaps one of the more *daunting* festivals. Its celebrations can be wild and cruel, and in many hidden corners involve sacrifice, as it had done thousands of years before, among humans. I don't mean that hara are literally slaughtered in the fields, but animals would be, their blood cast upon the growing crops to ensure their bounty.

As I thought of images and themes for a Cuttingtide festival for Gwyllion, I could not dispel the vision of the helpless har who had come to me at the Pwll Siôl Lleuad. Was he associated with a festival in some way, his trauma enacted upon a significant date? Without Wyva telling me, I couldn't see how I could find out, other than trying to communicate further with the entity itself – a thought that didn't exactly fill me with joy. His tragedy wasn't why I was here, and I could see clearly he could sidetrack me, and perhaps bring me into conflict with the

Wyvachi.

'Drop it,' I said aloud to myself, and dismissed all thoughts of the Pwll Siôl Lleuad from my mind. Wyva had been firm that I mustn't use any aspects of the story for my yearly round, so the field, river and glade were out. I thought instead of my initial impressions – a har rising from the mulch and leaves of the fallen year, blossoming into Feybraihatide. At Cuttingtide he must fall himself, but I decided not to make this cathartic or brutal. An arrow from his lover would fragment him into a storm of petals, which would blow across the fields and fall upon the crops. As a concession to the blood gift, I would make the petals turn red as they fell and sank into the soil. I needed a location in which to set my Cuttingtide drama, and as certain areas were off limits, this would require some exploration on my part.

The weather cleared late in the afternoon and weak, watery sunlight splashed down over the soaked landscape. Now I wanted to go exploring again. I'd been studying a framed map I'd found upon the wall of the spare bedroom. The map was drawn by hand in black, red and green ink and showed the extent of the Wyvachi lands, plus the village of Gwyllion. I was pleased to discover a shortcut to the village, which led through the farm, right to the inn where I'd arranged to meet Gen later on. This would be much quicker than the route I'd used earlier. Before my walk, I let Hercules out into his field and then set off, intending to explore some of the woodland nearby. I had debated whether to ride or walk, but had eventually opted for walking, since this would bring me closer to the earth, even though the damp might sink in through my boots. I'd copied parts of the map onto smaller, manageable bits of paper, and decided to begin my explorations with the Llwybr Llwynog, the Fox Run or Path, which covered a small hill two miles or so from the tower.

As I descended my own hill, in the opposite direction to the farm, the hounds started up their racket, seemingly more of them than ever before. There was an undeniable annoying note to their cries, which I found puzzling. Normally, the sound of hounds would have excited me. There was something primal about the concept of the hunt, associated with ancient pagan ways, that called to me. When I heard the voice of a hunting dog, I saw in my mind ancient gods and spirits riding the wind, rather than a struggling mass of yelping murderers intent on tearing apart one poor animal ahead of them. With these hounds, murder seemed more likely than a romantic vision; theirs was a cruel voice. I can put it no other way than that.

My walk to the Llwybr Llwynog was uneventful, yet I could not help but be intoxicated by the atmosphere around me, the breathing, living landscape. In every shadow I sensed elemental eyes; the very air shimmered with imminence. The colours of the new summer flowers were achingly vivid, glowing white and purple amid the forest lawns. Emerging from a copse to cross a stile into a field, it was as if the land was shouting its jubilation at reawakening. Birds wheeled in complex patterns above the growing wheat. A hawk rested on the air currents, high above me; the dehar Shadolan's creature. All this filled my senses, made me slightly drunk. I gathered items I thought useful for my temple room – a shard of tree bark adorned with vivid moss, some white stones I came across at the foot of an oak, pristine pigeon feathers, and so on. I visualised the dehar Elisin strolling through this wood, touching the trees, his bare feet conjuring forest flowers from the soil. I crossed a narrow stream, then decided to follow it, pleased to discover that when I reached the Llwybr Llwynog hill, before me was a waterfall where the stream fell into a pool. This was not some showy, gushing fall, but modest, somehow secret. Here, Elisin would pause, gaze at his shivering reflection in the pool. I could see right to the bottom of it, which was about two feet down, and was able to draw more small white stones from its floor; they seemed to glow with their own light.

As I was examining my finds, I heard childish laughter and turned round to see the brown faces of two harlings looking at me; they were partly hiding behind a tree. 'Good day, tiahaara!' I called, not wishing to seem in any way threatening or frightening. The harlings only laughed further, and then one of them threw a hard lump of moss at me, which bounced off my forehead. 'Hey!' I got to my feet, but the harlings were already off, scampering swiftly through the trees. Sighing at the rudeness of the harlings, I wiped my smarting forehead. Skirting round the pool, I found a path up the hill, which had a gentle slope and didn't look as if it would present any problems for somehar seeking its summit.

As I climbed, I thought about the cycle of Arotahar, as Flick har Roselane had named it, and how in many ways he had stuck to the imagery and ideas of earlier pagan systems. This lent itself well to adjustment, so that the beliefs of different areas could be incorporated. However, I wanted to avoid generic images and ideas for the spiritual system of Gwyllion. It would be too easy to drop into the ancient tropes of horned god of the forest and harishly-rendered forms of ancient goddesses. While these images had, of course, originally arisen from the land and its people, the hara of this landscape deserved something new while derived from the ancient, imagery more pertinent to modern times, reflecting our harish being. The major dehar should be *of* the land, yet of *us*.

I did not expect to come across this entity almost immediately.

I had wandered into the birch groves of the Llwybr Llwynog, where the sunlight came down in golden coins onto the sparse acid green grass beneath my feet. The sward was otherwise covered with a haze of bluebells. My eyes were concentrated mainly on my feet and what lay about me. I was humming to myself a tune that I was composing for Cuttingtide, embellishing its melody, inserting a line of lyrics when they came to me.

The sound of a horse's stamping hooves jerked me from my reverie. I looked up and saw what I first thought was the vision of a dehar – Shadolan in fact – before me.

He rode a tall grey horse, standing side on to me, whose mane was plaited into pairs of braids tied together at their ends with brass medallions. The rider's olive green cloak, fringed with what appeared to be rabbit fur, spread over the horse's haunches. This being looked down at me through narrowed eyes. His face was like something from an ancient painting, some fantasy creature: full-lips, perfectly-arched eyebrows, and sculpted face. The skin was darkish in tone, but I couldn't tell if that was its natural colour or simply a tan. His beech-brown hair, braided like his mount's, was gathered in an ornate silver fillet at his neck, two braids spilling forwards over his breast and three others cascading down his back. His shirt and trousers were of brushed leather, as were his boots. I saw scratches as if from brambles, and still smeared about with blood, on the backs of his hands where they lay idly upon the reins. He was harish, real and whole, no dehar – but what a har! His expression was difficult to determine – disapproval, curiosity, welcome, hostility?

'Good day, tiahaar,' I said, inclining my head.

The har continued to inspect me, and now that I had ascertained his corporeality, the gaze was insulting. He did not speak. The horse pawed the ground with a fore-hoof. I knew I wasn't on land I shouldn't venture into, since this whole forest belonged to Wyva's family. If anything, this other was the interloper. He was stationed right in my path and I'd have to walk round his horse to go further.

'Tiahaar?' I said.

His expression didn't change and it was clear he wasn't going to communicate. I didn't feel he wanted to hurt me, but I sensed my presence in what he took to be his space didn't please him. Still, short of running me out of the forest, what could he do? I had only to walk round him. Shrugging, to show him he didn't intimidate me, I took a wide path round the horse's head. I wasn't going to look back.

I pondered about him as I continued my walk. At first, I wondered if he would follow me and threaten harm, but eventually, when I did look back, there was nohar behind me. The har had oozed a kind of authority; he had looked down on me in more than one way. I laughed to myself. Well, there was my dehar, my version of Shadolan. Hostile, rude, or not, I saw a template there.

Consulting my fragments of redrawn map, I took a different path home, not wishing particularly to run into my dehar again. As to who he might be, later I could interrogate Gen, who no doubt knew everyhar within the local area. I had my own suspicions about the identity of the rider, though.

Gen had suggested we eat together at The Crowned Stag in Gwyllion, which was larger than The Rooting Boar, the inn I'd visited on my arrival in the area. The Stag was built of light grey stone, misted with mature wisteria, and faced the town green, where there was a wide pond fringed by ancient willows. Tables were set outside, but nohar sat there. When I arrived, which was early in the evening, there were only a couple of customers inside, who barely glanced at me, but Selyf, the har I'd met on my first night in Gwyllion, came out from behind the bar to greet me. Gen had told him I was expected. He ushered me into a private room at the back of the building, which overlooked a garden. Here, Gen was seated at a table by the window, drinking a tankard of ale. Soft globes of light illuminated the shrubs and trees outside as evening cast its veils over the land. I wondered what the purpose of this meeting was. Did he too plan a seduction of a new face? Or was I being too cynical, and he wished merely to extend a hand of friendship? He stood up to greet me and asked for wine to be brought to our table.

I sat down opposite his chair and he too reclaimed his seat.

'Is your work going well?' he asked me.

'Very well, thank you. This is an inspiring landscape. I'll have an arojhahn ready for Cuttingtide and hope everyhar will be willing volunteers for it.'

'Oh, they will. But surely you must begin preparations

soon? You should speak to Selyf, the keephar here, about what feast should be prepared, or perhaps that is the job of my family?'

I hesitated. 'Well, I hadn't been thinking of anything that grand. Is that what Wyva expects?'

'These hara are desperate for celebrations,' Gen said, grinning. 'Sorry, I didn't mean to alarm you. Perhaps I'm desperate for celebration as much as any.'

'The – er – catering side of things I took to be somehar else's responsibility,' I said. 'I just come up with the ideas, the words...'

Gen made a calming gesture. 'You're quite right. But you should speak to Wyva about it. He's as eager as all of us to begin our yearly round.'

I looked at Gen for some moments before speaking. 'I have to ask but... when your previous hienama left his post, why didn't Wyva simply continue the celebrations as they'd been before? I imagine Rey had arojhahns he used every year and majhahns for all other rites of passage? In my experience, in the absence of a hienama, the phylarch generally takes on the tasks of chesna-bonds, naming rituals and leading seasonal festivals.'

Gen too waited before replying. 'Let's just say that Rey told Wyva he must not.'

'What? Why?' My words came out too hastily and sounded abrupt. 'I'm sorry, that was rude of me. It's just... surprising.'

'No, I know how it sounds. It's difficult to explain.'

As many things seem to be in this place. I took a breath. 'You don't need to explain, it's none of my business. I'm here to do a job and I'll do it.'

Our wine had arrived, and Selyf poured it into our glasses. Despite waiting upon us, it was clear he was a prominent individual within the community, simply from the unmistakeable aura of authority that oozed from him. Unlike the proprietor of The Rooting Boar, he wasn't typical of the keephar kind, being somewhat ascetic of feature. I wondered if once he'd had an entirely different occupation. While he filled

71

our glasses, with deliberate slowness and continual dabbing of a napkin against the wine flask, there was a silence between Gen and me. Selyf said, 'Tonight, we serve venison with roast vegetables, tiahaara. Is this to your liking?'

'That will be fine,' Gen said.

Selyf inclined his head regally and departed.

Gen smiled at me with an apologetic expression. 'I get the feeling that all us Wyvachi do is cause problems for you. I heard Wyva had forbidden you from using certain legends in your work. It must seem as if our family is secretive and obstructive.'

'I'm sure you have your reasons,' I said dryly, taking a sip of my drink.

'We've sorely annoyed you, Ysobi.'

I shook my head, putting down the glass. 'Perhaps I'm just too curious. I wasn't sent here to solve mysteries, merely to help you.'

'There are few hara who can resist a mystery.'

Then don't mention it if you don't want me looking into it. I laughed softly. 'Maybe so.' I waited for a moment. 'Strangely enough, I came upon another mystery today, in the Llwybr Llwynog.'

'Oh?' Gen raised his eyebrows.

'I thought I'd stumbled across a dehar, a most unusual har, who clearly thought highly of himself. He was riding a great grey horse with an unusually plaited mane decorated with bright medallions, and he would not speak to me. Blocked my path.'

Gen sighed. 'Whitemanes,' he said.

'I thought as much.'

'From the description of the horse that sounds like Nytethorne Whitemane. Did he have hair braided into five plaits?'

'Yes. A striking creature.'

Gen grimaced. 'That's him. He's a prominent member of their household. The Whitemanes live upon our land but prefer to believe it is theirs, yet it's us who maintain it all, and they who benefit. You won't catch a Whitemane with his sleeves rolled up, working the fields at harvest, although Wyva is there every season. The Whitemanes are aloof, and unfortunately hara believe the image they've cultivated and see the Whitemanes as spiritual, mystical.'

'I can appreciate how this must grate on your family.'

Gen nodded. 'Yes. Wyva insists we must maintain our dignity and continue polite relations with the Whitemanes, but there's no love between our families. Whitemanes refuse to see themselves as Wyvachi. Nothing too serious, though. I'd call it a social dysfunction, if anything.'

I didn't believe that. Pondering what I'd heard, I thought this was even more of a reason why Wyva should have taken on hienama duties after Rey absconded. I was puzzled as to why he hadn't. Lacking a spiritual leader, it wasn't surprising the local hara would turn to those who fulfilled that role for them. What hold had Rey had over Wyva to forbid him to take on his enemies in this way? Gen was right; few hara could resist a mystery and me less than most.

Selyf brought our meal to us himself and for a few minutes we ate in silence. Soft, moving light from tall, narrow candles in pewter sticks fell over us. Perhaps those candlesticks had stood in this room for hundreds of years. Who else had dined here over the centuries? I would quite happily have drifted off into a meditation to try and find out, but then pulled myself back to the present moment. I must make the most of this opportunity to interrogate Gen, yet not press him too hard so that defensive shutters came down. I was struggling with how to open a new conversation, but then Gen provided this for me. 'You're happy with Dŵr Alarch?' he asked.

I nodded, dabbed my mouth with a napkin. 'Who couldn't be? It's an amazing building. Did Rey live there before?'

Gen ran the fingers of one hand through his dark hair, which was loose about his shoulders. 'Yes, it's traditionally the accommodation of the hienama.'

'Was Rey with you for a long time?'

Gen nodded. 'Yes, quite a long time. Maybe fifteen years.'

'Oh! It's strange he decided to leave you after all that time. How long has he been gone?'

Gen shrugged. 'Six, eight months maybe.'

I paused, took a drink, aware I mustn't fire questions at Gen too briskly. 'I'm surprised nohar tried to dissuade him from leaving.'

Gen ducked his head to the side, twisted his mouth. 'Oh, we *tried*. He and Wyva argued about it at first. Wyva didn't want to lose our hienama. But Rey is a strange creature. I wasn't surprised by what he did.'

I lowered my eyes, concentrated on cutting a piece of meat on my plate. 'Do you still see him?'

Gen didn't pause. 'No. He went off into the mountains and hasn't yet come back. There isn't a mystery there, Ysobi...'

I looked up, said nothing.

Gen took a breath. 'Rey is... *Rey*. He was never at home in a community, although he did his best. I'm sure he's happier now. He's first generation.'

'Oh.' I let the word hang darkly, with all its implications of instability, weakness and perhaps madness.

We ate again in silence for a minute. Then I said, 'Rinawne gave me a tour of the house yesterday. He showed me its most haunted room.'

Gen raised his brows. 'And which room was this?'

'The breakfast room.'

Gen laughed. 'It isn't.'

I returned his smile. 'Isn't haunted or isn't the *most* haunted?'

Gen made a careless gesture. 'The old place is probably crawling with ghosts and walking memories for those with the inclination to pick up such things, but no room more than any other.' He shook his head. 'Rinawne *does* like to tell a story – it's a trait of many Erini hara. What did he tell you?'

'That he saw some apparition pointing at him the first time

he ate in the room and that he spat at it in front of your entire family and nohar said a thing.'

Again Gen laughed. 'I recall that episode. He did spit, but there was no mention of ghosts, and the spitting was more symbolic than actual, if you get my meaning. You can imagine what we all thought, though – some strange Erini custom for eating at a new table or something. He was a wild young thing when he came here. We learned to expect anything!' He put his head to one side. 'I feel I should say something to you.'

'What?'

'About Rinawne.'

Momentarily, my flesh chilled. 'What about him?'

'Well, like I said, he's fond of telling stories – the harlings around here love him for it – but don't take everything he says as the literal truth. He rewrites reality sometimes to fit his own view of the world. He *embellishes*. This makes the stories more exciting, but remember – they will mostly just be stories. That's why you should be careful what you use of them in your work. The embellishment occasionally upsets hara.'

'When the stories are about themselves?'

Gen studied me, a half smile on his face. 'That's not what I meant exactly. The area... Well, I shall put it bluntly. When hara first appeared in these lands, whether they came from flying machines in the sky, across the sea, or were somehow just spontaneously created, as they were in Megalithica, there was great conflict between them and the human communities.'

'Wasn't there everywhere?'

'Yes, but here the people were already fairly tribal. With the breakdown in human society, the population here had closed ranks, drawn close, protecting each other from human threats, never mind anything else. When Wraeththu came, son was pitched against father and grand-father, nephew against uncle; it was an ugly time.'

I put down my knife and fork, folded my hands beneath my chin. Now I would *have* to be careful. 'Gen, where I come from... Jesith... I've lived there a long time, and to this day know little about how the community was formed or who lived there before. No doubt there was horror in the history – how could it be avoided? But the hara in Jesith don't... *dwell* on or in the past. They live for the present moment, nurturing the land, benefiting from its bounties. That is life to them, not ancient conflicts. From what I've seen, that's the situation throughout Alba Sulh – well, the parts I've visited. Why is it so different here?'

Gen dropped his gaze from mine. He seemed sorrowful, wistful. 'I don't know.'

I reached out and touched one of his hands. 'Perhaps what Gwyllion and the Wyvachi need is to let go of that past.'

Gen uttered a laugh that was more like a cough. 'How can we, when we *live* in it? We live in that house, upon this land, where it all happened.' He raised his eyes to me again. 'I'm sorry. I shouldn't be speaking to you like this. We shouldn't broach this subject. It's our burden, not yours.'

I opened my mouth to speak but he lifted a hand to silence me.

'No, you're right. The hara here should move on, and maybe you can help with that. But don't think of my family in that respect; they are locked into the past. To try and prise that lock free would...' He held my gaze for a moment, his eyes wide, not held in his usual slightly narrow, tricksy expression. 'I've said more than I should. Rinawne doesn't understand. He's an outsider, though much loved, of course. He doesn't mind his tongue and he could say anything to you. I'm asking you now not to encourage him, or to believe all he says. He knows nothing. He makes assumptions that are very... colourful.'

'I'm not here to rake over your family's past,' I said gently. 'Neither can I force any of you to abandon it. You will find your own way, in time, I'm sure.'

He nodded. 'Yes, in time.'

I picked up my knife and fork again. 'And believe me, I already have Rinawne's measure.'

Gen laughed, brightened. 'Please don't imagine I think badly of him. He's good for us. He just has his ways.'

I took a mouthful of food, swallowed it before continuing. 'All I'm concerned about is not treading on toes, which makes my work a little more difficult. But I've already decided to avoid the bloodier aspects of the yearly round. Such things can be implied but not emphasised. From what I've heard, and the feelings I get, it seems to me a lighter atmosphere needs introducing. Celebration of what is good about life.'

Gen frowned a little. 'Death is a part of the cycle, though.'

'Of course, but that doesn't mean it should be the main focus.' I cut some more meat, and spoke before eating it. 'The turning of the seasons, the movement from light to dark and how that affects our environment; that is what is important. How it affects us too.'

Gen again fell silent and I continued my meal. I could almost hear his thought: *But we are trapped in the darkest days of winter.*

He had taken off his trickster mask and laid it on the table. Had he meant to reveal his true self? I was quite sure he'd intended the meeting to be full of pleasurable flirting, not this. I could tell he was also afraid he'd said too much and this would get back to Wyva. 'Gen,' I said, 'this conversation we've had will remain between us. I appreciate you trying to explain the situation to me, but it's really none of my business. I know now what to avoid and how my work should progress. You've helped me.'

He looked relieved. 'I'm glad of that at least. I feel I've spoiled our meal.'

'Not at all. Thank you for inviting me here. The food is excellent.'

Gen poured me more wine. 'So tell me of Jesith, and what normal harish communities are like.'

I laughed. 'I don't think any harish community can be *normal* and Jesith has had its dramas too, but it's a good place to live. Sinnar, our phylarch, is in a way like Wyva – dedicated to the community and the land. He's a fair leader and well liked. We have good relations with all communities nearby and often celebrate together at the major festivals.'

Gen pulled a face, half wistful, half ironic. 'Sounds idyllic.'

'I suppose it does, but you know, I'm becoming fond of Gwyllion too, even after so short a time. This is a wonderful, atmospheric place, which is something Jesith lacks somewhat. I like the mystery here, and by that I mean of the land, not its inhabitants. It appeals to me. Jesith lies in what's traditionally regarded as one of the most mystical landscapes in Alba Sulh, but...' I shrugged. '... but here there is something else.'

'I sometimes think the land shaped the history,' Gen said, 'influenced us all, but no, we must not head back to that territory. Tell me of your family.'

So the rest of the meal was dominated by my tales of Jesith and the hara who lived there. I omitted all my personal drama, of course, because unlike Gen and his clan this was something I was working hard to put behind me. I was first generation, too. I didn't tell him that. But many in Jesith and its surrounding area had been incepted late. Such hara had gravitated towards each other and their desire to create a better life dominated all that they did. I could not think of anyhar in Jesith who brooded upon the ancient past or who even thought of human ancestors. Gwyllion was a different place entirely and only a fool would go blundering in and try to change things.

After the meal was finished, Gen and I moved from our table to sit beside the fire. Here we sat drinking a herbal liqueur in enveloping leather armchairs. Gen stared into the flames, the sculpted planes of his rather long face enhanced by the ruddy glow. I wondered whether it would be polite to invite him back to the tower, although I had little desire to do so. I sensed he was waiting for me to say something along those lines, though. He yawned, stretched. 'Well, this has been a pleasant evening. It's good to make new friends.'

'Indeed.' I put down my glass on the table at my side. 'I feel like I've been here for weeks. You and your family have been very welcoming. I appreciate it.'

'In amongst our quirks.' Gen grinned. 'I hope that you'll find fewer quirks and more reasons to be friends.'

'Oh, I have no doubt of it.' I adopted what I hoped was a more serious expression, although the alcohol I'd consumed simply made me want to grin. 'I know I have things to learn, and I don't want to go tramping all over your traditions, Gen. The idea is to create a system that everyhar is comfortable with and enjoys. Festivals are about celebration. We all have enough hardship to contend with in daily life, at least from time to time. I feel that when hara come together for the feast days, they should be rapturous hours, if you know what I mean.'

'I do. I agree.' Gen paused. Our drinks were finished. He too put down his glass. 'Well, I suppose I'd better get back. Thanks for joining me tonight.'

'Thanks too. I've enjoyed this.' I felt we were both waiting for something, so had to speak. 'I'm still getting over my journey, so I'm sorry if I look tired. I assure you it wasn't the company. I just need my sleep.'

Gen nodded, smiling slightly, interpreting my unspoken message. 'Would you like me to mention to Wyva about arranging the Cuttingtide feast?'

'Please. If your hara could organise that side of things, I'd appreciate it. Tell Wyva I'll let him see the ritual as soon as I've finished it – hopefully in a few days' time.'

Gen stood up. 'No problem. Will you be OK finding your way back to the tower?'

'Yes, of course. It's a straight path. I have only to pass through the hounds of hell to get there.'

Gen laughed. 'You mean Mossamber's hounds.'

'Who?'

'Mossamber Whitemane, their phylarch in all but name. He's hostling to Nytethorne, your spectre on the path.'

'Ah.' I was intrigued to learn the Whitemanes kept their pack of hounds so close to me, and wondered whether they might enact their own wild hunt. 'And these beasts are kept on Wyvachi land?'

Gen grimaced. 'Wyva is delighted, as you can imagine. But Ludda, who keeps the farm, is quite thick with the Whitemanes, while being an exemplary tenant for us. We can't really forbid it.'

'Awkward.'

Gen shrugged. 'As I said, we try to keep relations... polite.'

We walked to the inn door, bidding goodbye to Selyf as we passed the bar, where he was polishing glasses in a slow and meticulous manner. Rows of them gleamed on shelves behind him like crystal. Metal tankards, similarly buffed, hung in a row above him. There was no mention of the meal being paid for, although Selyf did ask me to visit The Stag again. I had a feeling I would never be asked to pay for anything either. Hara who were gathered around the tables fell silent as we went through the room, raised their glasses to Gen. He acknowledged each one with a greeting, a quick personal word. I was impressed he took the time to do this. I had no doubt the Wyvachi knew everyhar upon their land by name.

Once outside, I said to Gen, 'there's something else I'd like you to discuss with Wyva.'

'Oh, what?' He had paused by a line of horses tethered near the door, one of which must be his own.

'Well, the community needs a hienama, and that's not a duty I can take on long term. But I can train somehar up for you. Perhaps you and your brothers could discuss any likely candidates?'

'Well, all right.' Gen sounded uncertain. 'Really, we wanted somehar from outside, somehar who'd trained for... for a time.'

On the tip of my tongue, no doubt placed there by the fine liqueur and wine, was the suggestion that perhaps a Whitemane should be considered. Might that not do something to heal rifts and to give the family a role within the community accepted by the Wyvachi? Fortunately, prudence took hold of my tongue and kept it silent on that matter. 'I suppose I could write to my contacts in Kyme for you.'

'It's a pity you can't take the job on,' Gen said, and I sensed in his words the suggestion there was no reason for me not to become their hienama. And perhaps, really, there wasn't.

Chapter Five

My work progressed well over the next few days and I'd sketched out the body of the festival rite. All I needed now was to finalise locations. The hara of Gwyllion could begin their rite in the village, and then progress through a couple of pertinent sites, eventually culminating with a finale in the gardens at Meadow Mynd, where the feast could take place. Obviously, I'd have to check this plan with Wyva – he might not want so many hara at the house. But this was an aspect of the celebration that could easily be changed. Finishing off the songs would take a little longer, but I nearly had enough to show Wyva.

On the Aloytsday following my meal with Gen in Gwyllion, I decided to pin down my ritual sites, obviously avoiding any areas associated with the moonshawl. I needed a field, with a forest walk nearby that led to an open glade – both of which would have been perfectly provided by the moonshawl sites I'd seen. I suppressed irritation. There would be other sites. As usual, I elected to walk rather than ride – in the week or so I'd been in Gwyllion I'd only ridden Hercules that once. Now he grazed peacefully in the field below my tower, perhaps all memory of Jesith gone. He'd been made to work there, often.

Consulting my copied maps, I could see that the ancient river was flanked by fields on both sides. The river did not flow too close to Meadow Mynd, however. The house was surrounded by woodland on three sides, while on the fourth were the fields of Wyva's personal crops. These sites were quite a walk from the village. I needed a spot along the way where hara could pause and enact a small rite. Again, irritation shivered through me. Maes Siôl was close to the village and the pool not far from the trail through the trees that led to the Mynd. I felt that any sites I chose could only be second best to these eminently suitable places. Why couldn't Wyva put away the past and imprint new, positive memories over these areas, if bad memories were associated with them? Perhaps, if I grew to know Wyva better I could dare to broach carefully upon this subject, but not yet.

I planned to explore the woods between my tower and the house, hoping to find a picturesque and atmospheric glade. However, as I wandered, I found my steps taking me nearer to the Llwybr Llwynog, which was rather out of the way. I wanted to see what lay beyond the forest there, also what lay beyond the river. I was hoping to catch sight of one of the Whitemanes again. There was no point denying they fascinated me, mainly because of the way they'd been described to me. Also, perhaps part of me sympathised with the outsiders, as the Whitemanes were in the eyes of the Wyvachi. I knew how it was to occupy that role, to flex against it helplessly, full of resentment.

The Llwybr Llwynog was deserted of harish presences, although I sensed a watchful atmosphere. I stood on the summit, where I found the remains of a tumbled building, most likely a folly from the time of Wyva's human ancestors. From there, I could see much of the surrounding countryside. A pale band of fields hugged the glistening river and beyond the water I could see more hedged fields, occasional spinneys and in the distance the glitter of sunlight on glass. I shaded my eyes and stared at this place. Was this another elderly pile like Meadow Mynd, where once human families had ruled the land before falling into decline? Did anyhar live there? Beyond the wide river valley, ancient mountains soared mistily towards the sky, their flanks gold and russet beneath the sun.

I heard stifled laughter behind me and turned at once. Two small brown faces were peering round the mossy tumbled stones, grinning at me. I recognised the harlings of a few days before, who'd thrown the moss at me. 'We meet again,' I said amiably. 'Are you going to run off as before, or perhaps pelt me with missiles?'

Today not shy, the harlings came out from their hiding place and at first prowled around me like cats, examining me intently. They seemed barely harish, but more like supernatural forest creatures, born of loam and sticks. Their clothes were grubby; tunics and trousers of a mud-coloured fabric. They wore no shoes and their grimy toes were long. Their skins were as dark as the earth itself, yet their eyes were the vivid green of young moss. Their hair was a riotous black tangle, glossy, yet full of leaf fragments and twigs. 'Where are you from?' I asked them.

The harlings glanced at each other and laughed, and then began to caper about me in a mad dance. They swooped in to poke my legs with sharp little fingers, then wheeled out again to continue their circling. It made me dizzy; they moved so fast. Then, I had the presence of mind to grab one of the little pests when he swept in to poke me. He struggled like a wild creature in my grasp, a mass of flailing arms and legs and sharp little teeth. He lunged to bite my wrists but could not quite reach. His companion stood still, hands to his face, and began to screech. The noise both of them made was enough to wake the dead.

'Be quiet,' I said in a stern tone. 'Who are you?'

After a few more moments of caterwauling, both harlings suddenly became still, staring at one another. I felt they were listening to somehar – or something.

'Let him go,' said the harling some feet away from me.

'I think you'll simply run off if I do that,' I replied, somewhat harshly. The harling I held had gone limp in my hands. My shins hurt where he'd kicked me. 'I wish you no harm, but can't say the same about you concerning me. Do you treat all strangers this way?'

'Only playing,' mumbled the harling in my hold.

'Playing or not, it's rude,' I said. 'If my son had behaved like that at your age, I'd have chased him with a stick.'

Zeph of course would never have behaved like that. While being a somewhat eerie, mysterious harling, he'd rarely played up or been irritating. The harlings before me were now sullenly silent.

'If I let you go, will you stay to talk to me?' I asked. 'I have some lunch with me and we can share it.'

'All right,' said both harlings at once.

I released the harling in my hold and he ran to what was clearly his brother. They grasped each other tightly but didn't attempt to flee, simply stared at me with their uncanny eyes. I sat down and unpacked lunch from my satchel onto a small cloth I'd brought with me; cheese sandwiches, a couple of roast chicken legs and two apples, plus a stoppered flask of milk. Enough to last me for the day, I'd believed. After a few moments the harlings approached inquisitively.

'My name is Ysobi,' I said. 'Will you tell me yours?'

'Our names secret,' one of them said.

'Then I shall call you Twig and Leaf,' I said, pointing to each in turn. 'Help yourself to the food.'

The harlings squatted down and proceeded to take a bite from each sandwich I'd spread out. Then, leaving the sandwiches mauled, they started on the chicken legs, cracking the bones with their teeth. Regarding their filthy hands, I lost my appetite; they could have it all.

'Where do you live?' I asked.

One of the harlings, who I'd named Twig, pointed beyond the river.

'Is there a big house there?'

Both harlings nodded vaguely.

'Are you Whitemanes?' I asked, knowing instinctively they were. They shared the same strong, sensual features of the har I'd met upon the path before.

They looked up at me suspiciously, while continuing to stuff my lunch into their mouths. The chicken bones were discarded, now it was back to one bite from each sandwich at a time, until there were only crusts left, which they threw on the ground.

'I'm a friend,' I said. 'There's no need to be afraid. I'm

working here in Gwyllion for a time, and would like to meet your family... *if* you are Whitemanes.'

The harlings got to their feet, held each other's gaze for a moment and then beckoned to me. 'Follow.'

'Follow where?'

They came to me then, grabbed one of my hands each and started to drag me. They were laughing, jumping up and down in their eagerness to lead me forward. 'Now, wait...' I tried to resist them, but their grip was strong. 'Come now... where are we going?'

'Just follow!'

'Oh...' I sighed, smiled at them, 'all right.'

They set off at once, racing down the hill. I stumbled. 'Hey, not so fast!' But they only laughed at me wildly, and then I was laughing too and let them have their way. We ran down towards the open fields, faster and faster. I felt like a harling myself, although of course I had never been one. What would it have been like? These creatures were like no harlings I'd ever seen. They were wild and beautiful, beings of the land.

We came to the river, where there was a broad stone bridge, flanked with low walls, upon which hara might sit and gaze out over the water. My little Whitemanes led me to the middle of the bridge, slowing at last to a walk. The river was wide here and roiled with an almost muscular strength around the weed-wrapped struts below. I felt light-headed after my run, and disorientated – the unmistakable sensation that warned of the unseen. I didn't want to move an inch from the centre of that bridge.

The harlings complained, once more jumping around me, digging their sharp little nails into my hands. I had the irrational fear they intended to throw me into the water. No matter how much I tried to free myself, they wouldn't let go of my hands. I noticed then, at the other end of the bridge, facing me, two sentinel statues rearing high: white horses, each with eight legs, four of which mauled the air. Even from this distance I could see their stone lips peeled back from their long teeth in a snarl, their wild eyes. A shiver passed through me. At any moment, those beasts might spring to life and be upon me. The harlings, perhaps noticing I was mesmerised by the sight of these guardians, became quiet and still, as if waiting. Between the statues, I could see a well-trodden path through the fields ahead and then a band of tall trees, through which I glimpsed a hint of walls and windows.

'I must go back,' I said. 'Let me go.'

'No, come with us,' said Leaf in a deceptively sweet voice. 'Come home with us.'

'No... it isn't polite to do that. I'm not invited. If I *am* invited – properly – then I might come, but not this way.'

'*We're* inviting you,' said Twig. 'Come, little rabbit, we won't eat you.'

Both harlings grinned at me. I realised then that – farcically – I was afraid, but of what? Wasn't this what I wanted – a chance to see the domain of the Whitemanes?

'No, not today,' I said. 'I mean it. Now let me go.'

The harlings grumbled a little, unintelligible sounds, but clearly not happy ones. They pulled on my arms strongly, their fingernails still digging into the flesh of my hands. I was overwhelmed by a visceral desire to escape, to run. I couldn't pass those stone guardians ahead. I mustn't. I would never come back from what lay beyond. I felt as if I was a child again, held between stronger, meaner children. I was on the verge of tears: preposterous. Must I copy what my captive harling had done earlier and free myself with bites and kicks? But before I could attack my captors physically, (and I really would have done so), a figure appeared between the stone horses. He wasn't tall and at this distance I could discern little detail, other than that he was dressed in trousers and shirt of a dark colour and his hair fell in a glossy curtain to his waist. He carried a staff. As the harlings struggled to drag me onward, the har ahead put two fingers into his mouth and emitted a piercing whistle. The harlings let go of me at once and scampered towards the end of the bridge, without looking back. It seemed to me they occasionally dropped onto all fours like dogs, then sprang up again to their two feet, but even then, fuddled as I was, I told myself that couldn't have been possible. The harlings threw themselves against the har who'd whistled, gripping his waist. If they'd had tails, they would have been wagging. The har regarded me without moving. He too seemed young, not much older than the wild harlings, perhaps just past feybraiha. I was breathless, dazed, but managed to raise a hand in thanks, noticing it was smeared with blood from deep little cuts. Then, I turned away, went slowly back across the bridge, each step feeling as if I trod on blades.

As I left the bridge, I saw something I'd not noticed on the way across: two broken statues lying in the grass. Unwilling to stop moving, I merely glimpsed the lichened heads of eagles as I passed, then a lion's haunch, a smashed paw; gryphons. Whatever guardians had watched this end of the bridge had been toppled and vanquished.

When I reached the summit of the Llwybr Llwynog once more, I realised how shaken I was. None of what had happened during the last half hour or so seemed real. I found the remains of my lunch spread out and would not touch it, gathering up only the satchel and the cloth. My hands were smarting where they'd been scratched. I wanted desperately to wash them, anxious to reach familiar ground where I was welcome. Safe. I was sure now that this area was influenced wholly by the Whitemanes; it could not be regarded as Wyvachi land. As I made my way home, I heard again, as on the first day, the solitary tolling of a bell. I couldn't discern from which direction the sound came, but it was at once soothing yet unsettling.

Back in Dŵr Alarch, after I'd washed my cuts, I made myself strong tea and wrote up, with an unsteady hand, all I'd witnessed and felt that afternoon. Determined to examine the events rationally, I concluded I hadn't picked up any intention of actual harm or violence on the part of the harlings, other than a vague fear they might've tipped me off the bridge. But really, hadn't they simply been undisciplined and boisterous? It was absurd I'd reacted this way to their playfulness. I was unused to being around harlings. They were not like human children, (who themselves were very distant memories to me), and it was a mistake to compare them. Twig and Leaf had merely wanted to show me their home because I'd asked to meet their family. Why had I resisted so strongly? There was simply an uncanniness about the Whitemanes I'd met that repelled me as much as it attracted me. I was still shaken. I would have to meditate to calm myself, but then found that I was wary of what I might see in that meditation. I would take a bath instead, indulge in a more physical kind of relaxation. I went upstairs to the bathroom, shedding my clothes as I climbed the winding stair.

Presently, I sank into comforting warmth and scent. I sighed and lay back in the long, deep bath, only my head above the water. I was Ysobi har Jesith, a hienama of experience and knowledge. I'd seen many inexplicable and uncanny things in my harish life, but none – that I could remember – had unnerved me as much as those two harlings had, and the bridge, the rearing statues, the har who'd called the little ferals off me. The Whitemanes must be far more than the Wyvachi had led me to believe, or was it simply my imagination working too hard, dreaming up strangeness and magic because that was what I wanted to see?

I considered that if I'd not given in to my irrational fear and had crossed that bridge, met the har on the other side, everything might have been revealed as mundane. I'd have been invited to the house, met other hara there, maybe begun a friendship. Part of my reluctance might simply have been that I wanted the family to remain as they were to me, their mystery intact. I also thought about how it was likely they regarded me as a minion of the Wyvachi, and might have influenced me psychically to be afraid. Even I could succumb when unguarded to such basic bewitchments. If only all this had occurred to me earlier, but instead I'd given in to panic and had fled. Panic, yes, that was absolutely it. The ancient god Pan and the terror he could instil in the strongest heart. A god of the earth itself, the immanence of nature and her power. Panic could strike at any time in a landscape where the spirits were strong, especially at this time of year. I had been warned of this at the start. Now I must heed it, but not give in to it. There were lessons for me here.

Chapter Six

Rinawne arrived at the tower mid-morning the following day. His good humour appeared restored. I had hoped he'd show up, not least because I hadn't decided upon the ritual locations and wanted Rinawne, with his more intimate knowledge of the landscape, to help me with that.

'Have you got much work done?' he asked me.

'Yes, nearly done with Cuttingtide, but I'm struggling with the locations, since the moonshawl sites are out of bounds. I'm hoping you can advise me. I need a good field and a forest glade.'

Rinawne grinned. 'I see the problem. Now you've seen the moonshawl sites, which of course are perfect, it's difficult to replace them.'

'Exactly what I thought.' I was warmed by the fact his opinion echoed mine so completely.

As we walked down the hill, I told Rinawne about my encounter the previous day, making light of it. 'They seemed barely har,' I said, 'clearly allowed to run wild.'

'They are,' Rinawne said. 'Don't waste your time on that lot. They'll not be your friends, Ysobi, because of your association with us.' He then changed the subject, and asked how he could help me with my work.

'I was thinking the festival could finish up at Meadow Mynd,' I said. 'The other night, Gen spoke to me about the feast. Would Wyva be happy to hold that in the gardens of the Mynd?'

'I can't see why not,' Rinawne answered, somewhat shortly. 'How did your meeting with Gen go?'

'Pleasant enough,' I said, and then realised this would not satisfy my companion. 'I don't think it went quite how he planned, but it was an enjoyable evening.'

Rinawne expressed a snort. 'I knew he'd try it on with you.' He narrowed his eyes at me. 'That really doesn't work with you though, does it?'

I shifted my gaze from his. 'Well... no, not really, I suppose.'

'I wonder what it takes?' Before I could respond to that, Rinawne laughed and slapped my shoulder. 'Be as you are, Ysobi. Let's find your meadow and woodland dell.' He strode ahead down the hill.

Rinawne knew of an oak grove mid-way between the tower and the Mynd. When I saw it I realised rather grudgingly it would be adequate for my plans. I thought wistfully of the gleaming waters of the Pwll Siôl Lleuad, even though this other grove did have, beyond the oaken circle, a small pond on its western side, guarded by a single sentinel willow of great age. The oaks too were ancient; three or four had collapsed upon the ground.

'You can hear the trees creaking,' Rinawne said, sitting upon one of the fallen trunks. 'At any time a bough could plummet down and claim a life.'

'Well, *that* sounds safe for the festival,' I said.

'Oh, there's plenty of room. Hara round here know the ways of the grove and even harlings would recognise the wrong kind of creak and make a run for it.'

I walked around the grove, touching the trees, absorbing their being, their splendid age. These oaks had stood for hundreds of years, had witnessed the fall of humanity. They might even have been planted deliberately in this rough ring to provide a ritual space for humans. The trees were aloof but not malevolent. 'We should acknowledge the guardians of this site,' I said. 'Do you mind?' I walked to the centre of the grove and sat down.

Rinawne sauntered after me. 'What do you want me to do?'

I was surprised he didn't know. 'Just sit and close your eyes, and open yourself up to the spirit of place. I'll say a few words.'

'OK.'

While Rinawne sat obedient and quiet beside me, I didn't

pick up anything extraordinary about the site. I sensed the presence of ancient guardians, but they were slow and even a little sleepy. This was an undisturbed site in every sense, therefore perfect for my purposes. I ended our meditation and Rinawne blinked at the daylight. 'I've not done anything like that for years,' he said.

I opened my satchel, in which I'd stowed some wine, courtesy of the Wyvachi cellar. I'd even brought drinking vessels, albeit a couple of chipped tea mugs I'd found in the back of a kitchen cupboard. I hadn't wanted to risk breaking anything newer.

'Did you ever go through caste ascension?' I asked Rinawne, handing him a mug of wine.

He frowned, which was also a typical Rinawne smile. 'Some,' he said, and took a swig of his drink.

'By that you mean no,' I said.

Rinawne laughed. 'Is it for hara like me? I can't see it figures in my life. I'm har, I do what hara do, but I've no aim to be a mighty magus.'

'Like me?' I said, grinning.

'Yes, just like you. I bet you can throw purple sparks from your finger tips.'

'How else do I light my fires?'

He chuckled. 'Well, I'm probably not a very good example of a har. Do you think I'm squandering our gifts? Should I be lighting my own fires?'

'Some tribes take caste education very seriously,' I said, 'and it's important to them. I would never judge others about it. My job once was to teach in that way, and I can't say I have glittering memories of it. In my opinion, if you needed to call upon a harish power in a crisis, you could do so, whether you'd trained meticulously or not.'

'Now there's a relief,' said Rinawne. 'Despite my lack of education, though, I do know a lot about folklore, about beliefs, human and otherwise. That's my speciality, if any.'

'Have you always collected stories?' I asked.

He laughed. 'In a way, some collected me. I have a few tales to tell.'

'Perhaps they might be helpful for me.'

'Perhaps. As long as they are ones of which Wyva approves.' He grimaced. 'You know, I think it must be difficult to dream up a round of the year for a tribe like ours — well, for any tribe.'

'Not really,' I replied, gesturing around us. 'The raw material surrounds us.'

Rinawne wrinkled up his nose. 'What I mean is... in the human era there were legends going back thousands of years, about fairies, and dark creatures, ghosts and demons. Are those our legends too, and can we build our beliefs about them? Second generation though I am, and *uneducated*, I know we are young as a race – a *species*, even – so everything feels too invented and new, to my mind. I feel more affinity to Daghda than I do to any dehar.'

'I understand what you mean,' I said. 'But even in the relatively short time hara have lived upon the earth, they've created legends. I believe they bring new spirits out of the landscape, new thoughts and beliefs. They have always been there, but in a different shape. Now, we can put our own shape upon them.' I smiled, but Rinawne didn't look convinced. 'Come now, didn't you tell me you'd brought me out today to tell me more stories?' I put my head to one side. 'Didn't you?'

'Yes.' Rinawne grinned. 'You talk to me as if I'm a harling – clear to see you were a teacher. But most of the stories I know are about humans.'

'Tell me one.'

'OK.' He closed his eyes for a couple of seconds. 'Some people were digging the foundations for a new house near Gwyllion – before the Wraeththu era. They found beneath a rose garden a grave, two female skeletons twined together, as if they had been buried alive.' Now Rinawne punctuated his story with dramatic gestures to act it out. 'Their elbows and knees had been pierced with knives of black iron' He winced as if pierced by blades, clutched himself. 'This was to stop them walking, of course, or clawing their way out of the soil. They were witches.'

'And did digging them up free them? What happened to the bones?'

Rinawne spread out his arms. 'Well, of course they were reburied in the churchyard, but no one took out the iron.'

'Perhaps a wise precaution.' I laughed.

Now his voice lowered to nearly a whisper. 'They howled about it, though, as their sleep had been disturbed. Some people felt they should be dug up again and put back beneath the roses, but the parson said no. They must stay in hallowed ground so as to bind them thoroughly.' Now he performed the parting of curtains, peering through glass. 'Yet people saw distorted faces at their windows in the dark, and heard running feet along the roads, and the terrible voices. It took a while to calm down.' He paused, asked dramatically. 'You know that horses can be *hag*-ridden?'

I nodded, smiling at his performance. 'Yes, they're believed to be more susceptible to unseen presences than other creatures. Witches were said to entrance them and ride them to their sabbats.'

'Well,' said Rinawne, waving a finger at me, 'after the two skeletons were reburied in the church yard, every night a white horse would come and paw the ground above their grave.' This, he mimed. 'Eventually, it was traced to a house of the gentry, the gelding belonging to a lady who lived there. The horse had been hag-ridden and was drawn to its mistresses, perhaps always had been, when they were hidden beneath the roses. The lady had the horse slaughtered...' He drew a hand across his neck, uttered a choked gargle. 'Then all the ghostly activity stopped. The horse must've let the witches out somehow.'

'But how could they ride the horse, or even rise from their grave, if they were pinned by iron?'

'A mystery,' Rinawne said, 'but a good story, eh?'

'Can you show me the grave?'

'Yes, I can, but not today. It's some miles the other side of Gwyllion. It's not something you can use really, anyway.' He paused, finished his drink. 'Hara can be pinned by iron too. And they don't have to be buried, either.'

I looked away from him, sensing where this conversation was heading. 'I suppose so.'

'All the tortures of iron and fire; they can be wrought with words and deeds.'

I glanced back at him. 'Are you speaking from personal experience?'

'No, not me. I'm impervious to iron and fire.' He adopted a more serious expression. 'So who was the har who broke you with iron, Ysobi?'

My first instinct was to be angry – how dare he? – but then looking into his open face I could see no malice or slyness there. He saw me broken. He wanted to know. Simple as that.

'I don't speak his name, ever,' I replied lightly.

'Why not, is it cursed?'

'No, I'm afraid he might hear it.'

My grim, hollow pronouncement, which even made me shiver, only prompted Rinawne to laugh. 'Afraid he will trace the sound to its source and come find you?'

'Not that,' I said, somewhat irritably. 'We'll never meet again, but I don't want him to hear it. He should just be allowed to forget.'

'That must have been a powerful breaking,' Rinawne said, shaking his head in wonder.

'It wasn't his fault,' I said. 'And that's all I want to say.'

'Aww, come on, don't be angry,' Rinawne said, shaking my right arm a little. 'Don't bury it beneath the roses. Exhume!'

I couldn't help but smile.

Rinawne pointed at the willow tree drooping over the pond. 'She is the tree of grief and lost love,' he said. 'And she heard what you said. Maybe her roots will eat the words and make you lighter.'

I laughed. 'Maybe.'

And then, before I'd even started another thought, or begun another word, Rinawne threw me back upon the grass and kissed me. He was stronger than he looked. I lay paralysed, not sure what to think or feel. He wanted to share breath but mine was locked in my chest.

After a while, he released me, sat up and said, 'There.' He looked down at me. 'It's polite for a har to respond, by the way, not lie there like a corpse pinned with iron.'

'I was surprised,' I said feebly. 'It's... it's not why I'm here, Rinawne. I must be... careful.'

He snorted but in an agreeable sort of way. 'Who cares? No har need know. I'm bored to death. It will interest me.'

'Is this to be part of my duties?'

'For sure, make a dehar out of me. I won't mind.' He grinned.

'Perhaps,' I said, 'soon.'

Rinawne rolled his eyes. 'Soon? What does that mean?'

I was aware of the tightness that had come to my chest. Beneath my fingers, it was as if I could feel every single blade of grass. 'Look, you know little about me, but please respect that some things... I find difficult. I'm a recovering lunatic and need some space.'

'If you don't like me in that way, just say so.'

'No, it's really not that. Honestly. I find you very attractive.'

'Are you in the sort of chesna-bond where it's all "this is for life, forsake all others"?'

'No.'

'What is it, then?'

'By Aru, you are relentless!' I said. 'I just don't want to talk about it at this moment.'

He regarded me, his face still set in a humourless expression. 'That's the sort of chesna-bond I'm supposed to be in,' he said. 'The archaic sort.'

'Marvellous,' I said, and lay back on the grass. I laughed. 'Couldn't be better.'

'I've never abided by it, mind.'

'Of course you haven't.' I looked up at him. 'So why are you here?'

He sighed through his nose. 'Let's save that for another time, too. Want a new story?'

I closed my eyes. 'Yes.'

'It concerns the beansidhe,' Rinawne said. 'The banshee. It happened back in Erini... when I was a little harling.

I settled myself again, the tightness releasing its clutch within me. Rinawne's voice was jaunty as he began. I closed my eyes to listen.

'My friend Gadda and I, we snuck out of our houses one night and met in the dark. Gadda had two bottles of shine he had stolen from his father's store. We planned to find a barn and drink ourselves silly. It was an autumn night and the first frost was upon us. Some of the fields wore coats of mist. We followed an old rail track in a deep cutting, passing the first bottle between us. There was enough drink there to down a group of adult hara – gods knew what we were thinking.

'But anyway, we walked on, already tipsy. Gadda said to me, "Rin, you hear that?" and I said "What's that, Gad?" and he said, "just listen. Tell me you can hear that." So we both stood quiet, just the sound of our breathing, and I heard a faint mewing sound, like an animal in pain. "Creature in a trap," I said, taking a swig of shine. "Is it?" Gadda said. "Sounds like no creature to me." But still, he shrugged and we carried on walking along that old cutting – nasty places in themselves, the human tracks.

'As we walked, we were joking and pushing each other around, but then Gadda stopped and said, "Listen, Rin." The sound had got louder, a terrible weeping it sounded like now. "Somehar in trouble," Gadda said. He lurched to the side of the cutting and began to climb. I got watered up with this bad feeling and called out to him, "No, wait!" but he was gone like a rabbit, so I had to follow, him being my friend, and all.

'We came out into Mawna's Meadow, which was where

we'd been heading anyway, there being a great old barn there, full of fresh hay. But in the middle of the field, we saw a figure with its back to us, letting out these awful sounds. Gadda said, "That's no har", and I knew what he meant. It was a human woman, her hair sticking out all over. I could just *tell*. There were still old humans sometimes who lived among the hara of the villages, looked after until the end. The woman before us gave off this air of being very ancient, and oh, the grief that came out of her; it was the most terrible thing I ever heard. It made you want to cry, and run away, and go to her to comfort her, all at the same time.

'Gadda said, "We must help," and started to trot forward, but I went after him then, quick as I could, and pulled his arm. "No! Don't! Run!" He looked angry, but then he was looking back at me, and couldn't see what was before us – the shape ahead slowly turning round. I knew we must not see her face. "Just run, you roon wit, run!" I dragged him back into the cutting and we ran so fast back the way we came it was like we were flying. And all the time that awful shrieking rang in our heads.

'We ran till we got home, and then neither of us felt like drinking any more. "It was the banshee," I said and Gadda nodded, his hands braced on his thighs, his head almost between his knees. We were too scared to part, so Gadda came to my bed and until morning we just hugged each other, and couldn't sleep.'

I had been almost hypnotised by Rinawne's tale and had to shake myself out of it. 'That's an amazing story,' I said.

He shrugged. 'Yeah, it's a good one. Not much use to you as it's not of these parts, but I was never so feared in my life. She brings death, you know. She would've taken a soul, but maybe only a human one, I don't know. We never found out, and we couldn't tell our hara; we'd have been punished for sneaking out.' He paused, chewing on a grass stem, then said, grinning, 'But you know, to this day I wonder what her face was like.'

'I'm wondering too,' I said.

Rinawne got to his feet. 'Well, we have your forest glade, what else do you need?'

'A field,' I said. 'Near to the house, so the festival can finish up there.'

'There are plenty of those. Let's pick Dôl Cartref, the Home Meadow, since there's a path to the gardens from it. It's used for the horses, so it's grass not crops. We can shift the nags for a night, since a few of them have a hankering to eat harish flesh.'

'I've known horses of that type,' I said grimly.

We both laughed.

I stood up and Rinawne took me in his arms. I didn't resist. 'Don't leave it too long,' he murmured, kissing my brow. He was one of the few hara I'd met who was as tall as I am and didn't have to stand on a box to kiss my brow. 'I'm not being selfish,' he murmured. 'I've a feeling you need it.'

I sighed and leaned against him. 'It's like another kingdom to me now.'

'This I can tell.' He hugged me. 'Come on, let's look at the meadow.'

I'd expected an invitation to dinner at the Mynd as before, but after we'd walked round the field, deciding where the procession should pause and ritual actions performed, hidden from the house by towering elms at its border, Rinawne said, 'So when do I get the pleasure of a meal cooked by you, Ysobi?'

'I can't match your board,' I said.

'That's not the point. I'd like to sit in the tower at night and look over the land.'

I gave him a stare to show him I wasn't that stupid. He certainly wasn't going to allow me to "leave it too long", but how could I expect otherwise from an impulsive creature like Rinawne? Inwardly, I sighed, then came abruptly to a decision. 'All right. It might not be as good as you think likely, but all right.'

'You are a master of seduction,' he said. 'When?'

'Tonight.'

'Might as well get it over with then, eh?' He grinned.

'Might as well.'

'I have things to do this afternoon,' he said. 'I'll come over later, about eight o'clock. Is that OK?'

'Yes, that's fine.'

He shook his head. 'You're a wonder.' Then he sauntered off towards the house.

I stood in the field for a moment, staring at the grass, also mindful of the horses eyeing me from some distance away, some of whom yearned to be meat-eaters. Was this the right thing to do? I felt coerced, yet not. If anything, I felt like I'd tumbled into a stream and the current was carrying me; seemed best to go with it, see where it led.

I went down to Ludda's farm to order a chicken and to replenish my stock of vegetables; for the last day or so I'd been living on toast and eggs. I also requested a bottle of Ludda's best honey and herb liqueur. I knew he made it for Wyva, who had a vast collection of locally-made liqueurs, and that it was probably supposed to be just for him, but Ludda only gave me a wry look and agreed to supply the bottle. After that, and making preliminary preparations for dinner, I sat down at the kitchen table and wrote up the stories Rinawne had told me. I couldn't use them for anything at the moment, but I believe nothing that might be of use creatively should be thrown away or forgotten.

I felt extremely nervous and considered that part of my punishment in Jesith had been a kind of 'unharing'. Slowly and by degrees, the desire for aruna had faded away from me, almost as if I'd been given a drug to kill it. I didn't for one moment think any of my friends and family in Jesith had done such a thing, but that's what it felt like.

This had happened, I realised, even before I'd visited Kyme and the last fateful episodes with my nemesis, whose name I don't want to speak aloud or even write. And yet somehow I *did* want to write about what had happened, as if to purge some of it before Rinawne came to me. I wouldn't tell him any of this to his face, but would imagine him now as I wrote; a silent listener with no memory. Out came my notebook. I sat at the kitchen table, put a title at the head of a blank page: My History.

I'd had a towering reputation in Jesith once, and throughout the surrounding lands, but this had been destroyed, my character questioned. How? Through aruna, through love, or the emotion to which we give that name. I'd seduced one of my pupils... No, that's wrong, we seduced one another. But anyway, I should have known better, because he was mentally scarred by early life traumas. Without meaning to, I'd tormented him emotionally, because I hadn't been in the position to care for him, only to roon him secretly behind my chesnari's back. He had been, perhaps still was, indescribably beautiful, irresistible, an attribute with which his hurt psyche couldn't cope, because of the attention it drew to him.

Unfortunately, this har hadn't wanted a casual relationship, such as many enjoy outside of their chesna bonds, and with their chesnari's blessing. Like Rinawne, he had been relentless, but in this case he had been unswerving in his determination to have me completely, to remove Jass from the picture. Unhinged, of course. This ended with him trying to kill himself, messily, right at the time when my son's pearl was being delivered. Out of feelings of guilt and responsibility, I chose the wrong bed to sit beside and things went from bad to worse.

The young har, his mind battered, had been sent away in disgrace, to be educated in Kyme, to be disciplined and redesigned. The hara in Jesith saw him as a manipulative and selfish idiot, a soume shrew, who targeted weak, older hara who should know better. I'd been left behind to try and mend the mess, not at all successfully. You see, the worst thing about it was that my speciality in teaching was to enhance the arunic arts, to use aruna as magic and for self-development. Hara looked at me and saw an egotistic fool, who used his position to take his pick of young hara coming to him for education. It really wasn't like that, but that's how it looked. I was judged. They didn't pelt me with stones, or have me whipped, or even make me stand before a jury of my peers to receive punishment. They simply avoided me, crowded round Jassenah, the pious martyr, and judged me with their eyes. Left me out in the cold on winter's nights while they raised their Natalia cups to my chesnari and my son.

That should have been the end of it, but it wasn't. Fate took me to Kyme a year or so later and of course the path of my nemesis crossed with mine in that small community. Within the cloistered, antique atmosphere of our city of scholars, I'd wanted him still, with a yearning that was so profound it was unnatural. But I was bound somehow. I couldn't bring myself to initiate any physical intimacy between us, because I felt there was only a snow-blank void where once my sensuality had been. I could only torture him for my own loss and weakness. Even though the sparks took light once more, this was in an even more twisted and damaging way. The torture was suppressed desire; far more subtle and dark. We should never have met again, because our wounds from the earlier battle were still fresh. The skin could be reopened very easily.

I went slightly mad; no other way to put it. I punished that har for the way he made me feel. At times, I wanted to break him, because I saw in his beauty the ruin of my life. Eventually, *he* broke *me*, using harish powers that he had been trained by me to use.

Cursed and physically shrunken, I'd been taken back an invalid to Jesith by Jassenah, now regarded as High Martyr of All Martyrs by our neighbours. My life from that day forward had been that of the outsider. The other, I believe, came out of it better because he had made powerful friends in Kyme.

Hideously cruel. All of it. Yet desire had created the situation and had lit the bonfires that had heated the iron. My nemesis and I had been branded to the bone, and much had been lost. Thinking of it now, I felt angry for both of us. No punishment should be so harsh. I was first generation, perhaps hag-ridden by demons hidden so deep I was unaware of them, and he, the young one, had been beaten by life before he even reached Jesith for his education. Two damaged beings do not make a whole. We'd learned that in the hardest of ways.

Sighing, I closed my notebook and rubbed my eyes. Gwyllion had given me a new start. I hoped the same went for him, wherever he was. Part of that new start was standing before the mirror of what I was: har. We are told we need aruna, which is the current that sustains us, physically, mentally and spiritually. Without it, what am I? The truth was, I didn't even miss it.

I realised only a har like Rinawne was the right type to heal me in this regard. Irreverent, not particularly emotionally engaged with me, simply wanting a distraction. He didn't come with a contract of demands and expectations I was forced to sign in blood. True, he'd seemed jealous when he'd thought Gen might be trying to elbow his way into my affections, but I thought that was only because he'd wanted to elbow in first. Truly passionate love can be a heavy mantle, its lining laden with gloom and despair, as well as ecstasy and longing. I believe only the healthiest of hara can handle it correctly and without causing harm to themselves or those they love. Looking in from outside, it's like a disease that turns the brain to cheese. I didn't ever want to feel that way again.

Rinawne arrived around fifteen minutes late, during which time a part of me hoped he might not turn up. Perhaps my lack of eagerness had put him off. But no, at quarter past the hour I heard a thundering rap upon the door downstairs and seconds later Rinawne came bounding into the kitchen. I learned from then on that Rinawne would always let himself into my tower without waiting to be admitted. Well, I suppose it belonged to him more than it did to me, but I was used to the more restrained politeness found in Jesith.

'Door was open,' he announced, throwing himself onto a

chair by the table.

'Always is,' I replied, stirring pots needlessly at the range. 'Do you think it shouldn't be?'

'I'm sure it's quite safe.'

Over dinner, we both drank copious amounts of wine, and talked of harmless things, mainly Rinawne gossiping rather waspishly about the family, yet in an affectionate way. He made me laugh.

After dinner, I suggested we move from the kitchen table. For the first time since I'd moved into the tower, I'd decided to make use of the living room, which seemed a more suitable venue for intimacy than downstairs. The day had been warm so there was no need to light a fire, although part of me wished we could have had one. That would have set the archetypal seduction scene: aruna in the light of a fire. Yet the living room held the warmth of the day and, once the lamps were lit, became a cosy and sensual chamber, where even the vainest of Wraeththu beauties would have felt proud to bring his conquests.

Rinawne sprawled on the sofa. 'Do you have incense?' he asked.

I had in fact found a drawer full of it in the upper room a couple of days before, so went to fetch some, debating which scent was the most appropriate. I discarded the loose incense as impractical – I couldn't be bothered fiddling around with lighting charcoal. Some sticks of rather aged jasmine would have to do. I hoped they'd not gone musty.

Downstairs, Rinawne helped me light the sticks, which he stuck into the soil of the various fern pots around the room. Silvery smoke slid into the air. 'This reminds me of Rey,' Rinawne said. 'He always loved this scent.'

'Did you come here often when he lived here?'

Rinawne raised a brow at the hint of sharpness in my voice, smiled, but made no comment. Of course he'd come here often.

'One thing I'd like to know,' I said, sitting down on the sofa. 'How did you come to be here in Gwyllion, Rin? I don't get the feeling that once upon a time you met Wyva's eyes across a room and fell in love. If you're to be a visitor to my tower, I'd like to know the truth.' I set our liqueur bottle and glasses on the low table between the sofa and the fire.

Rinawne sat down again, next to me, and picked up his newly-filled glass. 'The Wyvachi have dealings with my family in Erini,' he said, without hesitation. 'Don't fill those words with dire meaning, by the way. When I was younger, it all seemed like an adventure – well, there was no *seemed* about it. I wanted to come. There were several young hara past feybraiha in our tribe. Wyva and Bronna, our phylarch, thought it would be a sign of loyalty and friendship to mingle our bloodlines, so a young har was chosen from Erini, and one here from Gwyllion, to be the consorts of the phylarchs. I believe the har from Gwyllion found more romance than I did!' He laughed. 'I don't blame Wyva. He just doesn't have it in him to be a moonstruck lover. He's practical, and in many ways so am I. Therefore, we work well together.'

'Yet you once told me yours was a chesna bond of the old-fashioned kind.'

He nodded slowly. 'And so it is, in some ways.' He frowned slightly. 'Let me put it this way. The har in Wyva accepts gracefully I should seek aruna with others; the human in him would not.'

'He's first generation?'

'No, but then in this place they don't need to be in order to carry around the worst baggage from the past, as you already know.'

I exhaled through my nose, drank some liqueur. 'You could say that.'

'When we made Myv, I evoked a dehar. I didn't take aruna with Wyva alone but the spirit of our race. I wanted to make a harling, have a son. I know we're told only the highest and most spiritual of loves can facilitate that, but it's not true. Dedicated will is just as effective.'

This had told me more than I wanted to know and

reminded me uncomfortably of how Zeph had been conceived – in the traditional, romanticised way. Or so Jass and I had fooled ourselves, perhaps. 'I think you're right,' I said. 'The making of harlings is seen as a rare and precious thing, with conditions having to be absolutely right, the moon in the right phase, all that. But this might only be a safeguard against Wraeththu flooding the world with harlings, among a race whose lifespans are perhaps five times greater than humanity's were.'

Rinawne laughed. 'Yes or... No, perhaps I'm wrong, and Myv's conception wasn't as cold-blooded as I remember, but the safeguard is there, all the same. Who wants another crowded world? It did humanity no good and eventually helped kill it.'

We grinned and clinked glasses. In that we were in accord.

Rinawne laid a hand on my thigh. 'Come, forget all this. Share breath with me. Share secrets, but not bad ones.'

At this point, I felt as if a part of me left my body and hovered against the ceiling looking down. I could see myself performing adequately all that was required of me to share what were supposed to be special, almost divine, moments with another of my kind. Rinawne was patient and skilled – as I myself once had been, and had been renowned for it – but even so a piece of me still felt obliged to escape, to observe and not take part. There is no greater pleasure for the harish body than that stimulated by aruna – we have been blessed by our gods in that something that was often base and crude in humans has been lifted to this unique and exhilarating experience: a true sharing of being. And part of me did share, swooning pleasurably beneath Rinawne's attentions. The ghost above the room could feel it, taste it, yet the experience was not truly his.

Rinawne did not appear to be aware of this separation. Afterwards, he held me close, no doubt believing me to have been exorcised of some kind of demon. He must've had glimpses into my psyche, because aruna allows little to be kept utterly private. 'You're not har-born,' he murmured as we lay entwined on the sofa in the soft sunset aruna leaves in the heart and mind. 'I thought you were.'

'No, hag-ridden,' I replied sleepily and buried my face in his hair, fragrant with wood smoke and the scent of young leaves. I had felt his strength, both of mind and spirit. Rinawne was a good ally to have and now, from the honesty of his breath and body, I knew he was truly this, yet still I had no desire to open my past to him, or indeed certain aspects of my present.

'It has a taste to it,' Rinawne said. He kissed the top of my head. 'It reminds me of walking into a long-disused room, and outside it is summer, and there is a church bell ringing, and birds in the air. Yet the room is so still, the cupboards shut fast, and it smells of dust.'

'Have you ever *heard* a church bell?' I enquired, somewhat scoffingly.

'Yes, in Erini the bells still ring as the twilight comes. Sometimes you can hear them here too, from some of the other villages. You'll hear them at Midsummer. The church in Gwyllion is a ruin, though. I think in some way it's connected with Wyva's dark past. He went peculiar on me once when I mentioned it.'

'I've heard a bell,' I said. 'Twice. Could it have been the Gwyllion bell?'

Rinawne shook his head. 'No. It's fallen, no doubt buried under shrubs and tree roots. I've been to the church. I didn't see it there.'

'Perhaps we should find and raise the bell,' I said. 'I think they're sacred. We could have a tower built for it.'

Rinawne laughed. 'Now there's a nice thought. Only aruna can make a har like you think of something like that.'

'I half mean it, too.'

Rinawne hugged me. 'I dare you to suggest it to Wyva.'

I raised my head, grinning. 'I can see his reaction now. "Argh, no, the bells! *The bells!*"'

This prompted further Wyva impersonations from Rinawne

until my stomach began to hurt from laughing so much. Then Rinawne sat up, wiping his eyes, and leaned towards the table to pour us another drink.

'Do you know Wyva's dark past?' I asked. If there was any time to interrogate him, now was it.

Rinawne glanced over his bare shoulder and stared at me in silence for several seconds.

'Don't answer if you don't want to,' I said, and reached out to touch him. 'I'm just curious, that's all. *You* have to live here.'

'It's not that. The truth is, no, I don't really know at all. I have ideas, but...' He sighed. 'I believe something happened here right at the start of harish history, something that bound Wyva's ancestors – harish, I mean – to that house and this area. It must have been something so bad we can't imagine it. Slaughter? Their beloved human relatives tortured and mutilated by wandering hara, or other humans, or even incepted family members? Perhaps the human ancestors shielded those who'd been incepted, and were punished harshly for it. Perhaps a harish community existed alongside the human one and it ended in tragedy. Or perhaps it was something else entirely. The Wyvachi won't say. They have a vow of silence about it.'

'What about other hara around Gwyllion? I assume some have lived here since the beginning too.'

Rinawne pulled a sour face. 'Oh, it's the typical thing. They won't speak to outsiders, as all newcomers will no doubt be for another hundred years. All I know is that the secret is so bad and dark it must never be spoken of, nor ever forgotten.'

'It must have been hard for you, living with that.' I smiled. 'You're as curious as I am. It must have driven you mad, not knowing.'

'Still does,' he said. 'I've scoured that house, its unused rooms full of dust, its empty attics, and I've found no clue. If there was any evidence, it was removed long ago. Only this generation live in the house. If there are harish ancestors they are dead or vanished. And they are never spoken of. I do know that Wyva's parents are dead, but nothing more than the bare fact of it. There are hurakin in the next county, but they don't interact. I believe these are the Wyvachi who chose to walk forward rather than stand in one place, and for that they were sort of cast out.' He leaned back against me. 'I have this awful fear that when Myv comes of age, Wyva will take him into some hidden, fusty room and chain the millstone of the family secret to him. I think it's passed down; that's how they remember it. And once it's heard, it's shut up inside like a canker.'

'Have you ever confronted Wyva about any of it?'

Rinawne grimaced. 'Of course. All I ever got was the hand to brow routine and "Oh, it is my terrible burden". Nothing will get them to speak, not even torture, I bet.' He smiled. 'Although to be fair I've not tried that yet.'

'You might reconsider that when Myv reaches feybraiha.'

'Myv is different,' Rinawne said simply. 'I sometimes feel he's the only one who can end this curse. Illogical, I know, him being such a fey and flighty little thing, but he's not like the other Wyvachi.'

'That's his Erini heritage,' I said. 'I hope you're right about him.' I leaned over to share breath with Rinawne once more, and this time, when our breath took us further, I did not feel as if part of me hovered outside. At least, not so much.

Chapter Seven

Cuttingtide crept ever closer and preparations for the feast appeared to have conjured excitement and anticipation in both the Wyvachi household and the community in general. Several times, when I went into Gwyllion, hara stopped me to thank me for the festival, even though they hadn't experienced my efforts yet. One har asked if I would be available to perform a blood bond between him and his chesnari. Looking into his face, full of hope and a small amount of trepidation, as if he knew my inclination was to refuse, it was in fact very difficult for me to say no. I knew the rite off by heart. All I'd have to do, in the absence of Gwyllion having a dedicated nayati building that might have to be prepared, was turn up at the designated site and conduct the ceremony. An afternoon's work at most. And yet, if I said yes to this request, I'd find it even more difficult to refuse others thereafter. I managed to stall the har by saying I was working very hard at the moment – despite the fact the population must have seen me wandering about the town and landscape a lot, apparently doing not much at all – but that after Cuttingtide I'd see what I could do. I knew for certain I had to speak to Wyva about this matter as soon as possible. His hara were crying out for a hienama and had every right to do so. Rites of passage were important for any community, especially close-knit ones like Gwyllion. I couldn't really believe there wasn't a single har among them who didn't have an interest in pursuing such an occupation and who wasn't suitable to be trained. Why had it been allowed to lapse for so long? I was surprised the Whitemanes hadn't started offering these services themselves. Wyva was perhaps lucky that they hadn't.

As I explored the town and small hamlets nearby, I noticed that all hara set protective wards about their homes and farm buildings, more so than would be done in Jesith, where such talismans would be seen more as decoration than protection. Contraptions of woven sticks, straw and feathers hung from every lintel. Sigils were painted across barn doors, and even the brands on sheep and cattle were warding runes. That suggested to me an overly superstitious, frightened community, yet in my conversations with hara, I picked up none of that. If I asked about the marks and talismans, I was told they were traditional, as if that was good reason enough. They were lying, of course, and I was an outsider, no matter what my profession was. The local hara didn't think it was my business.

Once, as I strolled home to my dinner, the weather changed suddenly. Summer storms generally creep up slowly, but in this case the air turned green and heavy almost immediately. I was walking through Gwyllion at the time, and saw hara come out their dwellings, workshops and stores to draw the shutters over their windows. Doors were slammed, and the gunfire report of bolts being shot rang out like artillery across the town. The hara had gone to earth. As I walked, my skin prickled. What walked with me? The smell of ozone filled my nose, but also a stench of burning flesh. The clouds above looked putrid, almost purple, like livid infected wounds. Needles of lightning pierced them, but weakly. There was no rain. Within minutes, the sky cleared. I reached Ludda's farm and saw he and his hara were gathered in the main yard. They parted silently to let me pass. Mossamber's hounds began to lament. The flesh on my back crawled as I climbed the hill. I was glad to shut the tower door behind me.

Rinawne had began to visit me a few evenings a week, leaving the tower before dawn, just as the grey light crept over the land. I felt he was taking too much of a risk staying with me so long through the night, but he insisted he wasn't. 'Wyva wouldn't really notice if I wasn't there for two days, never mind a night,' he said. And perhaps that was true. But what he didn't consider was all the other eyes and ears in the house, especially those of the staff who might be intrigued by gossip and speculation. Anyhar rising around dawn for their work – and this is of course common among farming communities – could see him coming home in the early morning, through the trees and across the wide lawn. I felt anxious about it, as the last thing I wanted was to live through any unpleasantness such as had happened to me before. For all I knew, Wyva might not care what Rinawne got up to, but appearances would mean more to him. If our liaisons became public knowledge, he might feel he had to act.

'Be careful,' I said to Rinawne one morning, as he put on his coat against the predawn chill. 'Don't let the staff get whiff of... us.'

Rinawne shrugged, clearly not bothered one bit about what the staff thought. 'You're as jumpy as a colt,' he said. 'Relax, will you? Nohar cares.'

He really didn't know about the attraction of gossip, or the harm it could do.

He came to me that night after the peculiar storm, and of course I asked him about it.

'There's a local belief that creatures walk in the storm light,' he said. 'There are similar beliefs in Erini; it's not that uncommon.'

'Hmm, I've never seen it before.'

He touched my face. 'Well, that's because Jesith lies in the enchanted heart of Alba Sulh, where all is the soft light of the otherworld, and bad things cannot dwell.'

'I've travelled around a lot over the years,' I said. 'The storm was *odd*. And I've not seen hara act like that before, so swiftly and so... I don't know... frightened?'

Rinawne shrugged. 'Well, you've seen it *now*. I told you hara here believe the land is cursed. They take precautions, that's all.'

I wasn't convinced and wrote up some notes after Rinawne went to sleep. *What* were the hara protecting themselves against? I didn't think it was simply storm spirits.

The following day, Aruhanisday, bloomed like a perfect flower as I made my breakfast. I'd been unable to get back to sleep after Rinawne had left, and the bed had felt cold, so thought I might as well get up and begin my day. The dawn was magnificent, gilding the tall beeches and oaks around the tower. I saw three deer come gracefully to the water trough down in Hercules's field, and drink there. Birds sounded intoxicated by the approach of summer, and even when the hounds started up their racket down at the farm, their voices had a softer note, so their cries too were more like a song.

The day felt enchanted from the start, and my heart was full of contentment as I prepared my meal. Perhaps Rinawne was right and I was too jumpy and paranoid – traits I should work to cast off. His presence in my life had given me comfort and had been healing; we weren't harming anyhar. We fulfilled a function for each other, finding happiness in each other's company. As long as we were discreet, no bad should come of it. The only problem was whether Rinawne was capable of maintaining discretion.

The Cuttingtide ritual was finished, and had only to be performed. Already my thoughts were turning to the next one, Reaptide. Some festivals have very powerful themes and images associated with them, while others provide a kind of lull in between. Reaptide was one of these. My main interest in it was the approach of what the old race used to call the Dog Days, and the approach to Reaptide Eve and the day after, when ghosts walked in the noon day sun. I wondered whether around here Reaptide might not be as uneventful as in other places.

Verdiferel, the lone dehar of the festival, being the transformed Shadolan, was rather a trickster god. At Reaptide he was released somewhat from the wheel of the year, the inevitable cycle of birth, life, death and rebirth; he could revel simply in his own power. That was what made him dangerous.

While I couldn't yet tune in to the authentic feelings of Reaptide, I thought it wouldn't do any harm to have a long walk through the fields, mulling over ideas. As always, I was drawn to the Llwybr Llwynog and the weeping birches around its foot. This was a light and airy woodland in comparison to the heavy armies of ancient trees in other areas; the atmosphere was sparkling. I always enjoyed walking through it, mostly perhaps because I might glimpse a Whitemane, like a spectre through the trees. Even the impish harlings would be a welcome sight, but since the incident on the bridge I'd not met them on my walks. I had a feeling they'd been told to avoid me, or perhaps just leave me alone. I had no idea what the Whitemane sentiment was towards me, really.

I saw movement through the slim birch trunks, which soon revealed itself as the swish of a horse's tail. Another scene like a painted picture was revealed to me. Was this a presentiment of Verdiferel? The horse was a grey, almost white, with thick mane and tail that tumbled like a har's hair. It was cropping the sweet grass of the forest floor. On its back a har half-lay, a Whitemane without doubt. The animal was unsaddled and the har's torso was laid flat, his chin resting on his folded arms, which lay on the animal's withers. His legs dangled down to either side of the horse's flanks, his feet bare. He seemed to be daydreaming, staring out at the fields and the silver river. His hair was a mane itself, the colour of autumn leaves, surrounding him like a shawl. Sunlight came down in golden spears about him, one striking his head to bring out the almost festive gleam of his hair. Around and above him, leaves were in their acidic green finery of early summer. He was a character in a story, waiting for something to happen, which inevitably it would.

This seemed too good an opportunity to miss. I would speak to him now, find out about his hara. He seemed too drowsy to urge his horse away.

As I drew closer, I could see more clearly what a beautiful creature he was. I considered he was like the perfect archetype of a har, like a Tigron, how Pellaz would have been in his early days. Such hara are the stuff of stories, hardly real, although I know they exist, had even been cursed by one. But such types are more common among tribes like the Gelaming than here in Alba Sulh. The har before me was young, and I thought he was the one who had stood at the Whitemane end of the bridge that day, who had whistled to the feral harlings dragging me across it. But then there might be many Whitemanes who looked like this. They seemed to me an enchanted race.

I was almost at his side, and he had not stirred, before I said, 'Good day, tiahaar.'

At that, he turned his head lazily and stared at me. 'Day to you, har,' he said and then turned back to gaze at the fields beyond the trees.

I patted the horse's neck. The animal ignored me and did not stop grazing. 'Beautiful creature,' I said, struggling for openings to a conversation.

The har on his back made a grunting sound, perhaps assent.

'I'm Ysobi har Jesith,' I began, but the har interrupted me.

'I know who you are.'

The harlings might have told him.

'I think I saw you before,' I said, smiling.

'When the lingies hauled you across the Greyspan. Yes, I saw.'

'Thank you for... calling them off,' I said.

'They hungry beasts,' the har remarked, somewhat casually, although the words made me shiver.

'Hungry?'

'Never still,' the har said, as if that were explanation enough.

'Are you of the Whitemanes?' I enquired tentatively.

The har laughed. 'I am of them.' He rose slowly to a sitting position and stretched his arms above his head. The movement seemed calculated to me since it showed off the lines of his body to splendid effect. 'You making for the river?' he asked, not looking at me.

'Not particularly. I'm working. Do you know why I'm here?'

'You're Wyvachi-called,' said the har. 'We know that. They throw you into the land. Call it work? See how they need to be told what they should know?' He made a scornful sound. 'How can you tell them? Work!'

'Well, they lost their hienama...'

'More than that. Lost what should be in them. A hienama can't lock it back in. You shouldn't bother. You're not of this land. A rabbit could see that. Or even a fish.'

'I'm not unaware,' I said. 'I was sent here to do a job and I'll do it. Beyond that, it's not my affair.' I paused. 'Perhaps you could talk to me about the land.'

'I'll not aid you, none of us will,' said the har.

A shiver of annoyance sliced through me, but I strove to keep my voice even. 'I'm not your enemy. If anything, while I'm here, I'd prefer to try and heal the rift among the community. I don't wish to sound presumptuous, but I can't see how this feud does anyhar any good. The hara in the village and countryside are divided, aren't they?'

The har looked me full in the face, which almost stopped my heart. No living har could look so perfect, surely?

'Stay on *his* side of the span,' said the har. 'Safer there. Leave what is not yours to own. Write pretty words for them, so they sing and dance and believe all is well.'

'Why are you hostile to me?' I persisted. 'I knew nothing of these hara before I came here. Nor of you. I'm impartial, like the land itself.'

'*That* is never so,' scoffed the har. 'You think it is?'

'Well, why don't you *tell* me?' I could hear the hard edge that had come into my voice.

'Not your affair,' he said, grinning.

'What happened to Rey, the last hienama? You think I'm destined for the same fate, to be sucked right into the land?'

The har laughed. 'No danger of that. For you.'

I also laughed. 'You're as rude as your harlings. I'll leave you to cuddle your secrets.' I patted the horse once more. 'Nice meeting you. Will you give me a name?'

He considered. 'One of them. You may have that. Ember.'

'Ember Whitemane,' I said aloud. 'Like a poem.'

He grinned again. 'You're right. Just like that. Wyvachi are a clag-heap of muddled words. We are poems.' With that, he clucked to his horse, who lifted its graceful head and then he was trotting out into the sunlight, towards the river.

I felt breathless, as if I'd been punched.

I went back to my tower and began to drink a bottle of wine, one of several that Rinawne had brought over the previous evening. I was disorientated, excited... Surely no coincidence that har had been there; he'd been waiting for me. The Whitemanes were playing a game. I must take care, and not be drawn into the feud between the families. Yet I could not stop thinking about Ember Whitemane. That he was beautiful beyond normal beauty was obviously a factor, but it was also the allure of the Whitemanes, their mystery. Having talked to him, I realised I felt privileged to have done so. Craziness! In the past I had several times become obsessed by surface beauty and it had always ended in catastrophe of one sort of another. Not least because beauty is simply a mask, an adornment, and what lies beneath it might not be so comely. Beauty does not guarantee accord; it is a blinding flash that can leave you sightless for a long time, and then when sight does return, the world has turned to ashes, your land is dead. I could see so clearly that Ember Whitemane might have that same effect on me; I was prone to it. At least now I was more aware of that weakness. It was as if the Whitemanes knew me intimately and how to manipulate me. But, as with Rinawne, I had their measure.

Restless and needing company, I rode over to Meadow Mynd in the late afternoon, hoping for an invitation to dinner and company through the evening. This was the first time I'd ridden to the house and Hercules seemed almost shocked when I fetched him in from the field. I fastened him into his bridle but left the saddle off. Whitemanes rode without saddles.

Rinawne was in the garden playing with Myv, and while surprised to see me, welcomed me warmly. 'What brings you here, esteemed hienama?' he asked as we led Hercules to the stables.

'I want to talk with Wyva. I didn't mention it to you before, but somehar in Gwyllion has asked me to perform a blood-bond. I think the question of the permanent hienama must be discussed. I also mentioned this to Gen when we dined together. Do you know if he told Wyva about it?'

Rinawne linked arms with me. 'Not that I know of, but then he'd be unlikely to tell me, anyway. You know that Wyva wants *you*, and *he* knows you don't want to take the job on. But he won't give up. He feels you're an old friend already, and he'd be uncomfortable with somehar new.'

I snorted impatiently. 'Oh come on, Rin. There must be at least one har in the whole tribe who would make a good hienama. Why get somehar from outside anyway? Come to that – as I said to Gen – why doesn't Wyva just perform the rites of passage and lead festivals himself? It's hardly difficult work. You just need a script and I can provide as many of those as he likes.' I decided not to mention what Gen had told me concerning the order Rey had given Wyva before leaving the community.

Rinawne made a flippant gesture with one hand. 'Wyva is fixed in his ways. He thinks we should have a proper hienama, and that's that with him. I doubt you'll persuade him otherwise.'

'Well, what makes a proper hienama? I had to train once and knew nothing when I started. All that's required is the desire to learn and to care about the hara around you in a spiritual sense.' I felt hypocritical saying all that, given how my pastoral care of a community had ended up, but despite my flaws, I believed what I said was the truth. I just hadn't lived

119

up to the standard very well.

'He wants *you*, Ysobi,' Rinawne said, grinning at me. 'Learn to live with that and go from there. In my opinion, get somehar from outside for us and work alongside him for a few months. That might mollify our demanding phylarch.'

'He wants me, yet so many secrets are kept from me,' I couldn't help saying.

'Well,' Rinawne began, 'if you'd commit yourself, you might be trusted enough to know some of these secrets. Perhaps there's more likelihood of that for you than there'll ever be for me. Had you considered that?'

'All right. I get your point. But it was never my plan to settle here.'

Rinawne raised a hand to his brow flamboyantly, threw back his head, and pantomimed sorrow. 'Ah, you think so lowly of me, Ysobi. I am nothing to you.'

'Don't say that. You know what I mean.' I squeezed his arm. 'You've been a healing draught for me. Don't ever think it's not appreciated.'

'Well, being a medicine is perhaps almost as good as being an object of adoration, I suppose.'

'Rin, just stop it. I love being here and have no plans to leave any time soon, but even so, I don't want to be a hienama in that way again. I enjoy the freedom of not being one. You must surely be able to imagine what it's like being on call for every soul around, twenty-four hours a day.'

He nodded. 'For sure. I understand. I'm just larking.' We had reached the stables and Rinawne let go of me. 'Myv, you take Ysobi into the house and I'll see to the beastie.'

Myv nodded gravely and – astonishingly – took my hand in his. The harling had wandered silently behind us and I'd forgotten he was there. Had I said anything imprudent that young ears could hear and young lips repeat? I didn't think so, but it unnerved me to think how invisible Myv had been.

The harling didn't speak as he led me to the back door of the house, half a pace ahead of me. He was humming to himself, and it seemed to me that the tune was very similar to one I'd composed for the festival that I'd revealed only to Wyva. Perhaps Wyva had remembered it and sung it to him. When we reached the door, Myv paused, one hand on the handle. 'I'd do it,' he said.

'What?' Other than the brief greeting on my first night here, I don't think I'd ever heard him speak before, but then, had I really been listening?

'The hienama job. I'd do it.'

'Really, Myv? That's, well... thank you for telling me. But you're a bit young as yet.'

'We don't always stay young though, do we,' he said, opening the door.

I followed him into the cool dim corridor beyond, which lay behind the kitchens. 'No, that's true. If you're serious, I could speak to your parents about it. There are some things I could teach you now for later in life.'

'I'd like to do that job very much,' Myv said.

I was so taken aback by his words I wasn't sure what to say. He was a harling; he might change his mind as he grew. But to belittle his desires now was a bad thing, I knew that much, even though harling-care had never figured greatly in my life. 'OK, let's talk about it, then,' I said.

'I used to help Rey all the time,' Myv continued. He'd let go of my hand now, as we approached the family part of the house. 'I'd help him gather things from the forest floor, and he'd teach me rhymes that the birds can understand. He taught me how to beguile fleas and sing to them so they leave a dog's coat.'

I laughed. 'Not even I can do that! How interesting.'

'He knows lots of stuff like that,' Myv said. 'I wish he was still here. He was my friend, and...' He frowned a little. 'He seemed more my age than Porter does.'

It occurred to me then that Rey should have resisted his urge to live the life of a hermit and perhaps waited for Myv's feybraiha and transferred the hienama role to him. What difference would an extra couple of years have made, when he could have bestowed a wonderful gift to the hara he left behind? I felt now that Rey was impulsive and selfish, a dreamer. He might have known the ways of the land and spoken with it, but he'd neglected the more mundane aspect of his duties, his responsibilities. I was impatient with that. But then, had he perhaps already started training Myv with the little things he'd taught the harling? Was I being too harsh? Did he *have* to get away quickly, had no choice? More mysteries.

I waited until after dinner before I approached Wyva. 'May I speak to you alone?' I asked him as we rose from our seats.

'Of course,' he responded, smiling. 'Let's go to the library.'

Rinawne winked at me as we departed and mouthed 'good luck'. I would no doubt need it.

In the library, Wyva fussed about getting us the right kind of drink, which was missing from the cabinet where he kept his liquor. I told him I really didn't mind what I was given, but he was deaf to that. So it took some minutes of housto calling and the tracking down of the particular pear liqueur Wyva wanted, which was eventually discovered in the kitchen where Dillory the cook had employed it to flavour a pudding.

'Ridiculous,' Wyva said, once the bottle was safely in his hand. 'It's not meant for cooking. At least he didn't use it all.'

The liqueur was indeed very good and warmed my insides beautifully. I complimented Wyva upon it.

'The recipe has been handed down for generations through our family,' he said. 'For hundreds of years.'

I glanced askance at the glass I held. He meant his human ancestors. 'Amazing,' I said inadequately.

'But no doubt your hara have similar recipes, given the main trade of Jesith.'

'Yes, they have a few, but none that old – that I know of.'

We both sipped reverently in silence for a few moments. Then Wyva asked, 'So what is it you wished to speak to me about? The festival?'

I put down my glass on the table next to my chair. 'No, that's all in hand. This is more to do with the hienama problem.'

Wyva stared at me expressionlessly. 'What are your thoughts on it?'

'Well, you know how I feel about doing the job myself, but I do consider it important I find somehar to fill that role for you properly. I've thought about writing to my friends in Kyme, as perhaps Gen might have told you, but really I believe the har should come from your own community. Today, an astonishing thing was revealed to me.'

Wyva raised his brows. 'What astonishing thing?'

'Myv told me he wants to do the job. It seems Rey might have started training him for such a role. Myv told me about some of what Rey's taught him. He does seem very keen, even though he is so young.'

'You're right, that *is* astonishing,' Wyva said. He narrowed his eyes a little. 'Even if I approved of this, and it could be done, Myv is far too young, not yet at feybraiha. Are you proposing you stay with us here until he's old enough and will train him then?'

'Well... I hadn't really considered that aspect. *Do* you approve of it... in principle?'

Wyva sighed through his nose, took another sip of his liqueur. 'Myv is a... *strange* little harling. It's come as a great surprise to me he spoke to you at all, never mind revealed all this. I suppose you're right – he must be very keen if he felt able, or was driven, to talk to you about it. But it warms me to know that he has ambitions, and is in that way... *normal*. He did spend nearly all his time with Rey, and was very upset when Rey went away. I hadn't even thought he might have been teaching Myv. It's certainly something to think about.'

'How far off feybraiha is Myv?' I asked.

'Oh, I don't know. It's difficult to tell, isn't it? He's older than he looks so maybe just a year or so, but then he is *behind* with some things, so I'd always thought it might take longer with him.'

I thought then that Wyva talked about his son as if he were a horse or a dog, who had suddenly displayed unexpected levels of intelligence and capability. He certainly did not talk like a hostling, who nearly always had strong bonds with their offspring, often more so than the father. Poor little Myv. He seemed a neglected creature to me. I thought about harlings in Jesith and how cherished and *included* they were. 'Perhaps you should talk about it with Rinawne,' I said. 'Even though Myv's not yet mature, he can start learning. As I said, it seems Rey had already begun the process. He knows how to charm fleas!'

Both Wyva and I laughed at this.

I was rather surprised Wyva had taken my suggestion this well, so blundered on, hoping to keep him in this compliant mood. 'In the meantime, perhaps I could help *you* with learning how to conduct everyday hienama duties, such as namings, bondings, and so on. Leading festivals is easy enough if you have a script.'

'No, that's not possible,' Wyva said in an even voice. 'Please don't ask more; it's simply not possible.'

'OK. Perhaps one of your brothers would consider it? Just until Myv is old enough?'

'Maybe.' Wyva sighed and pressed the fingers of one hand against his eyes. 'Oh Ysobi, I can sense your impatience with us. I don't mean to obstruct you. It's just...' He lowered his hand, looked down at empty hearth. 'Well, I can't go into it, I'm sorry. As you said, it can't be that difficult to follow a script. It's the obvious answer. Somehar must surely be happy to do that until Myv is ready.'

'I think it's important you find somehar sooner rather than later,' I said softly. 'And I think you know why.'

Wyva raised his eyes, fixed me with a gaze. 'What do you mean?'

I hadn't wanted to say it, and even now wasn't sure how to phrase it. 'Because... because others might slither in to fill the hole that Rey left behind, and not be of your choosing. I think we both know that in a small measure this is already happening.'

Wyva expressed another heavy sigh. 'I *do* know what you mean,' he said. 'I've tried to ignore it. Wrong of me. You're right in every way. Thank you.' He smiled at me warmly. 'This is why I wish it could be you.'

That night, I went to bed content. Blue starlight came softly into the room and I lay drowsing, mulling over the day. I had drifted off to sleep when partial wakefulness came to me. I was aware somehar had come into the room and had sat down upon the bed. Rinawne had come to me – dangerous perhaps, to sneak from the house this late at night, when noises were amplified for those alert enough to hear them. I didn't want him to be caught, but for now his presence was simply a comfort. I felt him slip beneath the quilt and press his body against mine. I uttered a soft sound. His right arm came about my waist, and I put my own over it.

What I found beneath my hand was not an arm of flesh and blood. My fingers gripped a skeletal limb that felt made of sticks and thorns.

Horrified, and fully awake, I leapt from the bed and plunged towards the light switch. At once the light revealed what I expected – the bed was empty.

Chapter Eight

When I woke the next day, my first instinct was to extend my senses and touch the spirit of the tower so I could judge its mood. I didn't pick up anything alarming or discomforting, so it hadn't felt invaded in the night. Had I dreamed those forest arms around me? There was no evidence in the bed of anything having been there, no hint of soil or twig. Perhaps unwittingly, I'd invited some minor elemental being inside, and it had simply been drawn to me. I didn't feel threatened, but would remain vigilant for further signs.

I remembered also the vestige of a disturbing dream. There had been firelight, but beyond it I'd not been able to see anything except a pair of shining eyes, staring right into me. I knew them, but could not recall the face to which they belonged. The dream, when I woke, left me uneasy.

As I made my breakfast, a resounding knock came at the tower door. My only visitor usually was Rinawne, who never knocked, so I went swiftly to see who was there. A har had come from Gwyllion with a parcel for me, which rested covered in a cloth on his cart. When I pulled off the cloth I discovered a hamper from Jesith. So Jassenah had bothered to send me gifts for the Wyvachi. I was quite surprised. I gave the post-har some coins and asked him to help me carry the hamper to the kitchen.

'Sent from home,' the har remarked. 'What is it? A whole cow?'

'No, I'm hoping for wine and other fruits of the vine.'

The har shook his head at what he no doubt considered affected southern ways.

After he'd gone I opened the hamper. Jassenah had been generous, hence the weight of it. There were two dozen bottles of wine, of twelve varieties, labelled beautifully in Jassenah's own hand. There were three stoppered vials of different scents derived from the grapes, some raspberry cakes in a tin, cordials of various flowers and fruits, and two rounds of Jesith cheese. There was also an elaborate Cuttingtide wreath, artfully contrived of dried flowers and grasses, with a note attached: 'To the hara of Gwyllion from the hara of Jesith. May your Cuttingtide be fruitful'.

I'd have to get somehar from the Mynd to come over with a cart and transport the hamper to the house, and was in fact eager to ride over there and tell the Wyvachi about the gift. But first, of course, I had to read the letter. It had been placed on top of the produce and I'd put it aside at once to examine the hamper's contents. Now it lay on the table almost accusingly. Sighing, I opened it and took out the single sheet of handmade paper.

Dear Ysobi

Thank you for your letter with all your news. It sounds as if you're settling in well.

I've drafted this letter so many times, and ultimately what needs to be said should be face to face, not with this distance between us. But that can't be done at the moment, and I wonder also whether the distance is perhaps not also a comfortable barrier across which we can speak.

I have to ask, and please answer me truthfully when you respond: Do you want to come back to me, or even to Jesith? I've had dreams of you drifting away in a boat upon a misty lake, me waving to you from the shore. I don't feel there is anger between us, or bitterness, but merely perhaps a knowing that it is time to part. We've not had a proper relationship for years, and I don't believe these words will come as a shock to you.

You were my light, Ysobi, my star, but stars

sometimes fall, and the light goes out. I want us to remain friends, to be there for Zeph until we're here no more, but I don't believe we have to keep up the pretence of a chesna bond to do that. I took care of you when you were at the bottom of that pit of despair, because I loved you as family, as your son's father, and I always will. But it was simply that. You're better now. There are new roads ahead of you and you're strong enough to walk them.

What I'm really saying, I realise, is that I don't want you to come back, and for us to carry on with that arid, pretend life. There must be new life and loves for both of us in our futures. All of your lovers made the same mistake, Ys – they wanted to own and consume you. I thought I understood you, but I didn't. I'll always remember fondly our good times, and many of those were ecstatic rather than simply good.

Think about what I've said. We do need to speak face to face at some point, but I don't want you thinking that's a leash reeling you back in. Enjoy the Cuttingtide. May it bring marvellous things to you.

In blood
Jassenah

I put down the letter, dazed. I stared out of the window for some moments. Then I spoke aloud, 'Dear Aru, I'm free...'

As I fetched Hercules from his field, my body felt barely anchored to the earth. I hadn't realised just how weighed down I'd been by my life in Jesith, my responsibilities there. I would have to keep Jassenah's letter secret for now, otherwise it could be used to badger me into committing myself to Gwyllion. I wanted to retain room for manoeuvre.

Wyva was still at the house when I reached it, having only recently finished his breakfast. 'What brings you here so early,

Ys?' he asked as he found me in the stableyard.

'A hamper's arrived from Jesith,' I said. 'A lot of produce we can use for the festival. I was just coming to ask if you could spare somehar and a cart to bring it over to the Mynd.'

'Yes, yes, of course. Take whoever you need back with you.' He mounted his horse. 'It's kind of your hara to think of us. I'll send them thanks. Now, I'm afraid I must be off to supervise the first cutting of the fields, but Rinawne is still at breakfast. The tea will still be hot.' He gestured at the house.

'Thanks. Until later, then.'

I saw Gen and Cawr come out of the stables to join their brother. After raising a hand in greeting to them, I went into the house. Whatever I'd expected of Gen had never materialised, since he'd not bothered to pursue a friendship with me beyond that night of the meal. Perhaps he was aware of my relationship with Rinawne. Anyhar with half a brain could work that one out.

That day was the start of everything, really. Endings, beginnings, the field set for battle.

Rinawne had work to see to that day too, so I only intended to stay at the Mynd for half an hour or so, long enough to pick at the remains of the Wyvachi breakfast and have a couple of cups of tea. 'You seem perky today, Ys,' Rinawne remarked, one eyebrow raised.

'I woke in a good mood,' I said.

'And were glad to hear from home, that's plain to see.'

'I suppose so.'

'Are you missing them? – your family, I mean.'

Rinawne had fixed me with the glacial version of his blue stare. I shrugged, acutely conscious of how I couldn't prevent my gaze skittering away from his. 'Of course, they're my family.'

'Uh huh...' He smirked at me, but there was an edge to it. I could read his thoughts as if he'd spoken them aloud; he feared I wanted to return home.

We talked then of minor aspects of the Cuttingtide festival and its preparations and when and how Myv's training would begin. Small talk, a little stilted. Then we heard a commotion outside.

'Dehara, what's that?' Rinawne muttered, rising from his seat. We were in the breakfast room, from where we couldn't see out over the yard. Did the air in that allegedly haunted room contract for a moment? Perhaps it was my imagination.

'Better go and see,' I said.

We could hear hara calling out, the nervous whinny of a horse, running feet. Soon, we were running too.

Wyva met us at the back door. His shirt was covered in blood, his hands similarly red.

'What's happened?' Rinawne demanded, his voice shrill. 'Is it Myv?'

Wyva closed his eyes briefly, shook his head, then turned to me. 'We need you, Ys. Thank Aru, you're still here.'

I followed him outside.

Hara were gathered around a cart, where a har lay redly on straw. It took me only a moment to realise this was Gen, but he was so bloodied, I couldn't determine at first what his injury was. However, as I reached the cart, and leaned over its side, I saw it was his right leg, a wound so bad below the knee it was nearly severed. Hara had already made a tourniquet around the thigh. Gen looked at me beseechingly with shocked, glazed eyes, but did not speak.

'Can you mend it?' Wyva was saying to me, over and over. 'Can you mend it, Ysobi?'

'Clear the table in the kitchen,' I said. 'Get him in there. We'll need boiled water, cloths, any medical equipment you might have.'

Myv came running to us, accompanied by Porter, as hara carried Gen inside.

'Is he dead?' Porter snapped.

'No,' I answered.

'Let me help,' Myv said, his face strangely expressionless,

his eyes fixed on the hara carrying his hurakin inside.

We went into the kitchen, where I washed my hands and told Myv to do likewise.

'Tell me what to do,' Wyva said.

'Wash yourself,' I said. 'You'll be ready then when I need you.'

I went to Gen and put a hand on his shoulder, projecting a wave of soothing energy, which I hoped would act as a mild tranquilliser. Some hara though, mainly through fear, can't relax enough to accept the current. I hoped Gen wasn't one of them. 'Everyhar else – out, please,' I said. Porter went to leave with the others. 'Not you,' I said. We locked stares for a moment.

'Shall I leave too?' Rinawne asked, from where he stood at the door, with Dillory's hands on his shoulders. I could see he wanted to go, was frightened by what he saw.

'Yes, you go.' I smiled at him and he turned away, let Dillory guide him. Wyva closed the door.

'What happened?' I asked Wyva. I removed the shredded remains of Gen's trousers using some kitchen shears I'd held hastily under the hot tap.

Wyva shook his head. 'The scythe,' he said.

'Well, I can see that, but how?'

He stared at me, his eyes strangely sunken. 'It was as if... as if...' He looked away from me. 'No, no...'

'As if, what? Just tell me!'

'As if it attacked him, all right?' Wyva's eyes were fiery with challenge now, daring for me to contradict him.

'OK,' I said simply, then put my hand on Gen's shoulder again, spoke to him. 'Well, I think I can patch you up and save your leg, Gen. We can prevent infection setting in from the start.' In humans, of course, infection had often been the worst hazard in serious injuries, especially before medicine became advanced enough to combat it. In hara, controlling infection was fairly simple, since the harish body is adept at healing itself. In the case of a deep, physical wound like Gen's however,

it would need some help. I could see the shinbone was broken –
cut through – as if from a battle wound. At least the break was
clean, but how could this happen in a hay field? Gen would not
be a fumbling amateur with a scythe, I was sure. None of the
hara out there would have been. I could probe that matter later.
First, the practical work. 'We need to set the leg,' I told Wyva.

He nodded.

'Fetch me something we can use as splints, also something
for Gen to bite on while I set the limb. Myv, boil all the tea
cloths.'

Fortunately, a huge pan of water was already simmering on
the stove, as Dillory had been in the process of making a large
batch of meat stew for the haymakers' dinner.

'Porter, fetch the most alcoholic drink you have in the
house.' He departed swiftly to do so, returning equally swiftly
with a bottle of Wyva's finest plum brandy.

When the equipment was assembled, I gave Gen a large
draught of the brandy and again put my hands upon him to
sedate him. I wrapped the wooden splints in the boiled cloth
and asked Myv to give Gen the piece of wood – a sawn off
section of a narrow tree branch – that Wyva had fetched for his
brother to bite upon. 'Be strong,' I murmured to Gen, then
gestured at Wyva and Porter. 'Hold him down, please.'

Despite the pain relief I'd tried to give him, Gen still
screamed and tried to writhe as I set the bone. The room
seemed to reel with his cries, strangely muffled around the
wood his teeth were clamped upon. The raw sounds echoed
throughout the building, so that even in the lulls as he drew
sobbing breaths, I could still hear them faintly, bouncing from
room to room. The walls of the kitchen shifted, creaked,
shuddered.

Myv was holding the injured leg. He looked up at me.
Something's here, he told me in mind touch.

Ignore it, I sent back. *It's attracted by the disturbance, that's all.
Do what you can to calm Gen, try to make him sleep.*

Myv was remarkably successful in this, because Gen

noticeably quietened down, his cries reduced to soft moans. Once the bone was in place, I directed agmara, healing energy, into the wound and instructed Myv to assist me in that. I approved of his calm, businesslike manner throughout. In mind touch, I informed him how to direct the energy more precisely, and he obeyed me without further questions. I could sense the agmara flowing from him easily, as if it was visible light. He was made to be a hienama, I thought, and wondered from whom he'd inherited these talents. Wyva was doing his best to be stoic, but I could feel panic hovering about him. Porter...? Well, Porter was unreadable, but did as he was told.

(*Is he dead?* I wondered about that question as I worked.)

Once we'd infused the wound thoroughly with agmara, I sewed the flesh back up. Myv watched me closely, in a decidedly detached and academic way.

'Will he be all right?' Wyva asked me. By this time, Gen had lost consciousness.

'There's no reason why not, but he must do his part too,' I said. Hara who'd stuck assiduously to caste training, of course, would be in a far better position to administer healing, whether to themselves or others, but I remained silent about that. This was not the time to make criticisms or judgements. I remembered something Ember Whitemane had said to me, though, about how the Wyvachi had lost something and turned to hara like me to try and get it back.

Once the job was finished, Myv and I removed the remainder of Gen's clothes and bathed him. Then I lifted him in my arms and Wyva directed me to Gen's bedroom. The healing now must take its own course.

Rinawne was in the bedroom with Dillory and stepped up to take over from us. Myv insisted on staying by his hura's side. Wyva meanwhile asked me to remain at the Mynd for a while. He was going to clean up but wanted to speak with me. I needed to wash too, and Wyva offered me a replacement shirt, since mine was soiled with Gen's blood.

'How did this happen?' Rinawne asked me before I left the

bedroom.
'Don't know yet,' I said. I touched his arm. 'We'll find out.'

In the library, Wyva offered me some of the plum brandy. 'Might as well finish this,' he said gloomily.

I stared askance at the glass he offered me, remembering only too vividly the image of it seeping from the sides of Gen's mouth, bloodied because he'd bitten through his lips and tongue. With difficulty, I took a sip. 'Try not to worry,' I said. 'You know we're hardy creatures, Wyva.' I wondered then why a second-generation har, born with the ability to mend so efficiently, would be as scared as Wyva was then.

'*Most* hara are,' he said.

'What do you mean?'

He shrugged. 'Nothing. Nothing.' He smiled at me unconvincingly. 'It was just a shock... Gen was standing there in the field with us all, laughing, talking, the next moment it was as if an executioner had struck him down.'

'Where was the scythe? How did the accident happen?'

'He was leaning on it,' Wyva said. 'Perhaps the shaft snapped or something.'

'You said earlier...'

'I know what I said, but that's not possible, is it?'

There was a feverish, angry edge to his voice, so I decided not to push him. 'Well, all that matters is that he heals. Myv did very well today, Wyva. He's an exceptional harling. I'll give him instructions to care for Gen.'

'Thank you.' Wyva put down his glass and came to embrace me. For some moments, he hung on to me as if he was drowning. 'The dehara sent you to us,' he said.

Porter and Fush were allocated to accompany me back to the tower and fetch the hamper. Fush was silent to start with, but then took to dire muttering halfway through the forest walk. He was a slight har around Porter's age, with delicate almost elfin features. His arms, however, were muscular, strong. 'The wards came down,' he said, to nohar in particular. 'That's what happened.'

'Shut it, Fush,' Porter said. 'Was an accident. Wyva said so. The shaft snapped.'

'Was the *ysbryd drwg*, that's what it was, and you know it.'

'I said *shut it*.'

'The what?' I asked.

'Old fairy stories,' Porter said coldly. 'Tales to scare harlings.'

'You're a pelking liar, Goudy.' Fush pointed at me. 'He should be told. Why have him here and not tell him?'

Porter grabbed Fush by the collar, pushed him against a tree. 'If you don't shut your mouth, I'll break all your teeth.'

'For Aru's sake!' I snapped. 'Let him go, Porter. No need to behave like a rabid dog simply because Fush believes in certain things.' I pulled Fush from Porter's hold and said to him, 'I know about the wards, Fush. I've seen them everywhere. I know also they're there to keep something at bay.'

'The *ysbryd drwg*,' Fush said, 'the bad ghost.'

'Pelking idiot,' said Porter.

'I know there's a ghost,' I said, 'or that hara believe there's one, but Fush, ghosts can't hurt hara physically.' He looked doubtful, to say the least. 'Really, I mean that.'

'This one can,' Fush insisted, glaring at Porter.

'Well, while I'm here it can't,' I said.

Fush gave me a look to say he wished that were possible, while Porter gave me a strange look I couldn't interpret at all.

Over the next few days, the drama died down. I went to see Gen every day, and even he told me the scythe had snapped so that the blade had sliced into his leg. 'Are you sure about that?' I asked him.

He held my gaze. 'Yes. I'm sure. What else could've happened?'

'How about the *ysbryd drwg*?'

Gen rolled his eyes. 'For Aru's sake, Ysobi, who put that in your head?'

I laughed. 'That's fine coming from a har who discussed the family curse with me.'

'Seriously, it was an accident.'

Yet still I couldn't forget the way the house had creaked and groaned around us as I'd worked on Gen's leg, and Myv's anxious mind touch: *Something's here.*

Wyva praised my healing, because it was clear Gen was mending quickly. As a reward for his own part, Myv was taken to Hiyenton market to pick a new pony for himself, whichever one he liked. Everything had turned out fine so Wyva was happy. He never mentioned the episode again to me.

Sometimes, I'd pass Fush in the corridors when I visited the Mynd and he'd give me a furtive glance, but it seemed he'd shut his mouth too. Still, whether the legend of the *ysbryd drwg* was a fairy tale or not, I noticed a lot more protective wards of grasses and twigs appearing in the hedgerows, along the lanes. Mossamber's hounds went crazy every night; eventually I became so used to the sound I barely noticed it. The land began to heat up as midsummer drew close.

The Wyvachi planned to hold their official Cuttingtide celebration on the evening of Pelfazzarsday. While traditionally, most would opt for the Aruhanisday instead, Wyva felt that the holiday aspect of Pelfday would be better. Hara generally expected not to be working all day then. The preparations had been made, the feast arranged, and my script had been carefully transcribed onto some handmade parchment Wyva had given to me and bound with a golden ribbon. I intended to make a gift of this scroll to Myv after the ceremony.

On the Hanisday Rinawne came to the tower for lunch – he and Wyva were making formal visits to other local leaders that evening, a common aspect of festival occasions. As we ate our meal, we talked about Myv and his aspirations. Rinawne was not surprised about any of it. 'Now we're talking about it, it seems to me we've been overlooking the obvious,' he said. 'Myv is different to most hara. By no means less intelligent or damaged in any way, but he walks his own path. He was very attached to Rey and Porter – still is. I've always known he adored the – er – less *communal* parts of Rey's calling – like he said to you. He'll gobble up the magical education like eating newly-baked cake, but the thing he'll have to work on is reaching out to other hara.'

'Wyva suggested Myv was a little behind in his development.'

At this, Rinawne laughed. 'That? No! Myv just isn't in a rush to be adult, such as you see with so many his age. He savours life as it is, and good for him, I say. Hara don't have the luxury of long childhoods like humans did.'

'Amazing. A reference to the human past!'

'No need for sarcasm, Ysobi. It's true, isn't it?'

'Very much so, but then humans took far longer to develop. Still, I do get your point. It's a shame harlings are suddenly hit with feybraiha and have to be done with childhood. My son, although named for the wind, is more like a river. He's flowed through life effortlessly, from harling to har. He never strained to be adult, either, but neither did it come too soon.'

'What's his name?'

'Zephyrus. We call him Zeph.'

'Is he like you?'

My laughter was tinged with bitterness. 'Not noticeably. He's his hostling's son, through and through.'

Rinawne put his head to one side, eyed me thoughtfully. 'You didn't see to much of his upbringing, did you?'

I sighed. 'Well...' *Time for revelations? No.* 'My work took me away a lot, so naturally Zeph spent more time with Jass. I regret that now, of course, because like you say the harlinghood is gone before you can blink.'

'At least you can make up for it now,' Rinawne said.

I took a drink of wine. 'Yes, at least there is that.'

There was a silence, during which Rinawne was no doubt

puzzling about all I'd *not* told him, because if his family had secrets so did mine, and perhaps their existence was as obvious. He did not try to pry, and for that I was grateful. Perhaps he imagined that as we drew closer to one another I would eventually open up to him, but the truth was I didn't want to drag any old baggage up here to Gwyllion with me. I wanted it out of the way, gone forever. And now that Jassenah had released me from our bond, I had more freedom to escape the past.

I think Rinawne would have been happy to stay for the whole afternoon and for us to spend most of that time in bed, but I'd planned to give attention to my temple at the top of the tower.

'Can't you do that any time?' Rinawne protested when I told him.

'No. I want to do it this afternoon, on the eve of Cuttingtide. I'll probably enact my own private rite there this evening, dedicate the upper room into a nayati. I've not done much with the place yet, and have a bagful of artefacts to arrange there.'

Rinawne pulled a face. 'Ah well, I suppose you're right, and I should go home and sort out gifts for those we're visiting later. Are you over at the Mynd tomorrow afternoon? I think Wyva would like it if you helped oversee the final preparations.'

'Of course. I'll be over around three. Have a good evening.'

Rinawne kissed the top of my head. 'See you tomorrow, then.'

After he'd gone, I leaned back contentedly in my chair, intending to finish my lunch wine slowly and simply stare out of the windows until my glass was empty. I was happy, utterly filled with a quiet joy. Not for a long time had I felt this way, part of a community, liked and trusted. I balked at conducting rites of passage, yet in Jesith nohar would even ask me to perform one anymore. Why was I rejecting what the dehara were so plainly offering to me? There were no impediments now. I could stay here until Myv's feybraiha, and then teach him – not in the way I'd taught young hara before, but as Rey would have done, out in the landscape, experiencing each facet of life through the prism of nature itself. Everything at last was slipping into place for me; it would be folly to fight against this. There was work for me here, and friends, and a kind of surrogate family. There was a new beginning.

Gwyllion had consumed me. Any thoughts I'd had of home hadn't been positive ones. I didn't miss Jass at all, especially not his domestic martyrdom, which he made all too plain. Perhaps even before I'd set Hercules upon the road north, I'd already left home for good. And now Jassenah would be relieved to hear I didn't intend to return. Zeph was another matter, and I needed to heal my relationship with him. It wasn't easy having a son who'd been educated only in the parts of my history of which Jass disapproved, and therefore regarded me through a film of judgements. Much as I loved Zeph, I wouldn't exactly be sorry to leave that behind too. I hoped there would come a day when Zeph might have enough distance to realise there is always more than one side to a story and would come to find me.

Mid-afternoon light was falling through my windows by the time my wine was finished. Then, rather woozily, I went upstairs to the nayati. Here I emptied the bag of items I'd collected from the woods and fields and began to arrange them on the empty altars around the room. I became aware of a watchful atmosphere, not altogether comfortable, which was completely at odds with the way I felt myself. Did this room, once so truly Rey's, not yet trust me? I didn't feel he had left a strong imprint on the place, because it had felt so empty, but walls absorb emotion and thought, and have in their own ways personalities themselves. This tower had stood a long time, and had no doubt seen many hara and humans within its rooms. Now somehar new was making his mark, planting his wards, his items of power; perhaps the temple was wary of that.

I sat down in the centre of it and began to hum softly beneath my breath. I composed a song of noble intention, of wonder and magic, of good deeds to be done. I sang of the sacred nayati, the church of Wraeththukind, and how this humble room would become again this holy thing. I could bring hara here for caste ascensions – assuming anyhar in Gwyllion would be interested in that – and could work rituals to help those in need of aid. Here, Myv could begin his education in earnest. I visualised him writing in a notebook, then calling upon the dehara in his clear young voice. I could imagine these shining beings hanging in the air at the quarters of the room, filling it with radiance and power. *This* was the purpose of the temple room; I hoped it liked my intentions for it.

Afterwards, the atmosphere did feel calmer, but I still detected a faint note of what I could only describe as anxiety. Why was the temple anxious? I asked the site spirit if there was anything I could do for it and awaited a response, but none came. I would just have to be vigilant and open, do what I could to heal this slight tremor in the nayati's ambience. I didn't think it was anything serious.

Chapter Nine

I ate a light dinner, because Rinawne and I had stuffed ourselves fully at lunchtime, and then wanted to be outside. If I was to perform my own private rite, I felt this should be done in the open air, beneath the Cuttingtide stars. The moon was a sharp sickle in the sky.

As soon as I stepped beyond the tower door, the hounds started up at Ludda's farm below, what sounded like hundreds of them now. They seemed to be singing rather than howling. I shivered. Perhaps Mossamber Whitemane was coming for them and would lead them across the land, even up into the sky as the Wild Hunt would ride. With this eerie song all around me I ventured down the tower hill, towards the forest, but ultimately I would let my feet lead me. I wondered whether the Whitemanes were celebrating Cuttingtide tonight or tomorrow. Were they gathering in the Maes Siôl? Perhaps so, but I wasn't tempted to head that way, uncomfortable that I might inadvertently gate crash a private rite.

I expected to be drawn in the direction of the Llwybr Llwynog, and while I wandered roughly in that direction, I found myself exploring a part of the woods I'd not yet visited. The trees were ancient deciduous, oak, sycamore and beech, with younger birches among them, the occasional holly and hawthorn. Everywhere was alive with movement; the rustle of undergrowth and foliage, the huff of deer. An owl called upon the night and slid like a phantom through the high canopy. I saw the flicker of bats against the sky. Power oozed from the very earth, exuberant and free. The solstice festival would last three days and during this time its influence would be strong. I felt as if I was caught up in a ringing yet silent song, uttered by a choir I could not see and only faintly perceive. Yet my body trembled at the sound that flowed through me, and tears started in my eyes. The earth truly was a goddess, beautiful beyond any means of description other than the ineffable words of other gods. Tonight she walked, arrayed in the garments – the forms – of the dehara, which were merely facets of what she had always been.

I thought of my human life, which seemed like a dream of childhood now, unreal. I thought about how the land had been scabbed and diseased then, with the last depredations of humankind. How quickly, comparatively, the world had taken back what had been lost. The green had spread over everything that hara had not claimed for themselves. Where now were the masses of vehicles that humans had used, the rail tracks, the field-covering roads? All gone, greened over, returned to earth. Houses had tumbled, towns and cities buried by vegetation, crushed and pulverised to dust. I felt a hundred years old and then realised, with some amusement, I actually nearly was. I'd lost track of the years, because time is different for hara than it had been for humans; it is less of an enemy. Humans had experienced each day as a step nearer to the grave, in what had seemed like a fraction of time that flashed past in an instant. In contrast, Wraeththu have been given the gift of longevity, a friendship with time.

I remembered my human grandmother, on my mother's side, once saying to me, 'We're a useless lot. Just as we become viable members of society, and are old enough to be wise, we die. If that's not a curse, what is? We'll never grow up because we don't live long enough to become truly wise.'

I realised how right she'd been, and that *had* been humanity's curse, always governed and influenced by the young, because no one had really been old. And those who had reached great age – which by harish standards had still been youthful – had been afflicted by infirmity and no longer had the vigour and physical strength to lead and make changes. So the young had prevailed. And the young, most often, though blessed with many golden qualities, are essentially stupid.

Smiling to myself, I strolled through the trees, laying my

hands upon them, absorbing their awareness and age. I did not think myself fully wise, but I was aware of gaining wisdom as life progressed. When I looked back on my days in Jesith, before Jassenah, my actions seemed like those of a hot-headed harling, yet at the time I'd considered myself to be a scholar and a sage, more knowledgeable than others. My reputation as some kind of aruna guru had been self-indulgent, supported by those who were hot-headed harlings themselves. In essence, we had still been wild inceptees, dancing around a fire in the dark, shrieking at the night and believing we were the all-powerful inheritors of the earth. Places like Jesith had been sanctuaries, little capsules of sanity in an insane, rapidly-changing world. Jesith *had* matured since its beginning, as had its hara, and now I suppose it really was an idyll, even though tainted with an air of righteousness – something the hara had yet to grow out of.

Gwyllion had also matured but had brought rank ghosts along with it. That was the difference, and here, despite all that I had done or believed, I *was* further along the path of life. Here, I was deserving of the reputation given me. I realised this was my opportunity to realise that, to be worthy of being har, to grow up. For that, I must work against being judgmental, because I could see that in myself. I must work against impatience with others.

These thoughts, I realised, were the Cuttingtide itself, the death of the worn out, that which should be discarded, to leave room for new growth. This was my private rite.

Sheer bliss at being alive spread through me like the sun's warmth. I would bring all of these feelings to the feast tomorrow. I wanted to inspire hara and considered that perhaps we should make some announcement about Myv and his future position within the phyle.

My feet had led my preoccupied mind and body to a forest lawn; I could see it through the trees. Small globes of light had been left around the perimeter, casting an eerie orange glow across the sward. Somehar was going to be here this night, and for what other reason than the Cuttingtide? The Whitemanes might be here soon, perhaps making their way from the Maes Siôl and the river. Who else would leave these lights burning here when the main Gwyllion festival took place tomorrow?

I was about to turn and leave when a shadow at the edge of my vision moved. I started in surprise, but then realised that somehar was standing amid the trees to my left, mostly concealed by shrubs around them. Whether they were looking at me or not, I could not tell. Then a voice hissed, 'Ysobi, Wyvachi-called, come here!'

I knew then it was Ember Whitemane who stood there, most likely waiting for his kin. I approached him and did not speak until we were close, afraid of attracting other hara's attention. 'I don't mean to intrude,' I said in a low voice. 'I was simply...'

'Looking for us?'

'No, no... I'm not celebrating until tomorrow, and merely wanted to take a private walk within the forest.'

Ember Whitemane made a snickering sound. 'Night of sacrifice,' he muttered. 'Search, you find.'

'As I said, I don't wish to intrude. I'll be on my way.'

'No, you can't,' Ember snapped. 'Not now. He comes. Can't change the pulse of it.'

Confused, I stared at him. He was peering out at the enclosed lawn, his body taut. I saw then he carried a longbow, half poised to use it, an arrow waiting there. The implications of this turned my blood to dry jelly. He meant to shoot something... somehar? I could not move now if I wanted to. 'Ember...' I breathed. 'What...?'

A rushing form burst out of the forest to our left: a har. He tumbled onto the lawn, arms flailing, glancing behind him. I heard the distant cry of hounds. *Great dehara, no!* I was powerless to run, as if held by Ember's word of command. *The sacrifice...* An ancient primal horror gripped me. I wanted to walk away, or fall to my knees and hide my face against the forest floor. But my feet had led me here, guided by my secret thoughts and *here* I was. There could be no escape, no turning of the eyes.

I saw that the har stumbling and scrambling across the forest lawn was the Whitemane I'd first met at the Llwybr Llwynog. There was no arrogance and aloofness to him now. He was, I felt, running for his life. He wore only a pair of hide trousers, and his hair was unbraided, whipping around him. His face and torso were daubed with painted symbols I did not recognise. As yet I could see no pursuit, but knew with grim certainty that it would come.

Ember raised his bow, aimed. In horror, I put out a hand to smack the weapon down, but Ember danced to the side and let the arrow fly. This pierced the fleeing har in the right calf, brought him to his knees. He tried to get to his feet, drag his body forward, but Ember was already readying another arrow, all the time dancing around me, so I couldn't stop him. The second shot took the har in the shoulder. He fell heavily to earth, face down. The yelping of the hounds drew nearer. I could hear the sound of horses' hooves. There were cries that were like the war chants I'd heard in early Wraeththu days; wordless, powerful, deadly.

For a moment, I could only stare, horrified, yet words can't convey my true feelings. There was a high-pitched whistling in my head. (*A Fire. Eyes. Eyes across a fire.*) My hands and feet were numb. I mumbled the phrase, 'What have you done?' which even to me seemed the most stupid words I could say. After only a few seconds – I assume – I retrieved my wits enough to try and go forward to assist the fallen har. I could see him moving feebly. Ember restrained me with a strong hand. 'No! Stay where you are.'

'I can't countenance this...' I struggled against him, but for one so slight he was surprisingly powerful.

'Don't wet yourself. He'll be fine. That's Nytethorne, my hostling.'

'What?'

'Morterrius falls at the hand of his son. Can't go to him. Blood must go into the earth. Then he'll be carried. Not yet.'

'How can you...?' I shook my head, pressed my fingers against my temples in utter bewilderment. 'He's hurt.'

'Won't feel it. Arrow numbs him. He's dreaming now. Dry your 'lim and dry your tears. This is the true song and dance of the season.' Ember hoisted the bow over his shoulder. 'Sing this to your Wyvachi on the morrow.' He laughed.

I knew then they'd wanted me to witness this, their barbaric rite. Morterrius falls to his son... his *lover*. My mouth filled with sour liquid, but I swallowed it down. 'I must go.'

'Where to? You can't escape the Cutting. Be har and follow us to the Greyspan. Come to our domain. If you dare.' His dark eyes reflected the wavering light of the nearest globe. I could see his wide white grin. He thought he had me, a terrified over-civilised har. Dehara knew what else they had planned to stupefy my mind.

'I have no place with your kind,' I said. I glanced at the body on the grass, the long feathered shafts sticking out of it, the fingers moving weakly on the deer-cropped lawn. *His hostling?*

'Your choice.'

Once he said this, a crowd of hara burst out of the forest from the same direction "Morterrius" had come. One was mounted on a great black horse whose polished coat shone as if wet in the soft orange light. The horse was surrounded by the inevitable hounds, which milled around its legs, but thankfully did not go to maul the har upon the ground ahead of them. I saw naked harlings prancing among the dogs, as much animal – to my eyes – as the hounds were. Ember gave me one sneering last glance then went to join his kin. I began to back away slowly into the cover of the trees, and as I did so saw the wild Whitemanes swarm around the limp body on the grass. Somehar tore the arrows from him, screaming in triumph, and each time a plume of blood jetted into the air. Once. Twice. I heard Nytethorne cry out. Hara painted their naked torsos with his blood, then lifted him onto their shoulders, held him high. I saw his arms dangling down, streaked with dark. Uttering whooping cries, the hara ran away with him in the direction of the bridge Ember had called the Greyspan. They were like raw inceptees from the dawn of our kind, revelling brutally in their new enhanced being, without compassion.

While all this was going on, the har upon the horse, who I realised must be Mossamber Whitemane, was turning his mount in a cavorting circle. When Nytethorne had been lifted and they'd begun to carry him away, Mossamber looked right at me, and it took all my will not to fall to my knees. His thick black hair was wild, as were his eyes. His dark-skinned face was that of a dehar, but a savage one. I could see he despised me. *Dress yourself up in expensive clothes, emulate the ancient ways of men, but this... this is what birthed you, what lies in the deepest corners of your heart.*

He did not speak the words aloud, of course, and neither were they a mind touch, but I knew them. Then, he dismissed me from his attention and urged his horse to leap forward. He overtook the lunging, baying crowd of hara and his white hounds tumbled after him like breaking waves.

Within seconds, as the wild sounds retreated, all was quiet, the forest lawn empty, as if nothing had happened. Nothing at all.

I sat down where I stood, because I had no fear the Whitemanes would return. Nausea still pulsed uncomfortably within me and my chest hurt. There had seemed so many of them. They couldn't *all* be Whitemanes, surely? They must have had village and farming hara with them, perhaps some of the same hara who would attend the Wyvachi rite tomorrow. As I strained to control my breathing, I heard the tolling of a bell again: loud, strong, clear. It held within its sonorous notes a voice of mourning, yet at the same time was sublimely uplifting. My breathing was synchronised with the chimes, which helped calm it to its normal rhythm.

I didn't feel restored enough to stand up for at least a couple of minutes. All I wanted to do was get back to the tower, shut myself in. Well, I'd certainly experienced a Cuttingtide rite, although not one I'd have chosen. I was aghast the Whitemanes were so powerful they could affect me like this. And how exactly had they done it? I'd been given no strange philtre, had entered no otherworld, and yet I felt as if I'd lost time and my head was not my own. It was like being drunk. I was weakened, barely capable of controlling my limbs.

Slowly, I began my homeward journey, passing from tree to tree, holding on to them, feeling their breathing warmth. I sensed they observed me scornfully. I saw faces in the foliage all around me. Echoes of memories cavorted across my mind.

Howling. Galloping horses. Smoke. Fire. Gutted buildings. Plumes of blood. Hoarse screams. A severed arm pointing from the earth. Then eyes. Frightened eyes. Not caring. Less than animal.

I didn't ever think of my early days of hardom. I didn't want to, and yet what I had witnessed that night had conjured back those times: our relentless driving urge to conquer, never ceasing our forward advance, like terrible sentient locusts armed with blades. Devouring, destroying everything in our path. No matter how I sought to suppress these recollections, they refused to be banished. How could I have been influenced and incapacitated like this?

Presently, I became aware of dancing, purplish shadows among the trees, and then saw a streak of magenta fire that trailed ribbons of deep pink smoke. The sight of it stalled the parade of hideous images in my head and in that way cleared it a little. The peculiar werelight fizzed round me, sometimes crossing my path some yards ahead, other times flickering through the trees. I felt it had intelligence, was observing me, teasing me. This, I felt sure, was a manifestation – or hallucination – of the *ysbryd drwg* that Fush had mentioned. I was mesmerised by its strange beauty, but knew I must escape it. Yet wherever I turned it overtook me.

Eventually, I gave up trying to get away. 'State your purpose or begone!' I said, mustering a voice of command. The apparition hung before me on the path, only feet away from me. For a few brief moments it adopted a vaguely harish shape: a mass of hair floating on the air, but no face. There were trailing arms like long thin fins, a robe of purple-black billows that faded to nothing above the dirt of the track. I heard a sound like the crackle of lightning, which might have been laughter. Then it was gone and the blackness was absolute, the landscape around me utterly silent, holding its breath.

I was so relieved to see the tower on its hill, I almost wept. By this time, my limbs had stiffened and my head was aching badly. Hara are rarely ill, but I was reminded of my human childhood, of the diseases of infancy that confined you to bed in a hushed room, of time ticking by, and the sweats of sickness, the boiling eyes, the soreness of throat and limb. I pressed my flaming face against the wood of the tower door, fumbling with the latch. Then I was inside, and it was as if loving arms reached for me, helped me up the stairs. I didn't pause at the kitchen, but went directly to my bedroom, where I flung myself on the bed, fully dressed. The Whitemanes had somehow *done* something to me, but what? I could barely move, afire with fever and pain.

I must have drifted into sleep, for I awoke not long before midnight, feeling perfectly fine. Whatever spasm had gripped me, or made me believe I'd been gripped, had vanished. The ancient memories had settled, become dim, and could be ignored. I went down to the kitchen and prepared myself some tea as well as three thick rounds of toast, for now I was ravenous. As I ate, I wrote up everything I'd experienced. Had Ember Whitemane managed to blow some hallucinogenic powder onto me? Had the lights on the ground been laced with some kind of drug that I inhaled? While it would be easy to imagine harm had been done to me on purpose, perhaps what I'd gone through was merely a component of the Whitemane ritual. All of them had been addled in the same way, running through the trees, amid the squirming hounds, carrying an injured har between them.

'Crazy hara,' I said aloud, shaking my head, and reaching for the comfort of hot tea. Only the dehara knew what had happened once that bacchanal band had reached the Whitemane domain. I imagined savage lust, fiery eyes, and the warm brown of Whitemane flesh. But there was no arousal in these thoughts; I was glad to be home.

Around an hour later, I went back to my bed, feeling comfortably drowsy and ready for wholesome sleep. The night was so calm, especially as Mossamber's hounds were absent from the farm. The eerie rise and fall of their spontaneous nocturnal chorus was not there to unnerve me and delay my slumber.

I remember I dropped off fairly quickly, for often I'm prone to lying awake for a long time before sleep comes to me. But then there was the dream.

As in the most disturbing of lucid dreams, I was convinced I was awake. I heard a noise on the stairs that woke me, and I sat up in bed. Clear azure starlight illumined the room. I saw the door swing open slowly, revealing an intense darkness beyond. I didn't feel afraid, only curious, but also sure of who would be standing there at my threshold. As I'd known, it was Ember Whitemane who stepped from the darkness. He didn't speak but came to me directly, half dressed in what might have been torn cloth or leaves. His hair drooped in matted rags over his breast and his eyes seemed wholly black. His stare reached right into me – wild, hungry, challenging – and inflamed me instantly and fully.

Again, a memory of the distant past, when aruna had been a mind-bending and potent drug, hara hungry for it continually. The power in it. I saw a pair of dark eyes gleaming, eyes across a fire.

Ember tore back my quilt and in a moment was upon me. I met him with equal hunger. We clawed at one another, snarling. What he gave me was gritty, part of the forest, scoring my insides, painful as much as pleasurable. I pulled his hair, trying to drag his face to mine, but he resisted. There would be no sharing of breath between us. This was some base, proto-pagan act, the culmination of whatever his bizarre hara had done that night, with nothing of finer feeling about it. It was as if he pulled from deep within my spirit some primal, savage entity. The ecstasy of this fierce coupling was so great, I was barely conscious. As waves of delirious arunic energy began to course through my flesh, I uttered a cry, a word. A name. But it was not Ember's. He took this from me, perhaps had visited me to seek it. I could not silence it, make him forget it, or pretend it wasn't the most potent of spells.

'Gesaril!'

Only once.

Enough.

When I woke the next day I wasn't as disturbed by the dream as I thought I should be, even though I could remember every detail. I knew it *was* a dream, that Ember had not visited me in reality. There were no leaves, or sticks or soil within my bed. My soume-lam wasn't torn. I wasn't bruised or scratched. But at the same time I was convinced Ember and his kin had *created* the dream. I was now sure the experience I'd had in the bedroom days before, of imagining that sticklike creature against me, had somehow presaged Ember's visit. His night raid of my sleeping mind, which I took to be mischievous rather than malevolent, didn't anger me or make me afraid, only left me somewhat dazed. I can't deny I'd enjoyed it, in an appalled kind of way. But what did unnerve me was that I'd spoken that name; my secret. I wasn't happy the Whitemanes had this name, but then, thinking rationally, how could they use it against me? My history with Gesaril – at least I was able to acknowledge his name now, as if a heavy stone had been lifted from me – was hardly likely to offend the Wyvachi should they discover it, because it *was* history, a sorry story of two individuals who'd acted impulsively. There is no record to say I was cruel.

After breakfast, I began to move clocks into the bathroom. One from the kitchen wall, one from the bedroom, another from the living-room mantelpiece. Why I was driven to do this, I couldn't then explain, but it felt right, as if the tower was speaking to me. I'd had a brief impression of the bathroom being used for ritual purposes when I'd first come here, and of clocks being somehow a part of that. I needed to bring these measurers of earthly time into that room, because it would initiate something. I had no idea what.

Chapter Ten

The celebrations for the Wyvachi Cuttingtide rite would begin in the early evening. I went over to Meadow Mynd in the afternoon to help with the preparations. In the garden, Rinawne came to me almost immediately as I wandered among the trestle tables and busy hara on the main lawn. He took my hand and said, 'Ys, are you all right?'

I pantomimed a double take, raised my brows. 'A strange greeting! Of course I'm all right. Why?'

Rinawne regarded me with suspicious eyes. 'I don't know. It's just when I first saw you across the lawn, you seemed...' He shook his head. 'There, I have no words to describe it! I suppose "out of sorts" will have to do.'

I squeezed his hand and let go of it. 'I'm fine. Just a little tired. Sat up far too late last night and there was wine in my store to help bring in the change of season.'

This was something Rinawne could understand and empathise with. 'Your own fault, then!'

I smiled. 'Yes. But never mind my self-inflicted hurts. There are so many tables here. Are you feeding several villages tonight?'

Rinawne laughed. 'We might well do. Word has spread. Hara are curious.'

'This means, of course, you and Wyva were publicising the event last night on your excursions.'

He shrugged a little. 'Well, maybe.' There was an excitement about him; he had some news. But I knew enough of Rinawne by now not to push him for it. He liked to choose his moments to astound. And from the look of him, the news could not be bad.

'How would you and Wyva feel about Myv leading the procession tonight?' I asked. 'I was thinking last night it might be a good idea to announce his intentions concerning the hienama role.'

'Sounds fine to me,' Rinawne said. 'I know Wyva would think the same. Word's got out already a bit. I think Myv must've mentioned it at the school, or to one of the househara who care for him.'

'Oh, what's the reaction been to the news?'

'Hara like the idea, or seem to. Why would they not? They've been gasping for a hienama for long enough, and...' He squeezed my arm, '...they have you to teach him.'

'Well...'

'All right, all right, we won't talk about that now. Anyway, I have to sort things out. Some of these tables are a mess. Keep me company, though.'

We roamed the lawn of Meadow Mynd, Rinawne inspecting tablecloths and other such trivia. While he talked with his staff about details, I mulled over the festival to come. I had decided that Myv should lead the procession crowned with early summer flowers and carrying a torch. I was glad rumours had spread among the local hara, and that there appeared to be no unhappy reaction to them. But then why should there be? Wyva and his kin were loved and respected. This could only be marvellous news to the hara of Gwyllion.

I wondered, though, what the Whitemanes might think about it. Could this announcement even put Myv in danger? I uttered a small sound aloud to dismiss the thought. I mustn't bring such ill-omened ideas into reality. A brief flash of Ember Whitemane's sly yet lovely countenance skittered across my mind. I had been determined not to think of the Whitemanes today, and must push images of them away sternly. The celebration tonight would be one of joy and gratitude for life itself, with no dark elements. The Wyvachi must be the future of hara in this area, not the Whitemanes. I was sure of that after what I'd witnessed the previous evening. The thought of Myv sticking Wyva with a few arrows, then his hurakin running off mad-eyed with the unconscious body, was in fact ludicrous. I was almost tempted to share what I'd experienced with Rinawne, but perhaps that was for another time. Today should not be tainted.

'What is it?' Rinawne asked. He was studying me and I'd not noticed.

'Nothing, why?'

'You made a strange sound.'

'Oh, just running over plans in my head. There are some words I wished I'd used for the main rite, but it's too late to change now.'

'Never too late to change,' Rinawne said, grinning. 'You should know that. Oh, this might fascinate you...'

'What?' *Here it came.*

'Well, on our travels last night, Wyva was in an extremely good mood, and in such moods might miracles occur! We passed the boundary into the next county and there are relatives of his in that place. He suggested we *call* on them.'

Rinawne's face was alight with pleasure, or perhaps just curiosity and love of drama, but I felt a strange twist of anxiety at the news. 'I didn't think the Wyvachi had any contact with other relatives.'

'Little,' Rinawne said. 'But it was in Wyva's blood to see them, so off we went. The domain is called Harrow's End, a beautiful old place, which was – I understand – a wreck when they first occupied it. Not so now, and a thriving community around it. They were celebrating their Cuttingtide last night. There were bonfires everywhere, sparks going up into the sky. We heard the singing long before we reached the house. We saw hara lurching and dancing all over the fields and gardens. Much wine and ale had flowed and everyhar was in generous spirit. The Wyverns were surprised to see us, of course, but embraces were exchanged, exclamations of delight. You can imagine. Some of them will be coming here tonight, because Wyva has told them the past is cleansed. I never realised what an expert liar he is.'

I frowned. 'Rin, isn't this... isn't this all rather *important*?

Perhaps a public festival isn't the right time or place for this family reunion.'

'Whyever not? Surely hara will be on their best behaviour if there's an audience.'

I shook my head. 'Because... something happened in the past to divide the family, *severely* divide it. Now you say it's all happiness and cheer again? Is that even... *right* without some sober and *private* discussion?'

Rinawne had assumed a slightly irritated expression, and had folded his arms. 'Only if we assume they fell out for a good reason, which I doubt.'

'Why assume it was a falling out at all? Maybe it was more to do with the situation here.'

Again Rinawne shrugged. 'I don't care. I'm impatient with it all, Ys. The secrecy, the melodrama. What reason is there for it now? Let them all get back together and see what a stupid thing the division was in the first place.'

'Well, let's hope that's the outcome,' I said.

I couldn't help but think of the Whitemanes again: the gleam of watchful eyes among the trees; swift, covert movement; the glint of an arrow. I was compelled to glance over my shoulder, at the dark mass of the thick shrubbery around the lawn. For a moment I sensed somehar there, watching me, the faintest tickle of a thought against my mind. Then it withdrew, the feeling passed. But after that, I had the clear and certain feeling that the problems of the Wyvachi were intrinsically enmeshed with the Whitemanes, more so than in mere history. Why this idea should come to me at that moment and so strongly, I had no idea, but I felt it was right. 'So who exactly is coming?' I said, trying to lighten the atmosphere. 'Prepare me so I can politely know names.'

Rinawne was looking at me in a slightly puzzled way, no doubt wondering why I'd looked behind us like a frightened cat. 'OK, well I've already told you that Wyva's parents are dead. As you might expect, details of this are scant and surrounded by much silent woe and hand-wringing. Maybe they were murdered, who knows? Certainly not me. The surviving hurakin are led by Wyva's hura, Medoc har Wyvern – that branch never lost the original family name. His tribe is vast and prosperous.'

'Yet in one respect like the Wyvachi, clinging to the past,' I said.

'What?'

'The family name.'

'Perhaps, although you don't get that feeling so much from them. Anyway, Medoc will come this evening, along with a half dozen or so relatives. Don't ask me to remember *their* names.'

I fixed Rinawne with a hienamarly stare, as he would call it. 'For Wyva's sake, for Myv's, this reunion has to go well tonight,' I said.

'Don't look so sombre,' Rinawne said. 'Everything was fine last night. Wyva probably hasn't seen his hura since he was a harling. His parents are gone, old feuds hopefully forgotten – mostly. Medoc has no reason not to re-establish relations with Wyva and his brothers. This should have been broached before.' He touched my shoulder. 'I feel it's you who's somehow brought about this change.'

'Don't blame *me* for everything.'

Rinawne laughed heartily. 'Blame? I was talking about gratitude.'

Later in the afternoon, after hours of niggling unease, I made a decision and asked Wyva if I could speak to him in private. He took me into the library, as he always tended to do when we needed to talk, away from the hubbub of the house and garden. 'You have something to say, Ys? You seem troubled. I hope all the arrangements are to your liking.'

'Of course,' I replied, 'I'm amazed at the extent of them! No, it's not that, Wyva, and I don't want to blow dark smoke over the excitement, but I must ask you this: will your estate be secure tonight?'

'What by Aru do you mean?' Wyva appeared shocked, almost angry.

I rubbed the nape of my neck, embarrassed. 'Rinawne told me about your hurakin coming here and well... I saw some *odd* proceedings in the forest last night. The Whitemanes. I hate to mention them, but I have to. What I saw... It's hard to explain, but when Rinawne told me your news I could only feel apprehension. I wouldn't want the Whitemanes spoiling your reunion with your family.'

Now Wyva laughed, apparently relieved. 'Oh, Ys, you're such a worrier! They wouldn't dare. But yes, as you mention it, I had planned to have hara patrolling our perimeter and the woods close to the house, just as a precaution. Prying eyes I could do without, and they might be tempted to spy, knowing – as they certainly will – that the first of your festival rites will take place tonight. Mossamber wouldn't be joyful if he learned Wyverns were present on this soil.' He paused. 'What exactly did you see last night?'

I shook my head. 'Only the dehara know really, but I witnessed their enactment of the Cuttingtide story, or part of it. I saw a running har brought down with arrows within the forest. He wasn't killed, or didn't appear to be. The Whitemanes carried him off, whooping like maniacs, like blood-maddened hara from the first days of our kind. To be perfectly honest with you, the sight completely shook me up.'

Wyva clasped my shoulders. 'Indeed. Bad memories revived. This is the problem with the Whitemanes, you see. They are...' He sighed, dropped his hands from me. 'Well, there's no other word but *primitive*. It's why I can't negotiate with them properly, why they want to maintain the bad blood between our families. I didn't want to say too much for fear you'd think I was exaggerating the problem, but now you've seen for yourself, and I need say no more. Stay away from them, Ys. You might think us Wyvachi live in the past, but the Whitemanes haven't changed since the first of them were incepted!'

'Did you know they... that their rites could be *bloody*?'

Wyva's mouth twitched a little. I could almost smell his distaste of the Whitemanes. 'Naturally, hara have seen things over the years. Rumours, even reports, have come to me. Mossamber isn't exactly discreet in these matters. Yes, I've heard before that they enact the Arotahar stories quite literally sometimes, although as you surmised I doubt what you saw was murder. Their ceremonies are known to be... *visceral*. I'm sorry to say it, but I believe that's why some local hara are drawn to the Whitemane festivals. Perhaps in some hara the germs of our creation and the memories of the first days are not that far from the surface.'

'I agree, especially so for first generation.' I paused, then had to ask, 'So how will the Whitemanes feel about Myv?'

Wyva uttered a scoffing sound. 'They will not care. Neither will they respect or acknowledge Myv's position in the community. As with everything to do with us, they'll ignore or spit on it. But if you're worried for Myv's safety, don't be. Barbaric though the Whitemanes might seem, they've never physically harmed any of us.'

'Never?'

Wyva dropped his gaze from mine. 'Well, let's just say not through bad intention.'

This was the trouble with life in Gwyllion. The moment one mystery seemed solved, another oozed out. Was it possible to harm a har with *good* intention?

The celebrations would begin in the village of Gwyllion itself, at The Crowned Stag. Here, Selyf and his staff would distribute hot spiced wine to everyhar who gathered there. I walked the path to the inn with the family around 7.30 in the evening. The hurakin would not arrive until later, once the ritual itself was over and everyhar had convened at Meadow Mynd for the nightlong celebrations.

Myv was excited, the most animated I'd seen him. Rinawne had dressed him in a moss-green robe and he wore a crown woven of early summer flowers and ivy, tendrils of which trailed artfully down his back. Wyva carried the procession torch, as yet unlit, which would be handed to his son for the ritual lighting. Everyhar associated with Meadow Mynd walked with us; Cawr and his chesnari Modryn, Porter Goudy, all the househara and those who tended the fields and gardens, who cared for the animals. Gen was allowed to ride, because of his healing injury. Dillory, the cook, began to sing a soft, lilting song, which I did not know, but gradually everyhar joined in, hardly more than a chorus of whispers. The notes conjured shivers along my skin, they were so beautiful. I was reminded of the song I'd heard drifting from the woodland on the evening when I'd first arrived. Perhaps it had been Dillory singing then too, down amid the trees below the tower, gathering herbs among the roots.

Now, bat shadows stitched across the early evening sky where the star of Lunil blazed alone in triumph. The lush foliage of the towering trees to either side of the path was almost wanton in its heaviness. The canopy of the oncoming night, of the earth, was ripe with the scents of nature, the forest lawns, night-blooming flowers. Even the dung of animals added another essential perfume. And we, in procession along the road, voices murmuring in song. The glory of this shared experience seduced me to tears. In the dusk, it was Wyva who reached for my hand, not Rinawne. I glanced at him through a film of water, squeezed his fingers. He smiled at me, with his eyes, his whole face, his whole being. *He is a good leader of hara,* I thought, more sure of it then than at any other moment before or since.

Hara were already gathered at The Stag, and stood in groups, drinking the hot wine. The scent of spices dominated the air. When the Meadow Mynd troupe reached the yard, everyhar cried 'Astale, Myvyen!' Yes, the news was widely known.

Myv clearly didn't know whether to be delighted or embarrassed by this greeting, which is how the dehara themselves are saluted during ceremonies. I saw Porter push him forwards with a hand to the back. Myv performed an exaggerated bow. The assembly clapped their hands and Selyf approached with his assistants and trays of drinks for us.

I noticed that protective wards hung plentifully from the eaves of The Stag, and that warding symbols had been woven into the Cuttingtide garlands that adorned the doors and windows. The hara of Gwyllion, clearly, were taking no chances this night.

Wyva gave a short speech on our reasons to be grateful for what life had given us, the bounty of the land, the gifts the dehara had imparted to all. I think he could have uttered a list of his tasks to do the next day and everyhar would still have listened in rapt attention, their eyes misty. At the end of it, Wyva gestured to his son, who stood at his side, and said, 'And perhaps the best gift we have this season is a hienama in making, my son...' he glanced at Rinawne, '...*our* son, who has offered himself, even at this tender age, for the role. Thank you, Myv. May the dehara guide your path. May the stars welcome you along their highways.'

The crowd uttered similar sentiments, and then it was, of course, Myv's duty to say something, as the hara called for him to do so. We should really have prepared him for this possibility, but he seemed comfortable with the attention. 'I will do my best,' he said. That was all, but it was obvious he meant it.

Looking at him, I knew then that his feybraiha would come upon him in the following year. I knew that Porter would be the har to guide him through it and beyond. Whether they ever became chesna did not matter. There was a closeness between them that would endure through life, however far apart physically they might become. I also knew that Myv's decision would bring him closer to his hostling, who had feared his own dark history had somehow blighted his harling's life. This fear had caused the distance between them. I could see it as if it was written on the night air in letters of glowing mist. I hoped

Wyva took recent events as proof that Myv was fine, untainted; he was separate from whatever darkness hid in the past and must remain so.

Then the moment came to light the torch.

An atmosphere of expectant calm fell over the entire group gathered outside the inn. Unspoken, the commencement of the ceremony had been felt, creeping upon us like a soft evening mist. Hara gathered around me in a circle, and I spoke the ritual words to bid farewell to the dehara of the previous season, Feyrani and Elisin, and to invite Shadolan and Morterrius into our reality to preside until the next festival. I drew the signs of the Cuttingtide dehara upon the air. Then I led the gathering in a short meditation, visualising Morterrius rising from the soil of the forest, blossoming as the flowers of the deepwoods did, voluptuous and luminous. His name, at this point of the ceremony, seemed incongruous, for there was nothing of death about him. We would walk with him through the woodland, our feet conjuring growth where we trod, to his appointed tryst with Shadolan; once his son, soon to be his doom.

After these preliminaries, Selyf handed me a flaming brand and with this I lit Myv's torch. 'Walk with the dehara,' I said, 'and we will follow you.'

Dillory began to hum a bittersweet tune, and this time his assistants, Fush and Barly, accompanied him. Presently, the whole company joined in harmony as we set off from The Crowned Stag. I had written two songs for the ceremony, because I knew that hara liked to sing at festivals. The first, a soft lament, would be sung at the forest glade I had chosen.

Presently, Myv veered off the path and led us towards this glade. While I joined in the flowing chant, I was alert for presences around us, both physical and etheric. I assumed Wyva had stationed security hara some distance off. I had no idea whether the Whitemanes were capable of harassing or even attacking a large group of hara in the midst of a spiritual ceremony, but I feared it. Seeing them in their full savagery the previous night made it seem all too likely.

As we went deeper among the trees, where the forest's breath was almost audible in the darkness, I thought again of my dream visitation the night before: Ember Whitemane standing in my doorway with his hair hanging down, his body smeared with the mud of the forest, perhaps even the blood of his hostling. I willed my mind away from such thoughts, concentrated upon the melody drifting around me like mist. The Whitemanes wanted me to think this way. They wanted me to be mesmerised, bewitched. Or was this all in my imagination, the product of my own fears and weaknesses? Cuttingtide was the time to rid oneself of delusions; I must abide by that. I must remember how I'd felt before I'd stumbled upon that forest lawn last night.

We came to the oak grove and here Myv stuck the torch in the mossy soil. Other hara, appointed by Wyva for the task, glided quietly around the edge of our circle, lighting small lamps to glow in a ring around us. As they did so, I spoke softly, but audible to all, for I am trained to speak that way.

'This is the time when the light draws away from us. Although the winter season is far in our future, we know the light is dying from this night forth, until the next solstice is upon us and light is renewed. Joyous yet melancholy are the days of high summer, when the earth dances in finery to the very edge of night. Astale, Shadolan! Astale, Morterrius! Reveal to us the secrets of the season, of life and death, rebirth and eternity. Astale!'

I led the hara in a visualisation of the dehara, similar in essence to the barbaric rite of the Whitemanes, but also different. Morterrius became the white hind that soared through the forest, her feet barely touching the ground. Shadolan, the archetypal hunter, pursued the hind and, with a single arrow, brought her down. But instead of collapsing to the ground to breathe her last, the hind transformed into a storm of white petals, which slowly became red as they fluttered to earth. The flower. The blood. Yet insubstantial as mist. (*Nytethorne's fingers moving feebly on the deer-cropped grass. No!*) Shadolan stood in a confetti of petals, his golden eyes luminous as those of a wolf. Now he was alone, the hunter in the forest. But instead of sending him off, brooding to some distant cave, I had him come to us, to stand before us. We sought his blessing and his counsel.

Everyhar sat upon the night-damp ground and I began to sing the first of my songs, the lament for Morterrius that was also a song of strength. Our dehar had not died but was simply transformed, to continue the cycle until he was born again. This was the way of our world, our home; the continual cycle we call Arotahar.

As the song died away, I allowed everyhar some minutes to commune privately with the landscape and Shadolan himself. The forest around us was full of subtle noise, but none of it was unnatural. I sensed no prying eyes, no slinking threat.

Then it was time to return to Meadow Mynd for the final parts of the rite and to partake of the feast that lay waiting. Dillory began to sing brighter songs and everyhar joined in as before. There was a sense of release around us, perhaps even relief. However it's dressed up, there's no escaping the fact that Cuttingtide revolves around Shadolan's slaughter of Morterrius, and what this symbolises. It is in nohar's interest to ignore the realities of existence, no matter how long our lives. Tragedy and accident can befall anyhar, and while the harish body is far more adept at healing itself than the human form had been, some injuries are beyond healing. This is what Cuttingtide reminds us, among its other messages. Now hara had faced that and could put it away in their minds for another year. There was no reason to dwell upon the darker aspects of the festival any longer. But as we walked, laughing and singing our way to the Mynd, I heard beneath the celebrations that distant bell once more. It seemed so close and yet not close at all, chiming from some distant spire.

Everyhar gathered on the spreading lawns of Meadow Mynd

and before we fell upon the food, Wyva began the passing of the ritual cup. Everyhar was to make a toast, and as so many were gathered there, this took some time. However, most elected to say simply 'to the dehara' or 'to the season' before taking a sip from the continually replenished cup. Only a few felt moved to utter longer toasts, and even these were not that prolonged. The rite was concluded, I sang the final song, hara joining in as they learned the tune.

The last strains of the song died away, but still seemed to throb upon the air. At that moment, almost as if they'd been waiting, hidden among the trees until the ceremonial aspect of the festival was concluded, the Wyverns cantered their horses onto the lawn. In the torchlight, I could see that there were five of them, led by a har on an exquisite palomino mare – a mount I'd have considered the Whitemanes might favour, seeing as the horses I'd seen of theirs had been showy. The har dismounted and Wyva went up to him immediately, embraced him. This must be Medoc har Wyvern. Wyva turned and beckoned to me, even before introducing Myv or any of his other relatives. I went forward and bowed my head. 'Tiahaara, best of the season to you.'

'This is Ysobi har Jesith,' Wyva said proudly, 'who is working with us at the moment in a spiritual sense. He won't allow us to call him our hienama but...' Wyva grinned and slapped my back, 'he is, in all but name.'

'I'm not ready to rush off,' I said, hoping that would suffice.

'This is my hura, Medoc,' Wyva said. Medoc was slightly taller than him, and slightly broader, but the resemblance was obvious. 'His chesnari, Thraine, his sons Ysgaw and Wenyf, his high-harling Persys.' I nodded to these hara, who were disturbingly similar and all looked to be the same age.

'Glory of the season to you, tiahaar,' Medoc said, his family echoing his sentiments in a respectful chorus.

Rinawne had appeared, beautiful in his ceremonial costume, small white flowers like stars in his hair. After formal greetings, he gestured for the Wyverns to follow him to the tables. There,

I could see Cawr and Modryn standing rather uncomfortably, with Gen in a chair beside them, equally uncomfortable, as if they were unsure how to take this revelation of relatives.

As we strolled to the food, Medoc hung back a pace or two to speak with me. 'So you are here as a teacher?' he asked. 'It's clear you're not local.' His tone held no hostility in it, merely a question.

'In a way,' I said, aware I must be careful of my answer. 'Gwyllion's last hienama opted for – shall we say – a monastic kind of life, which left the community without spiritual guidance. Wyva asked the hara in Kyme for assistance.' I assumed Medoc was worldly enough to know of Kyme and its functions. 'I'm here primarily to create a seasonal system for the Wyvachi, the first festival of which we celebrated tonight. But if I'm needed to teach, then of course I'll attend to that also.'

'Wenyf is our hienama,' Medoc said. 'One of my sons. He wasn't trained in Kyme, but he's a natural for it. I don't think any community should be without a har on the priestly path, do you?'

'Absolutely. We are part teacher, part physician, part advisor and... well, part whatever else might be needed from time to time.'

Medoc laughed, patted my shoulder. 'Indeed. I see you've worked long at your path. You are first generation, yes?'

Nowadays, that wasn't considered a polite question exactly. 'Yes,' I answered, holding his gaze steadily.

He rolled his eyes. 'I apologise. I meant no offence.' He touched his own chest. 'I'm first generation too, of course, but I'm under no illusion how pureborns regard us sometimes. And sometimes that regard is justified.'

'Unfortunately, that is so,' I said.

'But our knowledge of the past, and all that we witnessed, shouldn't be lost,' he continued. 'Perhaps we *are* tainted by it, but to forget what happened is to make yourself vulnerable. And old mistakes can be repeated. At least, that's what I think.'

He paused for a moment and gazed around him. 'Wyva has done well here. The hara are happy, the house stands proud. But there is blood beneath this soil, Ysobi har Jesith, and it has a memory. Just be mindful of that.'

I inclined my head. 'I understand.'

Again, he patted my shoulder. 'Enough of the past. Let's rejoice in mendings and happy hours for the future.'

'I couldn't agree more.'

We had reached the company. Several hara of the Gwyllion Assembly had clustered around Gen and Cawr – rather protectively, I thought. Conversation was cordial, yet a little stilted, perhaps to be expected under the circumstances. I took the opportunity to drift away from the family gathering.

I saw Myv near the fire, dancing around the flames with Porter and a tumble of harlings from the town, no doubt his schoolmates. Perhaps he had always been free and at ease among hara of his own age. To me that night he seemed like any other harling I'd met, carefree and joyous because he was at a party among friends. He spotted me and gestured for me to come over, and then asked me to dance with them. I hadn't drunk enough to feel comfortable being the only adult cavorting round the fire, so again made my escape. Myv didn't insist and turned back to his friends.

As I walked through the crowd that now covered the lawn of Meadow Mynd, hara called to me in greeting, showered me with blessings and good wishes. I was reminded wistfully of how I'd never really had that in Jesith. Even before Jassenah had come into my life, I'd been rather a recluse because of relationships that had gone sour, and my inability to deal with the fallout properly. Jass had tried to bring me into the light, and for a while that had been golden, but this hadn't lasted. Still, tonight was not the time for melancholy thoughts. I was here in Gwyllion and life was different.

I wandered into the woodland beyond the lawns, which comprised mainly aged rhododendron, unquestionably the sovereign in this part of the garden. Perhaps it had even witnessed the horrors of Meadow Mynd's history. The voluptuous blossoms were starting to look past their best, but they were late-blooming enough to grace the midsummer festival with their translucent beauty, and also being of a breed that released a faint fragrance into the air. I inhaled deeply as I walked the narrow path between them, conscious of the myriad dens of thick stalks and dusty leaves that were concealed in the heart of the overgrown shrubs. I remembered how I'd used to play in such hideaways when I'd been a boy. I'd owned a veritable labyrinth of chambers and tunnels in my grandmother's garden. Fondly, I reached out and touched a cluster of the glowing white flowers, bringing them to my face, taking in their scent. Petals came away in my hands, fell to earth. I was glad my grandmother had died long before her garden had been made a ruin.

Then a whisper came to me, 'Such fond memories, Wyvachi-called.'

Only Whitemanes would address me as that. I turned quickly, but could see nohar. My heart increased its beat, preparing to fight or flee. 'Are you such a coward as to not show yourself?' I said, equally softly.

There was a rustling and he came burrowing out of the dark leaves on the opposite side of the narrow path. He stood up. The starlight was so bright I could see him clearly, the dust on his clothes, cobwebs in his hair, the wet gleam of his eyes. He was tall, arrogant, sneering, yet with the features of a Classical god.

'I believe I have the honour of the company of Nytethorne Whitemane,' I said, bowing.

He laughed, shook his hair as a horse might shake his mane. 'So he perceives a difference among us, the Wyvachi-called.

'Why are you here?' I asked. 'The festival is over. It went well. You can report that.'

Nytethorne ignored my words. He smiled, and I couldn't tell what sentiment lay behind it. 'You grieved for my blood, my son said.'

And now they have sent you to continue his work.

I shrugged, more nonchalantly than I felt. 'I won't lie. What I saw last night shocked me, but then I am an over-civilised and weak har in your eyes. Blood rites do not figure greatly in my spiritual work.'

'Strange. Heard you spill blood quite regularly,' Nytethorne said, 'but not the physical kind.'

Again, I bowed. 'I'm flattered your family find me important enough to harass, tiahaar, but whatever you're plotting won't work. Unless you're planning to resort to physical harm, although Wyva assures me that has never happened between your clans, at least not – how did he put it? – *intentionally.*'

Nytethorne no longer appeared as confident as he had. I knew I had scored a point. 'No, they hurt their own more,' he said in a hard tone. 'Ask him about that instead.'

'Why do you care what I know or think? It's been made clear to me you despise me, and I've assumed that's because of my education and way of life, yet you can't leave me alone, can you? Why don't you just laugh at my *weakness* behind my back? Laugh at how stupid Wyva was to call me from Kyme, and leave it at that.'

'Didn't call you from Kyme, though, did he?'

My laughter was genuine. I no longer felt any shred of apprehension. 'You won't give up trying to unsettle me, will you? It's become a posture, Nytethorne Whitemane. Be civil to me or leave me be. I've no interest in any other kind of interaction between us. And that goes for all of you. Maintain your ancient hatreds if you must, but don't include me in your games.' I turned to walk back to the party, leave the spy to dwell upon what I'd said. I didn't expect him to follow and take hold of my arm.

'You know nothing, Wyvachi-called,' he murmured, close to my ear. '*They* called you into this. Can't turn the soil without finding worms. It knows you now. If you think we control that, you're mad.'

I shook myself free of him. 'I've no idea what you're talking about.'

There was a pause while we held each other's gaze, me waiting for Nytethorne's response. 'You've a leaning to meddle,' he said. 'Gets you noticed. Think you're quiet? You're not. You crash through the forest like a boar. Take heed of it. Learn to be quiet.'

'Because?'

Nytethorne held my gaze, and it was difficult not to be influenced by his appearance, the appeal that oozed from him. 'He went because he was wise,' he said slowly.

I was sure at once who he meant. 'Rey.' The name came out like a breath.

Nytethorne continued to stare at me. 'You be wise and do the same. Let the Wyvachi sacrifice their harling. Perhaps he's the one they wait for, but I don't believe in miracles.'

I realised this har, however disjointedly, was trying both to warn me and give me information. I also realised the Whitemanes must have an informant in the Mynd. Nytethorne's information was too precise. 'If Rey went because he was wise,' I said carefully, 'why did he leave his son behind?'

There was a moment's hesitation. 'Porter's never in danger.'

'Why?'

'Because of who his father is.'

I blinked. 'And that would be?'

I knew he wouldn't answer. He already regretted revealing too much. 'No matter,' I said. 'Keep your secrets. But as a har, and a parent yourself, if you have *any* information, however small, that would protect Myv, you should tell me. He's only a harling, not part of your family vendettas. Surely you have the honour to realise that?'

'*You* protect him,' Nytethorne said.

I stared at him, remembering that brief feeling of being watched earlier, the brush of thought against my mind. 'You were in the gardens earlier, weren't you? You tried to tell me something.'

'Nothing more to say!' And then he was sprinting away from me down the path, leaping in strangely long strides, until I could see him no more. He'd had merely the barest trace of a limp and yet only the night before he'd been shot in the leg. Not even hara usually heal that quickly.

Once he'd gone, I was shaken, flooded with disorientation that I'd managed to keep at bay in his presence. They had such a *strong* effect, these Whitemanes. It put my former reputation to shame.

I breathed deeply for a couple of minutes to calm myself, not wishing to return to the Mynd in a dishevelled mental state that somehar might notice. Once I felt in control of myself again, I retraced my path.

There was an ornate gazebo at the edge of the rhododendrons, and I saw that two hara were seated there. As I drew nearer, it became clear this was Wyva and Medoc. Something about their postures alerted me. I could hear no words, and neither of them was on their feet gesticulating, but all the same I sensed an argument was in progress. And because I needed information I crept up on them, keeping to the foliage, keeping quiet, until I could hear them. (Was I following Nytethorne's advice already?)

'Wyva, you must protect your own,' Medoc was saying. 'You've chosen to remain here, and you must continue to abide by the rules. Part of that is not challenging the past.'

'This is our home,' Wyva said in a controlled tone. 'Yes, it was our choice to remain here, while you chose to depart. But I don't see why, after all this time, we can't begin to put aside that grim history, truly take back what is ours.'

'Because you never can,' Medoc replied, his voice sounding genuinely sad. He put a hand against his chest. 'Wyva, I was *there*. I saw your parents after what happened. The terror in their hearts, their *souls*. Kinnard should have fled with us.

Remaining here cost him his life and that of his chesnari.'

'There's no proof of that... For Aru's sake, they didn't create my pearl then die. They had years of happiness... Cawr, Gen...'

'Oh, Wyva!' Medoc exclaimed. 'Will you blind yourself to that too?'

There was a silence after these words, as if Medoc had said something absolutely appalling or out of place. 'I'm sorry,' he said at last. 'I shouldn't have used that term.'

Wyva shook his head. 'My son wants to be hienama,' he said in a determined tone. 'This is a revered role and if he's called to it, he should follow the path.'

'Of course! But not here. It will turn the soil.'

I was reminded of what Nytethorne had said. *Can't turn the soil without finding worms.* What *was* this family's secret and how could it still affect the present? Was it merely a haunting, whether imagined or conjured from damaged minds, or something more?

'Medoc, part of me knows you are right,' Wyva said, still in that smooth, controlled voice that he must have perfected over the years, 'but it is *they* who perpetuate our curse. They feed it, never let it die. Is it right we should simply flee from that, turn our backs on it? What does that promise for the hara we leave behind? Do we abandon them to Mossamber Whitemane and his obsessions? Do you really advocate that?'

Medoc shook his head. 'No, but...'

'Somewhere in that house there is a shrine to Peredur,' Wyva said before Medoc could continue. He pointed out towards the river and what lay beyond. 'And nightly they worship before it, feeding whatever is left of those dire days.'

'You have proof of that?'

'No, but I don't need it. And in your heart you know that, too.'

Medoc sighed. He reached out and clasped Wyva's shoulder. 'My heart aches for you,' he said, 'and that's partly why I've stayed away from Meadow Mynd. I know I can't change anything and I can't bear to witness what might happen here, what will continue to happen until their thirst for revenge, their vision of justice, is quenched.' He stood up. 'If the fire of youth still burned in me, I'd muster an army from both our lands and lay waste to the domain of Whitemane, unearth whatever cankers its foundations and banish it. Don't think I haven't dreamed of that for nearly a century. But what is done is done. Kinnard made his choice. He did what he thought was right. He shot that arrow, and with it sealed the fate of our family.'

'Wouldn't you have done the same?'

'Instead of what Mossamber did?'

The question hung in silence.

Wyva shook his head. 'Mossamber thought he was liberating a corpse, and what he took was hardly more than that. You can't blame my hostling. As you said, you were there.'

Medoc made an impatient gesture with one hand. 'Wyva, the rights and wrongs of that are beyond debate now. It happened, and we can't change that. But the consequence was that we'd be cursed if we remained here. Kinnard chose defiance; I chose departure. And perhaps it seems to you as if things have gone quiet, somehow faded over time, but I swear that once Myv reaches feybraiha the soil *will* turn. Perhaps it's already doing so. *That* is what I must speak out about, no matter how you don't want to hear it. I also know you won't agree with me, but I have to say it to clear my conscience.'

'You wouldn't have come here tonight if I'd told you about Myv yesterday, would you?' Wyva said bitterly.

'Probably not. Our lives are long, Wyva. In comparison to our human forbears we have few children. For this reason, you've been able to carry on, believing all is well, because relatively few births occur to defy the malediction.'

'My hostling fought back. He protected his family.'

'A legend,' Medoc said, 'wishful thinking.'

'And yet this *wishful thinking* has magically sustained us.'

'I believe it has, because the will behind it was strong, but it's not enough, Wyva. All is *not* well, and Kinnard's original fire has flickered out. He's no longer with you with his ferocious beliefs, that power he had to protect his own. What you're proposing will only open it all up again.'

'I can't believe that,' Wyva said. 'My hostling is dead, but so is Peredur. He's been dead for a century. All that lives is Mossamber's hatred, which he's spread like a disease among his hara. I don't and can't believe there's anything wrong in standing up against that. To me, to do otherwise is simply cowardice.'

'Have you truly forgotten what happened when your pearl broke open?' Medoc asked softly.

Wyva paused before answering. 'No, but what I saw was with the eyes of a newly-hatched harling. How can I be sure that the memory is true and not just what my parents told me afterwards?'

'They did not lie to you. We all *heard* it, even if we didn't see with our own eyes. And many things happened afterwards to confirm the truth of that dark promise.' Medoc leaned down and again clasped Wyva's shoulder. 'Surakin, I know how badly you want everything to be right, to live here as a family should, leader of your hara, guardian of the land. But don't goad fate.'

'Your mistakes caused it all,' Wyva said abruptly. 'Peredur's, Kinnard's, yours. You turned on your human family, who still loved you, for no other reason than a mindless lust for destruction, the true curse of the incepted.'

Medoc sighed. 'There is not one creature who ever lived – human or har alike – who wouldn't have rewritten part of their history if they could. The early days were barbarous, Wyva. You'll never appreciate how much. The change was cathartic, terrible. Disgusting things were done – on *both* sides, as you know only too well. But to my mind, such things must be forgotten, left behind, and if that means leaving Meadow Mynd too, this should happen. There will always be a place for you in our home and for however many of your hara would follow you. Other than that, I can do nothing.'

'So this is it, then? You leave our domain and we continue as before, as if we were strangers?'

'No,' Medoc said softly. 'The estrangement was wrong, but please don't ask me to be part of what you're doing here. As I said, you're always welcome in our home, at any time. If you really can't bear to leave Gwyllion, at least consider finding a new house nearby. There are surely others that could be restored. That might be enough to protect you all.'

'I won't leave here, Medoc,' Wyva said. 'This house loves us and we love it too. It's the heart of our community and protects us every day of our lives.'

Medoc straightened up and looked around him. 'That might be so. How can I argue against such strong, personal conviction? I'm not you. But by the dehara, you can *feel* the resentment here. Watchful, cruel, vengeful, prowling beyond the boundary of your wards. The love among you keeps it at bay, but don't make the mistake of believing it weakened.'

Wyva said nothing, as if drained of words.

'Come,' Medoc said, 'let's return to the party. I hope you'll think about what I've said, but neither will we speak of it again.'

Wyva stood up, and he and Medoc embraced. Then they walked away.

I waited for some minutes before rejoining the party myself, thinking about what I'd heard. It sounded as if the Wyvachi believed the *Whitemanes* had cursed them. The history between the two families clearly went all the way back to the beginning. There had been at least three of the former Wyvern family who'd been incepted – or so I concluded. One had been Wyva's hostling Kinnard, another was Medoc, but who was Peredur, now dead? How had he died? *Mossamber thought he was liberating a corpse...* Had that been Peredur or somehar else? And what had happened when Wyva had hatched from his pearl? What had he seen, or been told he'd seen? How *did* it all fit together?

I felt strangely calm as I walked back across the lawns. Meadow Mynd stood strong against the night and I could feel its aura of protection as Wyva had described it. The hara dancing around the fire and who were clustered, talking loudly, around the tables clearly did not sense anything dangerous nearby, no prowling malice. Could Medoc be wrong, too influenced by his own past?

I noticed a pale figure standing a little apart from the others and saw it was Rinawne, his festival costume glowing in the light of the fire. It was not like him to be away from the heart of a gathering. I went to him and put a hand on his back. He jumped, startled, and then laughed when he saw it was me. 'Ysobi, don't creep up on me in the dark!'

'You seem thoughtful,' I said. 'Why are you here alone?'

He shrugged awkwardly. 'I think Wyva and Medoc might have had words. They went off together and now Wyva is upset. He snapped at me when I asked what was wrong.'

'They did argue,' I said, deciding on the spur of the moment to be honest, even though it was Rinawne I was confiding in, hardly renowned for his discretion.

'You were there?'

'I just overheard them when I was strolling past. I'd gone for a walk in the woods.'

'What did you hear?'

I took a breath. 'Rin, who's Peredur?'

Rinawne didn't hesitate before answering. He spoke the simple truth as he knew it. 'He was Wyva's hura, like Medoc, but he died. This was long before Wyva's parents did, or so I heard. I think he was killed during the initial struggle between Wraeththu and humans in this area.'

'Why didn't you tell me of him before?'

Rinawne frowned a little. 'There was nothing to tell. He's just a name, a dead name. Why?'

'I heard Wyva and Medoc discussing him. He's somehow

involved in this whole Wyvachi curse issue.'

'Leave it, Ys,' Rinawne said sharply.

'What?'

'It's just their stupid obsessions about the family history. Peredur's dead.'

'But perhaps not at rest.'

'Oh, come *on!*' Rinawne said scornfully.

'So says the har who once saw a banshee,' I said lightly. 'Maybe they want to be haunted, Rin, and maybe it's that. Medoc fears for Myv.'

'Well, he obviously fears a lot of things, which was why he fled all those years ago. Now he's feeding Wyva's fears. They should never have come here, and Wyva should not have visited them last night.'

'You've changed your tune since earlier, then.'

'And now you can say, all smugly, "I told you so". Gloat away!'

'Rin...' I put an arm around his shoulders. 'You're unsettled yourself, aren't you? Don't shout at me. We're allies, remember?'

Rinawne sighed deeply, leaned against me. 'I don't want any of it. I want us all to be normal, lead normal lives, for Myv to grow up, be the hienama he wants to be. What's wrong in that?'

'Nothing. But maybe some things need to be sorted out first. I'll help you. I promise.'

'I can't think what you could possibly do. Their wills are like iron!'

I kissed the top of his head. 'Don't speak to Wyva about what I've told you. Trust me on that. I need to find out what happened in the past to deal with it now, and we can't risk him becoming more defensive.'

'All right.'

'I take it Cawr and Gen are a lot younger than Wyva so won't know much, only what Wyva's told them?'

'I'd say so. You know...' He looked into my eyes. 'I think the

Whitemanes might be the only hara who can tell you what happened. Perhaps you could simply go and ask them. Knock on the door and interrogate whoever answers it.'

I laughed uncertainly to cover a kind of embarrassment. 'Why do you think they know?' I agreed with him, of course, but wanted to hear his thoughts on the matter.

'Because I'm sure they were mixed up in whatever happened. There's no reason for the hostility between the families, otherwise. And they've been here since the start, like Wyva's hara have.'

'You think I'll be safe just going to their house and knocking on the door?'

Rinawne grinned. 'Anyhar else, I'd say no, but you're different. Things just... *waft* over you somehow, and you're so down to earth, and tolerate no nonsense.'

He didn't know me very well nor, sadly, did he know the Whitemanes. 'I'll sleep on it,' I said. 'See what ideas come to me.'

'Can I come over tonight?'

I was torn. I could see he needed company. 'Not tonight. I need to be alone, not distracted. Tomorrow, certainly. We can talk about things.'

'OK.'

'I'll head off now, it's getting late. I won't be thought badly of if I don't do the rounds of saying goodnight to everyhar, will I?'

Rinawne put an arm about me, kissed my cheek. 'No, don't worry. Just go. Everyhar knows you're not a partying kind of har. Wyva won't think anything of it.'

I was glad I'd ridden over to the Mynd on Hercules, since the idea of walking home alone through the forest unnerved me. Whitemanes might still be lurking, and now I wondered about what else might be out there. I rode at a canter back to the tower. At one point – and only for the briefest of moments – a foolhardy part of me considered going to the Pwll Siôl Lleuad and trying to communicate with whatever had visited me there. Thankfully, my more sensible mind decided against this reckless idea. I must take this operation slowly, carefully. It would be better to visit that site in daylight, which clearly made no difference to whatever haunted that spot. Perhaps also I should meditate in the breakfast room at Meadow Mynd, since Rinawne had once seen something there. The house must retain memories of the past. I needed to coax them out.

I stabled Hercules and gave him a rub down, as the canter home had made him sweat. He munched contentedly on sweet-smelling hay as I did so, occasionally nudging me with his head. I was heartened to see how at ease he felt. If anything malevolent was around, an animal would sense it.

The tower was as welcoming as ever. I went to the kitchen to prepare myself some tea before bed and while the kettle was boiling went up to the bathroom to relieve myself. The room was in darkness and I did not turn on the light. When I'd finished, my back prickled unaccountably and I turned quickly, stumbling against the toilet. There was a dark shape standing between two of the windows. *Whitemanes!* I thought angrily, ready to lash out with words and even defend myself physically if required.

The figure stepped forward.

I stared at it mutely, unsure of what I was really seeing. This was not a har, I could tell that at once. This was a woman. She was dressed in shabby trousers and jacket, her dark hair drawn back behind her head. She was perhaps in her late thirties, and her dark-skinned face, though beautiful, was puffy with exhaustion.

'Who are you?' I demanded.

She frowned, spoke in a soft, cultured voice. 'Please... You must tell me... Is it still happening?'

'What do you mean? Is *what* still happening?'

But then I was merely interrogating starlight. There was no one in the room with me and the silence was broken only by the ticking of the clocks.

Chapter Eleven

Three days passed. I took time to prepare myself for what might be a battle to come. I worked in my nayati, avoided company as much as possible, and wrote up notes of all that I had learned and the suppositions I could make from that. Wyva was easily convinced that I needed a few days to think about the next festival and start work on it. I said I'd begin teaching Myv in a week's time. Rinawne, of course was difficult to avoid. I sensed he too was feeling the strain – a weird undercurrent that the solstice had brought with it or else awakened.

The woman did not appear to me again during this time. I was sure she must be connected to the Wyverns, simply because she'd manifested in their tower, but her skin was dark where theirs were fair, so perhaps not a blood relative. Also, for a ghost she'd communicated in a straightforward way. I had felt the will behind her question, her determination to *be* there to ask it. But she wasn't powerful enough. Not yet.

I put another clock into the bathroom.

During this time, I also replied to Jassenah, saying in the briefest of terms that I agreed with his assessment of our relationship and we should call it a day. I said that when my work in Gwyllion was done, I'd return to Jesith to retrieve any belongings he might not want cluttering the house, and conclude my affairs in the town. I was surprised at the anger I felt simmering inside me. I wanted to write *I'll be glad to see the back of the lot of you*, because that was how I felt. But I kept it polite. I wasn't the har the Jesithians thought they knew. They could carry on looking down on this fantasy for the rest of their lives. I'd be out of it.

When Rinawne came to visit me on the evening following the festival, I told him about my encounter in the bathroom. 'A ghost?' Rinawne asked, and his tone was strangely miserable for him. 'You must be pleased. It's all you've ever wanted since you came here.' I could tell he felt that life was turning in a way he didn't like. Wild and exciting tales were one thing; unsettling reality another.

'She's not a ghost in the traditional sense,' I replied, 'but she's a memory, certainly. For some time I've been compelled to put clocks into the bathroom. Remember how I had a strange feeling when I first came here about that room?'

Rinawne nodded. 'Yes, I remember.'

'Well, I had a feeling about clocks – time I suppose – and I'm sure this is meant, and will allow me to connect with the woman. A link through time. She might have been reaching to communicate for a while, hence my compulsion.'

'She'll be a Wyvern, of course,' Rinawne said. 'Connected by marriage, perhaps, given her appearance, but who else could she be?' He gazed about himself, shivered slightly. 'This place has always been theirs.'

I nodded. 'Yes, I think you're right. The tower will help me. Perhaps it too has had its fill of dark secrets.'

Rinawne laughed softly and touched my face. 'You're such a strange one, Ys. Most hara would find this place spooky and disquieting, but no, you find its spookiness somehow a comfort. Dŵr Alarch shares its ghosts with you.'

'Perhaps, but I think it's also a case of the tower resenting psychic intrusions.'

'What do you mean?'

I shrugged. 'Just that sometimes I feel and sense things that don't belong here, and the tower does too.'

'Does the woman belong here?'

'Yes, she does. The tower felt perfectly happy when I came home last night.'

Rinawne sighed deeply. 'I wish you wouldn't look into the past,' he said. 'I wish we could just live *now*. The Wyvachi's gruesome history doesn't belong here. Look at the summer unfolding around us, the beauty of nature. Smell the intoxicating air. Why should dark things have to exist in that?'

I hugged him. 'Rin, I don't have a choice. I really believe that now. I *can't* leave it – at the very least, for Myv's sake.'

Rinawne wriggled away from me. 'Now you make me sound like a bad parent, that I don't care. But I do! I just don't want Myv sucked into this self-indulgent melodrama.'

'I know how you feel, Rin. I'm not judging you.'

'Whatever's happening I can't help feeling the Wyvachi are encouraging and feeding it.'

'That might be true, but it still has to be dealt with.'

He let me share breath with him and felt vulnerable in my arms. I knew Rinawne was strong, so it was strange he was crumbling now. I thought he'd be more like me, determined to get to the bottom of it, sweep out the closet full of skeletons and put those bones to rest.

After our lips parted, he rested his head on my shoulder, and again expelled a deep sigh. Then he whispered, 'It's in the house, Ys.'

His words shocked me, but outwardly I remained calm, knew I had to. 'What is?'

'Something came in with the season. I can feel it. That room... it's in the drapes there. You breathe it into you even stepping into the room.'

'The breakfast room?'

'Yes.'

'Rin, I need to visit that room again, but not yet. I'd also like you to show me the rest of the house, perhaps before I open myself up to whatever's lurking around.'

'OK.' He sighed. 'I really don't want to, but I'm willing to trust you.'

I hoped he wasn't misguided and that I wasn't about to embark on a venture both needless and dangerous. But my instincts spoke clearly; I had to follow them. They knew the way.

On the fourth day after the festival, Loitsday, I decided I must now move out from my thoughts into the landscape. It was time for me to poke around more intrusively. Nytethorne had advised me to be quiet, but perhaps noise would flush the enemy from its lair. Let battle commence. I'd had time to gather my strengths. I felt ready.

I decided that I'd visit the Pwll Siôl Lleuad in the afternoon as I'd done before. In the morning, I'd go into Gwyllion, perhaps make some discreet enquiries. The Crowned Stag could correctly be called a Wyvachi inn, since its keephar Selyf had been appointed to the Gwyllion Assembly by Wyva and was an obvious supporter of his. The family tended not to frequent The Rooting Boar. I'd not been back there since my arrival in Gwyllion, but I remembered the keephar, Yoslyn, had been inclined to talk.

I arrived at The Boar around noon. Few hara appeared to visit it during the day, for as before there weren't many customers. Clearly, a couple were there simply to discuss business deals, farming business. There was no sign of the keephar but a young har not long past feybraiha was polishing the bar, humming to himself. He had a pixie-like heart-shaped face and glossy yet rather thin black hair drawn into a ponytail. I enquired whether his employer was available.

'That would be my hostling, Yoslyn,' he said, 'and no, he's not here at the moment. Can I help you at all?'

'Are you serving lunch?'

'Of course. Today being Loitsday we don't have hot food until later, but plenty of cold fare.'

'That will be fine. When will your hostling be back?'

'Not till sundown. He and my father have gone to Hiyenton to barter. It's market day there.'

Slightly disappointed, I found a seat for myself in a fairly dark corner of the main bar room, and thought I might as well enjoy a good lunch before heading off into the forest.

The young pothar brought me a plate of cheese, ham, bread

and dark pickles – typical country fare – and a tankard of pungent ale. The other hara in the room, who were within my line of sight, occasionally glanced up at me, but with no great interest. Some might be from out of town, of course. I smiled to myself; already I expected to be recognised. How many little conceits lurk within us?

The food was tasty and fresh, and quickly consumed. I got out my notebook and, while I finished the ale, jotted down a few ideas for the next festival. I always found Reaptide one of the most difficult to dramatise, if that's the word. Probably the most appropriate ritual would simply be for everyhar to walk alone in summer hills and see what thoughts and dreams might come to them. While most hara liked to celebrate at night, it occurred to me that perhaps a daytime festival would be interesting for a change. Festivities could carry on into the evening.

As I was pondering these possibilities, the inn door opened and for a moment somehar was framed in silhouette at the threshold. A jolt passed through me; it was Nytethorne Whitemane. Instinctively, I edged back into my corner, hopefully out of sight. Nytethorne went directly to the bar, where the pothar greeted him in an informal manner and handed him a key, which the young har had taken down from a board among the hanging tankards. I heard him say, 'The usual lunch, tiahaar?'

Nytethorne nodded, did not speak. He walked right past me, yet some distance away, and walked with odd slowness up a flight of uncarpeted stairs behind where I sat. I could hear his tread, which sounded tired. What was he doing here? Had he come for a secret liaison with somehar? Was a meeting of Whitemanes and their allies planned in this place?

I sat for some further minutes, feeling quite disorientated. The pothar walked past me, whistling rather tunelessly, a tray in his hands, a cloth over one arm. He went up the stairs, and I heard him knock upon a door on the landing above, clearly right at the top of the stairs, since it took him no time at all. The door opened, some brief words were exchanged and the pothar scampered back downstairs, not even giving me a glance as he passed. Nytethorne Whitemane was in a room above me, so close. Had he come here only to enjoy a private lunch? This seemed unlikely.

I went to the bar and ordered a half tankard of ale. I was almost bursting with the desire to question the pothar but resisted this impulse. I returned to my corner table and drank half of the ale quite swiftly. Thoughts thundered through my mind, so hectically I could barely take heed of them. Then I got to my feet, drink in hand, and climbed the stairs, knocked on the first door I came upon. The friendly tankard would make my appearance less threatening, I felt.

Nytethorne opened the door and stared at me in disbelief, said, 'What?'

I bowed slightly. 'Might I speak with you, tiahaar?' These words: as if I'd come to his home and knocked upon his door, on an ordinary visit.

Nytethorne glanced past me towards the stairs. 'You *follow* me here?'

'No, I was eating my lunch downstairs and saw you pass.' I didn't intend to apologise for the intrusion, although it was my instinct to do so. Let him think what he liked.

He looked directly at me again, eyes wide. 'There's nothing to say.'

I smiled. 'Of course. How silly of me. You're here waiting for somehar.' Still, I didn't turn away.

'I'm not,' he said. 'But makes no difference.'

I took a step closer. 'You sprang upon me in the Wyvachi gardens the other night. So now I spring upon you. Talk to me.'

He regarded me so steadily for some moments, I could almost see his mind working, wondering whether to admit me or slam the door in my face. 'What do you want?'

'The quite usual things in the face of mystery: answers.'

'What will you do with answers?'

'How can I tell until I know what they are? May I come in?'

He really didn't want me to enter that room and yet I could tell he was torn. Something made him say, 'Suppose so, but little I can tell you.'

Without further invitation, I walked into the room and sat down in an upholstered chair beside an empty hearth, cradling the tankard in my cupped hands. Nytethorne slunk past me and took a seat at the table beneath the window, where his lunch was still on its tray.

'So,' I said, 'I don't want to waste your time. Let me tell you something. Rinawne har Wyvachi advised me to go your house and knock upon the door, ask whoever answered it to tell me what happened between the Wyvachi and the Whitemanes in the past. He's a very direct har, is Rinawne, although he knows even less about local history than I do. Chance put you behind a door when I was close to it. We are both alone. What happened?'

'Is it your business, truly?' Nytethorne asked. He began to place the paraphernalia of his lunch upon the table, slowly and deliberately

'I have made it so, because of the harling, because of Myv.'

He grimaced. 'Don't think so. You've been curious from the start.'

'As have your hara about me,' I said sharply.

Nytethorne paid particular attention to a salt cellar he held in his hand. 'Curious? No. Mossamber will play games with Wyvachi toys, that's all it is.'

'Perhaps he fears me?'

Nytethorne laughed, in what appeared to be genuine delighted shock and now looked at me. 'Such proud foolishness will do you ill,' he said.

I shrugged. 'Not at all. Perhaps he knows an outsider could pry and find out all the secrets and point out to everyhar involved what idiocy this feud is. Perhaps he doesn't want you to realise you're being an idiot.'

'You have a mouth on you, Wyvachi-called.'

'My name's Ysobi. My friends call me Ys. We're not yet

friends, so stick with the longer version.'

'I know your name. As a har earns to call me by name, so he must earn for me to call him by his.'

'How delightfully medieval you are! It's as if your hara have read the most dramatic novels from human history and modelled themselves on the most pungent villains.'

'You know more of that than me,' he retorted. 'I'm pureborn.'

I put my head to one side. 'Not that... *recently*, however.' I made a dismissive gesture. 'But anyway, fascinating though this sparring is, I would really like to know why there is so much evil blood between the Whitemanes and the Wyvachi.'

Nytethorne breathed in deeply through his nose, looked out of the window, still turning the salt cellar in his hands. 'Hara have long memories. Injury is injury, despite the years. The Wyvachi are weak, always have been. Looked out for themselves, were cunning with the old tribal leaders. Little honour.'

I leaned forward in my chair. 'Is it all about land?'

Nytethorne glanced back at me. 'Mossamber doesn't want land, 'specially cursed land.'

'Then he wants the hara around here, he wants to lead them?'

'Not that.'

'Then what *does* he want?'

'For Wyvachi to be decent, raze the filthy hive that bred such evil.'

'What evil? Really, tiahaar, be more specific. Your words mean little to me.'

Nytethorne made a smothered, anguished sound, gazed once more out of the window for some moments, then turned to me, resolved. He placed the salt cellar carefully beside his plate. 'Will be truthful with you, *tiahaar*. You're no enemy of mine. Think you're crazed and full of yourself, but see you mean no ill. But this land... here... is full of ill. Hurts going back more than a century. Little snicks inflicted here and there over time. Wyvachi always looked down on my kin, even before any were har. Teeth bared between families. And then, Wraeththu happened. The soil roils with it all.' He stood up, clearly impassioned. 'Hearts were hot all those years ago, and what came from them fell into the land. Stored there.'

'And stored still in hearts.'

'Yes.'

'But what *did* happen exactly? How does the har named Peredur figure in this history, and what precipitated the Wyvachi curse?'

'Must not answer these things.'

I laughed coldly. 'You're a cliché. Stop pissing in the air. The mystery becomes dull.'

'You have no respect,' he said, almost beneath his breath, but I could see that faint shiver of uncertainty, the words held inside. Part of him wanted to speak. I could taste it on him.

'You warned me the other night,' I said. 'You care enough to do that. So let's leave the history and look at more recent events. Why did Rey leave Gwyllion? Tiahaar, put yourself behind my eyes, see what I see. Wouldn't you want answers too?'

Nytethorne closed his eyes. 'Things *come* to you,' he said in a voice barely above a whisper. 'If you are strong of heart, *let* them come. I can't be the one. Have no leave to speak.' He placed a closed fist against his chest. 'And *I* fear, tiahaar. Won't speak without leave – will be punished. And even here, never alone.'

I glanced around the room and its cosiness suddenly condensed in a weird kind of way. I felt a presence, as if Nytethorne had conjured it. 'I *am* ready,' I said, not just to the har before me. A thought came to me. 'Is this your sanctuary, tiahaar, this little room?'

He smiled then, with beautiful warmth. There was a brief transfiguration during which I fancied I could see the har Nytethorne Whitemane might truly be. 'Where I think,' he said. 'Where I write.'

'You write?' I could see my surprise nettled him somewhat – his warm smile hardened.

'Words are soothing to me,' he said. 'Here is nearest to alone.'

'Tiahaar,' I ventured carefully, 'don't you want this vendetta to end too, for the bad history to be healed?'

He put one hand upon the table, just the fingertips, and stared down at them. 'It can't,' he said. 'There's... a barrier.' He stared into my eyes as if trying to convey more than a few words. 'Rey tried.'

'Do you know where he is?'

He nodded. 'In the mountains. The air is clean there, and the soil.'

'Would he speak to me, do you think?'

He shook his head. 'No. He spoke with his feet. Has been granted solitude. Made a bargain, so I think.'

'And left Porter behind... Was that the cost?'

'No. He was asked to... for other reasons.'

'Who is Porter's father?'

Challenge came into Nytethorne's eyes. 'Me,' he said, without hesitation.

I absorbed this fact for a moment, and all its implications. 'You and Rey,' I said in a monotone.

Nytethorne shrugged.

This conversation was like pulling thorns from flesh. I felt that Nytethorne wouldn't volunteer information but would answer certain questions. If the questions were clever he might reveal more than he intended. 'So Porter remains because of you – do you see him often?'

Nytethorne shook his head. 'Not often. Not safe. And I'm not the reason.'

I nodded thoughtfully. 'He's Mossamber's eyes and ears in the Mynd, isn't he?'

A pause, then: 'No point denying. You're not stupid.'

'Does Wyva know you're Porter's father?'

Nytethorne shrugged. 'Doubt that. He'd not have

Whitemane blood in his house.'

I wasn't so sure about that. It occurred to me the eyes and ears arrangement might work both ways. Who knew how Porter acted to survive, and what Wyva might countenance to help preserve his domain? 'So Rey was in a relationship with you, yet working for Wyva?'

'Not that close,' Nytethorne said. 'He wanted to experience... certain things. Wanted understanding. He was Wyvachi-called, like you, yet Mossamber let him in. Won't do that again.'

A realisation came to me. 'Porter was made during a rite, wasn't he?'

Nytethorne nodded. He sat down again, rubbed his hands over his face. 'As you guessed. At a festival. Not intended. Just happened. Like you, Rey was inquisitive, but in a different way. You'd not do what he did.' He raised his eyes to me, gave me a curious look. 'Don't tell Porter what you know. Don't question him. Could be danger for him.'

'I won't. Tiahaar, what *is* the danger? Can you not warn me a little more?'

'You'll find out. Know you will. You finding me here is the start.'

'Oh no,' I said, 'it started way before this.'

'Might be meant,' Nytethorne said. He drew his full lips into a thin line, looked away from me. 'Reaching to you... maybe.'

'Is there a ghost, Nytethorne?' I asked, waiting to see how he reacted to my use of his name.

'Oh yes, *Ysobi*,' he answered, turning to me once more. 'Be sure of that.'

'Is it Peredur?'

Again, he turned away from me, as if aware his eyes might give away too much and he could only risk short contact with my gaze. 'Enough. Said what I can. Don't try to trick me.'

'That sounds much like a "yes",' I said.

'If only that simple...' He shook his head. 'Would you share my lunch?' He gestured at the table.

I stood up, went to the table, placed my tankard upon it. I put a hand on his right shoulder. 'I've already eaten, thanks. And thank you for what you've told me. I can see you're torn over this.'

He looked at my hand but didn't move away. 'You're brave yet foolish, strong yet at risk. Be wary, Ysobi. I can't come to your aid, should you need it.'

I patted his arm. 'Until we meet again, tiahaar.' With these words I left his room.

I wanted to stay, speak with him further, but realised cutting my visit short would have more impact and might draw him closer to me.

What Nytethorne had brought to the fore was that I might actually be *in danger*, and not just from petty etheric conceits designed merely to unnerve me. But in danger from what? Mossamber? Vengeful spirits from the past? As a hienama, I could not of course deny there is much beyond harish senses that make up the world, and that forces beyond our comprehension could be considered *hostile* in some circumstances – energies that might be found in the otherlanes, for example. Years before in Jesith, Gesaril had experienced a malevolent haunting that had derived from his harlinghood, but as Jassenah had said since, the frightening forms that had appeared to Gesaril could easily have been conjured by his own strong thoughts and feelings. We had no hard proof the manifestations were external. Perhaps the result was the same as if they had been, but the difference in what a manifestation actually *is* must have bearing on how to deal with it.

Examining what lay before and around me now, I considered that whatever might be manifesting could be an externalisation of the original hostility between Wyvachi and Whitemane, compounded by violent acts in the past. This poisoned energy had been allowed to thrive, being fed by the continued antagonism between the families. So now it had a form, and this might be the wraith I'd glimpsed at the Pwll Siôl

Lleuad, and the entity that had taunted me in the forest following the Whitemane Cuttingtide rite, and the strange stick-like being that had appeared just that once in my bed. Nothing had actually injured my body, or inflicted psychological hurts beyond uneasy feelings for a day or so after the event. (I still thought my disorientation in the forest had been caused by the Whitemanes in some way. I didn't believe that derived from an etheric entity.) As with all malevolent forms I'd ever encountered, their only weapon was fear. And surely if confronted without fear, they had no power whatsoever.

As I walked to the Pwll Siôl Lleuad, I considered that the Whitemanes, for some reason rooted in the past, did not want the Wyvachi on what they considered to be "their" land, despite the fact that both families had equal rights to occupy it. Meadow Mynd was regarded – as Nytethorne had put it – as a "hive of evil". Something truly bad must've happened there in the early days that had wounded the Whitemanes and had caused the death of Peredur, a Wyvachi har, it seemed, the Whitemanes had had an interest in. It seemed likely Mossamber had been fond of him. But whatever had caused the rift, it was so great and so deep it had never been healed. There *must* be some hara on both sides who thought, if only privately, the rift was an inconvenience they could do without. Yet it appeared nohar had ever acted to end it, except perhaps for... Rey. Yes, possibly him. He'd involved himself somehow, which I now believed had led to his swift departure. He must've been afraid. He'd left his son behind. How I wished I could speak to that har, hear from his mouth his reasons for leaving and also what he'd discovered.

From what I'd overheard between Wyva and Medoc, and all I'd learned since, it appeared true that a dire curse had been uttered in the distant past, with the suggestion that a dramatic event – perhaps the cursing itself – had taken place at the moment Wyva had emerged from his pearl. He had been Kinnard's first born. The moonshawl, then, was Wyva's. This artefact had been created to protect him, and all harlings of the family thereafter. A curse upon harlings: that indicated sore blood indeed. The Wyvachi believed in this curse – and who could blame them for being reluctant to test how effective it might be? As Medoc had mentioned, Kinnard and his chesnari might have lost their lives because of it. What sane har, however much his rational mind argued against it, would risk the life of his own harling?

I reached the pool and stared at its modest glade for some moments. Surely, the start of healing must come with honesty? The facts set out in order, shorn of sentiment and rhetoric. Of course, I wasn't oblivious to the fact that both parties might in some peculiar way enjoy this continued feud; it had become part of their being. Would it not have begun to strip the mystery of its power if Wyva had simply said to me about the moonshawl story: 'This is what happened in the past. Yes, it was bad, but we're not responsible for the actions of our ancestors. Yet nearly a century of bad feeling is hard to overcome. Please help me overcome it.'?

Well, I was going to try, whether he'd asked me to outright or not. How could he possibly believe a hienama could function in this place if he didn't know the whole truth? Perhaps Wyva secretly *wanted* me to delve and find out. In the face of his silence and obstruction, it couldn't then be said it was his fault if I stumbled on that truth.

I composed myself on the moist, springy grass next to the pool and for some minutes stared into its still waters to order my mind. I closed down irrelevant thoughts and sought a point of tranquillity within myself. This I visualised in my heart centre, the realm of love and compassion, because these were aspects sorely missing from the problem. No matter what frightening form the manifestation might show me, I would meet it with sympathy and sincerity. I would not flinch.

Satisfied, I slowly closed my eyes and focused upon velvet darkness before my mind's eye. *Come to me,* I thought, visualising my words drifting out like light, invading every corner of the landscape. *Come, Peredur, if it is you. I'm here to receive you.*

I could see now, in my mind, the Pwll Siôl Lleuad and its surrounding trees. As I concentrated, I saw the light change slowly from day to night. A mist, almost white, but tinged with lilac, seeped through the foliage at ground level, crawling towards me like a living thing. There was no sound, no smell. After a couple of minutes, I saw a form taking shape from the mist, at the same time seeming to rise up from it, but also walk *through* it. As it drew closer to me, I could perceive it was the har from my first meditation at this site – a har dressed in a white robe, his hair over his face. This time, he did not stumble or struggle, and his clothing was untorn. He drifted towards me, and the feeling that flowed from him was a mixture of curiosity and pity, coupled with a sense of hopelessness.

Why do you come to me, then, if you have no hope? I asked, not even asking him to confirm his identity.

The har drew himself tall, and with both hands, drew the curtains of hair from his face. I'd been prepared for anything, but what he revealed was refined and delicate features, a straight nose, a strong chin, thin yet well-shaped lips. His eyes though were completely white, like moonstones. I saw in him the traces of Wyvachi. I had no doubt this was Peredur.

What happened to you? I said. *Will you tell or show me? Why do hara still fight over you?*

In reply, he lifted his hands slowly to his face and to my revulsion dug out his eyes, held them out to me as if for inspection. Remembering I must not flinch, I looked at them. They were stones, hemispherical smooth moonstones that glowed in the darkness. He did not want me to see his empty sockets, for his hair now hung once more over his face.

Who blinded you? I asked.

He shook his head and raised his hands to his face once more, presumably to replace the stones. He pushed back his hair again, blinked at me. Though he was blind, he could still weep. I saw the moist trails upon his ivory cheeks.

I intend to heal the past, I told him. *Will you help me?*

Now, he shook his head violently, as if in fear, and despite his blindness turned briefly as if to glance over his shoulder. He held up his hands to me, to ward me off, and began to back away into the mist.

Wait, I said. *Simply speak with me. I am here to listen.*

NO! IT COMES! YSBRYD DRWG!

I could hear sound now, a low rumbling growl, as if the stones of the earth were angry. Peredur vanished into the mist and then something was rushing towards me in the place where he had been: an angry, spiteful entity. I could see its yawning mouth, the black holes of its eyes, abnormally long clawed fingers, splayed as if to attack.

I got to my feet within the visualisation. *In the name of the dehar Lunil and all things kind, begone!* I cried, and made the sign of Lunil in the air before me.

The entity wavered for a second, then spat out a string of black bile at me, uttered a hideous screech and spiralled up into the night sky, before vanishing in a flash of red light and a crack of dull thunder.

I knew it had not retreated because of my power, but because it had accomplished its task. Peredur was gone.

Chapter Twelve

When the sounds began, I was reading in my living room. I'd come home directly after my visit to the Pwll Siôl Lleuad, feeling as if I'd picked another layer off the scab of buried history, but what had been revealed to me I wasn't yet sure. Was there another entity involved apart from Peredur, or had the second manifestation merely been a different aspect of this damaged har? Part of his essence clearly reached out to communicate, otherwise I'd never have seen him helpless at the pool that first time. But perhaps another part, steeped in the enmity that had been nourished for so long, sought to banish this less hostile aspect. Only investigating further, on an etheric level, could tell me more. For now, I needed to rest, before facing whatever lurked in Meadow Mynd. This I intended to confront the following day.

I'd borrowed a few books from Wyva's library on local folklore and history, written back in the human era, and decided to spend the rest of the day reading, and making any relevant notes. The meditation at the pool had exhausted me, more so than I realised, until I sat down. After dinner, I went to the living room and here curled up on the sofa, pulling over my legs a fleecy blanket that was draped across the cushions. I was aware I needed comfort, but not harish comfort. A warm blanket would do. Wine was on the table before me and books were ready to read. This was how I planned to spend a lazy evening.

Immersed as I was in the old tales it took me a few moments to become alert to the noises, which sounded like hara talking outside. Strange conversation, though. And perhaps... only one voice. I heard soft laughter, then more words – somewhat angry – then a muted wordless cry. As my attention was focused upon them, the sounds grew louder, closer. They could almost be inside the tower.

I kicked off the blanket and stood up, every nerve tense and alert.

A book was still in my hand – it was, I remember thinking, my only immediate weapon. There was another short cry, despairing, echoing, as if bouncing off the cold stone walls of the stairwell. I had not heard the great door open below, but neither had I locked it.

I went to the door of the room and pushed it wide. The stairway was silent, its dim lamps revealing nothing. If anything was with me in the tower, it must be in the kitchen or the basement. From the farm, I heard the voice of the hounds rise in an ululating wave, and then they too fell silent.

Gripping my book, I ventured cautiously down the stairs, then paused before the kitchen door. Telling myself I was a powerful creature of magic – and why on earth was I nervous? – I steeled myself and opened the door, stepped into the room. The atmosphere in there was electric, the air so dense it could almost be *chewed*.

'Show yourself,' I hissed.

'Don't be angry again,' a wavering, childlike voice murmured. 'I'm here. I'm here.'

I saw then, huddled on the floor against the dresser, a quivering form, its arms over its face. My first instinct was that this was some benighted har who'd wandered into the tower, somehar ill or peculiar in some way, because it did not in the slightest appear to be a spectral creature.

'I'm not angry,' I said, putting the book down on the table. 'Who are you?'

The figure then lowered its arms and rose sinuously to a stand. 'Do you not know me, Ysobi?'

I jumped back against the heavy table so hard it skidded backwards a few inches. I couldn't speak. I saw a slim har with long dark hair, dressed in a tunic and trousers of what appeared to expensive viridian silk. His face was beautiful, his hands as he held them out to me expressive. I knew him well; he was my nemesis, my undoing. Gesaril. He could not be here. Did this mean he was dead and I was facing his phantom?

'This is not your place,' I managed to say eventually. 'You must go.'

Gesaril stretched out his pale arms, which appeared so horribly real, in a wide gesture as if to embrace, enfold me. I could see small hairs upon them, a minor scratch above the wrist. Could he *really* be here? 'But didn't you call to me?' he murmured, tears spilling down his face. 'Why must I be blamed for it all? You want my place to be here.'

'No,' I said and drew in a deep breath. 'Gesaril, are you now not of this earth? You must answer.'

For a moment, the image of him wavered, and that was the downfall of the plot. I knew then for certain I was dealing with a conjured being. 'You ruined me,' he said. 'You pulled me to you, then cast me away. So much of me died back then, but not all.'

'Where did we meet the last time?' I asked. My heart was beating so fast I could hear it throughout my entire body, and yet I was angry rather than afraid. Let this fetch answer the question; of course it wouldn't be able to.

'You made me a hated thing,' said the image of Gesaril in a whining tone.

The last time I'd seen Gesaril he'd been far from whining. He had virtually cursed me for eternity. What stood before me had been created locally. This was not a figment of the land, or of the tower; they were well disposed to me. This came from a har.

'Get away!' I cried. 'In the name of the mighty dehar, Agave, wielder of the sword of will, I command you to disperse into the thoughts that formed you!' I picked up the book and threw it hard at the figure before me. 'Be gone!'

And so he was, so swiftly he might never have been there. The atmosphere in the room was restored, and – I fancied – almost apologetic, as if the tower had been incapable of preventing the intrusion but regretted this bitterly.

I patted the table. 'Be at rest,' I told the tower. 'This disturbance is an insult to both of us. Trust that I'll discover its cause.'

Somehar – a Whitemane, and most likely Ember, or Ember with the help of an older har – had reached into my mind and drawn information about Gesaril from me, with the intention of using it against me. I'd been expecting something along these lines since my dream of Ember on the eve of Cuttingtide and was surprised it had taken him – or *them* – this long. What they'd conjured was a sickening violation, and to me it seemed petty and spiteful, not the act of somehar *really* wishing to hurt me. Did this indicate it *was* the youthful Ember behind it? Or was Nytethorne responsible? Had he told his family of our earlier meeting? I'd felt sure he wouldn't have done, that in some way he wanted my help, even if he couldn't voice it, but hara can be deceptive, especially if they deceive through the medium of a beautiful face. Still, I would not let this go unchallenged. The nerve of it!

Before going to bed, I set wards about the tower in every corner, not wishing to have my sleep or dreams disturbed further. I placed another clock in the bathroom, an old one I'd found in the basement. No one waited there. Not yet.

The next morning, I woke fizzing with energy and determination. My dreams must've been placid because I remembered none of them, which was unusual for me. My intention was to confront Nytethorne about the previous night's events, and I looked forward to this greatly, still furious at the intimate intrusion into my mind and past, which I remained convinced was the work of the Whitemanes. I had no idea whether Nytethorne visited The Rooting Boar every day, but as I didn't relish the thought of confronting the Whitemanes in their lair, the inn was the only sure way to get to him. If I had to wait a day or two, so be it. I'd been taking *my* lunch there until I saw him again. I refused to allow the

Whitemane clan to unnerve me. Until mid-day I'd work on my Reaptide ritual, putting all other thoughts from my mind. I sensed the tower's approval of my temper and decisions.

At noon, I was in no mood for walking, so rode Hercules down to Gwyllion. The pothar in the inn seemed both surprised and pleased to see me again – perhaps thinking I'd been impressed by my lunch the previous day. His hostling came through from what was clearly the kitchen and greeted me warmly. 'Good day to you, tiahaar. Would you like lunch?'

'I would indeed,' I said. 'I enjoyed yesterday's so much I thought I'd return. The ale was good too.'

'How about roast chicken? I have half a dozen already cooked, and the vegetables are done.'

'That would be perfect.'

Yoslyn spoke to his son, who then went to prepare my food. As garrulous as I'd remembered he was, Yoslyn ushered me to a seat beneath one of the front windows, and sat down opposite me. Today would be busy, he told me, because there was a livestock fayre just outside the village. I wondered if I should make an effort to be more aware of these local events, then smiled as I realised it was another thing that showed I'd decided to stay in Gwyllion longer than I planned.

Yoslyn made conversation while my meal was prepared by asking the usual questions: how was I getting on with my work, what did I think of Gwyllion, and so on. He didn't seem the slightest inimical to the Wyvachi – or to me – and yet I didn't remember seeing him or his son at the Cuttingtide festival, and the fact Nytethorne Whitemane had a private room here indicated in which direction the inn's loyalties lay. Still, if the keephar was prepared to be cordial, I would be so too.

The meal arrived – a plate heaped with roasted vegetables and half a large roast chicken accompanied by a pot of homemade relish; enough food to fill two bellies. As I began to eat, I considered that Myv's career choice must now be common knowledge everywhere in the district, so felt comfortable saying, 'It seems the village hienama problem will soon be solved. You've heard about Myvyen Wyvachi's offer to take the job?'

'Yes!' said Yoslyn, pouring ale into a tankard for me from a large earthenware jug his son had brought to us. 'Rather a surprise, but makes sense when you think about it.'

I nodded, took the tankard from him. 'Myv is rather young, of course, but his enthusiasm makes up for that. As you said when we first met, the hara around here really want a hienama again.'

Yoslyn took a sip of his drink. 'You'll be teaching him, then?'

'Yes, for some time.' I paused. 'Do you have no dedicated nayati at all here? I mean have you ever had one?'

'We've had several hienamas,' the keephar said, smiling. 'Flighty creatures, most of them, more concerned with burning the incense and plaiting their hair than serious matters, but I think the local... er... problems you've no doubt encountered made living and working here sour for most of them.'

I nodded again. 'You mean the feud between the Whitemanes and the Wyvachi.'

'Yes. I'm not a har to take sides, and in all honesty I don't think many hara in Gwyllion are, but the conflict has often caused difficulties for hienamas in one way or another, or so I've heard. Most of the original tribe don't like to speak of the past that much.'

'Well, I'm made of stern stuff!' I said, smiling. 'Although I do think a locally bred hienama will be best for Gwyllion. But anyway... a nayati?'

Yoslyn pulled a sour face. 'In the old days, at the beginning, hara had little time for being... spiritual.'

'Were you *there*?' I asked, in what I hoped was not too eager a tone.

'Not right at the start, no. I came here – what...?' Yoslyn turned his eyes to the ceiling for a moment and pondered. 'Well maybe forty or so years after Wraeththu took control in this area.'

'A lot can happen in forty years.'

'It can. But to answer your question, no, we've never had a dedicated building. One or two of the hienamas over the years have sought to use the old church, rededicate it if you like, but hara weren't comfortable with it – too many reminders of the human era, and outworn human beliefs.'

'I can appreciate that, yet most religious buildings were constructed on ancient spiritual sites, so they're not inappropriate for conversion to nayatis.'

'True, but prejudices linger.'

I nodded. 'All too often! I heard the original bell still lies hidden within the ruins of the church.'

Yoslyn grinned. 'Allegedly... and if a day comes when it is raised... well...' Yoslyn held up his hands, rolled his eyes in a comical manner.

'Oh!' I said. 'Is there a legend connected with it? Please tell me if so. I'm collecting stories of the area as part of my work.'

Yoslyn leaned forward, his arms resting comfortably on the table. 'There was an old song, probably invented round communal fires in the early days. I can't remember all the words but the start of it was something like...' He closed his eyes for a few moments, then sang softly a wistful melody. '"When the silver swan returns to the old domain, then the bell of Gwyllion will have throat again, but that day will never birth, for silver swan lies in the earth."'

My flesh tingled, and even Yoslyn seemed slightly affected by the song. He shrugged off the wistfulness. 'Well, it was something like that. There was more to it, but I can't remember the rest.'

'What or who was the silver swan?'

Yoslyn pulled a face to indicate he didn't know. 'Some tribal emblem, I expect. In this area, every ragged group unworthy of the word phyle had an animal or bird they venerated. I expect the song referred to some tatterflits being driven off or slaughtered by rivals, who knows?'

I retrieved my notebook and pencil from my coat pocket and wrote down the rhyme before I forgot it – also the word "tatterflit", which amused me. The keephar peered at the page as I wrote. 'Yoslyn,' I said, 'I often hear a bell in the evening. Do you know where it's rung?'

'A bell?' Yoslyn pulled a face. 'I've not heard one.'

'Perhaps it can only be heard from the Mynd area,' I said. 'No matter. I was just curious.' I paused. 'I don't suppose you know if the Whitemanes have a bell on their estate?'

'Not that I know of. That's not to say they haven't.' Yoslyn paused, then spoke in the most forced casual manner I'd ever heard. 'I hear you had business with Nytethorne Whitemane yesterday.'

I looked up. 'So? Whatever hienamas in the past were like, I won't take sides in local feuds.'

Yoslyn regarded me steadily, and I could see a smile somewhere in the depths of his gaze. 'You here for him again today?' He took a drink. 'Not that you are like... *previous* hienamas.'

To my great embarrassment I felt my face flame. I was sure the keephar's words were a reference to Rey and perhaps his relationship with Nytethorne. 'Do I look flighty to you?' I snapped.

Yoslyn raised his hands. 'Ooh, no offence, tiahaar. Forgive my humour.' He winked at me. 'But is the relish perhaps too hot for you? You look burned.'

I shook my head, smothered a smile, which was almost as embarrassing as the blush. 'Your sauce is somewhat hot,' I said dryly.

Yoslyn laughed heartily. 'Good luck to you, tiahaar!' He rose from the table and returned to his duties.

For a moment I put my face into my hands. *No, no, no, no...* I must collect myself. Was I incapable of learning from my mistakes?

As the afternoon rolled on, hara began to arrive at The Boar to eat. There was no sign of Nytethorne, however. I should have asked Yoslyn if he was likely to appear, but now the keephar was busy as the bar room filled up with hara ordering meals. I'd arranged for Rinawne to come over to the tower later on, but decided that while I was in a fighting mood I should instead go to Meadow Mynd and discreetly investigate the phenomenon Rinawne had told me about. Wyva would no doubt insist I stay for dinner and then keep me there far too late, talking, which would make it difficult for Rinawne and I to have time to meet that night. He wouldn't be pleased, but for now he'd have to put up with the situation. There were more important matters to attend to.

I'd finished my meal and the hubbub in the inn was now starting to get on my nerves. I thought I might as well leave and go to the Mynd. Confronting Nytethorne would have to wait for another day, hopefully tomorrow. But as I rose, with the intention of going to the bar to pay for my meal, I saw through the window Nytethorne tethering his horse to the rail by the door, where by now many other horses were tethered. I noticed him glance at Hercules, pause. He must have recognised my horse, perhaps because the Whitemanes knew everything they possibly could about me. Did it go through his mind then to untie his mount and ride away? Well, if it did, he decided against it and came into the inn.

As he reached the bar, he looked around the room, finally finding me amongst the sea of faces. He inclined his head, smiled in a hard, uncertain way. I raised my tankard to him, looked away, out through the window. I was aware my breathing had become fast and shallow and corrected this forcibly.

From the corner of my eye, I saw Nytethorne go to the stairs further down the room. He did not look back at me, and I found his mood difficult to read. Guarded. I waited only a minute or so before following him. The staff here were very busy. I doubted Nytethorne's lunch would be brought to him immediately. Perhaps he too had been at the fayre.

After I knocked on his door, Nytethorne opened it to me at once and stared at me in a completely unreadable way.

'Might I come in?'

'Why? Our business was finished yesterday.'

'Was it, now?' I pushed past him, stood in the centre of the room.

Nytethorne closed the door, pulled himself to his full height, crossed his arms across his breast. 'You have more to say?'

I didn't answer, but flew across the room and pushed him roughly against the door, one forearm against his throat. He yelped in surprise.

'Listen well, tiahaar,' I said, pressing my arm hard against him so he could barely breathe. 'I know your clan's little games. The show last night was impressive, but not for one moment was I deceived. Kindly inform Mossamber of this.'

'Release me!' Nytethorne gasped. 'No idea what you're saying.' He struggled, yet strangely did not retaliate. I'm sure he could have fought me off if he'd wanted to.

'You think I'm an idiot!' I said, but released the pressure a little. 'I'm not weak, Nytethorne. The horrors of the abyss have beaten on the doors of my mind many a time in the past. Whitemane theatrics can't touch me.'

'Ysobi,' he said, with difficulty. 'Let go. Tell me what you mean. If I know anything, won't hold it from you.'

I lowered my arm, moved away, but reluctantly. I felt as if I wanted to beat him senseless.

He stared at me. 'What happened last night?'

'An intrusion,' I said. 'A created entity manifested in my tower. The only hara who could possibly have known upon whom to base that form has to be a Whitemane, for no other around here knows of him.'

'And how do *my* hara know?' Nytethorne snapped, rubbing his throat with one hand. 'You've had no true conversation with us.'

I wasn't prepared to answer that directly. I too folded my arms defensively. 'Are you saying that your hara have had no interest in me since I came here? That they've not wished me gone, or at the very least have sought to unnerve me because Wyva brought me here?'

He had the grace not to lie. 'Were curious, yes. Mossamber knew Wyva would try to find somehar powerful. Wyva has his own plans, Ysobi. He's not told you.'

'And what plans are these?'

Nytethorne shook his head. 'Not my place to say.'

'Naturally. It never is *anyhar's* place to say *anything* around here. I believe Ember was instructed to *intrigue* me in certain ways, either to obstruct my work, confuse or frighten me. I don't think he acted alone. Were you part of this?'

Nytethorne looked disgusted. 'No! Why send my son to do a job I could do myself, a dirty job at that?'

That seemed to indicate he knew full well everything that had occurred. Self-justification had lowered his guard. Had there perhaps been an argument over this? 'You don't deny Ember invaded my dreams, then, was in fact instructed to?'

Nytethorne sighed, lowered his head. 'I wanted no part of this, Ysobi. Do my share from day to day, a good har for my family. I've no love of Wyvachi but...'

'Do you know who was responsible for last night's entertainment?'

He walked past me to the window, sat down at the table. 'No. That is truth. Knew the Cuttingtide plan, that was all.'

I followed him. 'Then I apologise for assaulting you. As you can imagine, my patience is somewhat frayed.'

He sighed. 'Understand. Would be angry too.' Again, he was avoiding my eyes, staring at the table.

'They are fools to attack me,' I said. 'I've no malice towards the Whitemanes.' I paused. 'Nytethorne, don't you want this senseless feud to end, as I do? For the sake of your son, and for Myv's, why continue it? Blood might not be shed, but a war is going on, beneath the surface, even in the etheric world. It is for *no reason*. Not now. Think about the community here, how good things could be if this ridiculous antagonism could be put to rest.'

He said nothing, still gazing at the table.

'You know, *this* is the downside of longevity. Petty squabbles of the young can take root and last for centuries. Grow up, Nytethorne!'

He looked up at me then, shook his head. 'So much guessing,' he said.

'Well, in the absence of hard fact, what else am I supposed to do?'

'How about leave well alone and go away?'

'I'm not going to do that, so don't waste your breath. You think I can ride out of Gwyllion and not have a second thought for the safety of an innocent harling?' I sneered at him. 'Oh, maybe you *can* think that.'

His eyes flashed with anger. 'I do for my son what I must. Part of that is silence and obedience. Pelk your blood, Wyvachi-called!'

I laughed coldly. 'Ah, hit a nerve, did I? That was a ripe insult.'

He put one hand across his eyes, rested his elbow on the table. 'You don't know,' he said. 'Squabble isn't petty, isn't now, never was. Beyond our control, but managed by us, as far as we can. Let loose...?' He raised his head, gazed at me wearily. 'You've no idea. Even *we* don't know. We *contain*...'

'What? What do you contain?'

He shook his head again.

'Is it to do with Peredur har Wyvachi?'

Nytethorne looked horrified at these words, and yet his response was odd. 'Was never Wyvachi... *Wyvern*, yes... don't say that!'

I sat down opposite Nytethorne at the table, reached out for one of his hands. 'Listen to me. I have a theory. The hostility of so many years can create a thoughtform, a being. I've seen it, Nytethorne, at the Pwll Siôl Lleuad. Is this what you refer to, the thing you can't contain, the thing you fear is being agitated by Myv's desire to be hienama?'

'What's out there – never *not* agitated,' he said, 'You're right, in a way. But's not what you think.' He took his hand from mine, yet only after he'd squeezed my fingers briefly. 'Long to tell you of it, but mustn't. Would make things worse.'

'Who *will* speak to me, Nytethorne? I believe I can help, but I need more information.'

He laughed bleakly. 'Only safe har to speak to is Peredur.'

'A ghost? I'm sure you know as well as I such apparitions can't communicate that clearly.' He said nothing and I considered. 'All right, I can perhaps get more clues and piece them together, but... just tell me this, no names, just yes or no... Does somehar know everything I need to hear?'

'Of course they do!' he said abruptly. 'You already know that. You tried Wyva, didn't you?'

'Well...'

'Mossamber is twice what Wyva is. Lives in the past, clings to it. Does that fill in a gap, answer a question?'

'Is he afraid?'

'No, responsible, maybe. In love, certainly.'

'With Peredur, still?'

Nytethorne nodded.

'The Wyvachi killed him, didn't they?' I asked gently. 'Don't answer, just look at me.'

He sighed, but he did look at me. 'Ysobi, you're a good har at heart. Can see you're passionate and mean well, but wish you'd turn from this tragedy. No good can come of it.'

'You're wrong,' I said. 'Much good can come of freeing future generations. There is a solution to everything, Nytethorne.' I took his hand again, shook it firmly. 'Work with me on this. All I want is your approval and support. I don't expect you to put yourself in danger.'

'You can't help.'

'I *can*. I'm not afraid. Dare to believe I can help.'

He smiled at me sadly. 'Wish it was possible.'

There was a moment's stillness as we looked at one another. I remembered the day I'd first seen him, my dehar on the path within the forest, his arrogance. Now, here he was, his eyes open to me. I let go of his hand, stood up. 'If you wish me to tell you what I discover, then I can meet you here again.'

He frowned a little. 'Yes, but... They – Mossamber – will find out. Might have already. Yoslyn and his kin have loose lips.'

'Then let your family believe you're playing me along to see what I'm up to. Don't try to hide our meetings: tell them. Even they can surely appreciate this is a more direct and effective method than creeping into my sleeping mind. Dreams are vague and fleeting. More can be determined from a meeting face to face.'

He nodded uncertainly. 'Will take that risk.'

'They won't harm *you*, will they, Nytethorne?'

He shook his head. 'My kin won't.' He sighed. 'Have responsibilities, Ysobi, within my family. Not your concern. You know where to find me.'

'That goes for me too,' I said. 'The tower.'

'*That* tower,' he said and laughed, slid his eyes away from mine. I realised then he had visited it regularly, once.

When I left The Boar, I found the day had darkened. Moody clouds were clotted across the sky and the air was oppressive, the light almost greenish. As I approached Hercules, the tethered horses suddenly became spooked, and jostled and grunted uneasily. I could not help but look behind me, yet nothing was there. For a couple of seconds, a pang speared through me. I thought of Nytethorne in the room above me. I thought of us touching. No! I banished the thought, and any associated images, before they could fully form. This *interest* in Nytethorne could be a further Whitemane attempt to befuddle me. Yet one thing I knew: in that moment he had thought of me in the same way.

I untied Hercules, swung into the saddle, and urged him to canter away, conscious all the time of eyes upon me, though there was really no way to tell whose eyes they were.

Chapter Thirteen

By the time I reached Meadow Mynd, thunder was complaining to the west, a storm coming in from the not-too-distant sea. Lightning shimmered across the clouds like cracks in glass. The ancient mountains beyond the river valley looked as surly, immense and threatening as offended gods. Perfect weather in which to investigate a haunting, I thought, amused. I rode to the stables and left Hercules in the care of Mynd hara, then went to the house. A few fat drops of rain were beginning to fall. As they landed upon the ancient sway-backed tiles beneath my feet, they were dark as blood.

Rinawne met me in the hall. He had been in the drawing room and had noticed me ride up. 'The elements conspire!' he announced, grinning widely. 'I take it you summoned this storm in order to provide the right conditions for ghost-hunting!' He seemed to have recovered his spirits. I didn't sense melancholy in him as I had before.

'I wish I could claim the storm is mine,' I said, equally lightly, 'but sadly no. Yet it *is* appropriate.'

Rinawne took my arm. 'Let's have tea before we begin. I feel like it's been too long since we saw one another in private.'

I sensed behind this airy comment a not too hidden desire to draw something from me – a word of endearment, perhaps, or an equal admission of missing him. I kissed his cheek briefly, unable to speak words that would sound sincere. Unfortunately, my mind kept returning to Nytethorne Whitemane, no matter how hard I pushed such thoughts away. 'Have you seen anything in the house since we last spoke?' I asked, hoping to divert him.

Rinawne held my gaze questioningly for a moment, and I dreaded he could see inside me, which could not be possible, for I'd raised every defence it's possible for a har to have. 'Well, it's ongoing,' he said, in a cooler tone than before. 'A feeling of unfriendly presence, of watchfulness. There are accidents all the time.'

'To hara?'

Rinawne shrugged. 'To everything. Plates breaking, soot on the floors, birds trapped in rooms when there was no way they could get in. Then, there are the little injuries. Nothing like Gen's but...' He let go of my arm and held out his hands to me. I saw cuts upon his fingers, still red. 'Knives are alive,' he said.

I took his hands, held them briefly, sent a soft surge of healing energy into him. 'Something's building up,' I said, 'like this storm yearning to break.'

'I feel that too,' Rinawne said, taking his hands from mine and rubbing his fingers. 'My dreams have been troubled. But the worst of it...' He sighed. 'I felt it in Myv's room. Twice. Menacing.'

'Did you ask Myv about it?'

'Of course. He said he hadn't noticed anything, but I know he's lying. Ys, I'm afraid for him.'

'What about Wyva and the others? Have you mentioned it to them?'

Rinawne shook his head. 'There's no point. I know what Wyva would say, which is to belittle my fears. Gen would make a joke of it and Cawr and Modryn look at me as if I've grown extra eyes.'

I smiled a little. 'You should protect yourself. I'll tell you how if you really can't remember.'

'Oh, I remember,' he said, brightening a little once more. 'I'm not afraid for myself, but for Myv. Tell me what must be done and I'll do it.' He took my arm once more. 'Come, let's talk in a more private place.'

He led me to the conservatory, after asking one of the house-hara to bring us tea. Here, we could watch the storm, which was prowling ever closer.

Until our refreshments arrived, we made small talk. Rinawne spoke of Myv and how he was looking forward greatly to the first of his lessons. Then the house-har arrived with the tea tray, and after his departure Rinawne broached the subject he was clearly itching to talk about, knowing we would not have any further interruptions.

'Have you found out anything more about the secret past?' he asked, pouring tea for me.

'Not much. Nothing that we hadn't already worked out for ourselves, but I'll tell you my thoughts. In the chaos of the early days, amid all that senseless fighting, Peredur Wyvern was slain. I think he might've had an attachment to Mossamber Whitemane, and that somehow Peredur's own kin were responsible for his death. But knowing what I do of the Wyvachi, and what I sensed about Medoc when I met him, I can't credit this was some deliberate cruel or evil act. An accident, perhaps? It's hard to know for certain, because hara weren't quite themselves in the early days. Anything is possible. Was Peredur's attachment to Mossamber seen as some kind of betrayal? Were rival factions competing for power in this area? These things are likely. I believe a combination of them is what lies behind the hostility between the families.'

Rinawne had listened patiently, now he said, somewhat sardonically, 'A love story. How quaint.'

'Love is a chaotic force,' I said. 'It might be the noblest of emotions, but in its darkest form can raze nations.'

Rinawne uttered a cold laugh and said mordantly. 'How outrageous that is.'

I felt I should steer the conversation away from this topic. 'So, my belief, if somewhat unformed as yet, is that the toxic energy, which has permeated this land for so long, has somehow coalesced into a malevolent force, in which both Whitemanes and Wyvachi believe, and this has extended to the local population. They are afraid of it, and in the Whitemanes' case perhaps also believe they are custodians who must contain it.'

'How do you know that?' Rinawne asked sharply. 'Have you spoken to any of them?'

I realised the folly of a lie. 'I have spoken to Nytethorne Whitemane, yes, but not in any great depth. He resists me, as you can imagine.'

'No, I can't actually,' Rinawne said icily.

'Anyway, I didn't go to the house. I spoke to him in Gwyllion.'

'What did he tell you?'

'Hardly anything. It was like pulling teeth. He would answer questions if pressed, but I felt as if I were playing some kind of game, where only the right questions would produce an answer.'

'Wasn't a brief conversation, then?'

I blinked at him. 'Rinawne, I detect a note of condemnation in your voice. What's the matter?'

'Wyva won't be pleased you've spoken with a Whitemane.'

I stared at him mutely for some moments. 'If there's a threat in those words, I'm puzzled by it. Wasn't it *you* who suggested I speak to the Whitemanes? I only did as you advised.'

Rinawne put his hands against his eyes briefly. 'Oh, I'm being stupid, I know. I can't help it.'

'I don't understand.' This wasn't exactly true, but I was acutely aware there was something I wanted to hear him say.

He shook his head. 'You know, I don't think you're aware of what you are, how you affect hara.'

'Oh, believe me, I am,' I said, with some bitterness. 'I strive now to affect them minimally.'

Rinawne uttered a snort. 'You might as well give up. Nytethorne Whitemane... is... No, I won't say it.'

'I insist you *do*!'

He sighed. 'Now I've angered you. I'm sorry. It's just I know you're only lent to me by life. I won't have much time with you. I'm no Nytethorne, I know that. He *will* desire you, Ys. How could he not? Look at you: tall, beautiful, strong, with eyes like the forest. Your hair...' He reached out as if to touch it, curled his fingers into a fist, withdrew. I couldn't help pushing my hair back over my shoulders, out of reach. 'You are...

helped me live again, and I hope we'll always be friends.' Inside, I groaned. Had I not said similar things to Gesaril, once? How in Aru's name had I ended up in the same situation? I'd tried so hard not to. But the fact was I *had* loved Gesaril, but hadn't been able to pursue it, for so many reasons. I did not, nor ever had, loved Rinawne. Now I had to limit the damage in some way. I realised that Rinawne was absolutely right in his assumptions and I didn't want him becoming an impediment. If he should betray me to Wyva... well, I didn't want to think about that.

I stood up and went to crouch beside Rinawne's chair, taking him into an embrace. He shuddered rigidly for some moments, then relaxed against me.

'Come now,' I said softly, hugging him and kissing his hair, 'don't be sad.' I pushed him away a little, still holding onto his arms, and smiled at him. 'Let's get on with our investigations, psychic sleuths as we are!'

Rinawne nodded, said in a voice striving to be steady, 'We've got all afternoon, Wyva's out. But he'll want you to stay this evening unless you leave here before he gets back, and I thought... tonight....'

'Let's appease Wyva today,' I said, squeezing Rinawne's arms. 'We can have a whole night to ourselves tomorrow. Come over for dinner.'

'Well, OK.' Rinawne seemed to cheer a little.

I went back to my seat, picked up my teacup. 'So, tell me what's happened here in detail.'

Rinawne blew his nose on the tea-tray cloth, grinned a little at this, then said to me, 'It was on the day of the festival, mid-morning. I was taking breakfast with Wyva – everyhar else was already out and about or eating elsewhere in the house. He left to start work on the preparations for the festival and I sat there to finish my coffee. That's when it crept up on me – this *disgusting* feeling. You know I'm not scared by these things, but in those moments, I was a harling again, running from a banshee in the dark. What I felt was not impartial. It was breathing down my neck.'

'Did you see anything?'

Rinawne frowned, considered. 'Difficult to tell. I felt light-headed, disorientated. The air seemed to shimmer, but whether that was the fault of my own eyes or something outside myself, I don't know for sure. I couldn't move. I *prayed* for release, Ys, but not to a dehar, to Daghda. Maybe that old god heard me, maybe he gave me strength, but my prayer broke the spell. I ran from that room at once.' He shook his head. 'Horrible feeling, and I resent it happening to me in my own home. I hated being powerless against it. I'm not easily scared, and maybe what I felt wasn't exactly fear, but it was fierce.'

I didn't doubt Rinawne's capability to withstand an etheric attack because he was – as far as I knew – very strong in that respect. The mere fact this entity possessed the power to affect him physically was worrying. So far, I'd scorned the idea it had any weapon other than fear. If the entity possessed the power to paralyse a body, how far could that go – a stilling of the heart, a stifling of the lungs?

'So what's happened since?'

'Well, for a start I've not returned to that room. I feel it's where the energy is strongest. Wyva clearly doesn't feel it, which is strange, but I'm glad of that. Other hara in the house appear to avoid the room, perhaps even without realising it. For me, there's a weird sense of being watched – everywhere, even in the gardens. And of course, I felt something in Myv's room, as I said. Did something get invited in, Ys? Did the festival cause this? Or Medoc being here?'

'A combination of it all, I think. Take me to the breakfast room. I'll go in alone.'

'You don't have to. I'd feel safe with you there.'

'No, let me see what happens. If there's anything there, I'll pick up on it. If there's nothing, it could indicate the manifestation is directed at you personally.'

'Now there's a comforting thought!'

'I'm fairly sure it's not that.'

Once inside the breakfast room, I closed the door behind me, leaving Rinawne in the corridor outside. The room appeared normal at first, although by now rain was coming down hard, so the light was dim. Thunder grumbled occasionally, and through the window I could see forked tongues of lightning licking the sky above the trees. The atmosphere of the storm alone made the atmosphere oppressive.

Breathing deeply and mindfully, I walked slowly about the room. Everything was still, oddly lifeless, as if I walked within a painting. In one spot, a flush of heat passed through me. I felt I was being observed, but in a calculating way. My measure, perhaps, was being taken. I didn't feel that whatever lurked there was the shade of Peredur I'd experienced in my visualisations at the Pwll Siôl Lleuad. This was a cool, brooding presence, more like an *intelligence* than a representation of somehar dead. Perhaps, though, it could be an aspect of Peredur as created by the warring families. I felt it was certainly connected to all I'd experienced.

I went to the window, looked out over the gardens. Rinawne had once felt something was in the drapes. I touched the heavy curtains, which perhaps had hung there for hundreds of years. In my ear, the softest suggestion of a sigh. *Peredur*, I thought, *is this you?* If it was, he was hiding in the dust and ancient threads, perhaps even held there by whatever else loomed over the room.

I put my forehead against the fabric of the drapes, breathed in, projecting feelings of compassion, of safety. Perhaps I could coax the wisp of Peredur out. Then, something grabbed my shoulder, and spun me round swiftly. Before I could take in what was happening to me, I was slapped hard across the face and then, unmistakeably, I heard the sound of spitting, and cold wetness sprayed across my eyes. For a moment, the burning pain was intolerable, I was blinded, but it cleared quickly. There was no other visible being in the room with me. On a sideboard, in the shadows against the far wall, something fell over heavily. The thick door to the room shuddered briefly, then became motionless. I staggered back against the window, gasping for breath, almost paralysed. Rain pattered on the panes, and I could hear water falling from a drainpipe nearby, outside. The room was utterly still, while my heart pounded so hard I thought it must burst. Then there was a raw, scraping scream, the most hideous sound I'd ever heard. Not in that room, further away, higher up.

The door was flung open and Rinawne ran into the room. 'Ys!' he cried and rushed towards me, took me in his arms. I collapsed against him, still struggling to breathe.

'Are you all right?' Rinawne said, lifting my head to examine my face. 'That noise! What happened?'

I held onto him, willing equilibrium to return and, thanks to my training, all feelings of debilitation flowed out of me. 'I was slapped, spat at.'

'I heard all that shouting, but I couldn't make out the words.'

'Shouting?' I pulled away from him.

'Well, yes. That awful voice, not harish, not even human, but cruel... so cruel.'

'I didn't hear that,' I said.

'You must've...'

'No. I heard only the softest sigh, here in the drapes, then I was grabbed by something else, and slapped. I heard a scream, but not in here. It came from higher in the house. Did you not hear that?'

'No. Just shouting in this room. I could tell it was a voice but couldn't make out the words.'

'Well that must mean – thankfully – the scream wasn't one of the family or staff being attacked.'

Rinawne closed his eyes briefly. 'You see how strong it is?' he said.

'Yes.' My voice was grim. 'I took it too lightly, didn't take enough precautions.' I grasped one of his arms and led him towards the door. He didn't resist. 'We need to go upstairs.'

'Is that wise? You look really pale. Perhaps more tea first, some wine even... as a restorative.' He smiled uncertainly.

'No, we must look. Whatever uttered that scream wasn't the vindictive force that hit me down here. There might be residue, a clue, a trail. Lead on, Rin. You know this house.'

There was nohar else around, as if the house was empty, although when I asked Rinawne about that, he said the staff must be in the kitchen area, the family elsewhere. This wasn't uncommon during the day. The storm had made night of the dark oak staircase that led to the first floor, but I sensed nothing dangerous there. On the landing above, a corridor stretched to both wings of the house, again virtually in darkness. The pale ovals of windows showed at the end of each corridor. 'It's not here,' I said, 'higher up.'

There was only one other storey to the house – the attics – as Meadow Mynd was a low and rambling building. The stairs to it were a short way to our left. Rinawne said that in the west wing about half the rooms were furnished and were the living quarters of the staff. The east wing comprised storerooms, or empty chambers, and had not been used since the human era – as far as he knew.

'It will be there,' I said, sure. 'From the earliest times.'

Rinawne continued to lead the way. I could tell he didn't feel disturbed at all now, as if whatever had manifested had passed, but I was still drawn to the top storey, and felt it was important to go there immediately.

The floorboards in the east corridor were bare and the ancient light fittings looked as if they didn't work, although we didn't need to try them. The storm was passing, and light was returning naturally outside. As on the first floor, a large oval window dominated the wall at the end of the corridor. Many doors led off to rooms on either side. Some were open, revealing clutter or emptiness. I tried every door, and even the closed ones weren't locked. There didn't appear to be a secret fastened away up here. Had I been wrong?

Then, with only a couple more rooms to explore, I knew I'd

found what I was looking for. We entered an empty room, no different to any we'd examined before, but the atmosphere was somehow wounded.

'Rin, I need to open myself up here,' I said. 'You can wait outside if you'd prefer to.'

'No, I'll not leave you alone this time,' Rinawne said in a determined tone.

I sat down on the floor in the centre of the room, while Rinawne leaned against the windowsill, watching me. Closing my eyes, I regulated my breathing, shut down sounds from the outside one by one, until all I could hear was the sigh of my own breath.

At first the images were fleeting and dim, like gazing down a darkened tunnel with flickering scenes at the far end. I heard a voice – female – say hurriedly, fearfully, 'She must not see this.' Then a pale, distorted face leapt out of the darkness, inches in front of me, snarling in fury. I was almost jolted out of my meditation, but held on.

It was my viewpoint, yet not me who witnessed what now lay before me. The scene spread out like a bolt of shining multi-coloured silk being unrolled, fluid at first then sharpening: a figure – har from the look of him – was restrained against the wall. I saw my own hands held out in front of me. The har lunged towards me again, as if to attack, but his bonds would not reach that far.

'My son,' I said, in terrible sadness, 'my son.'

'I am *not* your son,' he spat. 'No longer!'

His hair was ragged and matted about his shoulders, so fair it was almost white. His eyes were a deep gold and burned with a ferocious light. I could feel the pain of this woman through whose eyes I saw. She didn't know this wild creature chained to the wall, and yet she'd once carried him in her body, birthed him. Her beauteous youngest son, now taken from her. *Peredur.* Her instinct was to release him, let this wild creature free to leap from the window, leave this house and never return. She knew he wasn't safe here and yet... and yet...

The image faded and in its place I saw only another face, this one human and female. I knew it wasn't the woman whose experience I'd just shared. She appeared older than what I'd sensed the other woman's age to be, with dark hair worn in two thick plaits that framed her face. Her features were strong yet refined, and I could tell that in repose or when at peace she'd have been handsome, yet now her face was twisted with hate into a visage that was barely human. She looked right at me with wide, wholly black eyes, her expression full of contempt and loathing. 'Get out!' she hissed, 'Get out!'

At once, the open doors to all the rooms along the attic corridor slammed shut, including the door to the room we were in. The window shook in its frame. I gasped and opened my eyes, as if drowning and coming up for air. The room was freezing. I could see my breath, and also Rinawne's where he stood, stiff and wide-eyed at the window, glancing around himself. He noticed I'd come out of my meditation.

'It was here,' he murmured, rubbing his arms, 'great dehara, it was *with us.*'

I nodded and got to my feet. 'There's something I need to do before we leave this room,' I said.

'Can I help?'

'Just be calm.' I went to each wall and placed my hands flat against them, called upon the dehar Lunil to bring peace, to dispel hatred. I put as much will and energy into this task as I owned. Gradually, the air warmed up again, until the chill had fully departed. In its final wisps, I heard a soft sigh, a sob. I took my hands from the wall and stood straight, breathing deeply and steadily to centre myself.

'What did you see?' Rinawne asked, clearly aware my task was done.

'I think we need to know more about Wyva's human ancestors,' I replied. 'It begins with them.'

We went down to the library – with me relating what I'd seen to Rinawne along the way. 'Well, I think we can assume that

Peredur, after he was har, was confined here by his human family,' I said.

'And he was killed because of that?' Rinawne suggested. 'Perhaps because hara were not supposed to let humans get too close, discover their differences. I know that much.'

'I think there's more to it than that.'

Rinawne thought there might be records in the library from the human era. It seemed likely, given that Wyva's family never threw anything away. There were locked cabinets, of course, where no doubt any surviving documents were stored, but other clues might linger elsewhere. We found a few more books on local history I'd missed, which included information about Meadow Mynd, but were too old to give us details about the years we were most interested in. 'Look for a family Bible,' I said.

'A what?'

'It will most likely be a huge book, a religious text. Families used to record births, deaths and marriages in them, but whether that survived into the times of the Devastation, I don't know. Worth a look, though.'

We found nothing of that kind. Wyva or his parents had scoured the library of 'recent' family history. 'Does the Gwyllion Assembly keep any records, do you think?' I asked.

Rinawne shrugged. 'Not from that far back, I wouldn't think.'

'Oh, there will be records somewhere,' I said. 'Somehar, somewhere, always writes the history of a place. It's just a case of finding it. It need not necessarily be written in a book, but in letters, documents... all the minutiae of life.'

'Well, maybe so, but as we've no idea where such documents might be hidden it seems to me the only way to find anything out is to get Wyva to tell you, or one of his brothers.'

'I think we know those avenues are sealed.'

'Well, the Whitemanes will know, won't they?'

I pursed my lips. 'Hmmm... There's another route, and I've been working on it slightly. The woman I saw in the tower.'

Rinawne's eyes widened. 'Ah, yes! Could she be the presence we felt here today?'

'I think it's likely she's the one through whose eyes I saw, but not the mean-faced one.' I rubbed my face. 'But I expect that whatever – if anything – I can get from her will be fragmented, mere clues to puzzle us further.'

'That's the interesting part about it, though, isn't it?' said Rinawne. 'The piecing together, working out the mystery?'

'Interesting when it doesn't become threatening,' I said. 'I'd prefer to have hard facts now, so we know what we're up against.'

'Well, I can do some sneaking around here when it's quiet,' Rinawne said, 'try to open the cabinets, see what's inside. Between us, we might get enough information.'

'True, but don't take unnecessary risks.'

Rinawne had been looking through a chest of wide shallow drawers, which were mostly stuffed with Wyva's paperwork, but had once presumably held maps. The bottom drawer still did. 'Look!' Rinawne said, in a pleased voice. He withdrew a large sheet of thick paper, which in the human era had been laminated. When Rinawne placed this artefact reverently on the library table, I could tell it was a copy. The original had no doubt been sent to a museum and subsequently destroyed during the Devastation. Still, the copy was good and could be read easily.

'This is amazing,' Rinawne said, running his fingers across the dulled laminate. 'The field names... most of them we still use.'

'Most of them were used *again*,' I corrected him. 'It's common among harish communities to do that. Bizarrely, although all things human are scorned, their history holds a strange appeal. It's like a denial of the modern human era, as if by expunging its labels it can be eradicated from memory.'

The names on the map weren't written in the ancient local language, perhaps because Wyva's ancestors at that time didn't speak it. Landowners often came from across the border.

'Midden's Close,' Rinawne said, grinning, 'Poor Lady's Land. Those aren't used any more, but I love them.'

'Moon's Acre,' I said, tracing the spidery name. This wide field lay across the river and beyond it, Deerlip Hall. 'Is that...?'

'That is the Whitemane domain, yes,' Rinawne confirmed, his voice hardening.

'Do they still call it Deerlip Hall?'

'They simply call it The Domain, as far as I know. I've not had much social chit chat with them.'

'It must be incredibly old.' I looked for Meadow Mynd, found it; hardly more than a river and a few fields between them. Wyva's house, it seemed, had always been named Meadow Mynd. 'Have you never looked closely at Deerlip?' I asked, refusing to be put off by Rinawne's newly inflamed antipathy towards the Whitemanes.

'I rode across the river once, long ago,' he replied. 'I was curious, naturally, because I'd been given the "stay away from the Whitemanes" lecture almost the moment I arrived here. I wanted to see what it was all about, but as soon as my horse set foot on Whitemane earth, I was chased off by a pack of Mossamber's hounds. Hara came after them and threw horse shit at me. Shook me up. I rode home, stinking like a stable, and of course Wyva was angry with me. He warned me never to do anything so stupid again. He was right.'

I realised from that moment on Rinawne had adopted the Wyvachi view of the Whitemanes. He had been a young outsider, brought into this nest of hatreds, in much the same way that I had. Had Wyva not spread the family infection to him, Rinawne might've had the power to heal things himself, years ago. But perhaps he hadn't cared. He'd not had a son then, and had no doubt been immersed in being the consort of a very high-ranking har. And by the time he'd acquired the distance and maturity to reflect, it had been too late.

I was drawn to that delicate tracery of a name on the map. Nytethorne lived in Deerlip Hall. I wondered what it was like, whether it was lovingly maintained as the Mynd had been. At some point, I would see; I was sure of it.

Before Wyva came back from his tasks about the estate, I told Rinawne how to place stronger wards about the house – precautions of salt and iron, rather than grasses and leaves – and how to hide them so they would not easily be found by the house-hara or other family members.

He sighed. 'This is slow. I feel something terrible is building up, but we don't know how to fight it.' He clasped my arm. 'I'm such a roon-wit being jealous of Nytethorne. He does seem our only way to get any answers. I don't feel we can wait.'

'There are others, you know,' I said. 'Medoc, for one, and of course, Rey.'

'Rey?'

'I believe he tried to do what I'm doing now,' I said cagily, 'but was driven off.'

'You really think so? Why? All he told us was that he'd lived long enough as a community hienama and craved a solitary, spiritual life.'

'And you believed that without question?'

'No, of course not, not wholly, although at the same time I could see that potential in him. He was a fey kind of har. Wyva argued with him for weeks before he just took off. But I do think he spoke the truth, in a way...' Rinawne shook his head, smiled. 'However, let's say I wouldn't be surprised to hear he's now with some smaller community high in the mountains, living a life free of hostility.'

I made an emphatic gesture with one hand. 'So there you are – you've said it yourself. He was – at the very least – *uncomfortable* with the feud here.'

'OK, point taken, but what good does *that* do us? Even if he knew things, we've no idea where he is now.'

'*We* haven't, no,' I said.

Rinawne made a scoffing sound. 'I really can't believe the Whitemanes do,' he said. 'Rey was loyal to the Wyvachi. Why would he keep in touch with them and not us? After all, Porter is here. You're grabbing the air there, Ys.'

'Well, maybe...' I sighed. 'So all we have as possible sources are the ghosts, whatever they actually are, and the Whitemanes.'

'And Medoc, as you said,' Rinawne reminded me. 'We could perhaps visit him at his domain. I could act the concerned father, who's beside himself because the hostling won't tell him anything. He's desperate, and frightened for his son... It's worth a try.'

I could tell Rinawne would enjoy playing that role. 'It is, yes. At this point I can't see we have anything to lose, other than him telling Wyva about our visit.'

'I think we could ask for his silence,' Rinawne said. 'We go there on the pretext of seeking advice, and in the process hope we can extract information. It's not beyond our skills, I'm sure. I'm busy the rest of this week with things I can't easily get out of. How about next Lunilsday? I have that free.'

I grimaced. 'I said I'd start Myv's training then, and I don't want to let him down, or make him think he can simply be put aside. I want to get the Reaptide festival wrapped up before I start with Myv, so this week's out for me. How about the day after?'

Rinawne twisted his mouth to the side. 'Maybe, although I'm supposed to help with the open hall that day.'

'What?'

'Once every season, Wyva makes himself officially available to hara, settles disputes, helps with problems, or simply discusses plans... This custom has been in the family for centuries.'

'The tasks of a feudal lord!' I said, laughing.

'He takes it very seriously,' Rinawne said. He thought for a moment. 'Gen or Cawr would take my place if I asked, but Wyva insists hara like to see me there. I'd have to find a good excuse for a day away.'

'Visiting sites with me, of course. We need one for Reaptide.'

'He might argue we could do that any time... Trust me,

getting out of his precious community meetings isn't easily done.'

'I'll mention it later at dinner. You know I can get round him to a degree.'

Rinawne laughed. 'Aye, he likes to keep you as happy as he can. Let's see.'

Wyva was in a good mood that evening, so didn't put up much resistance to my suggestion. Cawr offered quickly to step in for Rinawne, and I suspected he probably enjoyed such events far more than Rinawne ever would. Watching Wyva over dinner, I was surprised he hadn't picked up on the strange atmosphere since Cuttingtide. Was he really so immune? Perhaps he blotted it all out, refused to acknowledge it, because to do so would give it power. If that was the case, I understood his reasoning, even if I might not approve of it.

Myv told me he was pleased his training would begin the following week. Now he'd put his heart into being Gwyllion's hienama, I could tell he wanted to start work straight away. This was fine; there were parts of the job he could fulfil for his hara before he reached maturity. Simply having somehar in the role would mean much to the community. I was keen to question him carefully about what he might have seen or sensed in the house, but a family dinner didn't allow the opportunity. I'd have to wait until next week. There was no doubt Myv was coming out of his shell, interacting more with hara around him, but that might also be the result of approaching feybraiha. Harlinghood would continue to slip away from him, soft as feathers, until the day he put it aside completely. I remembered my own childhood and how endless it had seemed. Did it seem that way to harlings too, who were children for far less time?

Chapter Fourteen

The next morning, I decided to visit the Pwll Siôl Lleuad again. To save time, I rode Hercules rather than walk. Each day the landscape became more fecund and lush as summer exploded within it. Soon, the heady time of Reaptide would be upon us, with all its daytime ghosts and shimmers of earthy power. Would this be the nexus point for what was happening? After so many decades of slowly writhing beneath the surface, whatever haunted Gwyllion and its hara was scratching towards the air.

I dismounted before we reached the pool and led Hercules slowly through the trees, absorbing the ambience around us. Today, it was benign, full of floating motes – feathery airborne seeds, tiny insects and flickers of light – and the trees displayed their gaudy finery beneath the sun, which filtered down in clear rays between the high branches. I wouldn't have been surprised to see dehara manifesting in these natural spotlights. And there was the pool ahead of me. I could smell its cool freshness; it seemed the land breathed softly. Birds called, but almost in whispers.

I was nearly upon him before I noticed he was there, sitting naked upon a rock, half turned towards me, his legs dangling in the water. His hair was unbound, sticking to his damp shoulders and back. Nytethorne. I held my breath. A dehar *had* manifested. Never had I seen a more beautiful and natural sight; this creature of earth, a son of the *new* earth, bathing like a naiad in a forest pool, combing his hair with long brown fingers. His skin was the colour of chestnuts and from where I stood seemed to have the texture of velvet. I saw a puckered mark upon his left shoulder – the quickly healed wound, where Ember had pierced him with an arrow at Cuttingtide – but this slight imperfection made him appear only more perfect. Even amazing, Ys. As beautiful as the Whitemanes believe themselves to be. Yet not proud or vain about it. Do you ever *look* at yourself?'

I felt embarrassed. My looks, whatever hara thought of them, had never brought me happiness. 'No,' I said. 'Doesn't interest me.'

Rinawne closed his eyes for a moment, sighed again. 'A stag in the forest, unaware of his own beauty. And Nytethorne...' He grimaced. 'Another fine animal, full of himself, yet glorious. I'm not stupid. How could you not desire him? If there are two hara in this county that have "pair" written on them, it's you and he.'

'Don't talk such rubbish,' I said. 'Honestly, Rinawne, I'm not looking dreamily for an idealised lover. Have you learned nothing about me?' But despite these stern, disapproving words, he had of course said exactly what my more honest – and foolish – inner self wanted to hear. My body filled with a pleasant warmth and, basking in this richness, I felt benevolent and reached out for Rinawne's hand. 'Please don't think this way. Emotions will cloud our judgement and our minds need to be sharp for what we're trying to do.'

Rinawne's shoulders slumped. 'I know. I said I'm sorry. But you asked, and I've told you.' Tears spilled from his eyes and he made a sound of self-reproach, tried to brush his tears away.

This was not good. Rinawne had already shown possessive tendencies and the last thing I needed was a vengeful, jealous har on my hands.

'Rin,' I said carefully. 'I think we need to talk.'

He continued to wipe his wilfully brimming eyes with the hem of his shirt. 'You're going to say something bad, aren't you? I'm not sure I want to hear it.'

I still held his hand. 'Look, I explained to you how things were with me at the start. You have your life in Gwyllion, and I'll probably be simply a brief interlude for you. But don't harbour bad feelings towards me because of that. You've reached me in a way I've not experienced for years. You've as I watched, and I must have done so for over a minute, he was drying off in the filtered sunlight. He gazed into the clear, deep water thoughtfully, and then a half-seen movement shivered the air behind him. I saw Peredur, a barely visible shade, standing behind him. This vision extended a spectral white hand as if to lay it upon the old wound on Nytethorne's shoulder. Nytethorne sighed, and the sound reverberated around the glade. Peredur withdrew and then had melted into the light and shadows.

Suddenly, as if released from an enchantment, Nytethorne sat up straight and turned, saw me.

'Excuse me, tiahaar,' I said awkwardly, raising my hands to him, 'I didn't mean to disturb you.'

He stared at me inscrutably for some moments. 'This is free land, Ysobi,' he said at last, which were disappointing words to me. I'd expected him to say something... well, I'm not sure what, but at least *meaningful*, mysterious.

'Would you like me to leave?'

'Depends why you're here, doesn't it?'

'I came to meditate. I've done so before here, picked up... certain things.'

He shrugged, drew his hair into a coil and wound it into a loose knot at his neck. 'How's your nosying going?'

I walked closer to him. There were only a couple of feet between us. 'Slowly, but then I get so little co-operation from *any* har who could aid me.' I hesitated a moment, then plunged on recklessly. 'I saw Peredur behind you a moment ago. He stretched out his hand to touch you.'

Nytethorne's expression hardened, almost imperceptibly. He emitted a forced laugh. 'Then where is he now?'

The question seemed stupid, as if he was stamping on the magical atmosphere of both the place and that moment.

'He vanished, of course, as ghosts do. Have you ever seen him here? I have. Twice.'

Nytethorne stood up, unashamed of his nakedness. He began to put on his clothes, which lay in a heap beside him.

'Seek to trick me as you think you've been tricked? Is that it?' He laughed again, a cold horrible sound. 'Don't waste your talent.'

'Why so hostile? I meant what I said. I wouldn't lie to you about something like that.'

'Then you delude yourself,' he said, sitting down on the rock again to pull on his boots. 'You didn't see him.'

'Well, I saw *something* and it definitely reached to touch you. I didn't feel it was malign. A har with long white hair who is blind.'

'He...' Nytethorne screwed up his eyes, uttered a sound of exasperation. 'Oh, think you're clever, don't you?'

'No... look...'

'No, *you* look. Some things are sacred, that's all. Mind your tongue.'

I remembered Wyva's words: *Somewhere in that house there is a shrine to Peredur...*

'I'm really sorry, Nytethorne. I assure you I didn't mean to offend you. I only said what I saw, what I've seen.'

He stared at me again, silent, his arms resting on his splayed thighs, and in his expression I could see his thoughts. He was wondering whether Peredur really had revealed himself to me, and if so, why. He could see I wasn't lying to him. Perhaps what offended him most was that his sacred dead har had chosen to communicate with *me*, an outsider. I could have said more, but decided not to; this would only rile Nytethorne further and that was the last thing I wanted to do. I remained silent, hoping to project my innocence of intent and the desire to make amends. Eventually Nytethorne exhaled through his nose in a great sigh and said, 'All is well. You can't help your mouth, can you?'

I almost protested, but then saw he was smiling. I risked another great impertinence and whispered to him in mind touch, *Of all things on this earth, I seek least to displease you.*

He raised his eyebrows, and responded, not with words, but with what I can only describe as a *purr*. 'Be on my way,' he said. 'Do your dreaming.'

I said nothing to delay him, merely watched as he folded into the restless shadows of green and black. Then I sat down on the rock where he had sat.

No more information came to me that afternoon, but then my mind was too active. Rather than concentrate on Peredur or the history of the land, I faced up to the inescapable truth that I was attracted to Nytethorne greatly; it seemed I was incapable of leading an uncomplicated life in that respect. But this must inevitably be no more than another emotional flash, like the sky filling with a thousand glittering explosions, only for those lovely sparks to fall to earth and fade. I had no faith in love any more. The desire, the chase, was more meaningful. Gratification was a brief if marvellous flare in the darkness, but in the end became only a damp firework, lying spent on the ground of day. For this showy yet intrinsically meaningless folly, I should not be prepared to cause trouble for myself again. But try as I might to be sensible and firm, the desire – the *feeling* – remained; the delicious yearning that compares to no other experience in life. The touchpaper, as yet untouched.

I went back home determined to carry on with my Reaptide work and not pursue silly romantic thoughts like a harling approaching feybraiha. It was clear Rey had had dalliances with both Nytethorne and Rinawne, and surely at the very least I didn't want to follow where he'd lain, as it were.

I'd decided to go for a daytime ritual as I'd originally thought. I'd found one or two things in the local folklore books I might be able to do something with. I'd found a story of some high summer spirit being drawn from a pool. Perhaps that was how we could bring Verdiferel to us. I needed to meditate, rehearse my scenario, find the threads for it and weave them all together.

Before I started work, I took a bath, and while I lay there, as ever made blissful by the warm perfumed water, I opened myself to any energy that might lurk there. I thought of the woman I'd seen, and spoke aloud to her. 'If you can hear me, if you're there, I've sore need of your help.' But nothing came, and the clocks ticked on.

I got out of the bath and dried myself, caught a glimpse of my reflection in the tall, freestanding mirror. Because of what Rinawne had said to me about myself, I paused to stare, trying to see this *thing* he'd described. I don't think I'm beautiful in the way Nytethorne, his relatives, or even Gesaril is beautiful. But I don't *mind* myself, however peculiar that sounds. My appearance has never been a great concern to me, but then I'd never had to bother with it. Inception had done all that for me. All I ever really needed was a hair brush. Now, my hair, normally a dark auburn, looked darker because it was wet. I admired the way it clung to my shoulders, back and chest, and this inspired a vision of the dehar Verdiferel arising naked from water. I felt hara would like that image for the Reaptide ritual. I turned to admire my back view, and thought how much I'd like Nytethorne to see the gifts inception had given me, learn that I could be a real har, a sensual creature of mystery, like we're supposed to be, not just a pompous, boring academic. Then I had to chastise myself harshly for wandering into moonwit territory again. 'Grow up, Ysobi!' I told my reflection and turned away from it.

Once dressed and sitting at the kitchen table, I wrote up some notes. A few bars of a tune had come to me, and I began to hum them. I found I wanted to put the words of the bell song to the forming melody and did so. The tune Yoslyn had sung wasn't very good, I thought. I could do better. But, as far as Wyva was concerned, no doubt the bell was locked in the same drawer as the moonshawl. Could swans be brought into the ritual, though? I closed my eyes and imagined a silver swan gliding upon a dark pool, the rippling arrow of its trail in the water. Its eyes were moonstones that shone in the night and in its beak it held a white rose. This must mean something. I opened my eyes and wrote another note. Then, as I prepared to ponder some more, I heard the tower door open and Rinawne's step on the stair. Surely he couldn't be here just to pester me? I sighed, turned to a new blank page to hide my notes.

When Rinawne erupted into the room, as was his habit, I could tell he was excited.

'Good day and what is it?' I asked, rather testily, my pen held pointedly above the page.

Rinawne glanced at the table. 'Oh, you're working. I'm sorry, but this couldn't wait.'

'What couldn't?'

'Put the kettle on, Ys. We'll need tea while we ponder these.' He took a satchel from his back and emptied its contents on the empty half of the table. Documents, bound with ribbon, and letters, other papers.

'You've been pilfering!' I said.

'You bet I have,' Rinawne announced in triumph.

'You're right, we need tea for this august occasion.' I put down my pen and stood up.

As I saw to our refreshments, Rinawne tidied the papers, putting them in different piles.

'Have you read any of them?' I asked.

'Briefly, enough to tell me I'd hit gold,' he replied. 'Ys, I found the original document from the instatement, when the Wyvachi were given leave by Wraeththu leaders to keep their land.'

'The letters derive from that time too?'

'Some, but even better than that, several are from Medoc to Kinnard, after he left the Mynd.'

'My dear Rinawne,' I said, grinning, 'that is not gold, it's diamonds! Well done!' I hesitated. 'These must be returned before Wyva discovers what you've done.'

Rinawne laughed. 'Don't worry about that. I covered my trail. Now... where shall we start?'

The document I wanted to examine first was the most

ancient, the deed that had been written up, back in those early days of formation, that granted the Wyvachi phyle leadership and also parcelled up the land in the area. While the document itself didn't reveal anything other than that the Wyvachi became leaders in Gwyllion with the sanction of the local Wraeththu commanders, it was accompanied by letters from one of those commanders, whose name was Malakess. 'Great Aru,' I murmured.

'What?' Rinawne asked curiously.

I tapped the document. 'This name, Malakess. I knew a har in Kyme with that name. I wonder...'

Rinawne's eyes widened. 'If it's the same one? If so, maybe you could get more information from him.'

'Well... possibly.' I made a dismissive gesture. 'He's no longer in Kyme. He moved to Almagabra to work for the Gelaming.' There were other reasons I didn't particularly want to contact Malakess, not least his own relationship with Gesaril, part of the whole sorry mess. Still, it intrigued me Malakess might have been part of the administration in this area. Everyhar has a history, and incepted hara more than most.

The letters from Malakess had perhaps been preserved because they were 'evidence' of discussions that had taken place back then. They were dated, so I read them in order.

Dear Kinnard

I've thought more about your suggestion that the Wyvachi should return to Meadow Mynd and restore it. I understand your reasons for wanting to make it your headquarters. I agree that while we are striving to create a new society, hara will feel comfortable with familiarity, what they already know and respect and, as you rightly pointed out, Meadow Mynd has been the heart of the community in your area for a long time. My only reservations stem from the fact that these connections were established in the Human Era and part of me feels such ties should be cut completely. But as the Mynd offers so much opportunity to help hara create a new community in the area, not least its established farmland, I'm prepared to put my reservations aside in this case. I liked your analogy of how, in the distant past, religions seeking to suppress previous belief systems built their churches over existing sacred sites, in order that people would feel comfortable with the new, and that your situation is similar. Indeed it is, and I see the wisdom in your decision. Please take this letter as formal permission to return to Meadow Mynd and establish your phyle there.

Your concerns about Mossamber har Whitemane will be addressed, but if I am to step in and take your side in these negotiations, you must be willing to compromise. I'm sure I don't need to remind you that Mossamber and his hara were instrumental in securing this area for us, and for that alone they deserve compensation and the granting of their own desires for the future. While my fellow commanders and I feel that the Wyvachi are the best candidates to lead in the Gwyllion area, this must be with the co-operation of the Whitemanes and their inclusion in plans and decisions for the community. The only object of importance is the development of Wraeththu in Alba Sulh. Personal issues must be put aside.

I will call on you next week for further discussions. My aide will send you a message as to the exact day and time. Please invite Mossamber and his highest-ranking hara to join us. I think this would mean a lot coming from you, rather than me, and will perhaps do something to calm the troubled waters between you. Give Mossamber his due, Kinnard. Don't let pride stand in your way.

In blood
Malakess har Sulh
First Commander of the West

Well, I could certainly hear Malakess's voice in that letter. It had to be the same har. I smiled, wondering if he'd ever been a fierce young thing. Somehow I found it difficult to imagine, but no doubt hara thought the same about me and many others like me. We had glossed our histories with a thick pigment of respectability, and whatever Malakess might have lived through, as he'd fought to establish Wraeththu in this area, in his letter it was plain he had already been striving to be something other than a wild warrior. He'd wanted to be a politician, not a tribal chief.

There were other letters and documents detailing arrangements for various hara in the area concerning the allocation of land and similar matters, none of which had much to interest me. But then came a missive decidedly more appetising.

Dear Kinnard

I cannot, in all conscience, involve myself in the personal matter upon which you requested my jurisdiction. While I appreciate that you and several members of your erstwhile human family comprise the leadership of your phyle, I must remind you that human ties have no bearing on your situation now. Medoc is your fellow har, as are those who were previously your cousins. You are all part of one family —Wraeththu. And this includes the Whitemanes.

The circumstances you described to me are essentially the province of Mossamber har Whitemane. He was Peredur's chesnari, and as such is responsible for making decisions that Peredur is no longer able to make. That is all I have to say on the matter, and pray that you will put history aside and respect the wishes of your fellow hara as they are now.

You have my condolences, and I understand that your abrupt letter to me reflected the pain you feel, but nevertheless I feel strongly that this matter is outside my area of authority.

In blood
Malakess Har Sulh
First Commander of the West

I read this letter out to Rinawne.

He grimaced. 'They wanted Peredur back, didn't they?' he said. 'That's what the letter says to me. Remember what you heard Medoc say to Wyva at Cuttingtide. *Mossamber thought he was liberating a corpse.'*

Since the festival, I'd told Rinawne everything I'd heard during that conversation. 'There's also another implication in those words,' I said, 'namely that Peredur wasn't dead when Mossamber *liberated* him... whatever that means. But from what I heard at Cuttingtide, the Wyvachi and the Wyverns are sure Peredur didn't survive, but perhaps he died later from his injuries.'

'So maybe Kinnard asked this Malakess to intervene because Mossamber refused to give up the... remains.'

I nodded. 'It could be read that way, yes.'

Rinawne gave me a curious look. 'Could this be why Peredur is not at rest?'

'And that all we need to do is bring him back to the Mynd for reburial?' I grimaced. 'Seems too simple. Plus his body might have been cremated.'

Rinawne pantomimed a shudder. 'Or it could be preserved at Deerlip Hall, forever enshrined – a dried out mummy. All the Whitemanes worship it.'

'Thank you for that image,' I said dryly.

'I think it's entirely possible,' Rinawne said, grinning.

'*Maybe* you're on the right track. Wyva said he suspected there was some kind of shrine to Peredur at Deerlip. I thought he was speaking metaphorically, but perhaps not. It could explain the Whitemanes' *sensitivity* over Peredur.'

Rinawne gave me a hard glance. 'Nytethorne said

something, then?'

I didn't want to tell Rinawne what I'd seen at the Pwll Siôl Lleuad earlier, because I sensed that revealing I'd met Nytethorne again would bring on a dark mood. 'Well, not in so many words. I tried to talk about Peredur, but Nytethorne got defensive about it. I've already told you the meeting I had with him was difficult.'

Rinawne sniffed in a surly manner. 'Read the other letters. These will be the meat of it, I'm sure. The ones from Medoc.'

Medoc, it appeared, had tried five times to communicate with his brother and had then given up. Or if he had continued to try, those letters had not been preserved.

My dear brother,

Too much time has passed since we saw one another. I trust you and your hara are in good health. I have no way of knowing, yet am certain if anything bad had befallen you, I would've heard from somehar.

I had hoped you might try to contact me, but now, after two years have passed, I realise I must be the one to make the advance. You are in my thoughts constantly. I know you must believe I betrayed and abandoned you, and that I seduced our cousins into leaving the Mynd with me, but the truth is every har who came with me that day felt it was the right thing to do. I didn't have to persuade them. That was our decision, and we stand by it, but I respect yours too, and appreciate why you stand by it in the same way.

We have founded our phyle at an old domain named Harrow's End, some miles over the county border to the east. Things are going well for us, if slowly, but we are content. You would be most welcome here at any time, and even if we cannot reconcile our differences in terms of where our hara should live, I hope at least we can mend our relationship.

To this day, I'm not sure what I really experienced that night at the Mynd, but I knew then, and still know now, that I cannot live in that place. I admire that you have the strength to carry on there, despite everything that happened. I know you are right: It is our domain, but all I questioned was the rights of the dead, as it was theirs too. Perhaps you don't want to hear my excuses, as you'll no doubt call them, but I feel I want to explain and wish we could speak face to face. Please let me know if we can meet, if only halfway between our domains.

In blood and in love,
Your brother, Medoc

The second letter was around four months later.

My dear brother, Kinnard,

I'm saddened you didn't respond to my letter and apologise if anything in it gave offence. I wish only to see you again, and to meet your son. Summer is blooming here and I thank the spirits of the land that I live amid such beauty and peace. Please come to visit us. We don't even have to speak of the past, but only of now and the future, the time for our sons. We have gone through too much together to remain estranged.

In blood and in love,
Your brother, Medoc

The third letter indicated Medoc still hadn't received a response from Kinnard, but he didn't mention this. He spoke only of his land, of his hara, and the way his community was developing. The fourth letter was similar. I wondered whether Kinnard, reading these letters, had envied Medoc his peace and liberty, and for this reason couldn't bring himself to make contact. Perhaps he didn't want the greater part of his family to have escaped the malediction and to be living happily free of it elsewhere. The fifth letter was different and was dated some seventeen years after the previous four.

My dear Kinnard,

Forgive that I write to you again after so long, for I realise you must have no wish to hear from me, but word has come to us of Yvainte's passing, and I had to contact you. Please know that my heart breaks as yours must be broken in losing your beloved chesnari. I am so sorry that such a light has left us under such tragic circumstances. My domain is always open to you. Know that you can arrive here at any time of day or night and will be welcomed, without questions being asked. Though many years have passed since we last saw one another, in some ways it feels like only a few days ago. If you want me now, I am here. I will always be here for you.

In blood and in love,
Your brother, Medoc

After I'd read the letter aloud, both Rinawne and I were silent for some moments, then Rinawne said, 'That's so sad. I wonder what happened?'

I sighed, shook my head. 'Well, whatever happened, one thing's certain: Kinnard was stubborn as a mule.'

'Maybe he *did* go to see Medoc.'

'Maybe.'

'He kept the letters,' Rinawne said wistfully, picking up the last one.

'We'll learn more when we visit Medoc ourselves,' I said, gathering the documents into a neat pile.

'You know...' Rinawne said, 'I wonder whether Mossamber

has kept correspondence from Malakess too. If so, they might shed more light on the Peredur aspect.' He glanced at me. 'Much as I hate to suggest this: Would Nytethorne help with that, do you think? Would he look for you?'

I uttered a scornful laugh. 'Has anything I've said indicated Nytethorne would in any way be helpful?'

'No, not in what you've *said*,' Rinawne replied sharply. 'I was just thinking. There's nothing to be lost in asking and perhaps something to gain. Maybe it's time *I* made contact with Nytethorne. It could be up to us pureborns to put the past to rest.'

My entire body went cold at the thought of Rinawne blundering in, messing things up. 'No, don't do that,' I said.

He gave me a severe glance.

'Well, not yet. It's delicate. Let's talk with Medoc first.'

'I don't think you're being direct enough,' Rinawne said, 'you just shilly shally around with Nytethorne. He might respond better to somehar being straight and open.'

'I *have* been straight and open,' I retorted, feeling my face grow hot at the memory of throwing Nytethorne up against a door.

Rinawne regarded me speculatively. 'Uh huh.'

'Please, Rin, let's concentrate on Medoc for now. I don't want a dozen cans of worms opened, emptied, and wriggling around in a great big mess.'

He narrowed his eyes at me. 'Do you question my ability to be diplomatic?'

'Quite frankly, yes,' I said. 'Rin, you've no idea how awkward Nytethorne is. He doesn't really want to speak to any of us at all.'

'But can't stop himself speaking to you, of course. Any excuse for that.'

I put my head in my hands for a moment. This reminded me painfully of similar arguments I'd had with Jass in the past. 'Please stop this. It's nothing to do with what we need to concentrate on.'

'You've seen him more than once, haven't you?'

I stared at Rinawne for some moments. I couldn't be bothered to lie and have to try and cover it up. 'Since I've been in Gwyllion – four times. On three of those occasions, we've spoken for... oh, at the most a scandalous fifteen minutes, at the least a rather tense five minutes, during which he accused me of making things up. So, there we are. The extent of my relationship with Nytethorne. Are you happy now?'

I wondered then whether Rey had ever endured a similar conversation to this.

Rinawne put the letters and documents back into his satchel, his face pinched. 'I only asked.'

'And I only answered. Thank you for bringing the letters over, Rin. I think we've learned a lot.'

He nodded vaguely. 'I'll get them back now.'

'Yes, you'd better.'

Rinawne hooked the satchel over his shoulder, looking down on me where I sat at the table. 'I'm sorry,' he said.

I made a gesture with both hands to indicate acceptance of the apology, but said nothing in return.

After Rinawne had left, I was in no mood to continue working. I was furious he'd disrupted my day, even though he'd brought the letters over. I knew with a heavy certainty I had to end the physical aspect of my friendship with Rinawne, but I also knew this wouldn't be easy. The chances of him turning spiteful on me were, I thought, great. He could ruin everything for me here. I cursed the moment I let him "have his way" with me, to use a quaint old term. But then he'd let me believe he'd wanted only a casual dalliance to liven up his life. Perhaps he had even meant it to be so, at the start. I thought of Gesaril, the hara before him, the temptations that had been offered me, which had turned out to be poisonous. I couldn't add Nytethorne to that pathetic list. If hara needed aruna, I needed a friend who would be uncomplicated and undemanding and with whom I couldn't possibly fall in love. I realised I'd probably have been wiser to take Gen up on his far more guarded advances. I might've also learned more to help me. Too late now. Here I was in the same old mess.

Sighing, and feeling miserably sorry for myself, I made more tea. Then, I went to my nayati to calm my thoughts.

Chapter Fifteen

I spent the next couple of days keeping to myself. I didn't go over to the Mynd, nor down to Gwyllion. I strolled in the woods near the tower for relaxation in between bouts of writing, and one evening even went to swim in the Afon Siôl Lleuad. The only hara I saw on my daily walks were those I didn't know very well, who'd only offer a brief greeting before carrying on with their own business. That suited me fine.

Each evening, I meditated in the bathroom, hoping to bring out the woman I'd glimpsed there, but even though sometimes I felt sure some kind of energy was straining to reach me, nothing manifested. The landscape held its breath, I thought, remote storms rolling in from the ocean. Heat was building up, stifling the air. I was relieved Rinawne kept his distance, no doubt having realised he'd annoyed me greatly – fatally, in one respect.

I decided to wait until the weekend, then break the silence and visit the Mynd. I didn't want Wyva thinking anything was amiss. I would take him what I'd written, because my Reaptide rite should be complete by then. I could also discuss with him my plans for Myv's training. Rinawne I would deal with as the opportunity arose. If he went so far as to inform Wyva of our relationship, then I'd have to deal with that too and claim I'd been misled, and that once I'd realised my mistake I'd ended the arrangement. As a har, Wyva should accept that – I hoped. If not, well... if I was meant to be here, as I thought, then nothing would impede my ability to carry on my investigations. I had to trust in that. Having made these decisions, I felt greatly relieved.

On Hanisday, I decided to ride over to Hiyenton, the town nearest to Gwyllion, take lunch there and walk around. It was a busier place than Gwyllion, being a market town. After I'd browsed all the stalls of the indoor section, buying myself some candles for my nayati, some night-scented stocks to plant outside my tower, and also a couple of small clocks to add to my bathroom collection, I wandered to the large inn I'd noticed on my arrival and where I'd arranged to have Hercules stabled for a few hours – The Swan with Two Necks. The name was so intriguing, I couldn't lunch anywhere else. The place was ancient, and its ceilings dipped like the backs of old mares. It was full of hara, all talking loudly. Hemp smoke thickened the air. Two fiddlers played fast and complex tunes that wove through the hubbub. As I made my way through the throng to the bar, I found myself jostled up against a har I knew: Nytethorne. He stared at me in disbelief for some moments, and I expect I looked at him in the same way.

Then he said, 'Ysobi,' and I responded 'Nytethorne.'

It was then I realised he had Ember with him, who was regarding me with a quizzical expression on his face. *Do I move on or say more?* I wondered.

'You see, he lived,' Ember said in a sarcastic tone, patting his hostling's shoulder in the place where it had been wounded.

I smiled. 'Unless he's a very convincing ghost, yes.'

'Shut it,' Nytethorne said to his son, although I could see plainly he was relieved Ember had spoken.

'Are you here for the market, tiahaara?' I asked.

'I'm here to buy arrows,' Ember said, smirking at me.

I raised my brows. 'Oh, really? I think you make your own, young har.'

'He does,' Nytethorne said.

Beside his hostling, Ember appeared very young and less mysterious than on the other occasions I'd met him. He did not seem to me the har who'd visited my dreams, simply a good-looking youngster, unruly and impertinent. But then, of course, in my eyes Nytethorne now outshone him. Whatever brief spell Ember had cast had dissolved.

'Care to sit with us?' Nytethorne asked.

'Er... well yes, of course.'

'Ember, get ales,' he said. 'I'll get seats, if they're to be found.'

To my surprise, Ember obeyed without answering back. Nytethorne put a hand gently upon my waist. 'Outside,' he said. 'There's a yard.'

I pushed through hara in the direction he'd indicated, eventually emerging into a walled courtyard dominated by an immense and ancient fig tree. Worn stone steps ran up the sides of two walls, no doubt leading to accommodation. In the back wall was an open wooden gate leading to the stables. Flowers bloomed in blackened oak tubs rimed with moss, and there were half a dozen pine tables with benches. Two of these, near the gate, had no occupants. I went to the furthest and sat down. Nytethorne sat opposite me. Wide-fingered fig leaves littered the ground around us; several lay on the table. The air smelled green and slightly damp, despite the heat. 'This is a pleasant surprise,' I said.

Nytethorne made a huffing sound and smiled. 'We come here once a week, sometimes more.'

'Do you know what the name of the inn means?'

'The river splits outside the town, very old. Curves like the necks of swans.'

'Oh, I was hoping for something more... strange.'

Nytethorne took out a pipe from his pocket and began to pack it with smoking materials of some kind. I wondered whether to broach the subject of my investigations, but was reluctant to. I didn't want to spoil the atmosphere by putting Nytethorne in a defensive mood. But then he said, 'Got very far?'

'Taken a few steps,' I replied.

He put his head to one side, struck tinder for his pipe. 'And?'

'Seen a few letters from the early days, and the document that formalised Wyvachi settlement of the land.'

'What letters?' Herbal smoke plumed before his face.

'I don't want to say, because I'd quite like to spend some sweet moments with you without you getting angry, scared or mulish.'

He huffed out another short laugh. 'I see.'

We held each other's gaze for a few moments, then I mustered my courage and said, 'A har named Malakess, who was a local commander in the early days, wrote to Kinnard on a number of occasions on matters concerning both the Wyvachi and the Whitemanes. Do you suppose Mossamber might have kept similar letters?'

Nytethorne's teeth tapped on his pipe. His eyes had narrowed. 'Maybe.'

'Well, if such letters did still exist, I think it would help my investigations a lot to see them.'

'Expect it would.'

Behind him I saw Ember emerge from the inn carrying our drinks. His arrival was opportune. I'd said what I had to say.

Making small talk with the Whitemanes that day was one of the most difficult social challenges I'd faced, not least because the obvious things we could discuss were taboo. I couldn't talk about my work, or Myv, or my investigations into the past. Mentioning their interpretation of the yearly round and their associated beliefs was unthinkable. Even asking about their home might be taken as sinister interrogation. But I wanted to make the most of this coincidental meeting – if not to further my enquiries, then to establish more of a friendship with these distrustful hara. The fact I'd been invited to join them and Ember hadn't protested said a lot. Perhaps Nytethorne had indeed been open with his family about meeting me, and now this was to be encouraged. So, in desperation for something to talk about, I began to tell them about Jesith and the vineyard. Whether this interested them or not, I can't say, but they were polite enough to listen with some attention. I mentioned Zeph and Ember said at once: 'You have a son?'

'Yes, preposterous as that might sound.'

'Why that?' Nytethorne asked.

I shrugged. 'Well... I don't think I'm really the parent type.'

Ember laughed at these words. 'Is he like you?'

'Not much, no. He's not a harling anymore.' *No, just an adult I don't really know.*

The thought was unguarded and I sensed Nytethorne pick up on it; the wisp of a comforting feeling brushed against my mind, but he said nothing. However, I liked that he was alert to my thoughts, ready to scan them if they were available to him.

'You decided to stay here longer,' Ember said. 'We didn't scare you off.'

'Despite your best efforts, no,' I replied lightly, taking a sip of my ale. 'I wonder, Ember... If I'd followed those harlings across the bridge that day, and had come to your domain, what would have happened?'

'We'd have eaten you!' His bright, amused eyes told me he still thought I was easy game to be intimidated.

Nytethorne made a sound of annoyance. 'Don't be a whelp,' he said, and cuffed his son round the head. Ember yelped, but then laughed.

'It's fine,' I said. 'Believe it or not, I know that wouldn't have happened.'

'You didn't come, though,' Nytethorne said. 'Did you?'

'Would Mossamber welcome me there?'

Nytethorne didn't answer but Ember said, 'No. You'll always be Wyvachi-called to him.'

'Yet not to you?'

'Didn't say that,' Ember said, taking a drink and looking away from me.

'Well, thanks for the ale, anyway.' I raised my glass to them.

'You returning to Jesith soon?' Nytethorne asked.

'I have no immediate plans. My work here isn't finished.'

'Still here come Shadetide, watch us roast a har on the bonfire,' Ember said.

'What an appealing invitation. I can't wait.'

'Might see more than you barter for,' Nytethorne said,

carefully.

'Really? Shadetide is a long way away.'

There was a silence.

I could sense the fragile camaraderie between us fizzling out, the conversation, such as it was, dying. It was time to go. I'd not had any lunch, but could manage until I reached home. I'd laid some groundwork, I felt, and to prolong this difficult encounter wouldn't help. I got to my feet. 'Well, thanks again. Good day to you, tiahaara.'

Nytethorne smiled at me then, in such a way that the skies might've opened and rays of glorious colours come streaming down from some far realm that was the essence of bliss. I picked up my shopping bag, and wafted out of the gate into the stableyard beyond.

As I rode home through the searing summer haze, the air alive with floating motes around me, I considered it was perfectly fine to be dazzled by a har, as long as it didn't descend into sticky, painful situations. Nytethorne could be my muse. He might stay that way if we didn't end up together. That was unthinkable anyway. We weren't alike at all.

Once home, I planted my new flowers and did some tidying of the ground around the tower. It didn't have a garden as such, because nohar had bothered with it, but there was plenty of room for one. In one of the sheds behind the tower, I found some rusted but serviceable gardening tools, so perhaps in the ancient past somehar, or someone, had nurtured this little patch of land.

I mulled over the last of my Reaptide ideas as I worked with the soil. This festival is the second of the harvest festivals, culminating with Smoketide in the month of Harvestmoon. I'd decided that to begin the ritual, participating hara would meet at The Crowned Stag. From there, everyhar must wander off alone or in small groups, out into the forests and the ancient hills beyond. They must follow streams and the tracks of sheep, until they come across a place where they will commune with

Verdiferel. His totem creature is traditionally the white owl who flies by day. Hara should be alert to appearances of this bird. Perhaps Verdiferel himself, in the guise of some mysterious har, might cross your path in the afternoon heat. He might try to trick you, but if you best him will give you knowledge or some other gift. As the sun begins to set, so hara will commune at a pool – the one we'd used for Cuttingtide would be adequate – and there we'd call upon the essence of Verdiferel. White owls would come down from the sky and glide across the hills, conjuring a sweet-smelling ground mist. The hara would stand around the pool, singing one of the songs I'd been working on. I ached to include the swan; it seemed intrinsic. I decided to slip that in and see whether it passed Wyva's scrutiny. I wouldn't mention it was silver. The swan could turn into Verdiferel, whose essence we would bind into the water so he could do no harm. But we would offer him gifts instead, the bounty of the land. We would offer him aruna. This thought came unbidden to me, but I realised it was pertinent. Harlings, of course, could not participate in that aspect, but older hara could disappear ghostlike into the landscape to perform this part of the rite. I'd be happy to remain behind to keep an eye on the younger hara.

After this, a feast would be held again at Meadow Mynd and songs would be sung. If Wyva wanted more than this, which admittedly was quite freeform, we could discuss it. It occurred to me then we could have our own book to sit on the shelves beside Flick Har Roselane's archetypal work. The yearly round of Gwyllion. I was sure Wyva would like that idea.

When I was hungry I put away my tools, and went to prepare dinner. I thought it was about time I visited the Mynd, but only when I was sure everyhar there had eaten dinner. I didn't want to feel Rinawne's accusing gaze across a table. But despite that, I was looking forward to having company, being still high on the meeting with Nytethorne and unable to settle to pursuits such as reading or painting.

I was just braiding my hair in preparation to leave when I heard a sonorous knocking on my tower door. That couldn't be Rinawne, but who else?

I went downstairs, resisting the temptation to ask 'Who's there?' before opening it. This was Gwyllion; nohar wishing me harm would knock.

Nytethorne stood on the step. I was surprised, and yet not. Now was the time to be careful. 'And so faintly you came tapping – tapping at my door.' I smiled. 'Hello, Nytethorne. To what do I owe this pleasure, may I ask?'

'Nevermore,' he responded, grinning, but clearly to show me he knew that quote from a very ancient poem.

'Well, without more preamble, and supposing you bring no dire omens, please come in.'

He walked past me into the tower, looked around, no doubt reminiscing about previous visits.

'I doubt it's changed much,' I said.

He ignored that remark. 'Brought you something.'

'Come upstairs.' I began to head for the stairs, then paused. I went back to the door, removed the key from the hook just beside it and locked it, leaving the key in the lock. Nytethorne gave me a quizzical look. 'Don't worry. You're not a prisoner. It's just that Wyvachi tend to charge in here without knocking. I'm not sure it's a good idea any of them see you here.'

'I understand.'

I took him into the friendly kitchen, feeling the living room would be too intimate, and somewhat imprinted with memories of Rinawne, never mind recollections of Rey for Nytethorne. 'Would you like tea?'

'Yes. Please.' He sat down in what I assumed was the chair he'd always taken at that table. We are such creatures of habit. He had a heavy hessian bag with him, embroidered with stylised willow trees. The work was exquisite.

'Did one of your hara make that?' I asked.

He nodded. 'All of it, yes.'

'Beautiful work.'

'Grow flax. A lot of it. Make dyes too.' He smiled and withdrew from the bag a package, bound in fine linen – no doubt also of Whitemane manufacture – which he unwrapped. There were letters, not many, but perhaps more precious than what Rinawne had shown me. 'You asked,' he said.

'I hope it wasn't difficult... dangerous...'

He shook his head. 'No. Not under lock and key. Knew where to look. Mossamber keeps things neat, so he can lay hands on anything, any time.'

I couldn't wait. While the kettle was boiling, I sat down and drew the fragile papers to me greedily. The first one was clearly in response to a missive Mossamber must've made to Malakess, after he'd been informed the Wyvachi would be the ruling phyle in the area.

Greetings Mossamber,

Thank you for your letter, which was brought to me this morning. I understand your position on the matter of division of land and power, but trust that with my assistance all can be resolved to a degree of mutual satisfaction. As I've said to the Wyvachi, the future of Wraeththu as a whole must be the only consideration, and what will work best for bringing order, routine and stability to your locality.

I know it is difficult to put away human notions so soon after inception, but ask you to step back and consider things impartially. I know also you have suffered, as have countless others in our struggles to establish ourselves and heal this world. Your suffering is no less valid to me than any other har's in my care.

It is my opinion, and that of my fellow commanders, that Kinnard and Medoc har Wyvachi are the natural leaders in the Gwyllion area and surrounding lands. At one time you were brothers in arms, and I ask you to look into your heart and rediscover that amity you once enjoyed. Remember you share a mutual grief, however you might view it. I shall see to it that the Whitemanes will be given all that they require in order to run their own domain, but under the overall leadership of the Wyvachi.

I consider it my duty not to leave this area until the matter of leadership is settled. I will remain here as arbiter until that occurs.

In blood,
Malakess Har Sulh
First Commander of the West

I wondered how Mossamber had responded to that. Not in a particularly cooperative way, I imagined. There were several more letters, almost repeating the same thing but in different words. Mossamber must've questioned everything, the dominion of every corner of land, the division of the tiniest of spoils. I could almost hear Malakess's patience fraying, as the letters became shorter and more abrupt.

Such as:

My dear Mossamber,

I think we have covered this ground too many times. Kinnard has already agreed that the spring in the copse of Moon's Acre shall be yours. Please don't mention this again.

Malakess

And then, when things really were becoming too much for him:

Mossamber,

The thoroughfares throughout the Gwyllion area, excepting

*the roads to your respective domains, are communally
owned and will be maintained by the Gwyllion Assembly,
via tithes and labour from the population. I thought this
was made clear at our last meeting. It is neither acceptable
nor convenient for the Whitemanes to have their own
private roads across common land.*

*It is your choice not to accept a position on the
Assembly, when to my mind you should do so. Then you
would not have to write to me over these trivial matters but
could take part, firsthand, in any discussions and decisions.
Please address any further enquiries of this nature to
Kinnard har Wyvachi or to the Assembly.*

Malakess

But then, as I'd hoped, came the treasure. And because the
wound it addressed still rilled with blood, Malakess's tone
was gentle.

My dear Mossamber,

*Rest assured I will not take the Wyvachi's part in this
dilemma. I have already informed Kinnard that as Peredur's
chesnari any decisions concerning him are yours, in the
absence of him being able to make decisions himself.*

*But please be mindful of the fact that Peredur also
means a lot to Kinnard and Medoc and those who were
incepted with them. Their request is not to slight or anger
you, but to assuage the grief they feel themselves. I know it
is hard, if not impossible in the rawness of sorrow, to put
aside human feelings at this time. This goes for all of you
concerned. But as your commander, all I can advise is that
you attempt to find release among your hara, the comfort
you need. However harsh this might sound, I wish for a
swift resolution. His wounds cannot be healed, my friend.
You know that and it has to be faced.*

254

I would like to say that in the short time I knew Peredur,
I found him to be a profoundly spiritual har, with limitless
generosity, wisdom and ability. What befell him was a sore
loss to our kind as, like you, I believe he had a wondrous
future ahead of him. I can only imagine the pain his fate has
caused you. You have a lot of work ahead of you,
Mossamber, and have a duty to the hara in your care. You
need to mourn before you can take up your life again.
If there is anything you need from me, please ask.

In blood,
Malakess

That was the last letter. After I'd read it, I placed it on the table. Nytethorne had already seen to making the tea – he knew where everything was kept. Now he sat opposite me again, his arms folded on the table top.

'The wounds must've been... very bad,' I said, 'if they couldn't be healed by the hienamas, or Peredur's own harish body.'

Nytethorne nodded. 'Very bad,' he said. 'Hara heal well, but none can grow back what's lost.'

I closed my eyes. 'Dear Aru.' I knew he wouldn't give me specific details if I asked. I could tell simply from his demeanour it had cost him to bring these letters to me, and he was uncomfortable revealing what little he had. A part of him hadn't wanted to do it.

'Mossamber took him home to die,' I said. 'That's the truth, isn't it?'

Nytethorne nodded almost imperceptibly, his gaze on the table.

'Did it... did it take long?'

He glanced up at me, his expression pained.

'I'm sorry to ask, Nytethorne. I'm trying to keep it as simple as I can.'

'Some things never die,' he said and then, in a soft

melodious voice, he chanted, '...On this home by Horror haunted – tell me truly, I implore – Is there – *is* there balm in Gilead? – tell me, – tell me, I implore. Quoth the Raven, Nevermore.'

He looked so sad, I reached out impulsively to take hold of his hands. He did not resist. 'Thank you. That's a beautiful way to put it.'

He squeezed my fingers, then let me go, folding his hands away.

'You like poetry?' I asked. 'Even human poetry?'

'Art is beyond human or har,' he replied, shrugging. 'It survives.'

Peredur had died so long ago, and yet to the Whitemanes, apparently even more so than to the Wyvachi, his death seemed recent. I could tell this by Nytethorne's sorrow, even though he had never met Peredur. He must have been an amazing har to have had such an impact. Mossamber still loved him, after all this time, and having created harlings with others. He had passed on the memory of his beloved through time. It survived. How could this cherished thing be malign? That was the mystery of it, really.

'Nytethorne, I can't thank you enough for bringing these letters to me.'

He shrugged. 'Thought about it. Decided if it's meant, it's meant. You'll release us. If not, nothing changes. Seemed worth the risk.'

He held my eyes, his expression both inscrutable and plain. Yet there was a table between us, and to rise from my seat and cross that distance would break the spell, I was sure of it. 'Nytethorne,' I said softly.

He closed his eyes, his brow furrowed, his head dipping towards his chest. 'Food is eaten, it is gone,' he said. 'Soon not even taste remains.' He looked up at me. 'I want to be more than food.'

I became aware that, in his own strange way, Nytethorne felt the same way I did. For him too, glorious sunsets had become grey, cold dawns, a listless swamp where nothing lived. Even to approach a har seemed fraught with the danger that this *blight* would devour the blissful landscape, leaving only barrenness behind. And regrets.

'I know,' I said.

'Yes.' He smiled wanly. 'To look is enough. To *be*.'

'In the early days we were taught that love is canker,' I said.

'Hush!' Nytethorne said.

'But I want you to hear it. My own teacher, who claimed to have been taught by Thiede himself, said that we must not succumb to petty human emotions but strive for something greater. I wonder if somehow many of us have lost sight of that.'

'Maybe teachers were wrong. We're not capable.'

I smiled at him. 'Well, *you* should be, as you're pureborn, and not a mess of bad memories and traumas like us incepted hara.'

'Raised by them, though.' He stared at me in silence for some moments. 'Don't feel pureborn. Wonder if any of us can, my kin.' Again a pause. 'Wyva and me – could never have it. Weren't allowed. The moment we sucked air, we were old, as old as the earth.'

'Are you saying it wasn't just the Wyvachi...?'

'No! Saying nothing.'

I dared to murmur. 'Show me. In your breath.'

'No.' He put his hands against his face and I longed to go to him, comfort him, but knew I mustn't.

Instead, I said, 'I'm going to see Medoc in a couple of days.'

Nytethorne raised his head. 'You think he'll speak?'

'I don't know, but he has distance, Nytethorne. He might feel able to.'

'When?'

'Calasday, next week.' I hesitated then said, 'perhaps we should meet afterwards, some time.'

He nodded vaguely. 'No doubt will.' He stood up, gathered up the letters and replaced them in his bag.

I stood up to see him out, but he said, 'Don't trouble yourself. Know the way.' He smiled then, came to me and kissed my cheek. 'Care for yourself.'

'I will.'

How strange it was not to obey harish instinct and reach for him, draw his body close. But I knew he would only pull away and I'd risk breaking some rare magic between us. I sat down and listened to him leave the tower. Afterwards, there was a great silence, the world stilled.

I knew I couldn't leave the situation with Rinawne as it was, and that I would have to be the peacemaker. The day following Nytethorne's visit to me, Pelfday, I thought I should go to the Mynd. Wyva liked it when I stayed for dinner at the weekends, and we could discuss the Reaptide festival. The weather had continued to heat up, making the air indoors stifling and unbearable. Even with all my tower windows open, I could barely breathe. Evening brought some respite, as the air would cool and a soft breeze steal across the land. On Pelfday, the sky began to darken around six o'clock. A storm was coming to land. I hoped this would freshen and clear the air.

I planned to ride over to the Mynd around seven, since the family would generally eat around eight on this day. I pottered about the kitchen, gathering my notes together and stuffing them into my satchel. Then suddenly, the whole tower shook as the mightiest peal of thunder I'd ever heard exploded overhead. I jumped in shock, and it felt as if I was thrown across the room, because the next moment I'd collided with the cooking range, banging my hip sharply upon it. The storm had charged towards us, faster than I thought possible.

Rubbing my hip, I went to the windows to shut them. Outside, the sky was dark purple and green, and the air felt as if it was made of lead, so heavily did it weigh upon me. There was no rain. Not yet. I stood at the window, mesmerised by the peculiar light, the prowling thunder, which now growled menacingly in a lower tone. The lightning, when it came, at first crawled uneasily amid the clouds, illuminating them in a sickly light. Then, as if a dehar of storms had thrown a trident, a triple fork of immense size was hurled from the sky. I'm sure I heard it land with a mighty crack somewhere in the direction of the Mynd. My first thought was: *the house!* I grabbed my satchel and ran down the stairs, wondering even as I did so whether it was sensible to go outside. This storm wanted to injure and damage; I felt this strongly.

In the field, Hercules was standing with flattened ears, wild eyes, and a froth of sweat on his withers. He seemed petrified. I called to him in a soft voice and he came to me willingly, apparently relieved to press his long nose against my chest. Reluctantly – because of the metallic bit – I put the bridle on him, then vaulted onto his back. Whether this trip was safe or not, I was compelled to get to the Mynd.

We cantered through the trees along the forest path, and it felt as if the undergrowth was alive around us, crawling with hidden, mysterious life. There was now continuous low yet echoing thunder that sounded almost like the tolling of a bell, or perhaps the bell was sounding alongside it, an alarm from some distant village.

Even before we reached the exit from the trees where a wider path led to the Wyvachi estate, two hara on horseback came galloping towards me. One of them was Cawr, the other a har I recognised by sight but did not know. 'Thank Aru!' Cawr exclaimed upon seeing me, his horse skidding to a halt at Hercules's side. 'We were just coming for you.'

'What's happened?' I snapped breathlessly, dreading what he might say.

'I fear you're too late,' he said, 'but then it would have been too late from the start.' He saw my expression of horror and added, 'The family are safe, it's one of the stable hara. Well, *the* stable har. He's been with us for decades. Come. We must get back.'

I urged Hercules into a gallop and followed Cawr and his companion to the house. The lightning played games with us, striking the path only inches ahead of our straining horses. The animals were virtually uncontrollable, bolting in panic, but thankfully in a direction we wished for them to go.

I expected to see smoke or flames, or both, but upon reaching the Mynd there was no sign of structural damage to the house or outbuildings. But in the stableyard, the cobbles were covered in oily soot that was almost like tar, and a terrible reek of burned flesh hung in the air. I couldn't prevent myself gagging but fortunately managed not to vomit.

Cawr led me to the kitchens, where it seemed only a short time ago we'd been tending Gen's injury. The har on the table this time, however, was beyond my help. They'd laid him on a thick canvas sheet. His right side was burned completely, the limbs merely charred bent sticks, while his left side was unblemished. He stared at the world through one remaining eye, which was quite dead. Wyva was in the room, and Gen, both of whom greeted me gloomily. Myv stood beside the corpse, looking helpless. I went to him and put my hands upon his shoulders. 'Lighting strike?' I asked him.

He looked up at me, clearly relieved to see me. 'Yes. It pierced him in the middle of the stableyard, cooked him where he stood. We couldn't do anything.'

I remembered Fush's words: the *ysbryd dwrg*. I could visualise it prowling around the house; the lighting was its death-bringing gaze, the thunder its murderous voice.

'The *ysbryd* plays with us!' Gen suddenly blurted out. 'Injures me, but lets me live, then makes me witness this. Am I supposed to feel guilty?'

'Hush now!' Wyva said, taking his brother in his arms. But Gen remained stiff, straining away from Wyva's embrace.

'This is beyond your skill,' Gen said, staring at me with wild eyes.

'It's an accident,' Wyva said in a calm tone. 'Calm down, Gen, it was just the lightning. Could happen to anyhar.'

Gen screwed his eyes shut, shook his head. 'No, I won't believe that.'

'Ysobi...' Wyva appealed to me. 'Tell him.' The meaning in his gaze was clear: Convince him, because they all need to be convinced of their safety at this time.

I didn't want to lie to any of them, but then I didn't really know what was out there – not yet. 'It's a fierce electrical storm,' I said carefully. 'Anyhar out in it is at risk.'

'But *there*,' Gen said, his voice now little more than a sob. 'In that place. In that *exact place*!'

'Could happen anywhere,' Wyva said, turning to his other brother for support. 'Isn't that so, Cawr?'

'I suppose so,' Cawr responded, guardedly.

Gen fought free of Wyva's hold. 'Fool yourself if you must, brother,' he said, 'but there will be more. Pray to the dehara it isn't your son.' With these words, he left the room, slamming the door pointedly behind him.

Wyva shrugged at me. 'He's afraid,' he said. 'He's not over his own injury.'

There was an uncomfortable silence in the room. Myv seemed oblivious to his hura's comment and his hostling response, staring only at the dead har. Outside, rain had begun to pat softly at the windows.

Wyva sent to Gwyllion for the coffin maker and the corpse was wrapped and placed in an adjoining sub-kitchen until this har came to fetch it. Mourning friends and relatives filed silently into the tiny room to keep a vigil with the deceased until he was taken away. Myv stayed with them, sprinkling dried rosemary and torn rose petals upon the winding sheet.

Wyva ushered me into the main part of the house. 'Terrible thing to happen,' he said.

'The storm is very... strange,' I said inadequately. Was now the time to broach the matter of the *ysbryd dwrg* with Wyva? I could tell his defences were up and felt sure anything I said would simply bounce off him.

'Nothing we can't deal with,' Wyva said, with appalling heartiness. 'It's only a storm.'

I choked back a humourless laugh. 'What? Wyva... Somehar is *dead*...'

'I know,' Wyva snapped, turning to face me. 'His name is Briar and he's lived with this family for over twenty years. I saw him break from his pearl. You think I don't care? I do. You think I'm not afraid? I am. But I can't afford to show it!'

I stared at him, shocked. 'I'm sorry...'

Wyva shook his head. 'It doesn't matter. Leave it, Ysobi. Just leave it.'

He took me to the drawing room where Rinawne was sitting with Modryn, both of them looking subdued and pale. Rinawne gave me a look of naked appeal and I smiled at him, blinked slowly to indicate there was no bad blood between us.

Dinner was subdued that night, eaten late at ten. By this time, we'd all drunk rather a lot in the drawing room, and I don't think any of us really felt like eating. I didn't have the will to bring up the topic of Reaptide. I made excuses to leave early, around midnight, and Rinawne saw me out to the stableyard. The rain had washed the soot and smell away. Rinawne took me in his arms. 'I love you, Ysobi,' he said, 'enough to let you be. I just want you in my life, in whatever way.'

'I'm not going anywhere,' I said, and again a needling lance of remembrance shot through me. My own lightning strike. I'd once said that to Gesaril too.

Chapter Sixteen

On Lunilsday, Myv arrived at the tower alone at noon. He banged the great knocker on the door several times, no doubt enjoying the portentous clunk of it. When I answered the door, I laughed and said whoever made a sound like that must surely be a supernatural creature! I thought it had been the dehara seeking entrance. Myv smiled at me, pleased. I told him to put his pony in the field with Hercules and then come up to the kitchen. This he did obediently. Upstairs, I watched him from the window taking off the pony's saddle and bridle, his precise way of moving, the fuss he gave to the pony's ears as it pressed its head against his chest. Hercules had wandered over to investigate – he was always a placid animal – and I saw Myv give him some kind of treat from his pocket, again rubbing the horse's ears and laying his face against the broad neck. *The future,* I thought. *That small being will grow into a har and the weight of a community will rest upon him, as it does upon his hostling. May the dehara give me power to ease that way for him.*

I decided that for today we wouldn't do any work in the nayati upstairs. This would be an introductory session so we could start to get to know one another. I sat Myv at the kitchen table and offered him tea and a slice from a cake Rinawne had given me, fresh-baked from the Mynd kitchens, the day before. Myv accepted these offerings gravely. I could sense how seriously he took the job ahead – and could see his hostling in him strongly then. The adherence to duty, the ability to focus upon it.

I had no idea what Rey might've told him about the hienama's calling, but first I wanted to establish Myv's own spiritual leanings. I asked him what he believed in spiritually, giving him credit he'd know what I meant.

'Rey said to me we see and hear more than humans ever

did,' he replied, 'mainly because they let that part of themselves wither and die. But we do more than see and hear better – we have other senses that allow us to see... beyond normal everyday things.'

I could hear his previous teacher's words in his voice. He recalled his lessons well. 'And do you feel yourself that this is true?'

'Yes. There's so much all around us, all the time, that we can't see or hear. I practice sensing. Rey said you can pretend you're an animal and *feel* the world how they would feel it. This makes it easier to strengthen your senses.'

'Do you know about the dehara?'

'Yes. Rey said they are like the statues humans used to make of their gods, things we can put ideas into, a face for the natural forces around us. He said I should seek the dehara for myself, because they are something different for every har. He said also that I must be mindful of this when speaking with other hara. We shouldn't always think we're the ones who are right, because there are lots of versions of right.'

So, it seemed like much of the groundwork had been done, mainly in that Rey had encouraged Myv to *think*, not just accept received knowledge and seek no further. Once invited, Myv loved to talk. He was bursting with ideas and experiences.

'I saw some harlings from the other side of the river once,' he said. 'They were somehow like I practice to be, except I want to be as I *am* most of the time. Those harlings are like animals always.'

'Did you speak to them?'

'No, they didn't want to speak, and they often want to hurt you. It's best to stay away from them, like you'd stay away from an animal who'd hurt you. I know their paths across the land and they know mine. We don't meet now.'

This, to me, seemed encouraging. Harlings from both clans appeared to have a rudimentary mutual respect in terms of territory. This could perhaps be a foundation upon which to build. Myv talked of his observations concerning the creatures, plants and trees of the landscape. He perceived spirit within them and found it no more unusual to speak to a dandelion than he would to a har. This, he explained, was part of the hienama's way. 'We do the speaking other hara can't,' he said.

As I listened to him, I found more and more that I wished I could meet Rey. I approved of the education he'd given this harling. I liked his view of the natural world. He was altogether intriguing. Suddenly some words came out of my mouth that I hadn't planned to say. 'Do you know where Rey went, Myv?'

His gaze slid away from mine. 'Not... *precisely*,' he said.

I knew then he'd once made a promise not to say. I wouldn't pursue it now. As a hienama, Myv would have to keep many promises and secrets, and I didn't want to start bullying him into betraying them. He already knew when it was important to hold his tongue. I respected that.

'You know, Myv,' I said, 'most of becoming hienama will be through experience alone. Rey has taught you a lot already, I can tell, and I will teach you more, but at the end of it, none of us can prepare you for what your calling might throw at you – the individual problems and situations. All we can do is help you prepare the tools of your trade and tell you of our own experiences. You'll make mistakes – we all do – but you'll learn from them. The trick is not to judge yourself because of it...' I paused. One day I'd learn to practice what I preached. I couldn't help smiling.

'What is it, tiahaar Ysobi?' Myv asked.

'I was just thinking what I say is no more than a basket of words. I judge myself, I still make mistakes. I'm still learning. I'm sure Rey would say the same. Just be... *kind*, to yourself and others, but at the same time be firm – even harsh – when you need to be. Kindness is not always about giving in.'

Myv nodded. 'Rey once said our instincts are like a tracker. They already know the way, and can read the signs, but our everyday selves can talk very loudly and can argue against what our instincts know. We need to understand the difference. Sometimes, the everyday self has useful things to say, sometimes it's just afraid.'

'I agree with all of that,' I said. 'I wish I could meet Rey. He seems a very interesting har.'

Myv grinned. 'He'd say you were a bit stiff.' He covered his mouth with his hands. 'Oh, tiahaar, I'm sorry... I meant...'

I laughed. 'No offence taken. He'd be right!'

'I think he'd like you, though, after he'd talked with you.'

'Well, perhaps one day that will happen.'

Myv said nothing, and again I didn't pursue it.

'We might as well begin your caste training soon,' I said. 'When you reach feybraiha you can take the Ara initiation.' Given what Myv already knew, I felt sure it would be best, and most meaningful, if his first caste ascension took place during this rite of passage. I was confident that would happen the following year, if not before. He'd started growing before my eyes in the past few weeks. Perhaps Nature herself would accelerate his maturing, because he would need to be adult to fulfil his role properly. There was a vacuum within Gwyllion, and as the ancient saying goes, Nature abhors a vacuum.

'Are you going to stay here until my feybraiha?' Myv asked, a certain edge in his voice.

'I intend to,' I said smoothly. 'I can't make promises, because we never know what life might throw at us, but whatever happens, I'll make sure you have access to a mentor. High caste hara can communicate over distance using only their minds and the ethers.'

'Can you do that?'

'I've not used it for a while,' I said, 'but if I had to, I could.'

'Don't you speak to your family that way?' Myv asked, in all innocence. 'Your son?'

'They're not that highly trained. I send my son letters,' I answered glibly, knowing this young har would wonder afterwards why the son of a hienama *wasn't* trained in that way. He'd wonder why we didn't want to keep in touch with one another all the time, other than through the lengthy process of written letters.

I considered also that the instruction of a young hienama was not a short job. Myv would need the support of a trained har for years, at least until he'd ascended to Acantha. Many community hienamas didn't progress beyond that level – and it provided what they needed to function – but if Myv wanted to train further he'd need the assistance of others. Even in my own mind, I continued to hedge around how long I'd stay in Gwyllion. I still didn't think of myself as a permanent fixture in this community, and yet here I was embarking upon work to which I really should commit myself for a long time. It was almost as if I was waiting for something else, something my inner tracker was already aware of, something that would lead me away from these hara. I knew now I wouldn't return to Jesith. One solution to the problem would be that Myv could visit me wherever I settled a couple of times a year for caste training and ascensions, but we'd have to see. There was much to live through first.

Towards mid-afternoon, after so much talking, I sensed we were ready to conclude our first training session, such as it was, and told Myv we could continue in two days' time. Then his education could begin in earnest and I'd test his capabilities, particularly concerning healing, since that was most called-for in communities, not least for hara's livestock. He had already showed his aptitude for this when he'd helped with Gen's injury. Myv asked to use the bathroom before he left. While he was out of the room, I cleared away the tea things, considering I'd ride part of the way back with the harling and then leave the path to visit the Pwll Siôl Lleuad, see if I could pick anything else up. Rinawne would be over for dinner, but I had plenty of time.

Myv had scampered up the stairs to the bathroom, but when I heard him returning, his step was slower, heavier. This alerted me immediately. He came into the room, and for some moments looked far from adulthood, once more a tiny harling. His face was pinched and white. I went to him at once, and hugged him. 'What is it, Myv?' I asked.

267

'There was... a strange har upstairs,' he said, and then began to cry, a heart-rending sound of utter grief.

'Sssh,' I murmured, patting his back. I wasn't the most expert at dealing with harlings, especially those in distress. 'Are you hurt? Did this har speak to you?'

Myv sniffled, and I let him go to fetch a cloth for him to blow his nose on. Now, he looked embarrassed, clearly mortified he'd burst into tears in front of me, when he'd spent all afternoon proving to me how capable and knowledgeable he was.

'It's OK,' I said gently, handing him the cloth. 'You know there's nohar else here with us, Myv, so what you saw wasn't a living har. It's natural to be upset and shaken by that. Come on, sit down again for a minute. Tell me about it.'

He drew in a shuddering breath and went back to his seat at the table. 'He made me feel so sad,' he said, 'like I was nothing *but* sadness. His face was a like a picture of tears.'

'Tell me what he looked like.'

'He was dressed in shabby clothes, just standing there, looking at me. He said "Tell me if it's still happening" and every word was like a pin in my heart. I had to turn my back and get out, slam the door on him. That was wrong, wasn't it? Shouldn't I have stayed and asked questions, found out who he was and why he was so sad? I knew it wasn't real, tiahaar, and yet more real than anything.' He shook his head. 'I'm sorry.'

'Hush now, no need for that.' I sat down at the table and pulled my chair closer to his. 'Myv, I think what you saw was a human woman, not a har. I've seen her up there too.'

His eyes opened wider, and now curiosity began to suppress his fear and sadness. 'Really? Who is she? A ghost?'

'Well first, yes, *really*. Second, I think she might be an ancestor of yours, from the human era. And third, I'm not sure she's exactly a ghost. She's not alive here and now, but I think what we see is somehow more than a spirit.'

'What does she want?'

'Well, the answer to a question, don't you think? Something

bad happened here in the past, Myv, and she's tied here because of it. My inner tracker says to put clocks in that room. Don't ask me why, but I believe this will draw her out. That might be why you saw her today, so clearly, in daylight.'

Myv smiled in a watery way, his eyes still wet. 'I did wonder about the clocks! So you're helping her.'

'I hope to.'

'Can I help with that too?'

I hesitated. 'Well, we'll see.'

He looked crestfallen, perhaps thinking he'd failed a test.

I put a hand on his arm. 'It isn't because I don't think you're capable, Myv. It's just that at the moment I don't know what I'm dealing with, and I don't want to put you in danger. Let me find some things out for myself first, then perhaps you can help.'

He nodded. 'All right.'

I realised that Myv – as the future generation – deserved to be part of what I was doing, but I had spoken the truth. He should be intrinsic in the cleansing of this community, but must also be protected. It was a tricky and precarious situation. There was also another delicate aspect to consider. 'Myv,' I said, 'Please don't mention what you saw here at home. I don't like asking you to keep it secret, but your hostling is extremely sensitive about past history. We mustn't worry him yet, mainly because I don't know why that woman's here. Do you understand?'

'Oh yes,' Myv said firmly. 'Rey told me long ago that some things I see I should never mention to anyhar.' He looked at me earnestly. 'He said it was to protect my family.'

Again, the urge to probe and question, but I let it lie. 'Then heed what he said. I'll not keep you in the dark for any longer than is necessary, I promise.'

'Rey said the same,' Myv murmured bitterly. 'Then he was gone.'

I paused for a moment, then asked. 'Myv... have you noticed anything strange at home recently, similar to the woman you just saw?'

'There has always been... strange things,' he replied.

'What like?'

He shrugged. 'Feelings, mostly, not all of them good. Sometimes I see shadows that move, or pale things moving within shadow. Rey told me they were part of the past, that I shouldn't mind them.'

'And he told you not to speak about them as well?'

Myv nodded. 'It's best the others don't know. I know my hostling worries a lot. He hides it, but I can hear him thinking. He dreams badly too.'

'Can you see his dreams?'

'Only by accident sometimes. I don't try to, because they're horrible. Monsters without faces that can scream.'

'Has he always had these dreams?'

'Yes, but I don't think he remembers them when he's awake.'

'Let's hope not.' I took Myv's shoulders in a strong hold. 'Listen to me: I'd like you to take extra care at home now. Did Rey teach you anything about self-protection?'

Myv looked almost insulted. 'Tiahaar, I have *always* done that.' He paused. 'Is something going to happen?'

'Yes, I think it is. I'm going to see your hura, Medoc, tomorrow. Again, please don't mention this to anyhar. I'll tell you what I can afterwards. I know this involves your family, Myv, and I won't hide things from you if I can possibly help it.'

The harling's eyes had widened, excited. 'Is it to do with that woman upstairs?'

'Yes, I believe so. She has something she wants to tell us about your family's history, and I'm hoping that will help us deal with what's building up now.'

'It's me, isn't it?' Myv said, his shoulders slumping. 'Rey warned me things might change as I grew older.'

'Yes, I think you're part of it, through no fault of your own. But I also believe it isn't something we can't deal with. Do you trust me?'

Myv drew in his breath, straightened on his chair. 'Wyva asked the dehara for a hienama. You came to us. I *have* to trust you.'

Although I'd planned to ride part of the way home with Myv, I now let him leave the tower ahead of me, mainly because I knew he'd want to ask more questions about what he'd seen and about his family's past. I didn't want to deal with this because I didn't want to lie to him, but neither would I feel comfortable confiding in him fully just yet. It was his right to know, of course, but he was still so young and what I'd sensed in the Mynd, and in the landscape itself at certain times, was cruel and strong. I'd prefer not to have Myv tested by that at such an early stage in his training. Something had awoken and had come inside the Mynd, perhaps *back* inside. I watched from the kitchen window as Myv rode his pony back into the forest. He was a sturdy soul. I hoped this was enough to keep him safe.

Rinawne arrived early, and despite our air-clearing at the weekend, I could tell he was trying to disguise a fretful state of mind. I reminded myself he was my ally and friend. He wanted more than I was prepared to give him, but appeared to have accepted that situation gracefully. He deserved my full attention. Yet even so, I had to fight the sly little thoughts that slipped through the cracks in my mind, which selfishly wanted only to think about Nytethorne Whitemane. It was a difficult evening.

Over dinner, we made plans to visit Medoc the following day – the Wyvern domain was around a two-hour ride from Gwyllion if we went at a steady pace and didn't exhaust the horses. Wyva would be fully occupied with his community meeting until mid-evening. After farming out all his daily chores, Rinawne would have the entire day to himself. But behind our light-hearted discussions I could sense that Rinawne's discomfort lay brooding. He merely played with his food, eating little. I decided to tell him about the woman I'd seen – but for now omitting to mention Myv had seen her too – and my idea for drawing her out. 'She must know everything,' I said.

Rinawne frowned at me, a fork drooping from his hand. 'Why didn't you tell me about her before?'

I spoke without hesitation, and gilded my words with a white lie. 'Well, I wasn't sure what I was seeing, but I glimpsed her again earlier. I've never sensed her during the day before. Maybe she's the obvious key to everything, which I've overlooked.'

'Well, yes, I'd say she sounds pretty important! Can we go to the bathroom later? See if she'll show herself to me?'

'I think – if you're serious about that – you should go alone. Two living energies would be too much. I sense she's tenuous, even if her ability to manifest is strengthening.' I smiled at Rinawne over the table. 'I take it your scepticism has taken something of a beating?'

He grimaced, nibbled a morsel of food. 'You could say that.'

But my ghost didn't want to meet Rinawne. Although he spent nearly half an hour sitting in the dark there after midnight, he saw and sensed nothing. We'd spent most of the evening in bed, which had taken considerable effort on my part. I'd had to guard my thoughts, and withhold myself during aruna, because all I could think about was Nytethorne. Rinawne must have known I was holding back. I wasn't happy with myself over this.

I lay staring at the ceiling while, a floor below me, Rinawne tried to commune with my peculiar visitor. I realised that despite my best intentions, I wasn't remaining as impartial and sensible about Nytethorne as I'd so smugly thought. My muse? Ha! Where was this higher feeling my teacher had spoken of so long ago? I didn't want to be this har who fell into love stupidly, as if unable to avoid bottomless pits along the path of his life. I'd learned these passions led only to disruption and misery. When I fell, I fell fully, headfirst, heedless of danger or consequence. These passions, when they take a hold, have a life of their own and will not be denied. They put their hands over their ears and sing loudly to themselves to drown out the voice of reason. And now I could feel this creeping up on me, and my sanity stood like a horrified bystander, watching the inevitable collision draw close.

Rinawne left early, around one, because of the fairly long ride ahead of us the next day. I went to bed after clearing the kitchen, which didn't take long. By half one I was asleep. By quarter to two, I was wide awake, sitting up in my bed, my heart pounding as if I'd been running. The air was still and watchful around me. I got out of bed and faced the stairs.

Chapter Seventeen

I knew it was time. The tower didn't speak to me; it didn't have to. In the stairwell, there was an underlying calm to the air, yet also a subtle nuance of challenge. The light was bluish, the narrow windows channelling starlight. The bathroom door stood ajar. There was no sound but the ticking of the clocks, which in themselves created a strange orchestra. All sound from outside was muted. She was there, waiting for me.

I pushed open the door, which creaked alarmingly loudly, not a single creak but a series of small ones. I heard a sigh that swept around the room like steam. She was lying in the bath.

I approached, my breath stilled. All I could see was the back of her head and the dark water. She had cut her wrists, of course. The image was in black and white, but then there were splashes of dark crimson within it – the water itself remaining like ink. A smudge of red upon her pale shoulder. A few scarlet spots on the black and white tiles of the floor, and there the blade she'd used, with a rime of ruby along its cutting edge. The clocks ticked on, marking the hour of her passing. As she'd sunk from life, so her breath had matched the rhythm of the clocks, but becoming slower as they had not.

I looked into her face – her head had drooped onto her right shoulder. She had been lovely, as I thought. What had driven her to this? The answer was of course the answer to everything, or at least part of it. Then a whisper came to me, and I saw in fact that her lips were moving.

'I don't want to stay here.'

I wondered why she'd been held, in this moment between life and death. Had she done this to herself, or had some other force inflicted it upon her? I knelt beside the bath, my knees in her blood. 'If I can help you,' I murmured, 'I will.'

She said nothing more for some moments, and I wondered

274

whether I'd heard all I was going to hear, but then she sighed again. 'Cut it,' she whispered. 'Cut me free.'

'Cut what?'

'The cord of time.'

I knew this was *my* time, and whatever suffering she'd endured had led to this moment, me kneeling beside her in this room of red and black and white. 'Speak to me,' I said. 'In order to free you, I need to know about the past. Can you tell me what I need to know?'

Her lips trembled, but her head did not lift nor her eyes open. 'Cut it... Can't speak here in this midden... Don't want to...'

I had to steel myself, because only a heartless torturer could do this without flinching. 'You must tell me... Who are you?'

For a moment there was only the sounds of the clocks, and her shallow breath, which filled the whole room, felt rather than heard. Then: 'Arianne.' The beautiful word was horrible coming from that broken body.

'Arianne, I am Ysobi. Why did you do this to yourself?'

There was a distant echo of sad laughter – hers, although it did not derive from what was left of her in the bath. And yet the voice, when it came, was stronger. It appeared to emerge from what lay in the bath, and *was* her voice, yet the flesh did not shape the words, it was merely a conduit. 'Why does anyone? Certainly not because I am happy and my life full of joy.'

'Do you live at Meadow Mynd?'

'Not any more. I did. Now I am here, and now it is over. But I'm trapped. Cut it! *Cut it!*'

At this moment, something occurred to me, and I spoke from instinct. 'You are dead to mortal life, Arianne. There is no need to remain in this terrible moment. You are free to be what you choose. I have seen you standing in this room. Get out of the bath. Nothing's holding you there.'

For some seconds, everything stilled, even the clocks, as if holding their breath. I experienced a brief stab of pain behind my eyes, and my sight was occluded for a couple of seconds. Then it cleared, and I saw there was no one lying in the bath. Had I released the poor creature before I'd interrogated her? I hadn't thought she'd just disappear like that. Then I became conscious of being watched and got to my feet, turned round.

She stood at the window, illumined by starlight; not a ghost, but a woman at the end of human days, dressed in dark shirt and trousers, heavy boots, her long hair pinned up on her head, somewhat unsuccessfully. I glanced back at the bath; it was empty and clean. When I turned once more to her, she was gazing out of the window at the forest below.

'How beautiful the land is at night,' she said, one hand pressed against the glass.

'Do you remember all that happened?'

She laughed bitterly. 'My curse not to forget.'

'Will you tell me about it?'

She stared at me. 'This is strange. I feel alive, a person, but I'm not, am I?'

I didn't feel as if I were conversing with a spirit, but a real living woman. The clocks were ticking again, perhaps holding her together, anchoring her here. 'To be honest with you, Arianne, I can't answer that. I wouldn't say you're a ghost as such, in the traditional sense, because usually they can't communicate so freely. They're generally just memories we can see. I think this room allows you to talk with me, the part of you that still lives, perhaps the greatest part of all, which we're not meant to know about in our mortal lives. But that's not what I want to ask you about.'

She smiled sadly, gazed at me, a woman conscious of her own beauty yet not vain about it. A natural. This disturbed me, because I didn't recognise traits of Wyvachi within her, but bizarrely of Whitemane. Even by starlight, I could tell she was darker skinned than the Wyvachi.

'You're one of them, aren't you?' she said, matter-of-factly.

I knew what she meant. 'Wraeththu? Yes. But not one of the kind you ever saw. A hundred years or more have passed.'

'I can see that you're different, very different.' She sat down on the tiles and patted those in front of her. 'Come here, by me.'

I sat down in front of her, gazed into her dark eyes. Still that look of the Whitemanes about her, their rich, sensual beauty. Was she an ancestor of theirs?

'My name,' she said, 'is Arianne Wyvern, widow of Tobias Wyvern. I came to their house from across the river, because there is a bridge between our families.'

'You were once of the Whitemanes?' I asked, somewhat breathlessly.

'That wasn't our family name.' She frowned. 'I find it hard to remember, because everything across the bridge is hazy.' She rubbed her face. 'Let me think... My name... yes, it was once Arianne Mantel.'

'What happened to the Wyverns when the Wraeththu came?'

Arianne shook her head. 'Terrible things. My sons were taken, my husband killed, many others also. My daughters...' She pressed her hands to her eyes. 'It was yesterday, yet a hundred years ago, and it feels to me like both.'

'We have all the time we need,' I said. 'I want to know... all of it.'

What she told I later wrote down, sitting up for the remainder of the night, because I knew if I delayed the account through sleep I would forget details. She talked for perhaps two hours, but in that time, concisely, told me the history. Now it is a chronicle, in print.

The matriarch of the Wyvern family in the early days of Wraeththu aggression was Vivyen Wyvern. She had been a great socialite in her youth and was known as Vivi to friends and family. Her husband had died when fairly young, through one of the diseases that ravaged humanity at that time. She had three sons: Vere, Tobias and Erling. Tobias, the middle son took a wife – controversially – from 'across the river' from another land-owning family, the Mantels, who were regarded locally as eccentric and wild. They were not local people but had come from somewhere else. Arianne Wyvern, nee Mantel, had six children with Tobias, four boys and two girls; this was a boon in days when human fertility was waning. For this reason, Arianne was much loved and revered by the Wyverns, and regarded in some way as sacred. It was commonly assumed that Arianne's husband would take over the family once Vivi passed on, as the eldest son, Vere, was sickly. As well as physical illness he was mentally delicate, and for years had had to be kept confined to the house because of his occasional ravings and other eccentric behaviour.

As human society continued to break down and the first horrifying rumours of the Wraeththu began to circulate, many human communities reverted to a kind of feudalism, since the remaining (very few) old landed families were often prepared to take local people into their estates and fortify them against threats. Generally, this threat was all too human; looters were common. Both the Wyvern and Mantel estates became fortified in this way, although there was much commerce between them. Differences were put aside in the face of common peril. They made a vow to defend each other's families, and the people dependent upon them, from the specific threat of Wraeththu.

Family members from far-flung corners made their way to these estates, seeking shelter and safety. Many had lost their homes. Vere, like some demented prophet, told anyone who would listen that Wraeththu would soon over-run the entire world and that all was lost for humanity. Vivi refused to countenance this outrageous idea, believing Vere's pronouncements to be no more than fanatical drivel. She strengthened her land's fortifications. The Wyvern wall could be seen from far away. Beacon towers were built on both sides of the river so that the Mantels and Wyverns could warn each other of attacks and if necessary send aid. They had many fit and able fighters between them, prepared to fight to the death for their land and homes.

For years, no Wraeththu presence came close to their isolated corner of Alba Sulh, and some among the families dared to think the plague had passed them by. They believed they were safe within their walls and alliances. What they had not accounted for was the Call.

One midsummer, it came. The air became very still, all animals and birds were silenced. Sentries on the estate walls were alert for enemies creeping towards them. Great torches had been lit so that none could hide in the immediate countryside. But no enemies revealed themselves. Vivi herself patrolled the wall, her hunting hounds beside her, but no one saw a thing. They just *felt* it. From the house came the eerie chanting of Vere Wyvern, uttering prophecies of doom. Vivi is reputed to have said to her estate steward, 'Either you silence that boy in a civilised way or I will do so permanently.' (Vere was at this time over forty years old.)

Vere *was* silenced, not by violence but by a drug that Arianne gave to him. The night passed without apparent incident, but in the morning the beds of Arianne and Tobias's sons were empty. Kinnard, Medoc, Gwyven and Peredur: gone. No one had heard or seen anything. At first, there was an intensive search, people believing the boys were hiding because they'd been afraid, but they were not to be found. A rider came from across the river to say that several of the Mantel boys had also disappeared, among them Bryce, Thorne Mantel's eldest son.

'They will be found,' Vivi declared furiously. 'If we have to scour every inch of this county, they will be found.'

Arianne, silently, left the family gathering and went to Vere's room. She woke him and asked, 'Were my sons taken, Vere?'

He replied. 'I don't wish to wake from the next sleep you give me, and pray you may gift your sons with a similar release.'

This was all she needed to know.

Arianne returned to the family and delivered the news. Predictably, Vivi would not believe it. The boys could not be snatched from a secure stronghold in plain sight. There was no way enemies could cross the wall unseen.

'Then search for tunnels,' Arianne said dully, but she sensed they had come by no means known to humankind.

Vivi ordered a search of the estate at once, as did the Mantel patriarch, but no trace of tunnels was found.

The Mantels were indeed eccentric and wild, and also different to the Wyverns in other ways. They were not 'old blood' in a nobility sense, and had come into money some time earlier, which had enabled them to purchase their estate. They came from what Vivi regarded as 'disreputable stock', and because of this they did have means at their disposal to conduct a different kind of search to anything the Wyverns could attempt. Their wily scouts, underworld bred, reported that a large gathering of Wraeththu was camped twenty miles or so beyond the borders of Wyvern and Mantel land. It was clear they had been collecting recruits. The Wraeththu were regarded as a sinister cult into which impressionable young boys were brainwashed. Other rumours about certain 'changes' being made to converts Vivi dismissed as superstitious nonsense. Both she and Thorne Mantel were determined to retrieve their boys. They would launch a rescue mission when the Wraeththu next went hunting.

Careful surveillance by the Mantels' subtle trackers revealed when the camp was most vulnerable. The Wraeththu did not go out daily to kidnap people, but appeared to venture forth less regularly on small raiding parties, during which only a few would be captured. The Wraeththu would then spend a couple of weeks enacting peculiar ceremonies with the captives, which were presumed to be the technique through which these unfortunates were indoctrinated.

When the news came that the camp was emptier than usual, Vivi and Thorne knew they would have to respond quickly. Vivi herself led her people north. Mindful of her own estate being left vulnerable, everyone who could hold a weapon was stationed upon the walls or ordered to patrol the perimeters, whatever age they were.

The desperate savagery of the Mantel/Wyvern attack was mostly successful and they managed to liberate around twenty boys they found in a bad state, apparently infected with some kind of wasting disease. Many of the Wraeththu left behind in the camp were slaughtered, as they'd been taken by surprise. (This was presumably because they were a fairly neophyte group, lacking the powerful leaders who would have sensed impending danger.) During the attack, one of Vivi's own grandsons – Peredur, almost unrecognisable – joined the defence put up by the Wraeththu. He had clearly already been converted. Vivi shot him in the shoulder and had him taken away from the scene of battle at once, believing that whatever had been done to him could be reversed.

Unfortunately, Peredur was the only boy of the Mantel and Wyvern families who was found. The others, it was assumed, had gone out raiding with the Wraeththu or were dead, or confined elsewhere.

Just as Vivi had known she'd have to act swiftly, once the Wraeththu were fully aware of the attack they reacted equally swiftly, fighting with a ferocity and speed the humans had never seen before. Reinforcements slunk in from the fields and forests, perhaps part of that particular tribe or called from other groups by unknown means. Their unearthly cries instilled terror, and caused many of the Mantel and Wyvern party to panic and run, or simply drop in their tracks to be butchered. Eventually, realising they had got the best they could hope for from the raid, Vivi and Thorne ordered a quick retreat, streaking back across fields and through forests to their strongholds. They had made rescues, but only one of their own kin.

Arianne attended to her injured son, along with two members of the family staff, while Vivi helped with the other boys they'd brought back. She'd found they were terribly sick with an unknown disease that was ravaging their bodies and had in fact appeared to have eaten them partially away. Due to these deformities, it was not immediately apparent what had happened to them, but to Arianne, caring for Peredur, it was obvious. He barely even looked the same, more like a beautiful wild animal in the form of a young *person* – she could no longer call him a young *man*. She felt she had been bleached out of him, for his once golden skin was now white, as was his hair. He was like no earthly creature. The only way he could be approached was when drugged, and Arianne kept him in a virtual coma, concealing what she had learned from other family members and pressing her staff to secrecy. But after a few days, one of the women told Vivi what she'd witnessed, and Vivi went herself to see what had happened. Peredur's gunshot wound had healed already, but stranger than this were the physical changes to his body. He was no longer completely male but some kind of 'intersex freak', as his grandmother referred to his condition. Vivi ordered him to be confined in a room in the attics, and that for now nothing should be further revealed to anyone else. Family members and household staff must be kept away.

The other boys who had been rescued died in excruciating agony, their bodies malformed, their flesh rotting upon their bones. Unknown to their human liberators, these were half-completed inceptions and without Wraeththu hara to tend them through the change, they had no hope of survival.

The Wraeththu retaliation, when it came, was devastating. Only Vivi's strength of spirit kept the Wyverns fighting. Fairly soon all contact with the Mantels was lost. Nightly, waves of attacks would come, with weird screams through the night that sent guards running from their posts. Many threw themselves over the walls, their hands clasped to their heads, to be slaughtered by those waiting below. Vivi sought out those who were deaf, either from birth or through old age and infirmity. These she sent to guard the walls and in some measure this was successful, since the battle cries did not affect them. But there were not enough of them to patrol the entire estate. Experiments with blocking the ears of guards were sometimes effective, while in some cases seemed to make no difference.

Refugees flooded to the Wyvern Estate, and despite dwindling supplies, Vivi ordered that all should be allowed within, after a body search to make sure no Wraeththu attempted infiltration. To Vivi, this was a means to get more troops rather than an act of charity. More boys began disappearing without a trace, and Vivi decreed that any who remained should be drugged and incarcerated to save them from whatever hideous fate awaited them at Wraeththu hands.

One night, a couple of months after Vivi and Thorne's attack on the Wraeththu, the beacon fire of the Mantels was lit, and at first the Wyverns believed their neighbours had survived, as they had, and that this was a signal. But it quickly became evident this was not the case. A swarm of Wraeththu attacked the wall. They made sure to light the Wyvern beacon, which Vivi believed would summon even more of them. As her people fought for their lives against quicksilver attackers who were ferocious beyond measure, she ordered that the fire should be extinguished as a matter of priority. This action probably saved the survivors.

Wyvern defenders recognised Wraeththu who had once been their kin and friends, now not even seeming to know who they were. Entreaties were met with savagery. Relatives were cut down without compassion, even the girl children. Boys were spared and taken. But Vivi would not accept defeat, rallying her ragtag army. Through some miracle, as the sun was rising, they drove the attackers back. But so much had been lost, and the soft daylight revealed the extent of the carnage and structural damage. It was obvious to all that another attack could not be survived.

Enraged and grief-stricken, after witnessing so many of her family slain, Vivi lost much of her reason. She believed that Peredur had called the Wraeththu down upon them. She ordered him to be brought out into the stableyard before the people, along with all the other incarcerated boys. She had Peredur stripped naked and tied to a stake. Then she fetched from the kitchen one of her grandmother's silver desert spoons and a meat knife. Arianne was locked in the attic, whether to protect her from seeing what would happen or to prevent her interfering, Vivi did not say.

She mutilated Peredur herself, in front of everyone. She took out his eyes, hacked off his genitals. To her, he was no longer her grandson, but a disgusting interloper in his body. She regarded Peredur as dead, and what lived on was an abomination. Let his fate be a lesson to all. Any boy who turned traitor in the coming days would be similarly punished.

After this torture, Peredur was left in the stableyard of Meadow Mynd, as an example. Arianne was forbidden to tend to him, or go anywhere near him, although she was released from imprisonment. Vivi needed her to care for Vere, who would tolerate no one else near him. Often, he just lay on his bed, screaming, as if all that Peredur had gone through had happened to him instead. He bled from the eyes. He pissed blood incontinently.

Witnessing all this, sitting beside Vere's bed, weeping out her heart, helped Arianne make her decision. The only regret she had was that she could not reach the yard where Peredur still hung, nearly dead, but because he was Wraeththu unable to die quickly. Her husband and daughters had been slaughtered, the fate of three of her sons was unknown. The last one, Peredur, was dying slowly, in terrible pain and fear.

Two nights after Peredur's mutilation, Arianne

administered a fatal drug to Vere, as he had asked her. She sat with him until he died. Then she fled to Dŵr Alarch, and there took her own life, unable to bear any more of the horror, or to witness the inevitable, unspeakable end to it all. But then there was no escape and she was held, as if in some endless nightmare, alive only to her memories.

Until I came to her. Until then.

This was all that Arianne knew. Once she'd finished speaking, I took her in my arms; she felt like a woman of flesh and blood.

'I can't go yet,' she said, her face pressed against my chest.

'But you *are* released,' I said.

'No. I don't know what happened afterwards. *That* must be what holds me here. Something else. The horror didn't end with my death.' She pulled away from me, wiped her face. 'You will help me, Ysobi.' This was a simply stated fact. She and I both knew I would.

I left the bathroom, and went down to the kitchen, where I recorded Arianne's account in as much detail as I could recall. When I'd finished, I put my arms upon the table and buried my face within them. I wept as Arianne had wept. I thought of what I'd seen at the Pwll Siôl Lleuad, of what had happened in the stableyard of Meadow Mynd, of the slaughter of the human Wyverns and those who depended on them. How *could* Wyva still live there, knowing about these atrocities? I thought now that Medoc had done the right thing in leaving that blighted ground.

I didn't have the end of the story – exactly how Peredur had died – although it seemed obvious to me his own kin, those who had become har, had killed him as an act of mercy. And now it seemed Peredur lived on in hatred and resentment... or....? The shade I'd seen hadn't radiated anything like that. There was so much more I needed to know.

I woke up around nine in the morning, still at the kitchen table, roused by the scent of cooking bacon and toasting bread.

Groggily, I lifted my head, expecting Rinawne to be there, but no. Arianne was at the stove, as if she was living a normal life, as if she'd come to the tower all those decades ago, not to die but merely to live here, safe. I was astounded. This was no ghost.

'Good morning, Ysobi,' she said, turning to me. 'You see, I remember your name. I didn't want to wake you. You've been up nearly all night, haven't you?' She smiled, even though sadness would always be etched into the history of her face.

'How...?'

'I don't know. After you left me, I wanted to sleep. Yes. Real sleep. I think it was in your bed. I hope you don't mind.'

'This is... I can't believe you can leave the bathroom. Arianne... is it possible you are again alive?'

'How *can* that be possible?' She grimaced. 'It isn't, but here we are. How do you like your tea?'

'Strong... very strong. And sweet.'

She placed a full cooked breakfast on the table before me. 'Eat. You know, I'm going to think of you as a woman, if that's all right with you. It will make this easier for me.'

'Of... of course.' My mind was in such a whirl, I couldn't decide if I was awake or dreaming. I reached out and grabbed Arianne's arm. Yes, felt real enough.

'Come with me,' I said.

She raised her eyebrows. 'Before breakfast? I haven't eaten for a hundred years.'

'Please... just a moment.'

She gave me a quizzical glance, appearing less unnerved by this inexplicable situation than I was. I led her onto the stairs and down to the front door. 'Open it,' I said.

She did so, still looking at me.

'Now go outside. Just onto the step.'

I could see she tried to, but it didn't work. She couldn't put a foot outside the tower. Bizarrely, this reassured me. I couldn't accept a woman coming back from the dead and taking up life as if she'd never left it. Strangely, it seemed I *could* accept a woman coming back from the dead and being stuck in a building like a regular ghost, if there is such a thing.

Arianne frowned. 'Perhaps I can only... *be* here.'

'I just needed to know,' I said. 'Maybe you did too.'

She hugged me briefly, and I realised how much I liked her already. Whitemane woman. Incredible.

We went back upstairs and ate breakfast together. 'One thing is better now,' Arianne said. 'Today I feel like all I told you last night happened to someone else. I'm me, yet *not*. It's like I've just been away, but have forgotten all about my travels. This is my tower. I always used to come here.' She looked around herself, smiling, then back at me with an arrow of a glance. 'So... what are *you* doing living in it?'

'There is so much to tell you,' I said. 'And I really don't know where to start. Purely about me...?' I shrugged. 'I work for your family, your descendants. This tower came with the job. I'm like a... priest, a doctor and a teacher combined. That's the work I do.'

'And everyone is a Wraeththu now?'

'Just about, yes. Humanity has all but died out, although some hara seek to preserve them.'

She grimaced. 'How grotesque. Like in a zoo?'

I laughed. 'No, not like that. Communities. Some humans live among hara in the great cities.' I took a breath. 'Arianne, I have to tell you something. One of your sons is still alive. Medoc.'

Her eyes widened, and she flushed, perhaps uncomfortably reminded of all she was trying to forget in these pleasant moments at the breakfast table. She swallowed. 'How?'

'Well, hara have much longer lifespans than humans, if that's what you mean. Other than that, he survived the early days. He doesn't live here now, but in the next county. He has sons.'

'You... *breed*?'

'Well, yes. We're androgynes, Arianne. We're quite capable.'

'That's... *something*,' she said, clearly not sure whether to be disgusted, amazed, delighted or all three. 'So I'm the Neanderthal,' she concluded. 'All but extinct, and this newer race came to replace me.'

'That's about it, yes.'

'And I'm still a mother.'

'Won't you always be that?'

'You know what I mean, but it's all so... *distant* to me now. That has to be a blessing under the circumstances.' She shook her head. 'This is like being drunk. How can I feel this good? How can I *be* at all? It's as if I've come back as I was before everything bad happened.'

'Well, I hope to find out how all this possible. I think your original family know, or will at least be able to work it out. But they're not great talkers. They certainly won't talk to me.'

'The Mantels?'

'Whitemanes now. Their phylarch or leader is Mossamber, but I doubt that name means much to you. I imagine he's Thorne's son, so you're his aunt.'

She shook her head. 'So much to take in. Why the name Whitemane?'

'Most hara took new names when they were incepted, as your sons were, but it seems *they* didn't change their names. The family split in two. Those who live at the Mynd – Kinnard's descendents – are the Wyvachi. Medoc's hara are still Wyverns.'

'Kinnard didn't survive? Gwyven...?'

I closed my eyes briefly. 'I'm sorry... I know Kinnard died, but he had sons before that happened. I don't know what happened to their other brother.'

Arianne simply stared at me. I couldn't imagine how all this must sound to her, this weird Sleeping Beauty who had just woken up from an enchanted slumber. I took a breath. 'The Wyvachi and the Whitemanes hate each other. This is because of what happened in the past, and it's to do with Peredur.'

'Don't talk about him!' she said abruptly, raising her hands. 'Not now. Not yet.' Panic had come into her face, and a kind of transparency as if she was on the verge of fading away.

'All right,' I said soothingly. I wondered whether hara other than me would be able to see Arianne. Perhaps this was just *my* weird dream of reality. 'Much as I don't want to think about it – and I'm sure you don't either – we don't know how long this *existence* will last.' I paused. 'If you want to see Medoc, I can try to arrange that.' Assuming he wanted to see her, of course. How would he greet this news? How, for that matter, would Wyva feel about it? Even as I was thinking this, I heard Rinawne's familiar quick step on the stairs. He had let himself in, as usual. Arianne froze, eyes wide.

'It's all right,' I said, standing up. 'It's Rinawne. Your... *grandson's*... partner.'

'I'm afraid.'

She could say no more. Rinawne hurled himself into the kitchen, said, 'Aren't you ready? We've got a long ride.'

I wondered if Arianne would simply vanish, or if Rinawne wouldn't be able to see her, but then he noticed I had company. That was one question answered at least.

'Hello,' he said sweetly, 'who are you?'

Arianne merely stared at him in a kind of horror, as if the reality of her situation had finally hit her.

'A friend,' I said.

Rinawne's eyes narrowed a little, his expression hardened. 'You look familiar,' he said. 'Let me guess... Whitemane?'

'In a way...' I said.

'What's the matter? Can't he speak? I don't think I've seen this one before, but the dehara know their domain is overflowing with them. We've no idea how many there are.'

'Rinawne, shut up,' I said. 'This is Arianne, Wyva's... grandmother.'

'His *what*?'

'It's true,' Arianne said, standing up in a challenging manner, hands braced on the table top. 'I am Arianne Wyvern. Believe it or not, as you like, but Dŵr Alarch brought me through time.'

Rinawne looked at me. '*This* is your ghost?'

I couldn't help feeling smug. 'Beats your banshee, doesn't it?' I said.

Chapter Eighteen

Thoughts in Retrospect:

Medoc har Wyvern had fled Meadow Mynd in the grey light of predawn, allowing his hara only an hour to gather whatever belongings they wished to take with them. They had fled in fear, with the harsh words of Kinnard still ringing in their ears. Medoc told me that when he looked back, he saw his brother struggling in the grip of his chesnari, Yvainte, in the driveway of Meadow Mynd. Yvainte was holding him back. Kinnard's eyes were wild, almost senseless. He looked violent, but whether because he wished to cause the deserters harm or was furious with himself because he couldn't go with them, Medoc isn't sure, even now.

Whatever Kinnard might have believed, he *could* have left Meadow Mynd then. He could have started a new life beyond the reach of the past's hungry claws, those dreadful hooks that had sunk not only into his own flesh and that of his hara, but into the very fabric of the house they called home. These claws hid like thorny seeds beneath the soil of the restored gardens, from which the debris of war had been erased. They scratched beneath the fields where the Wyvachi now cultivated crops for any hara in the area who might need them, and the meadows where the placid cattle grazed, ignorant of the old blood that had soaked far beneath their cloven hooves. The claws lingered in the gorse of the ancient mountains that rose in their deceptively gentle slopes towards the clean sky. They clung to the smooth white stones at the bottom of the swift-running river and floated invisibly in the air that hara breathed. Medoc knew these things. He felt the claws scratching him in the night. And on that one night, when the terrible cacophony started up, and Kinnard and Yvainte's son broke from his pearl, and the curse fell upon them all, Medoc knew he could not stay. He was honest about it: he was terrified. No matter how strong he felt, no matter how contentedly he could reflect upon his glories, and bask in all that he and his hara had achieved since the early days, he was too frightened to fight.

Unlike Wyva, Medoc wasn't secretive about the past, not in the face of a genuine need for information. But this was because, of course, he'd got away.

Rinawne and I rode along the high-hedged lanes that were little more than dirt tracks. The day was glorious, so much so that even the inexplicable and unacceptable held no terror. The sun shone fiercely in a cloudless sky, but the air was a little cooler than of late, fanned by scented breezes coming in off the fields. As we rested the horses at a walk after faster travel, we talked about Arianne. Rinawne felt we couldn't just blurt the news out to Wyva. 'It seems too unbelievable,' he said. 'I can't help feeling she'd simply not be there if we fetched witnesses.'

'Yet *you* are a witness,' I said, 'and you saw her. You spoke with her. You touched her. Did she seem in any way spectral to you?'

He shook his head. 'No, but... I find this really hard to believe. As hara, we accept the unseen, the world beyond our senses, because for us it is more real than it was for humans. And yet this... it's beyond anything I've experienced or even heard about.' He stared at me. 'Ys, maybe you should contact somehar... you know, one of your high-caste friends. Arianne changes everything.'

'Let's see if she's still there when we get back,' I replied. 'I'm struggling as you are. It wouldn't surprise me if the tower was empty on our return.'

Rinawne grimaced. 'I'm worried that it won't be. This is huge, Ys.'

'Huge, yes, but we already know there are forces at work around Meadow Mynd that aren't part of everyday life. As we said, a storm is brewing. Arianne is part of that. Perhaps it's necessary for our cause that she's returned. Perhaps it's meant.'

As we'd travelled, I'd related to Rinawne everything Arianne had told me. At the end of it, his skin had taken on a yellowish tinge. 'I don't *ever* want to walk through the stableyard again,' he'd said. 'How could Wyva and his brothers just live there, cross it every day a dozen times, knowing what happened there? It's sickening.'

But that was all he said. It was easier for us to talk about Arianne's reappearance than the horrors of the past, because she appeared healthy, whole and sane. Neither of us wanted to talk, never mind think, about Peredur. I didn't mention that the stable-har Briar's death had most likely occurred in the same spot where Peredur had been tortured. Gen had virtually said so. I'd no doubt Rinawne had realised that too.

We passed a sign for Harrow's End, Medoc's domain. Our journey was nearly over. 'Well, we have to decide, Ys,' Rinawne said. 'Do we tell Medoc about her or not?'

I drew in a sighing breath. 'Well, personally I want to talk to him first, see if we can draw him out. I want to gauge whether he'll accept what we have to say, and guess at his reaction.'

'I've only met him twice, so I have no idea,' Rinawne said. 'He might just order us out, think us mad, or lying trouble-makers.'

'Well, let's see.'

I wondered whether to tell Rinawne that Myv had also seen Arianne, albeit before she'd manifested properly, but decided against it. At the very least, he'd be annoyed I hadn't mentioned this when he'd last visited. And yet, withholding that information made it a lie, and lies can be found out, and then there is trouble and upset and recriminations. But not today. For now, we had to focus on Medoc.

Harrow's End was more like a castle than a house, and had stood for perhaps a thousand years. Its walls were high, its windows narrow and it was built in a quadrangle around a central courtyard. A deep green moat surrounded it, over which a permanent bridge had been built, now mossy with age. Over the centuries, the buildings had spread and these formed the heart of a village surrounding the house. The formal gardens had been carefully restored, but were open to all, rather than only to those who lived in the house. That too, we quickly found out, had no silent or neglected corners. The past had no space to brood at Harrow's End, for it was a living, thriving community.

Medoc's security hara had told him two unknown riders approached the estate, and he rode out to meet us alone, no doubt curious as to who we were. The fact he had no escort indicated how safe he felt in his domain. He was surprised to see us, of course, and said, 'You have business with me, clearly. We will talk about this at home.' These words sealed the topic of our visit until we had been installed.

On the way back, Medoc told us about the house. We learned that when he and his hara had found it, it had been a virtual ruin. There had been, in fact, other large houses in the area that would have been more suitable for occupation, but Medoc fell in love with the ancient feel of Harrow's End. 'There are chambers inside it that haven't changed since the days of its construction,' he told us proudly. 'Naturally, I've been restricted concerning how much I could preserve in its original state, since Harrow's is now a home, a community.' He gestured at the house ahead and smiled in a somewhat dreamy fashion. 'History took place within those walls: political conflicts, betrayals, murder. But it also embodies love and continuity, strength and family. Fine old house, who's hung on despite all odds, while the race who built it fell to dust.'

Approaching it, I could see Harrow's End was imposing and solid, an edifice to take on challenges. This made me realise how wounded Meadow Mynd was in comparison; it did not stand tall and proud against the trees and sky, but rather huddled, cringing, close to the ground.

Hara gathered curiously as we rode over the moat bridge and beneath the dark archway into the courtyard.

'These are kinshara,' Medoc told them in a ringing voice, 'from across the county boundary.'

Everyhar would have known then: we were Wyvachi. I saw glances exchanged. Hara would wonder if Wyvachi were to be common visitors now. At midsummer, Wyva had crossed not only the boundary of the county but of the past. I could sense the Wyvachi were regarded as peculiar by the hara here – emanations of this opinion washed over me in an almost physical wave. But of course, as far as the Wyvern hara were concerned, the Wyvachi were cursed. This no doubt made them feel uncomfortable as we walked upon their land, entered their home. We endured a gauntlet of stares as we walked to the main entrance of the hall, and I wished Medoc had qualified his announcement to include the fact Rinawne and I weren't blood relatives.

Medoc took us to his sitting room, which was a room on the first floor, away from the busy hustle of the ground floor. This chamber overlooked the gardens to the back of the house, where there was an ornamental lake. Looking out, I saw harlings playing there, splashing in the water. Black-headed geese strutted among them, occasionally hissing and raising their wings at any who came too near. Beyond the gardens I could see hara busy in the fields, and carts of produce being driven along the winding lanes. A row of hara fished the river two fields away and between the water and the house were spreading reed beds. All around was a sense of industry and purpose, but also contentment and order. Meadow Mynd should be like this.

Rinawne came to stand beside me at the small-paned window while Medoc saw to refreshments for us. We exchanged a wordless glance. Rinawne sighed deeply. He was wondering what his life – and Myv's – might have been like if

Wyva hadn't clung on to Meadow Mynd. No resentful Whitemanes, no curse.

Medoc came back into the room. 'Please sit down, tiahaara. I've ordered a late lunch for you. You should have arrived earlier!' He wreathed this faint criticism with a smile.

'Thank you,' Rinawne said. He sat down where Medoc indicated, at a small round table near the door, which at present was cluttered with ledgers. I sat beside Rinawne, drawing my chair closer to his, closing ranks.

Medoc stood at the empty hearth, his back to it. He studied us disturbingly for some moments. 'You may tell me the purpose of your visit now,' he said at last.

Rinawne glanced at me, and I nodded slightly, implying he should be the one to speak. 'Tiahaar, I seek your advice,' Rinawne said. 'As you know, my son Myvyen is training to be hienama of Gwyllion, but I'm afraid for him. Things have... *happened* at the Mynd. Wyva won't tell me anything about the past, what instigated the alleged family curse, or even what form it might take. His brothers are also silent on the matter. I have no har else to turn to but you, and as we met at Cuttingtide I risked coming to speak to you. I felt you would at least listen to me.'

Medoc said nothing, while Rinawne waited in clear discomfort for a response.

'Something is in the house,' Rinawne said to break the silence, and then, either genuinely or in an attempt to touch Medoc's heart, Rinawne put a hand against his eyes and quietly wept. He looked lovely as he did so, his hair tumbling around his shoulders.

Medoc remained stern-faced to this display. 'Tiahaar, please don't,' he said gruffly and then took a breath, softened his voice. 'I'm not sure what I can do, but if I'm able to help you, I will.'

Rinawne raised his head. 'All I want is the truth,' he said, blinking his wide dark eyes. 'I'm of Erini blood. Once I know my enemy I will stand against it, but all I face is fog. I need to see through it.'

'What do you want to know?' Medoc asked.

'The full story,' Rinawne said. He looked at me. 'Please, Ysobi... would you tell him what we've learned?'

Without mentioning Arianne, or indeed any source for our information, I related that we knew of the Wyvern history up to the moment when Peredur was maimed. 'It goes without question the curse is associated with Peredur's fate,' I said, 'and perhaps directed by the Whitemanes, but we don't know the details. We don't know exactly what haunts Meadow Mynd.'

Medoc didn't respond, watching me carefully, betraying nothing. I went on to tell him what I'd seen at the Pwll Siôl Lleuad and some of what I'd experienced in the tower, and then related the accidents that had occurred at the Mynd, and the various signs of haunting.

When I'd finished my story, Rinawne took over the narrative and told Medoc about Rey and his disappearance. 'We believe Rey discovered something, and whatever it was frightened him away, or at least convinced him it was wise to leave.' He smiled at me. 'So Wyva brought Ysobi into this position, and he gives me the strength to fight, to learn, to mend. I want to believe it's possible to mend. I have to, for Myv's sake.'

At this point, as if waiting outside for an appropriate pause in the conversation, one of Medoc's househara knocked briefly on the door and came in with a tray for us. Medoc indicated this should be laid out upon a larger table that stood near the windows, where the summer light fell caressingly into the room. The househar worked swiftly, then left. Medoc indicated we should move from our rather uncomfortable and cramped seats and take our places in the sunlight. He had clearly come to a decision while he'd been listening to us and now came to join us in these friendlier seats. He poured out three tankards of cold ale from a sweating blue stone jug and handed them round. Then he drew in a deep breath.

'Wyva should have told you everything,' he said simply. 'I

can't see why he hasn't.' He sighed through his nose, somewhat impatiently. 'My honest opinion is that he should pack up that house and abandon it. He should find another property in the area if he wishes to stay near Gwyllion. But it's clear he won't do that. Given what you've related, I'm prepared to do his job for him and tell you the rest of the story, sorry tale though it is.'

And so the second part of the Wyvern history began, which I'll write as faithfully to what Medoc related as I can recall.

'I remember that when we rode to Meadow Mynd to take our revenge, it was as if the wind itself had taken on a voice, so great was the clamour. We shrieked and howled and sang. News of the undefeated humans had reached the ears of local harish commanders, and they didn't take the news lightly. From their perspective, if humans came to think they could take a stand against hara and win, it would make Wraeththu's task to control Alba Sulh more difficult. The Wyverns – my family – therefore had to be contained. The next time hara flung themselves at the Mynd's protective wall, it wouldn't be a motley bunch of random, loosely-allied phyles; it would be an organised attack, led by Malakess, the highest-ranking har in the area.'

I had to interrupt, just to make sure. 'Malakess? Do you mean the har who became High Codexia of Kyme? He is... was... a friend of mine.'

Medoc shrugged, clearly irritated his narrative had been interrupted. 'That I can't tell you, tiahaar, only that this was the commander's name.'

I apologised and indicated he should continue.

'The harish leaders were interested in people like my brothers and me, because we were... well... educated, and sons of a fairly powerful human family.' He raised his hands, perhaps at Rinawne's expression of disapproval. 'I know how that might sound, but trying to establish organisation within the nascent Wraeththu tribes wasn't easy. Hara were needed as figureheads, hara whom others would be glad to follow. We – and the incepted Mantels – were exactly the kind of hara Malakess and his fellow leaders were looking for, since those who'd been incepted with us had gravitated towards us, probably simply because they knew us. Both the Mantels and the Wyverns had protected people for a long time. Newly-incepted hara couldn't help but remember that. They trusted us. Kinnard, Peredur and I were the only remaining Wyverns, since our brother Gwyven had not survived inception. The Mantels, perhaps a stronger breed than us, had lost none to the inception knife. Malakess held all of us in high regard. He included us in his plans to subdue the remnants of our human families.'

'And you... just... went along with that?' Rinawne asked, his eyes wide, further disapproval oozing from him. 'You just... *killed* them, even children?'

'You have to bear in mind,' Medoc said patiently, looking directly at Rinawne rather than at me, 'that in those days newly-incepted hara were savages. In frenzied euphoria, we had cast off everything about ourselves we considered human, and this included ties to our families. We were young, and believed ourselves to be superhuman, capable of anything. Humanity represented everything that was wrong with the world – we sought to reclaim it. We weren't wrong, but our methods were. It was destined the world would become ours – we didn't have to slaughter to get it – but we didn't know that then.'

'But...' Rinawne had no idea what the early days had been like. So easy now for him to judge those who'd lived through that madness.

Medoc sighed. 'Look, I'm not going to go into excruciating detail about what happened to our human families, because I'm sure you can imagine it. Every single one of them, regardless of age or gender, was killed.' He looked at me and said bitterly, 'That is the shame of first generation hara. Is there one of us who wasn't part of that attempted genocide? No. We were all responsible. Is that not so, Ysobi?'

'Yes,' I said simply, my mouth dry, forcefully repressing unpleasant memories. 'Terrible scenes live within the minds of all who created our race.'

'We made a slaughterhouse of Meadow Mynd,' Medoc said. 'We left the bodies where they lay. Friends who'd been incepted with us took from Kinnard and me the task of disposing of our blood kin. They did this without being asked, because they *felt* for us. A cowardly way on our part, because we did not demur. We wouldn't have the blood of our sisters on our hands, but neither would we save them.'

'Did you feel *nothing* for them?' Rinawne asked.

'We felt very little,' Medoc said. 'Only that eradicating humanity was essential. We were half mad with the way we'd changed, conflicting personalities raging through us and the worst of both genders bursting out. It's impossible to explain to you really, because I can't go back inside the head of that har I was. But I suppose we must've cared in some ways, otherwise we'd not have flinched from doing the killing ourselves. Vivi was a different matter... I had no care for her then, and don't now, but the others... my mother...' He shook his head. 'We never found her.'

Rinawne shifted nervously beside me, but I pressed my leg against his, sent an arrow of mind touch. *Not now.*

'Deerlip Hall had already fallen,' Medoc continued, 'but all that consumed us, as we cut our way to the heart of the Mynd, was the dying screams of those who had been under our protection, the inceptees who Vivi and Thorne had stolen and let die. Their pain and terror had reached out to us through the ethers. We could not save them but we were there to avenge them.' Here, Medoc paused and poured himself more ale. He drank slowly, his eyes on his tankard, while Rinawne and I waited, almost holding our breath, for him to carry on.

'What you really want to know about is Peredur, isn't it?' he said. 'Now I'll tell you. We knew he was still alive, because we and Bryce Mantel, the erstwhile eldest son of that family, could hear him. Peredur called to our minds, in our dreams, as fragments of sound upon the waking air. This had almost driven Bryce mad, because he loved Peredur. They had come together very soon after inception. Bryce's only objective that day was to reach his beloved, come what may. If armies of iron had stood in his path, he'd have cut his way through them.

'But Kinnard and I weren't without our own perception of our brother's fate. The cries of Peredur's spirit were a raw shout in our minds; they haunted us constantly. We couldn't shut him out. We knew he'd been maimed horribly, *unspeakably*, even if we weren't sure of the exact details. We knew Peredur wanted to die but still lived on. Kinnard, particularly, couldn't stand the thought of this. He wanted to get to Peredur as desperately as Bryce did, but not for the same reason.'

Medoc drew in a shuddering breath. 'You have to understand that there was no way in a merciful world that Peredur should have survived. You don't have the full story about what Vivi did to him, but we found out... later, from the unincepted boys we took from the Mynd. She took his eyes the first day, his ouana-lim the second. On the third she... it was a torch of burning tar... So much damage.' He grimaced. 'Every day she intended to remove or ruin another part of him.' Now he paused to swallow, visibly nauseated. 'When we rode into that courtyard of death, Kinnard did what I would have done if he had not been the one with a bow. He shot Peredur in the chest. He was a good shot, always had been...'

There was a silence then, although we could still hear the harlings playing outside beside the water. Rinawne reached out to touch one of Medoc's hands where they were clasped on the table.

Medoc pulled his hand away before Rinawne could touch him and continued. 'Bryce... he simply rode through the bodies, the limbs, the chunks of meat on the bloody ground. It was like time had stopped. He cut Peredur's body from the post and rode away with it. You can understand then why he felt the way he did about us.'

'Yes,' I said. 'Bryce was... *is* Mossamber Whitemane, isn't he?'

'He was. There was never a great love between our two families, because the Wyverns had always felt the Mantels were beneath them. Circumstances had made us reluctant allies. But the reason Bryce hated us so much wasn't just because Kinnard shot the har he loved. It was because of what happened afterwards. Peredur was still alive.'

'He survived all that?' I asked, shocked.

Medoc closed his eyes briefly and nodded. 'For a time, but there were other matters to deal with that drove the Mantels and us even further apart.'

'Ah, the political side,' I said.

Medoc nodded. 'Malakess wanted to organise hara in the Gwyllion area. The idea originally was that Kinnard and I – with the Mantels in high positions within the community – would lead the newly-created phyle, but from the Deerlip domain. Bryce Mantel would hear none of that, and neither would we, in particular concerning our headquarters. We felt strongly we should be allowed to return to Meadow Mynd and establish it as the centre of command in the area. The place had suffered considerable damage, the outer protective walls had been torn down, but we wanted to restore the house, most of which still stood. You have to appreciate that ours was an old family, who had held that land for centuries. We had no intention of letting it go and were prepared to fight for it, even if that meant the risk of offending Malakess. Kinnard insisted that local newly-incepted hara would trust and follow us more than they would the Mantels, and that Meadow Mynd had been the heart of the community for a long time. Wiping away the worst aspects of the past was one thing, but equally important was a sense of foundation, of familiarity, on which to build anew.

'Malakess was eventually swayed by Kinnard's words, and agreed we could return to the Mynd. Bryce and his hara would be accountable to us, because it was important to establish a hierarchy, a leadership. Malakess insisted that personal feelings must be put aside, for the sake of Wraeththu as a whole. Resentfully, the Mantels agreed to the arrangement, on the understanding they would be able to retain their domain as well.

'Around this time the Mantels began to create their phyle identity, making themselves clearly separate from the Wyverns. We adopted Wyvachi as a tribal name. The Mantels took the name Whitemane and, as was generally the custom, also took new personal names. But we didn't do that.'

'Why not?' Rinawne asked.

'Because the names our mother had given us were ancient, mythical. We felt they suited our new being as much as the old, for we were very much drawn to the ancient history of our land. Our choice over names was perhaps – unacknowledged, as it had to be back then – our tribute to our murdered family.' He took another drink. 'Anyway, the negotiations had taken a few days, and by the time the future of Meadow Mynd had been established, we wanted to deal with family matters, and Kinnard wasn't shy of asking Malakess for support. We knew Peredur had survived and was being kept in the Whitemane domain. We found this abominable, because we were aware what state he was in, and no amount of Wraeththu healing could put that right.'

'Did you have no healers?' Rinawne asked. I could tell he didn't like hearing about Peredur's injuries and had asked the question perhaps to delay details he could barely cope with.

'Yes, we did,' Medoc said. 'Hara had been forced quickly to learn how to heal back then, although our abilities were primitive, not fully understood. Even those drawn to the healing path were merely exploring their capabilities rather than being masters of them. Peredur was dying, but slowly, kept alive yet not mended by the arts of the Whitemane healers. Nohar knew how long it would take for him to die. Can you imagine how we felt about that? We asked that Peredur be returned to us. Mossamber refused. At this point, Malakess withdrew his support, as he felt the matter was outside his jurisdiction. He told us emphatically that even though Peredur was a blood relative of ours, the ethos of Wraeththu was to discard old human relationships, even when family were incepted together. Everyone was har, one family. Peredur was Mossamber's chesnari, and it was Mossamber who should have last word on matters concerning him, should Peredur not be in a condition to make his own choices. Human blood ties didn't count. We were furious about this, and some of us even considered trying to take Peredur by force, but even Kinnard was sensible enough to realise we should push Malakess no further. The truth was, the Wyvachi had come out of the conflict well. Perhaps Peredur was a sacrifice we had to make, horrible though that was to us.'

Medoc rubbed his hands over his face. 'So life went on,' he said wearily. 'We burned the dead, we cleaned the land, we rebuilt, we organised, we created a community. We took in refugees, many damaged in mind and body. But we were always mindful of Peredur, a deep and suppurating wound we could not heal. We felt he should be with us. But Peredur had not asked to come home – we had to suppose he was capable of at least making himself clear about that. *And he would not die.* The seasons passed, our community grew and then... Then news came to us, not directly from the Whitemanes, but clearly Mossamber wanted us to know...'

Medoc stared at us for a few moments. 'I have not spoken of Peredur himself, what he was, *how* he was. As a child, he'd been fey, somewhat effeminate, yet brimming with life and energy that was infectious. You could not help but love him, in a weirdly helpless way. When we were incepted, he became this... *radiant*, almost ethereal creature. I can describe it no other way. I saw from the beginning he was made to be har, perhaps had partly already been so, simply waiting for the day of inception. We were all sure he was destined to be a great leader, but in a spiritual sense. What most interested him about his new being was the otherworld. I remember him once saying to me, "Meddy, we've become *other*. We've become what I've always sensed was out there in the land. Elemental."

'He always believed, during those early heady days after our inceptions, that Wraeththu would become something marvellous. He said we were still covered with the dirt of our humanity, but that eventually it would fall away from us, revealing new skin, as althaia reveals the new skin of a har. Hara could sense it in him, this connection with the natural world. They called him Silver Swan.'

'The song!' I said, unable to keep the words in. 'Somehar sang it to me, about Peredur...'

This time Medoc merely smiled at my interruption. 'When the silver swan returns to the old domain, then the bell of Gwyllion will have throat again, but that day will never birth, for silver swan lies in the earth.' He spoke the words rather than sang them. 'Somehar wrote that after his death.'

He sighed deeply. 'What we learned was that Peredur could bear his life no longer. He wanted only to die, yet could not. The gruesome fact was he had *half healed*. He couldn't be the har he believed he should be but was trapped in his ruined and barely functioning body. Nowadays, of course, he would have been nursed effectively, so as to have a full and productive life. We've learned so much, but then... We had no Gelaming... no true understanding of our abilities. All Peredur knew was that he was helpless; viciously blinded, unsexed, crippled, constantly in pain, hidden away, dependent on others for everything. All the wonderful potential of his new life had been murdered by Vivi. He asked Mossamber to let him go... no, more than that. To be merciful. You know what I mean.'

Medoc paused and again we could hear everyday sounds beyond us, outside: that beautiful day.

'They made a ritual of it, at midsummer, what we call Cuttingtide today. We didn't witness what Mossamber did, nor even heard how it happened. We turned away from it, never tried to find out, because Kinnard said if we knew, if *he* knew, he would have to kill Mossamber himself. But despite not knowing how, we knew the time of it.' Medoc again had to pause as memories came back vividly. When he spoke again, his voice was jagged.

'On that night, we built a fire outside the Mynd and sang sad songs. Hara came out of the twilight to join us. Somehar rang the bell in Gwyllion, in the old church, though there was not much left of it even then. But at midnight, the bell fell. It died. The har who rang it could have been killed; it just fell like a stone before him. Didn't even crack. Yet was silenced.'

I couldn't think of anything to say, my mind was numb. Rinawne looked as if he'd just witnessed a murder; his face was sallow.

'I can't say any more,' Medoc said, 'not now. Please excuse me...'

He rose from the table and left the room without another word.

For some moments, Rinawne and I sat in silence.

'It's like a cairn,' Rinawne said at last in voice that was barely more than a whisper. 'We discover stones to build it, one by one. A monument.'

There were still questions I wanted answering. Why had Arianne's body never been found? Presumably somehar would have visited the tower not too long after her death. The body should surely still have been there. And also... the bell. When the silver swan returns to the old domain, the bell will ring again. While the song spoke of a day that would never come, did it not also convey a different message? Could the end of the curse be as simple as returning Peredur's remains to the Mynd? I couldn't speak my thoughts, because – to say the least – it would have been inappropriate at that moment. Grief hung in the chamber like a gaunt ghost, even though Medoc had left it.

'He still hasn't told us about the curse,' Rinawne said. 'Do you think he will?'

'I believe so, yes. The impression I get is that, painful though this is to him, it's a purge.'

But Medoc did not return to us in that room. After some minutes had passed, his son Wenyf came to us. I don't think Medoc had told him anything, because he appeared cheerful and courteous, as if this was merely a social visit on our part. 'My hostling wishes me to show you around,' he said. 'Have you finished with your lunch?'

The day crept on. While I was fascinated with seeing the workings of Harrow's End and enjoyed everything Wenyf showed me, Rinawne was fractious and fidgety and could barely keep up a pretence of interest. I knew he wanted only to talk more with Medoc, find out about the curse. What was the use of us knowing Peredur's history if the narrative stopped at the part that would be most useful to us?

As dinnertime drew near, and Wenyf mentioned the family would like us to dine with them, Rinawne's patience snapped. 'I need to speak more with your hostling,' he said. 'It's why we're here. Could you ask him for me, please, if that's not too much trouble?'

Wenyf was taken aback by these words – and their tone. 'I will, of course, ask...' He glanced at me, and I made a discreet gesture to indicate I understood his surprise. Hienama to hienama.

'Thank you,' Rinawne said, 'unless you can tell us what we want to know?'

I put a hand on Rinawne's shoulders. 'Hush, now. Don't be an unruly guest, Rin.' He really did have the capacity to spoil everything.

'I don't know what you discussed with my hostling,' Wenyf said, trying not to sound stiff. 'What was it?'

'It doesn't matter,' I said quickly. 'We can perhaps talk with Medoc again after dinner.'

'It's clearly important,' Wenyf said. 'I'll speak to him for you, make sure he knows.' He indicated the stretch of the gardens. 'Please explore where you like. You'll hear the bell for dinner from here if you don't wander too far.'

Rinawne wasn't happy. After Wenyf had left us, he said, 'We *can't* stay for dinner. I have to get back. Seeking Reaptide sites isn't a good excuse for being away, once it gets dark.'

'You go back,' I said impulsively. 'I can stay. Perhaps it might be better if I try to speak with Medoc alone.'

Rinawne eyed me coldly. 'Well, much as I want to say "we're in this together", I can't make such assumptions with you. I suppose it makes sense for you to stay.'

I felt like leaping up and punching the air, as a harling would who's just been granted his dearest wish. Or maybe it was just relief.

'Shall I go to the tower after dinner?' Rinawne asked. 'See if your visitor's still there?'

'Yes, good idea,' I said. 'If she is, it'd be good for her to see somehar. She's been alone all day.' I paused. 'If she is there, Rin, please be careful what you say to her about today.'

Rinawne expressed a snort. 'You think I'm stupid, don't you?'

'No, I just think you trundle in sometimes, when a careful tread is more appropriate.'

Rinawne shrugged. 'I guess that's true.' He sighed. 'Well, I'd better get going, otherwise I'll be late home.' He hugged me briefly. 'Good luck. I hope to hear lots of interesting things from you tomorrow.'

'I'll be over,' I said.

Chapter Nineteen

Dinner at Harrow's End was a far more raucous affair than meals held at the Mynd. For a start there were around two dozen hara present, not all of them family, but members of the estate staff and various guests. The dining room was a vast hall in the centre of the building on the first floor. While the Wyvachi favoured subtly-flavoured foods, artfully arranged, Wyvern cooking was more along the lines of heaps of meat and vegetables thrown into immense serving bowls, from which diners helped themselves. One sauce, a gravy made from the meat, was provided in brown jugs that were interspersed among the tureens. Wine and ale were consumed in abundance. I was seated next to a har who worked in the stables. He told me Hercules was a fine horse, but then went on to recommend various dietary changes for him.

'He... just eats in the field where he lives,' I said. 'Isn't that enough?'

The har gave me a "look". 'Try what I said,' he advised patiently, 'then ask if it's enough.'

Medoc sat at the end of the table, far away from me, with his chesnari and sons, but he acknowledged me by raising his tankard to me several times during the meal.

At the end of it, after huge bowls of milk pudding had been brought in and devoured, Medoc stood up. He gestured to me and I rose from my seat, went to him.

'Come to my living-room,' he said. 'I'm sorry your friend had to leave before I could finish our talk.'

'That's all right,' I said. 'He had to return to the Mynd because of business... and...'

'Because Wyva didn't know he was here,' Medoc finished, smiling.

'Yes.'

'Well, in all honesty, I'll feel more comfortable continuing the story to you alone,' Medoc said. 'I could tell Rinawne didn't like a lot of what he heard today.'

'He's pureborn,' I said, 'and from what I can gather, until now his life has been easy and uneventful. He was... shocked.'

Medoc grimaced. 'These things were clear.'

Before we left the room, Medoc insisted I meet his immediate family, some of whom, of course, I'd met briefly at Cuttingtide. Thraine, the chesnari, asked how long I'd be staying. 'Just overnight,' I said. 'I have work waiting for me at Gwyllion.'

'Your training of young Myv amongst it?' asked Thraine, meaningfully.

'Yes, amongst it...'

I think Thraine would have said a lot more, but at that point, Medoc made our excuses and herded me away.

He led me to a low-ceilinged yet airy room next to the chamber we'd spoken in earlier. This was more of a family room, and I could tell he shared it with them from all the clutter left lying about. A pile of lean cats lay tangled in contented sleep on the long sofa and two hunting hounds were sprawled out on the rug before the empty hearth, which was flanked by two armchairs.

'Would you mind if I took notes, tiahaar?' I asked. 'If that makes you uncomfortable, please say so.'

'No, do as you wish. You should have said if you wanted to earlier.'

'I have a good memory,' I said, 'but remembering two long conversations might stretch me a little!'

Medoc smiled and indicated I should take a seat beside the hearth, while he went to fetch us drinks from a sideboard between the windows. He opened the panes upon the evening. Sweet-scented air, slightly cool, drifted in. 'It must've seemed stupid, me running off like that earlier,' he said. 'I apologise.'

'Please. No need to,' I said, taking out my notebook and pen and ink. 'It must be harrowing for you remembering what happened.'

Medoc smiled, glancing around the room, 'And here we are at harrow's end! You want the full story. Now you shall have what's left of it.'

'I appreciate this,' I said. 'I know in some ways you hate to speak of it, but I hope in others it provides a release.'

'Well, our skeletons are kept neatly in their cupboards,' Medoc said, his words again mellowed by his gentle smile. 'They are polished bones, brought out occasionally so they don't accumulate dust or start to rot and cause problems.'

I returned his smile. 'Then I'm ready to continue the ritual viewing.'

Medoc sat down opposite me. 'One thing's for sure, Meadow Mynd will always be haunted by knowledge of the past, but those of us who lived there in the early days of the Wraeththu era just got on with our lives. We established the community, built trade links with other phyles in the area. We reclaimed some of the ruined towns and villages and rebuilt them, leaving others to be swallowed by the green, nature's devouring wave. We salvaged what we could from what humanity had left behind, discarding all that we felt should be forgotten.'

He took a drink, stared at the iron grate where in winter time logs would burn. Perhaps he saw a fire there, from long ago. 'In those days,' he continued, 'procreation was rare.' A glance to me. 'Well, of course you know that.'

I nodded. 'I've always thought this was a deliberate act of nature, because – let's face it – few hara at that time would have been suitable parents.'

'Yes, very true. But then, once we'd learned more about ourselves as hara, so nature gave concessions and the first harlings began to appear. Do you remember how miraculous and strange we used to think that was?'

I laughed at the recollection. 'Very much so. Somehow, we blundered through. Hienamas were thrown into dealing with delivering pearls, as if we were experts, yet we had no more knowledge than the hara in our care.'

'I know... Well, around thirty years after Peredur's death, Kinnard found he was with pearl. None of us realised it for a while, not even him. I knew, because he'd told me, that he and Yvainte had *experimented* with aruna, because they wanted to have a harling, yet their success took them by surprise. But once the pearl was confirmed by our hienama, our hara rejoiced. Here was the living proof that Wraeththu were truly the inheritors of the earth. We would continue once humanity had vanished completely. That is, in fact, a moment in a har's life that's as pivotal as awaking from inception – or it was then.'

'I know. The first time I saw a pearl I couldn't quite believe it. Even watching a harling crawl from its broken covering some weeks later seemed like something from a fairy tale, part wondrous, part grotesque.'

Medoc took a long drink, pulled a comical face. 'I felt the same. Squeamish! Anyway, Kinnard's pearl attracted the attention of hienamas and tribal leaders near and far, who wished to study the phenomenon, to acquire knowledge for their own hara. A kind of peace reigned in Meadow Mynd. It was like...' Medoc's expression became wistful, '...the tranquillity after an atrocity has taken place and the storm of grief has passed.' He sighed. 'It was a delicate peace, but we cherished it. We lived in something like a capsule of time, in an Alba Sulh that had perhaps only existed in the dearest dreams of men. The fields grew high, the summers were long. We learned to love again.

'When news of the pearl was made public, Kinnard and Yvainte were praised and adored, almost like religious figures. Congratulatory messages came in abundance, but none from Deerlip Hall. This didn't surprise us. We understood that Mossamber would feel bitter – the chesnari he loved had died under terrible circumstances. He and Peredur would never have harlings, the ultimate expression of love. But bitterness is one thing, resentment another. Some of us were under no doubt that Mossamber wished the Wyvachi ill and were convinced he did not want us to experience happiness.' He put the fingers of one hand against his lips, again staring silently at the grate for some moments. I let him have his silence.

Eventually, he said, with an emphatic gesture, 'This is what I think: the earth *had* changed during the Devastation. Energies that had lain dormant awoke, because they were no longer suppressed. Hara embraced the 'other' as humanity could never have done, not even those who were drawn to it. Perhaps Mossamber did his own etheric delving at that time. Historical griefs had soaked into the soil; buried but not wholly dead. My belief is that Mossamber was *partly* responsible for what happened next, even if unconsciously. But I need to be clear that I have never *wholly* blamed him, no matter what others thought.

'I understand,' I said. 'That's what I'll record.'

Medoc nodded. 'Good. Anyway, Kinnard delivered his pearl in the early summer. As far as its care was concerned, all we had to go on was hearsay that pearls took several weeks to mature, like eggs, and had to be nurtured in the same way. Daily, hara went to inspect the pearl, from the family to the hara who worked in the fields. Kinnard either lay with it in bed or, when his strength had fully returned, carried it around with him strapped to his body.' Medoc narrowed his eyes. 'We could perceive it *growing*, the uncoiling life within it. So strange...'

Again a pause.

'The weather changed as the pearl matured. The summer haze was extinguished by heavy rainstorms and gloomy air. Many of our crops were ruined. The river burst its banks and seethed over the meadows. Further towards the sea, it lunged destructively through villages. Dozens of homesteads were flooded. But we were determined not to see bad omens in these disasters. Summers *could* be bad. This had happened before and would happen again. We would cope with it.'

Now Medoc leaned closer towards me, lowered his voice, as if somehar – or something – might hear him.

'And yet in our home, all was not well. Inexplicable sounds were heard in the Mynd, curious scratchings and dragging in the walls. Hara heard thuds and scrapings in rooms overhead while they were on the ground floor. But if anyhar went to investigate these sounds, they found nothing. Several of the staff reported hearing groaning sighs in the attic corridors, sighs that followed them. Some took to sleeping in the stable block, because they came to fear the top storey. But even the stables weren't safe. The horses were spooked every night, and in the yard the rain made the cobbles rusty, as if with blood.'

Medoc shuddered, and now his voice was hardly more than a whisper. He gazed at his hands. 'I could *feel* him there, Ysobi, and was sure that if I didn't concentrate very hard, every time I crossed that stableyard I would *see* him, tied to that stake, the blood running from him to make the cobbles red. I kept my eyes on the ground, always. I didn't want to see...'

He looked up at me. 'Kinnard refused to succumb to anxiety. He was like iron. He said to me that if Mossamber and his kin were indeed responsible, sending evil thoughts our way, making our house feel the way it did, then we must fight them. He wouldn't be intimidated, and I could see he despised the fear in me. "Medoc, if you give in to terror, they have won," he once said to me. "Ban this feeling from you, refuse it!' But the truth was, I *couldn't* share his resolve, although I pretended to. I was also sure Yvainte felt as I did, but he kept quiet, avoided my eyes. I believe he knew that to voice the fear would help make it real, give it power. I knew it too. I was afraid to speak.'

Medoc lay back in his chair, tapped one arm of it with his fingers. 'In those days, four Wyvern cousins who had been incepted lived also at the Mynd. Beiryan, Caerwyn, Edryd and Meilyr. They too had hara who were loyal to them and in this way there were factions within the Wyvachi. The cousins weren't shy to announce their belief that we were under psychic attack from the Whitemanes. They claimed that Mossamber would seek to destroy the pearl before it could offer the world its gift, and that we could not stand idly by, refusing to admit we had a problem. They knew that approaching Kinnard with their fears – and their ideas for solutions – would be pointless, and so instead they came to me.'

'"We should make a stand," they said, "show Mossamber what we're made of. Instead of waiting here while he throws haunts at us, we should ride to his domain, fight back."'

Medoc rubbed a hand over his face, sighed through his nose. 'Part of me sympathised with them, of course, and yet I couldn't agree with their suggestion. I said that we couldn't invade the Whitemane domain on a whim, because we had no true evidence that the Whitemanes wished us ill.

'But my cousins insisted they had plenty. They reminded me of all the slights and insults the Wyvachi had endured over the years. For example, if any of our hara should come across a Whitemane in the business of his day, the Whitemane would jeer and laugh at him, make crude insulting gestures. Whitemanes openly spat on the path before a Wyvachi. Gradually, over the past couple of years, all commerce between us had ceased, where once there had been precarious trade. Lower ranking hara of both clans, who had still maintained a show of friendly relations – being once brothers in arms – now turned away from one another. If this wasn't evidence, what was?

'Meilyr was our cousins' spokeshar. He was of the hienama type, if not officially so. He suggested that rather than assaulting the Whitemane domain, the bridge between the two estates should be shattered, since it was, after all, a symbol, a connection between the families. Mossamber might be using its symbolism to further his aims on an etheric level. But I didn't think antagonising Mossamber at that time – in any way – would be helpful.'

'But I've seen the statues on the Wyvachi side of the bridge,' I said, 'well, what's left of them. Did Mossamber have them toppled?'

'Oh, that,' Medoc said caustically. 'He did that on the day he took Peredur home. With his own hands, or so we heard.'

I imagined then a grief-stricken har, his strength engorged with anger, smashing those gryphons to pieces. After he'd done that, had he fallen to his knees upon the bridge, roared his grief to the sky? This image seemed real to me. 'So, how did you appease the cousins?'

Medoc smiled sadly. 'I remember Meilyr saying to me once, "Don't become like the old cat who dozes by the fire, cousin. Remember the dog can leap on his back and break his spine."

'And I replied, "A cat is not a dog. He uses stealth rather than brute force. That is his natural way. He might appear to be asleep by the fire, but he is watching."

'But while I was proud of these words, Meilyr wasn't impressed. He insisted that Mossamber didn't want Kinnard to have a son and said to me, "If you refuse to believe this, you're a fool. He wants all of us to suffer as he does, as Peredur did. And don't question me, Medoc, I *know* this, as strongly as if Mossamber had told me himself."'

Medoc gestured with both hands resignedly. 'He was fired up, but then he'd always been of the fiery kind. I couldn't ignore him, because all our hara respected his power and his honesty. So, I offered a compromise. I asked hara with the strongest psychic talents to observe what they could of the Whitemanes. I wanted to find more evidence.'

'And was this plan successful?' I asked.

Medoc shook his head. 'Not really. My spies picked up shivers of energy that felt vaguely threatening, but obtained nothing definite. The Domain had strong wards around it, blocking intrusion on any level. Perhaps the fact they'd installed these defences was evidence enough of bad intention, but I couldn't be sure. As the days went on, and nothing happened that was worse than peculiar sounds and vague feelings of threat, I dared to think that perhaps all Mossamber was capable of was a grumbling sky, the symbol of his displeasure.' Medoc fell silent.

'That wasn't true though, was it?' I said, to encourage him.

He stared at me for some moments. 'Ysobi, to this day, I can't say for sure who or what was behind what happened. I can only relay what I experienced. On the day that Kinnard's harling began to break from his pearl, the sun reappeared. Everyhar took this as auspicious. I wanted to as well, but couldn't feel reassured. If anything, I felt worse than before: utterly unsafe, unable to relax.'

A stillness came into that room, then, and I too could feel how Medoc had felt, all those years ago.

'The house creaked,' he murmured. 'There were crackings in the timber all around us. Perhaps the ancient wood was simply drying out from the constant downpours, but it didn't feel that way. The Mynd *shuddered*. There were smells, as of burning, but also fires that had been dampened and the smoke gone sour.' Medoc shivered. 'The light inside the house went *green*, although the sun shone strongly outside. I can remember feeling at one point as if the whole building was under water, and had taken us with it. It was so hard to breathe it was like gulping dark water. I wondered if we were still alive. Can you imagine that?'

'Yes,' I said softly, and in my mind, a minnow of thought: *Mossamber drowned him. That's how Peredur died.*

Medoc now lay back in his seat, blinking at the ceiling, his hands resting on the chair arms. 'As evening came on we were drawn like ghosts ourselves to the upper room, the bedroom where the pearl lay. Kinnard, Yvainte, our hienama Arynne, all the cousins... They gathered around the pearl. They sang to it. Within each of them was the single, focused desire to shower this emerging child with their love, with their fierce drive to protect it. I never reached them to add my voice and will to theirs.'

'Why not?' I asked, when I sensed him pausing again.

He frowned, tapping the tips of his fingers together, spoke slowly. 'I remember climbing the stairs, or trying to, but my limbs ached and it was difficult to take the steps. Around me, the Mynd groaned and rasped like the timbers of a ship. The stairs seemed to rock beneath my feet as if we were at sea. I kept thinking if only the pearl would break, it would be over. The harling would be safely in the world, and the shining power of this new, purely-created being must surely eclipse all shadows of the past.

'But before I reached the room, the din started up.

'Out in the yard, the dogs started to bark and howl. I could hear the horses screaming, as if on fire, kicking at their stalls. I heard all the chickens squawking desperately. Later, hara told me they had tried frantically to fly, feathers falling from them in a cloud. They told me cats had streaked hissing from the house and run to the forest.' Medoc paused again, and I could feel his deep reluctance to relive these moments. He looked me in the eye. 'And beneath the terror of the animals, there was another sound: a moan, rising in timbre that sounded neither human nor harish, nor from any natural creature. I had heard nothing like it – ever.

'For some moments, I was paralysed. I clung to the banister, which shook beneath my hands, as if an earthquake convulsed the land. I could hear this *loathsome* voice, in my head, rather than my ears. There were no clear words exactly, just a series of terrible sounds like... like out of tune musical instruments and fragile things smashing. I can describe it no other way, yet even that doesn't really convey what I heard. But the sentiment within those sounds had the clarity of polished glass.

'This is what it told me: We would never thrive in Meadow Mynd and our offspring would perish. We were traitors, becoming fat on the suffering of others. If we wished to save ourselves, we must leave the house, burn it down, so its timbers would join with the ashes of those who had been cremated in its fields. It would never belong to us, nor to anyhar. If we defied this curse, we'd bring death upon our hara, starting with he who had just been born.'

Medoc shuddered. 'Oh, it was more, far more, than that, every atom of hatred and cruelty you could imagine. That terrible wordless voice screamed at me, and I knew the essence of it meant simply, "Get out ! Get out!" I hung half dead upon the banister, the only sure thing in my existence for those moments. Blackness closed in around me until I could no longer see. It was like no blackness you can imagine, for even with your eyes closed there are spots of colour or movement before the mind's eye. This was total, *dense* blackness. Dead. I thought then that was my curse – I had been blinded as Peredur had been. I couldn't even save myself, run out of that house, because I didn't know where to turn and the stairs were writhing beneath my knees.'

Medoc rested his head upon his hands for a moment.

'You can take a rest,' I said gently. 'Medoc... please...'

He looked up at me, and his eyes were bloodshot. Now that he'd started I could see he was unable to stop. 'I didn't see what manifested in that upper room, but heard about it from Yvainte later. He said that as the pearl broke, the light in the room became dim, almost purple in colour. This happened quickly, yet seemed to take a century. A shadowy shape gradually formed, so immense it had to crouch with its shoulders pressed against the ceiling, and its arms spread out to the corners of the room like the branches of a dead tree. It was a terrifying spectre, thin and gaunt, writhing within the space too small for it.'

Now Medoc pulled back his lips in a snarl. 'Think about it, Ysobi. That vision, that *horror*, was the first thing that Wyva har Wyvachi saw in this world. The first sound he heard was that foul cacophony. And yet, even with that memory, which I don't believe has ever left him, he chooses to remain at Meadow Mynd. And why? Because of his hostling. Because Kinnard drummed into him from day one that he must fight.'

'What happened in that room?' I asked, unnerved by the ferocity of Medoc's expression. 'How did it end?'

Medoc sighed raggedly, and the fierce glow faded from his eyes. 'Yvainte told me that all he'd been able to do was fall to the floor and huddle into a ball. He'd covered his head with his arms. The hienama – Arynne – had been thrown against the wall and lay slumped against it. The cousins had been similarly tossed aside, and were barely conscious. Yvainte heard them whimpering. But Kinnard?' Medoc closed his eyes for a moment. 'Oh my brother, my brother... After laying eyes on that *thing*, Yvainte and everyhar else in that room – but for Kinnard and the harling – had been blinded as I had been. But Kinnard... he roared his fury, picked up the harling, and ran from the room with it. He must've passed me on the stairs, but I didn't see him. I couldn't see anything.'

'How long... how long did it last?' I asked.

Medoc drew in a breath. 'I believe we were held in that blindness for perhaps two or three minutes, but it felt like an eternity. Without light. When Yvainte could see again, the apparition had vanished. But odd shadows remained.'

For me too, listening to his ghastly tale, the room around me had become weirdly shadowed. I found it hard to draw breath, felt disorientated. 'Medoc,' I said, with difficulty, 'what they saw in that room... was it Peredur?'

Medoc grimaced. 'That was the first thing I asked Yvainte,' he said. 'But he couldn't say for sure. It did have holes for eyes, but then its mouth was also a gaping black maw. The rest was shadow.'

'Do *you* believe it was Peredur?' I asked.

Medoc shrugged. 'It was partly him, I think. But more than that. *She* was in it.'

'She?'

'Vivi,' he snarled. 'I could *smell* her. She had never left us. If Mossamber hated and resented the Wyvachi, she detested us and craved vengeance.'

I sat up straight. 'So, what's happening now... you think it's her too?

Medoc shook his head. 'Not exactly. I think the spectre of Meadow Mynd is Peredur, Vivi, and perhaps all the others combined. A maelstrom of pain that has survived like a wasp's nest in the eaves of that house.'

'Including your mother?' I asked carefully.

Medoc glanced at me. 'No, not her. She wouldn't. Neither would Vere. Dehara bless them – they were gone. And I'm glad of it.'

'So Kinnard ran with Wyva and sought aid from the ethers,' I said. 'And that's how the moonshawl came to be.'

'Yes. It was Kinnard's belief, his *will*, that protected Wyva. I'm not so sure about the shawl itself – that was merely a symbol of Kinnard's potency.'

'Yet it protects the Wyvachi harlings to this day,' I said, 'and Kinnard is long gone.'

'Such is the power of faith,' Medoc said. 'But now...? I think it's too old and has lost its power. The thirst for revenge is gaining strength. I could feel it when I visited. The years have not diminished its craving.'

I hated to keep asking questions, because of Medoc's obvious pain, but knew I must. 'The shawl... I assume Kinnard had it made, that it wasn't just given to him by a spirit?'

Medoc nodded. 'Yes. The next day he visited somehar in the town who had a gift for such things. He demanded that har work day and night to create the shawl as quickly as possible. But... as I said, that was just his symbol. The *real* shawl was his ferocious will.' He stared at me. 'If your friend Rinawne has any sense at all, he'll take his son and leave that blighted place, because it's clear that Wyva won't do so. You must tell him this. Don't take any risks with a young life.'

I nodded slowly. 'I'll tell him all you said.'

'That answer isn't as clever as you think,' Medoc said harshly. 'You think you can fight it, don't you?'

I held his gaze. 'Yes, I do.'

'That delusion might be deadly.'

'Medoc, I'm no proud fool. I know my limits, but I really don't think this is beyond them. I'm not taking it lightly, believe me, and I'm aware of the strength of... whatever's there... but that land has to be cleansed. You must know that.' I paused. 'Would you prefer to stop here, or can you tell me what happened to Kinnard and Yvainte?'

Medoc drew in his breath. 'If I'm to relive this, I'd rather get it all out of the way tonight. I'll tell you. The truth is, though, I didn't witness their fates firsthand. This was because before morning I fled the Mynd, taking my hara with me – our cousins and others who decided to heed the warning. As we left, Kinnard told us not to come back. He would fight alone. Only a lunatic would have stayed, in my opinion, but Kinnard was always stubborn. He saw the curse as a challenge to his authority.'

Medoc sighed, ran his hands through his hair. 'Over the years, and once we'd established ourselves here at Harrow's, we sought reunion with Kinnard, but it never came to anything. However, whatever he'd done had been effective: Wyva lived and thrived. Kinnard had driven that malevolent force underground again and undoubtedly thought I was a coward to have run from it. He had fought and won, while I had abandoned him.'

'And yet... he died,' I said. 'How did it happen?'

Medoc pulled a sour face. 'Well, you have to appreciate that, even though our domains weren't that far apart, those of us at Harrow's never heard the full story about anything. We did learn that after a couple of years Kinnard tried to mend things with the Whitemanes, simply because the hostility was an inconvenience at times. Neither did he want the local hara to feel torn. You see, Kinnard and I had both felt very strongly we should be fair leaders – not tyrants, not some grasping throwback to human history. We were Wraeththu – above all that. I know Mossamber shared that ideal and most likely still does. But he couldn't bring himself to mend the hurt, no doubt because of his own pain. He didn't murder Kinnard and Yvainte, if that's what you're thinking.'

'I've never thought that,' I said.

Medoc groaned, rubbed his face. 'Now, I wish I'd done more to keep in contact with Kinnard, but after several rebukes I stopped trying. Yvainte died first – poisoned. Yes, you heard that right: a *har* – poisoned. They said it was something picked up from the land, as if the Wyvachi lived in an area where humans might once have hidden or used weapons that could kill like that. They didn't.'

'Were there no suspects? Did nohar look towards the Whitemanes?'

Medoc made a gesture with both hands. 'Yvainte cut himself on an old iron nail in the stables at the Mynd. That's what we heard, and I've heard nothing different since. It was hidden beneath the hay. Anyhar could have scraped against it, or they might not. Could have simply seen it, removed it, and not been hurt. Yvainte's wound became infected and his body couldn't fight it. The hienamas couldn't cure him. He died. And it happened very quickly, unnaturally.'

'What about Kinnard?'

Medoc stood up, turned his back on me wandered to the window. 'Well, he killed himself. Or that's the story.'

'Yvainte was dead, perhaps that...'

Medoc turned once more to face me. 'Nohar knew Kinnard better than I. He would *never* have taken his own life. I'm not saying he didn't love Yvainte or his family, but to Kinnard the tribe always came first. He believed wholeheartedly in his destiny to rule it justly. Also, it happened years after Yvainte's death.'

'So... what happened?'

Medoc came to sit opposite me once more. 'It appeared he rode his horse off a cliff and fell to the gorge below. Is it possible to make a horse do that? Unless... unless it was galloping in terror?'

'Pursuit does seem the mostly likely explanation, since there are far easier ways to kill yourself.' I paused. 'The death must've been investigated. Why was suicide the conclusion?'

'He left a note,' Medoc said bitterly. 'The note said, "This will be the end of it, for all time." I don't believe he was talking about his own life exactly. Perhaps he feared he might perish during what he intended to do. But his hara...' He gestured widely. 'They interpreted it as a suicide note and who of the Wyvachi would listen to me? I lived miles away, had run from home. But I'm convinced that Kinnard tried to take on that malevolent power, end the curse once and for all, and he failed. He was vanquished.'

'How old would Wyva have been when this happened?'

Medoc shrugged. 'Around sixteen or so, I think. Well past feybraiha, in any case.'

'I wonder how much Kinnard told him.'

'Well, some of it, obviously,' Medoc said. 'I talked with Wyva at Cuttingtide and it was clear he knew the basic story.'

I shook my head. 'He's a puzzle. He saw both his parents die under very suspicious circumstances. He knows the full story, yet like Kinnard refuses to budge.'

'That, my friend,' Medoc said, 'is perhaps as much a part of the curse as anything.'

'Hmm, to know the danger, yet lack the will to escape it.' I gazed at Medoc meaningfully. 'There might be more to what you said than you think. Kinnard kept your letters. I know because I've seen them. If he didn't care, or still resented you, surely he'd have destroyed them. So perhaps he *was* tied there, and a wedge was driven between you of more than personal feeling.'

'He never replied.'

'I gathered that. But perhaps he felt, deep inside, that what you'd done was for the best, and for all the hara who departed with you. Perhaps he made no contact so you were free to create your own new lives, far away from that twisted nest.'

'I'd like to think that,' Medoc said, unsure.

'I believe you should think that, no matter what.' I put aside my notebook. 'Thank you, Medoc.'

'Don't thank me. Now I'm wondering whether I was a fool to tell you the story, because it's only confirmed your belief you can fight this evil, this *ysbryd drwg*.'

'Oh, it was confirmed before I came here,' I said. I felt I couldn't tell him about Arianne at that moment because enough dramatic information had filled the air for now. It might be she'd faded away without me there to anchor her; I had no way of knowing till I returned to the tower.

'Do you really think you can win?' Medoc asked.

'Yes. I wouldn't go so far as to say it's a certainty, but the odds are on my side. I have the confidence of one of the Whitemanes.'

Medoc's eyes widened. 'You do?'

'Yes, and Myv is a sturdy little soul. I hope that between us we have the means to banish this historical parasite, this bad ghost, once and for all.'

'You have to wonder,' Medoc said, 'whether Wyva and Mossamber will thank you for it, if you succeed.'

I smiled grimly. 'If they don't, I can live with that.'

Medoc was silent for a moment, staring at me. 'If you have to, if you need a place, you are always welcome here.'

'Thank you. I hope, though, it's not needed.'

Medoc stood up. 'I'm weary now, wrung out like a wet cloth. I'll show you to a guest room, but stay up if you wish to. Hara will still be down in the hall, I expect.'

'No, I'd prefer the quiet of a bedroom. I want to write up notes from our earlier conversation, then sleep too.'

'Stay for breakfast, then. Don't rush off tomorrow.'

'I won't. Thank you.'

Medoc led me to a small but comfortable room that looked out over the farming land, the river, the distant trees and the even more distant mountains. Laughter came from the hall below. Before I began writing, I sat for some minutes on the window seat, gazing out over this placid, fecund land and prayed to Aruhani, dehar of aruna, life and death. 'Extend your hand, Aruhani. Be kind to those who have suffered.'

Chapter Twenty

The following day, I got home around noon, by which time summer was having one of its moods and had pulled curtains of petulant clouds across the sun, but at least this was a natural phenomenon, unlike the previous recent storm. Rain began to fall as I let Hercules into his field. Before I entered Dŵr Alarch, I stood for a few moments looking up at it, thinking of its history, its character, and wondering what might happen next. Because there had to be a next, now.

When I went into the kitchen, I found Rinawne sitting there with Arianne. If anything, she seemed more real than before, so much so it wasn't even disorientating, which in itself was odd. She was my visitor, a person who'd returned to a home in which she'd once lived. I did wonder though, what she and Rinawne had talked about.

'I take it Rinawne's been looking after you,' I said, as I took off my coat and hung it on the hook next to the door.

'I wish you wouldn't say that as if it were a bad thing,' Rinawne retorted.

Arianne and I exchanged a meaningful glance, and I had the feeling Rinawne had spent considerable time complaining about Wyva and the secrecy surrounding the past. She said to me, 'If it's possible, I would like to meet Myv.' So *he* had been one of the subjects.

I nodded. 'Yes... I didn't tell Medoc about you.' I shifted my travelling bag next to the door. 'The main reason being I don't want to disappoint him if it turns out your visit here is... only temporary. But Rinawne can get Myv here in twenty minutes.' I stared at her. 'And Wyva?'

'A bit at a time.' She grimaced. 'I can't shake off the feeling he won't believe I'm who I say I am. I don't want to deal with that.'

Thank you, Rinawne, I thought.

'But Myv...'Arianne said softly, 'a child born of... *not* a woman. Yet my great grandson. This little miracle I want to see.'

'Technically he's your grand high-harling,' I said, 'and yes, he is a little miracle.'

'Rinawne explained a lot to me,' Arianne said, sending a warm glance across the table to him.

I noticed he glanced at me furtively before smiling back at her. He could sense my thoughts.

'This new world is strange...' Arianne continued, oblivious to the undercurrents in the atmosphere, 'a return to some kind of idyllic past in some ways, yet in others utterly alien, as if people have come here from a different planet and taken the place of humanity.'

I smiled at her. 'Despite the upheaval, I like to think the world is happier now. There is room to breathe.'

'Humanity destroyed itself,' Arianne said. 'Some of us could see it coming and to be perfectly honest, I'm not sorry it's gone. Selfish, greedy, cruel, ignorant...' She shook her head. 'Wraeththu was both our punishment and a cure for us.'

'Hara aren't perfect,' I said. 'We can be all those things you just listed, as well as stupid. We're humanity's second chance, really, and we need to work hard not to ruin it.'

Arianne smiled. 'What I've seen so far gives me great hope.'

I was warmed by her words, but all the same, she'd only met two hara. She had no idea what was out there, the bad things that still happened, the power struggles that continued to be fought. Still, for now, I was happy to let her keep that feeling she called hope but was in fact relief.

There was a fresh pot of tea on the table, so I sat down and helped myself. 'Well, such thoughts aside, we might as well get to the meat. I'll tell you all I learned from Medoc.'

'From your face I can tell you've learned a lot,' Rinawne said, who had remained uncharacteristically quiet for some minutes.

'Oh yes!' I said, somewhat grimly, and turned to Arianne. 'I apologise in advance for some of what you're going to hear.'

She shrugged. 'I want the truth as much as you do. The pain I lived through was far worse than anything you can tell me now. Remember, I *saw* some of it.'

As I was speaking, relating the facts impartially, I wondered when in fact I'd have to reveal what I knew to Wyva. He'd be angry, of course, that I'd investigated his family's past without his permission, but would he be prepared to face up to what was happening now? A new generation of Wyvachi reaching maturity, the curse revived from whatever dank corner in which it had slept? He *had* to face it, and I didn't agree with Medoc's opinion that the Wyvachi should just run away. Whatever haunted the air around Gwyllion and Meadow Mynd was *wrong*, a remnant of a past best forgotten that should be erased. And if Medoc was right, and Vivi Wyvern was part of this lurking malevolence, there was even more reason to fight, to send this damaged fragment of a soul on her way.

When Rinawne brought Myv over to the tower, later in the day, Arianne held out her arms to him and he went to her willingly. She enfolded him, smelling him, perhaps holding him too tightly. But he allowed this. Rinawne had clearly explained what he could to his son on the way through the forest, and Myv being the har he is had simply accepted it. 'I saw you in the bathroom,' he said to Arianne. 'Did you see me?'

'Not that I can remember,' she answered, 'but I'm seeing you now.'

'You're here to help us,' Myv said firmly. 'This means we must win.'

I caught Rinawne's eye and he gave me a pitiful look, clearly not sharing his son's confidence.

'Now we must begin to make plans,' I said, indicating everyone should sit at the kitchen table. 'I can only use techniques I've employed in similar situations, which – I have to be honest with you – were far less... *entrenched.*'

'What techniques?' Arianne asked.

'Fighting will with will,' I replied, 'but making ours the strongest.'

Arianne nodded. 'I understand. This is what we called magic.' She grinned. 'Yes, I was known as something of a witch in my time. The power of the will... the connection between all things... Are we not on the same path?'

I smiled back at her. 'Yes, I'd say we are.' I was glad I wouldn't have to explain too much or – worse – have to explain to a sceptic what I wanted to do. 'We know more or less what we're up against. We can visualise the *ysbryd drwg* as a condensed ball of badness, whose skin we've got to pierce. First, we'll need to lure and confine it somehow. This can be done with focused imagery – again, our combined will. When we accomplish this, and the skin is breached, it's likely the badness will emerge. We'll have to transmute it into a different kind of energy and then disperse it.'

'Sounds simple,' Rinawne said sarcastically.

I ignored his tone. 'The main difficulty is that when the *drwg* – the bad – does come out, it will most likely disorient us or incapacitate us in some way. Fear and the fact we believe in it might be the *ysbryd*'s only weapons, but they are strong, despite not being physical. We'll have to support each other to keep our defences intact.'

'We'll have to give something also,' Myv said. 'A sacrifice.'

'What kind?' Arianne asked him sharply. 'Not a life... don't say that.'

I let Myv continue without interrupting him, not quite sure myself what he meant.

'No, not a life,' he said, 'but something meaningful.'

'You're wrong,' Rinawne murmured.

'How?' Myv asked, somewhat sharply.

Rinawne stared at his son. 'The face of the banshee.'

Arianne frowned at him. 'What?'

'That's what we'll have to face,' he replied. 'We have to make her turn round. And she will demand her price.'

Rinawne asked for a private word with me shortly after this dire pronouncement. 'Outside,' he said.

We went to stand on the tower's terrace, surrounded by my rudimentary attempts at gardening. 'There's something we've not discussed,' Rinawne said. There was an unfamiliar seriousness about him.

'What is it?'

'My son,' he said. 'Now, don't say anything – just listen for once. Over the past few days, we've accepted the unbelievable. We talk about taking on nebulous, possibly deadly entities, as if it's some little adventure. You've included Myv in this and because you have this glamorising effect on hara I've gone along with it. But just now, in there, it hit me. Should a harling be involved in this? He sees it as a game, I'm sure, and he's loving the way you've drawn him in, treated him as an adult. But Ysobi... *really*...' He pulled a sour face. 'If Wyva knew of this, he'd put a stop to it – and your work here. You'd be lucky to leave Gwyllion with your skin intact. Stand back a little, will you? Just think about this?'

I stared at him, seeing in his face that he'd braced himself for my retaliation, expecting to be beaten down with words. 'You're right,' I said.

He narrowed his eyes. 'I'm right, and then suddenly there are all the reasons that, even though being right, I'm wrong?'

'No, you're absolutely right. We're taking immense risks and if Wyva found out, the least he'd do is banish me from this place.'

'But...?'

'There isn't one. I just don't think we have a choice. Myv will be involved whether we keep him informed or not. He's always been involved, Rin – seeing and sensing things around the house, speaking with Rey about it all. All we can do is stand by him and protect him to the best of our ability. Cutting him out of our discussions would simply be unfair and disrespectful. Also, I like to think including him will do more to protect him than keeping him in ignorance.'

Rinawne grimaced. 'That was a paragraph of "buts".'

'No, it wasn't. I'd rather Myv was with us than alone at home with his hostling, who's in denial. I understand your fears, Rin, and I'm not belittling them. You've a right to be afraid for Myv, but you're strong and grounded, and an essential part of our team. You're his father. Who else could be more adept at protecting him?'

Rinawne smiled uncertainly. 'You assume that when whatever it is we have to face turns up I won't be running off screaming.'

I smiled also. 'Oh, come on. You're fierce. You wouldn't do that now, not if Myv was in any danger.'

Rinawne appeared partly reassured by these words, but really I didn't blame him for not being wholly convinced. 'Do we even know what's going to happen?' he asked.

'No, but we can take action and help guide events. We can't wait passively to find out, hoping it's something we can cope with. We have to make plans. We have to be firm. I'll put all I have into protecting Myv and freeing Gwyllion from this blight. That's all I can say.'

Rinawne sighed deeply. 'I remember the fear, Ys, from when I was a harling and that *thing* I saw began to turn round. The fear was irrational and consuming. I'm not sure making plans will help in any situation like that.'

I squeezed his shoulder. 'You were a harling. You're not now. Neither am I, nor Arianne. Maybe you had that experience for the very reason you'd be facing this situation now. Maybe it was meant.'

Rinawne expressed a scornful snort. 'That would be too convenient. No, it was just an experience, as all the things you've gone through as a hienama are experiences, and perhaps what we've learned from those things will help us now. That's the best we can hope for, I think.'

'Then that will be good enough. We start work now, today, building our defences, unifying our group. I hope that'll make you feel more confident.'

Rinawne laid a hand upon my chest. 'So do I. Don't be get me wrong. I want to be brave, and I'm furious this blight, as you put it, is threatening my family. I agree with you entirely we have to try to put a stop to it, once and for all. I just don't want to let the rest of you down.'

'I know how you've felt since Cuttingtide,' I said. 'You wanted it all to go away, have a normal, uncomplicated life. Yet you're here now, prepared to fight. That's courage enough for me.'

He smiled, stroked my face. 'When the time comes, just hold my hand and don't let go.'

The four of us spent the rest of that day meditating together, trying out various visualised scenarios, combining our intention. Arianne could not mind touch as a har can, but because three of us could put concerted effort into including her in unspoken communication, she was able to pick up enough to work with us effectively. Also, as she'd already told us, she was familiar with work of this nature, although she'd never had to deal with anything like the *ysbryd drwg*. 'Love spells, healing, divination... that's as far as it went,' she said. 'But I can feel what you talk about, Ys. I've no doubt it's out there. And I'm here now to help fight it.'

She wasn't scared, but why should she be? As far as Arianne was concerned, she'd already lived through the most terrifying things a mortal life can throw at you. I did manage to ask her privately during that afternoon how she felt about the fact part of what we faced might be a remnant of her mother-in-law.

She set her face in a firm expression. 'It's *not* Vivi. If there *is* anything of her in it, it's her grief, her fear and her anger. But it's not her entire personality, if you understand what I mean.'

I nodded. 'Yes, but whatever part of her it is, it will no doubt recognise you and seek your vulnerabilities.'

Arianne laughed coldly. 'Ysobi, I lived with Vivi Wyvern for many years. I learned how to cope with her then – and she *could* be a monster. I'm not going to let her bully me now.'

My little team had enough enthusiasm and courage for a group of ten, yet I was worried for them. I had fears I hadn't been prepared to admit to Rinawne because I didn't want to feed his doubts. Ferreting out information and putting the story together was one thing, but now that the time had come to act, we seemed so small in comparison to what we might face. This was a power that could engorge the skies and command the elements, could strike a har dead. We were one hienama, a har who'd never trained but had once seen a banshee, a human woman who might or might not be a ghost, and a harling not yet at feybraiha. I did wonder during that afternoon whether I was mad, and Medoc was right, and I was about to throw these good hara – and woman – into something far bigger and deadlier than we imagined. Still, what other choice did we have? If I went to Wyva, or even Mossamber Whitemane, and revealed my plans to them, I was sure I'd be met with scorn or disbelief or anger, or all three. This negativity would disperse all that we were trying to build up. I couldn't risk it. We had to remain focused, pure of intent and strong. Whatever happened, I would have to take responsibility for it.

In my room, before I went to bed, I performed protective and strengthening exercises of both mind and body – the Yogic Salute to the Sun, the ancient Cabalistic Cross, and the more recent Aegis of the Aghama. I prayed to the major dehara, visualising taking their qualities into me. I had instructed the others to perform similar exercises before sleep. To do this alone was important, for we must learn to muster our strengths in solitude as well as when together.

'To those benign powers who hear my voice,' I whispered into the darkness, 'guide my steps and those who walk the path with me. Stand at our side and lend us your vigour. Ward us from evil intent. In the name of He Who Walks Beyond the Stars, let it be so.'

My group and I must work to protect and strengthen ourselves from this day forward until Reaptide. Now, I must put all the might at my disposal to the test, draw upon my training, be what a hienama can ultimately be. The investigations, I felt, were over. Now was the time to act upon what I knew.

I was wrong. There was still more to learn.

Chapter Twenty-One

I woke up from a dream of drowning, gasping for breath, sweating so heavily my body and hair were soaked. There was an echo of a voice in my head: *Come find me, now...*

In the distance, outside, a dull boom of thunder belched across the sky. A flash of light rippled faintly across the ceiling of my room. Dream recollections trickled through my mind. In nightmare, I had relived images of the past, those early days of carrion stink. The echoes of cries both fierce and pitiful still haunted me. I recalled the hunger of flames in the night, cold laughter, and the wet glint of sultry eyes by firelight. Him – some ancient nemesis of mine, his name forgotten, the first of many eyes that had spoken across a fire, setting a pattern for my harish life. I remembered that I dreamed of him often, yet the memory rarely survived into waking life – before being here in Gwyllion. In the dreamscape, I had slunk by captives – not human, but hara. They'd been bound, mutilated, some dead, the casual victims of tribal rivalry, territorial dispute, execution. These buried scenes now blew through my mind like feathers in a storm. I remembered. Everyhar was to be feared back then... everyhar. We'd been capable of anything.

I sat up in bed, regulated my breathing. Those days were gone, far gone. Greened over. Forgotten. New lives had been pasted over them; respectable, thoughtful. We were *hara* now properly, elevated above the dross of history. This new sleek race, these angels of light, of freshness and clarity. The demons were buried now, stamped underfoot, groaning in whatever deep hell we'd squashed them into. Except... in our hearts...

This is the time. Now. Find me...

Dŵr Alarch was quiet, hesitant. I got out of bed, dressed myself slowly, with purpose. As I went out into the stairwell, the tower creaked a little, bringing to mind Medoc's recollections about Meadow Mynd on the day Wyva entered the world. A wind had started up, a hurrying wind, shooing the distant storm away. Rinawne and Myv had returned to the Mynd. Arianne slept, oblivious. I went outside.

In the rustling night, I whistled to Hercules in his field and, as always, he came to me trustingly. I put a bridle on him, then vaulted onto his back and urged him to a gallop. We followed the forest path to Pwll Siôl Lleuad. Around me the land was majestic and beautiful; trees had never been so tall, shadows never so deep, the sky never so high, nor encrusted with such vibrant stars. I didn't want this world to be an illusion. We *had* made it happen, reclaimed it, set it free. We'd paid in blood.

I heard through the rushing air a faint skein of music, a plaintive tune, sometimes so faint I could barely hear it; this drew me onwards like a light. As I reached the pool, the wind died down, and the scraps of cloud that had skittered across the sky fled to the south. Moonlight fell severely into the glade, creating hard angles, not entirely natural. I dismounted and pressed my cheek briefly against Hercules' neck. 'Wait for me,' I murmured. He at once lowered his head to graze.

I composed myself beside the pool, brought my heart rate down to its regular beat. Immanence sizzled in the air around me. Again that voice breathed into me. *Find me now...* And so I would, beneath these dark waters of the pwll.

I closed my eyes upon the world, went inward. At the same time, I offered myself to what would come. No holding back. Completely open.

In my mind, through history, I could feel hara approaching on all sides. I heard a low melancholy song on the air, and the muted thump of a hand drum, soft like the swishing of blood in the ears – that balcony we have over the inner workings of our bodies. In the distance the mournful tolling of a bell. I was drawn out of myself, sucked almost, the very essence of me. Into *him*. Peredur. And this is what he told me.

Mossamber held me before him on his horse, his arms so tight about me. His breath in my ear. *I will always love you, always.* He wanted someone to pay, but how was that possible? I was just a part of everything the world had become. I did not like the choice that had been made for me, but I had the power to refuse it. This was the way it must be.

Mossamber dismounted first and then held out his arms to me so I could drop into them. He was so strong, like a wiry hound is strong. I always felt safe in those arms, but they couldn't save me.

I knew the water was ahead of us, but only because I could smell it. But... was it just that? Then, it was hard to tell. I had no eyes, so how could I see? Merely a memory of that place? Yet there was Mossamber's face before me, the most beautiful face that ever lived. I *knew* that love in his eyes, in every cell of his being. I could touch and hear it, smell it, taste it.

He helped me walk to the edge of the pool, because walking was more difficult for me than seeing, even though I had the working parts to move. He waded into the water with me and I stroked his mind with the words, *Don't think it, Moss. You must go on.*

He smiled sadly into my mind: *I won't let you die alone.*

And I knew he was strong enough to survive, even if he stayed with me in the dark until the very end.

This place. This was where it must happen, where things had often happened so many years ago. This place, where first I'd discovered the unseen world, where a creature of water had spoken to me and changed everything. It had warned me though, even as a human child, that one day I would come here to die.

But what is death?

I heard those words beneath the water as we sank down to the secret depths, where once I had seen green eyes glowing amid the waving weeds. They weren't Mossamber's thoughts.

He kissed me, sharing breath with me, pouring into me his strength. Even now – hoping. *I don't care,* he told me. *I don't care about it. Please, Peri, please...*

But I care, my lovely one, I said. *I live with this ruin, not you.* I pulled away from him gently, touched his face. I could feel around us a cloud of hair, his dark, mine the colour of light. Water beings. Holding onto his hands, I drifted, breathed in.

I knew it wouldn't be easy, that it would hurt, that my body would fight. I was prepared for it. Then, the watery voice in my head.

Yes, that's it. Slowly... Breathe in... Breathe out... Let it go...

I could see the bubbles rising, like something from a swamp, disgusting. I breathed in the sacred water, I breathed out filth. It *did* hurt, but I'd experienced worse. Of course I had. I even laughed then, and a ribbon of tiny bubbles escaped, filled with blood. A fine moss of bubbles clung to my bare arms. I could see them shining. I could see...

The pain grew sharper. I felt I must burst.

Mossamber and I were flailing in the water together, in a maelstrom of silver spheres. The water churned, as if some wild underground spring had suddenly broken through the rock beneath us.

Now, said the water spirit. *Now, my son...*

I came to with a jolt, coughing, spitting out water. My clothes were wet. I was still sitting on the bank of the pool, but had I somehow wandered into it during my trance? My body shuddered and I had to lean over and vomit into the grass; muddy water, sticks and stones. I heaved out the contents of my lungs and my stomach for over a minute, then had to sit with my head in my hands for a further minute or so just to ground myself, regain my balance. I could still feel Peredur all around me. What he'd shown me filled me with a sense of apprehension and dread. By the dehara, he was powerful! I felt as if he'd reached inside me and squeezed my brain with a long-fingered hand.

I sensed a shadowy presence creeping around the edge of the glade, a predator, hungry yet cowardly. I knew for the moment I could let it be, until I'd returned to normal. I took a drink from the pool, which helped restore me and soothed my grazed throat. The unseen creature still prowled. When I felt the time was right, I got to my feet and summoned my strength. I formed a globe of light within me and then exploded it around me, crying, 'In the name of the dehar Lunil, master of the west, banisher of darkness, be gone!'

I heard a snarl, a faint whimper, then sensed it retreat. Some creature of *hers*, I felt. A watcher. So: she would *know*. Let her.

Now I would follow the trail: a faint ribbon through the trees, a scent of cut foliage, a wistful melody so distant I barely heard it.

My clothes were dry now, perhaps had never been wet.

Hercules was standing nearby, his posture alert, yet he was not too discomforted. He *had* waited for me, and horses aren't fools. He wouldn't have stayed if he'd been in danger. I called and he came to me, pressing his nose against my chest. I remounted him and turned him toward the river.

The Greyspan glowed in the moonlight. Still vibrating inside with an echo of Peredur's despair, I had to dispel the fear that if I set Hercules upon the bridge, the bricks would turn to mist and we'd drop into the churning river below. The broken gryphon statues on the Wyvachi side seemed to me like the bodies of real animals in the half light; dismembered, wings broken, tawny feathers scattered through the grass. I extended my senses beyond these shattered sentinels. I could perceive no guards ahead, other than the wild-eyed equine statues on the Whitemane boundary. There were no lights visible beyond the river, as if the domain on the other side was empty, unlived in for a hundred years. But then the foliage of the summer trees was thick, hiding everything.

'Well, my friend,' I said to Hercules, leaning towards his ears. 'Here we go, into the heart of it.'

Even without my urging him, he trotted onto the bridge, ears pricked, steps high, cautious, his hooves echoing loudly as if there were a high wall around us. Below us, pale sinuous shapes twisted and rolled in the water.

We passed between the stone guardians, and their cruel stone hooves did not come to life and strike us. They were lichen-covered, frozen in the act of lunging forward, their eyes blind.

Beyond the bridge, a wide gravelled path led into the gardens, beneath an ornamental arch covered in ancient ivy, wound with honeysuckle. I rode out onto an immense lawn, neatly kept, and populated here and there by yews, cedars and oaks. White deer grazed, ghosts in the moonlight. They shimmered away from me, as if walking on air. A folly temple glowed shyly white to my right, modestly revealed amid concealing yew hedges. And still I could hear that faint thread of music, a voice beckoning to me through the night.

The house was huge, larger than I imagined, and certainly not in decline. Built of grey stone, it was three stories high, with four rounded turrets, one at each corner of the domain. Lights burned dimly in a few windows. I could see a vast complex of outbuildings behind the main house.

I could perceive now that another river flowed behind the main building, not so wide as the Moonshawl flow, but that undoubtedly joined with it near the Greyspan. I rode to this river's edge, which came very close to the Domain itself. Here, I dismounted and tethered Hercules loosely to a birch tree, its trailing summer tresses rivalling those of the elderly willows that wept into the water along both banks. I again asked Hercules to wait for me, reinforcing my request with mental pictures. *If anyhar draws near, find cover...*

I followed the river towards the back of the house, considering it prudent to seek a way inside from there. I passed what were clearly farm buildings – a dairy, stables, a dove cote, buildings dedicated to cloth making and dyeing. In a few hours it would be dawn and hara would be out in these yards, seeing to the business of their day. I heard, coming from the south, across the Greyspan, an unnatural gulping yelp. Three times it called, then fell silent. The creature that had come sniffing at the pool could not cross the water, I thought. More distantly, Mossamber's hounds began their song at Ludda's Farm. After some moments, those cries too died away.

I edged towards what I took to be an entrance to the kitchens. Beside a half-paned door, a sneering gargoyle dry-retched into a water tub, an occasional drip falling from its lips. A boot scraper stood to the other side of the door. Perhaps Nytethorne had cleaned his soles there, a brown hand braced upon the old stone of the wall. He was inside this place.

I tried the door and it was unlocked. Attempting to fade myself as much as possible, I slipped within. I must be a ghost in these corridors. I must follow my nose, my ears. The music that had lured me was stronger now, sounded real; a wistful tune played upon a piano.

I didn't yet know precisely *what* led me, other than the sound, but my whole being, from the moment I'd awoken from my dream, had been a single driven purpose: Pwll Siôl Lleuad, the Whitemane Domain.

As I passed through the sleeping passages of Deerlip Hall, I felt as if many eras existed all at once, overlapping. Here, Arianne had grown up, a girl born into the end of human days. Before her, people who'd not been her ancestors had lived here, families going back centuries. Someone had lost it to gambling – that had been common. Before that, political terror, people in hiding, religious conflict. And then, way way back, before the first stones were raised, a village had stood on this spot, and a rough keep house had been home to one of the first lords of this land. I sensed it all, the lives coming and going, the small details, the births, the marriages, the deaths. Tears and laughter. Betrayals, the greatest of loves. All the ancient houses of Alba Sulh have these epic stories, forgotten and unread, unless you are prepared to open their pages.

I passed beyond the domestic areas, out into the main hall of the house. A lamp was lit upon a table by the door, emitting a soft orange glow. Boots were thrown in a heap around the table legs; gloves lay upon its surface like empty hands. I imagined boisterous Whitemanes shedding their outer clothing here, bringing in a scent of rain or snow or new mown hay.

Nohar stirred. Was this unnatural or simply because the Whitemanes were, amongst themselves, at peace, unconcerned about intrusion?

And then I was climbing, drawn towards the rear east wing of the house, drawn on by that skein of music. The stairs were grand at first, sweeping up from the ground floor, but then, above the first floor became narrow like the attic stairs of Meadow Mynd. I saw nohar, nohar living, although sometimes ghosts stopped to stare, or perhaps people in other eras who believed they could see a ghost.

I came to the tower door, and now the music seemed to come from all directions. I knew the tune, yet I'd not heard it before. A heavy scent fingered its way around me, redolent of summer gardens and flowers that bloom by night. I was like the prince in a fairy tale, slipping through an enchanted slumbering palace, up the tight winding stair to a room with a spinning wheel and a sleeping princess.

Mossamber would be waiting for me, I was sure. This is what I expected. He would live here in his shrine, surrounded by his memories and perhaps – as Rinawne had suggested – Peredur might lie enshrined in a glass tomb. Whatever I found, this was the only place I must be – the 'next' I'd known would come.

The tower was similar to my own except that it comprised only two floors and was smaller in circumference. The music became louder still as I climbed the stair. I had no doubt that it was real. I opened the first door I came to and emerged into a room with bare floorboards, except for a wide faded rug upon which stood the piano. Owl light from the sinking moon flooded the room through tall windows that overlooked the lawn. I couldn't yet see who was playing the piano, as they were hidden by a large music stand, but the melody flowed effortlessly, like water. I drew closer slowly, taking in further details of the room, the patchy walls, an immense gilt-framed mirror that was dappled with dark silvery blots, a sway-backed sofa draped with fringed shawls before a gigantic cold fireplace. A table between the two windows held a china jug of white lilies, petals fallen on the wood; their voluptuous aroma filled the air.

The music stopped.

I sensed the musician pause, aware he was not alone. I sensed trepidation, but also relief. I thought for a brief moment, *Nytethorne.*

Then the har at the piano rose, up like a pale ghost, hair around him in a moonshawl. He had stones for eyes. It was Peredur.

For several breathless moments I stared at him and he stared back with those sightless orbs, yet I had no doubt some part of him could see me well enough. Had I known this, suspected it?

343

Yet perhaps I shouldn't be surprised. Who else would I find in this enchanted room? 'Don't be afraid,' I said softly, 'I'm not here to hurt you.'

He came out from behind the piano, moving surely, his slender body erect. 'I know,' he said. His voice, of course, was beautiful, as he had been, or perhaps still was. I saw no horror before me, only this ethereal, surreal figure, with that abundant platinum hair, his features somewhat ascetic. He was Wyva viewed through a strange glass. 'I must say also, don't be afraid,' he continued. 'You're no shock to me, Ysobi har Jesith. You're only here because I allow it.'

'Am I the first?' I asked, needing a point from where to proceed.

'Rey saw me, if that's what you're asking,' he replied. 'Nohar else, beyond these walls.'

'But why...? Why keep yourself hidden, letting everyhar believe Mossamber killed you? Did you want to perpetuate the idea of a curse?'

He grimaced. 'The *idea*? Have you learned so little, Ysobi?' He came close to me now and in the meagre light I saw the scars upon his face, very faint. His skin was white, otherwise flawless but for those traces like claw marks, down his eyelids and cheeks. His lips were likewise pale, the same shape as Wyva's. Those stones that glowed where his eyes should be seemed to gaze right into me. Were they only stones? He wore a loose white shirt that hung off one shoulder, cream linen trousers, no shoes.

'What do you want of me?' I asked.

'For you to stop being a pest,' he said. 'Leave it be. I know you won't until you've ferreted every last morsel off the bone, so here I am. Now, be satisfied, and leave it be.'

'If you know me so well, then you also know I won't do that.'

He sighed. 'Even Rey had the grace to give up before you did. He'd be dead if he hadn't. He meddled too, through the *best* of intentions. It's not just *me*, you understand. You think you can come here and somehow heal everything?' He uttered a cold laugh. 'Impossible. If you care so much for the harling, steal him away, ride fast. She'll have him otherwise.'

'Vivi,' I said. 'Is that who you mean?'

He stood perfectly still, only his mouth moving. 'Who else? You've learned that much.'

'Why can't you stop her? What hold has she over you?'

'None. We are simply of the same fabric. She wants to be loose, but I won't let her. That is my only control.'

'So you hide here, denying yourself a life, but also denying her freedom.'

He smiled coldly. 'Well done, you get it. Part of it at least.'

'But Vivi, unlike you, is dead.'

Peredur exhaled through his nose impatiently. 'Nothing dies here. The land is a storehouse. Oh, we cursed each other well enough, she and I. We were bound from the moment she decided to dismantle me. As she took from me, so I took from her, not least the ability to move on. So she's my curse and I am hers. There are curses everywhere, to go with all the others uttered over the millennia in this land. Gods and heroes, goddesses and witches, all set free now the world is new again.'

'It must be possible to end this particular curse,' I said.

'You'd think so, wouldn't you?' Peredur sauntered to the sofa, his only betrayal of blindness the minnow quick reach with a hand to touch it. 'Sit with me,' he said. 'Let me taste across the air between us what has Nytethorne in such a bother.'

I sat down, conscious of the flush across my face, glad he couldn't see it. 'I'm not the first in that respect either, am I?' I couldn't help saying.

Peredur put his head to one side, a coquettish gesture that teetered dangerously close to being grotesque. Somehow, he managed to get away with it. 'So you're as afflicted too,' he said. 'Jealous? Worried you can't measure up to he who came before you?' He stretched his arms out along the back of the sofa.

I didn't enlighten him as to the true nature of my concerns about Nytethorne, and was glad he hadn't worked that out for himself.

'Don't worry,' Peredur said. 'They weren't close for long. Rey, like you, thought he was being clever, *detecting*. Then he found out the truth and realised he wasn't clever at all.' He smiled, more warmly now. 'Mossamber likes to play with your kind. He thinks you're like kittens chasing toys. Charming, really, but sometimes the claws do scratch and the kittens have to be put outside for a while, where they can't hurt anyhar, so they learn not to scratch.'

'I'm not here to play,' I said. 'As you allowed me in, do me the courtesy of finishing the story. You faked your own death, I take it.'

The smile fell from Peredur's face. 'How crude you are. If you must know, I truly intended to die, but what lives in this land, its genius loci that has nourished me since birth, wasn't ready to let me go. The water spat me out. Reluctantly, I was reborn. Mossamber had the idea that we should let the Wyvachi think I'd gone. They'd leave us alone then, and we could deal with Vivi ourselves, keep her busy, away from them and anyhar else.' He pursed his lips. 'This was not wholly successful, obviously. She's straining at the leash now, and power is building up that she can feed on. I don't know what will happen.'

'And you're quite content just to let that... occur?' I said, disgust purposefully injected into my voice. 'You'll let her harm Myv?'

'Oh Ysobi,' Peredur said, as if with pity, 'don't make the mistake of thinking I'm still what I was, that ingenuous, floppy fool. The Silver Swan, as they called me, gliding down an endless, peaceful river. The truth is, I don't care about anyhar beyond this domain. They bring disasters on themselves.'

'If you really think that, why have you and Mossamber worked to contain Vivi all these years?'

'Didn't you listen to what I said? It's not just her who has to be contained. She's simply a part of it, as am I. And you.'

'And me...?'

'Yes. You have made it so.'

'But what is *it*, in plain terms.'

Peredur sighed impatiently. 'I thought you knew. It is the *ysbryd drwg*, in the old language, an egregore of the past, created and moulded by those who suffered and died, and those who fuelled it thereafter. Tragedy goes back a long way in these valleys. The land as it is now, free of humanity, flexes its muscles, releases old memories. As I said, we're all part of it.'

I drew in a breath. 'Right, so let me get things straight.' I marked off my points on my fingers. 'There is a malign egregore and you *are* partly responsible for it. You say you contain it, yet you haven't done anything meaningful to actually stop it, even after all these years. Is there something about it that amuses you? Is it revenge, resentment, what?'

Peredur grimaced. 'It's just the way things are, a stage we set almost a century ago. The Wyvachi are as responsible for it as I am.'

'So you're saying both sides are prepared to allow Myv to be sacrificed on the altar of this poisonous belief?'

Peredur slapped the sofa with one hand. 'Keep up, Ysobi! It's not a case of what we can allow. None of us control it, not even Vivi. It's in the soil, the sap, the waters. Hundreds of human voices crying out, hundreds of hara. Did you know that the Wyvachi and the Whitemanes, under Commander Malakess's instructions, razed several phyles around here they thought *unsuitable* for this land's future?'

My face must have expressed my shock, and it was clear Peredur didn't have to wait for words to illustrate my feelings.

'Quite. You didn't know. Even in Wyva's early days there were still occasional purges. Nohar speaks of *that*, of course. They wring their hands and pull on their hair and weep about curses and terrible burdens. Perhaps they wanted the curse, in order to appease their guilt.' He shrugged. 'It's a wormy mess, isn't it? And so inconvenient now we're established and civilised.'

'So Medoc was right,' I said. 'He's worked out a lot of it for himself.'

There was a silence that again informed me Peredur didn't know *everything*, not for example that I'd visited his brother.

'So how is it you have the ability to contain this force yet can't dispel it?' I asked.

Peredur made an insouciant gesture. 'I'm alive *simply* to contain it. Hadn't you thought of that?'

'And yet you say you don't care...'

He sighed, somewhat irritably. 'All right, it's a nuisance. I wish it was gone. Mossamber *does* care, especially about the harling, although he'd rather die than let Wyva know that. Myv is the first harling to be born to that house since Wyva and his brothers. And now he's nearly at his feybraiha, his potential.'

'And events are building towards a climax,' I said. 'What will happen exactly? Do you know?'

Peredur nodded. 'At Reaptide, Verdiferel will be unleashed, and he is the guardian of the land at that time. He will inevitably merge with the egregore, the *ysbryd drwg*, and together they will bring a purge. None shall emerge unscathed.'

'So in some ways, this year Verdiferel will be a manifestation of every etheric force lurking about?'

'You could put it like that. We can go for years – decades even – when things are quiet and it's easy to maintain balance in the land, but times are changing. Myvyen har Wyvachi is reaching maturity. You must feel dark energy building up around you. I smell it everywhere. I can taste it in the air, hear its breath. It threatens all of us, not just the Wyvachi, though it's doubtful they will survive it.'

I felt as if pieces I'd been missing from my puzzle were falling into place. I'd sensed and guessed so much, but now I sat before the oracle, who knew far more than I did, who confirmed my intuitions. But oracles could be tricky. I must proceed carefully. 'I see. So how does Mossamber intend to protect his family from this *purge*? You must've discussed it, surely?'

'Yes... We've discussed *you*, as it happens.'

I raised my brows at him. 'Oh, really? Why, if you've only summoned me here to warn me off?'

Peredur laughed coldly. 'I wanted to hear what you'd say.' He leaned towards me a little.

'Wait...' A light went on in my head. 'Rey... me... All this time, perhaps with hienamas before us, Mossamber has been trying to find a solution, hasn't he?'

Peredur shrugged, a slight smile on his face. 'Yes, I suppose he has – not that it did any good. Nytethorne has particular faith in you, although I did tell Mossamber it's unwise to trust the judgement of the besotted.'

'I agree, yet here I am.'

He nodded. 'Yes. There is a strong flavour to you, I can taste that. So...' He paused. 'As I said, there are cycles. We've experienced... risings... before. My brother Kinnard was the casualty of one of them.'

'He tried to do something about it.'

'Yes, although he had no chance to succeed alone. We worked hard to *manage* the rising then, and push it down again. Some of us were ill for weeks afterwards, weakened.'

'Why didn't you join forces with Kinnard at that time?'

Peredur sighed, shook his head. 'Do you really have to ask that? Yes? All right... It was because Kinnard would rather have murdered Mossamber than work with him. And because I didn't want Kinnard to know I lived. And also because Kinnard was the only Wyvachi who really understood what was happening. The others would have rejected any overtures from Mossamber, except perhaps for Medoc. But he'd already taken the sensible way out and had fled.' Peredur clasped his crossed knees with his hands. 'Part of the problem is that although the Wyvachi believe in their curse, it's almost a romantic ideal for them. They cherish their burden, yet they *don't* act. They are in denial.'

'Nytethorne intimated Wyva might have plans this time...'

Peredur nodded again, thoughtfully. 'I believe so, because I've sensed this. But they won't come to anything and he'll lose his son, possibly others, even his own life.'

'But surely,' I said carefully, 'the families acting together is the only answer. You must know this, even if the task seems impossible. I can't understand why you haven't encouraged this, worked for it, even if you stayed out of it yourself?'

Again Peredur sighed deeply. 'Why do you make me explain things you already know? Or are you perhaps not as quick as I thought you to be? I haven't bothered because my Wyvachi kin are stupid. They are unable to get over their prejudices enough to be of any use.'

'And the Whitemanes *are* able?'

Peredur laughed softly. 'I take your point. No.'

'Yet when so much is at stake? It seems almost wanton to maintain this feud. Aren't the Whitemane harlings as threatened by this egregore as much as the Wyvachi ones are?'

'Of course. That's why we observe the festivals in the way we do. It's an ancient pagan tradition, an attempt to appease the gods, so they won't wreak havoc. It works, in its way.'

'Or has done.' I remained silent for a few seconds but Peredur waited for me to continue. 'So, are you going to tell me the real reason I'm here?'

He remained perfectly still for a moment, the moonstones gleaming. 'I find it interesting that Mossamber allows Nytethorne near you. Initially, he'd decided that Wyvachi-called were no longer any use to us, and in fact rather a hindrance. Nothing good had come of Rey, or any of his predecessors, so why bother with the next one? But something has changed his mind.'

'Have you asked him?'

Peredur nodded. 'Of course. He laughed. Talked about making the Wyvachi-called puppet dance. Yet both of us know that's not entirely true.' He paused. 'He knows you're here, by the way. I told him I'd be meeting you tonight. He said nothing. That in itself is interesting.'

'You could simply have invited me over,' I said. 'You know I wouldn't have refused, yet still you had to pull the strings. I hope you're suitably entertained.'

Peredur regarded me expressionlessly, remained silent.

'Aren't you bored of hiding?' I asked abruptly, because I could sense within this har a great restlessness. Also, he was not as callous as he made out. There was a part of him I could feel shivering, unsure. He put up a good front, though.

He yawned carelessly. 'No, I don't particularly want hara to see me. I have my rooms, my amusements. I have my chesnari... and his sons.'

That you could not give him, I thought and perhaps uncharitably didn't take much trouble to keep it quiet within me. I think if he could possibly have gone paler, he would have done then.

'You don't know how bad it was,' he said, in a low hard voice. 'Poisoned by my own body because I was burned *shut*. I won't tell you more, because nohar should have to hear the details of that and how we coped with it. Losing the possibility of harlings was a minor thing in comparison. Being able to eat and process food properly took years to mend to a bearable level. You have no idea what we all had to go through.'

'I'm sorry,' I said. 'I...'

He waved a hand at me. 'So long ago. I was somehow meant to survive and I did. My body fought to repair itself enough to function. The waters of what they now call Pwll Siôl Lleuad helped as much as they could.'

There was a silence, then I said. 'Peredur, why didn't you just summon me from the start?'

'You caught me unawares,' he said, his head thrown back as if he were gazing at the pitted ceiling. 'I was asleep one day, dreaming in the afternoon, in my roof garden. I found myself back at my pool, but for some reason I'd forgotten everything. I was just sightless, terrified, blundering about. Then there you were, telling me not to move, that you'd come to me.' He smiled. 'Well, I decided to believe it, see if you could.'

'You believe more than that, don't you?' I said softly. 'You don't want to, but you can't stop yourself. I won't let go of the bone until I've crushed the marrow from it. You *know* I can help.'

He didn't reply for some moments. 'Rey tried,' he said at last. 'He really tried, but he's not... *seasoned* as you are.' He laughed. 'Like a big old oak tree. That's how I see you in my head, with your autumn leaf hair, those dark summer eyes. But you are rooted, through experience. Rey was too young, too idealistic. One fierce storm and he was torn from the ground.'

'I'd like to see that tried with me,' I said, almost as a growl.

'Be careful,' Peredur replied. 'Don't be angry, for that is weakness.' He inhaled deeply through his nose. 'The truth? Yes, I want to believe. I set you a test. If you uncovered the mystery, followed the clues and found the treasure – that is, me, albeit not a very glittery one – then you would have a chance. I threw tricks all around you to see if you'd falter, but they seemed only to increase your resolve. If you can't help, I'm sure you'll die trying.' He put his head to one side. 'I made it like a story from legend. The hero has to complete tasks before he is worthy.'

'Ask me, then,' I said.

'What?'

'You *know*. This is part of the legend too.'

He sighed through his nose again. 'Very well. Ysobi. For God's sake, get rid of it for me, will you?'

'Gladly,' I said.

Peredur stood up. 'So, there is our pact.' He walked back to the piano, played a few wistful notes. 'Mossamber had this repaired for me. In the early days, it was the only thing that kept me sane. Then, as I slowly recovered, I found my skin, my touch, could perceive colours – not very strongly to start with. I found there were other ways to see, that taste and smell and touch were in themselves a way of seeing. All this strengthened over time. Gemstones help me focus. Mossamber had the idea of the eyes. He had many made for me. Different coloured gems, with different properties, that I could wear as I liked. Moonstones for my music, rubies for play and for love, black obsidian for serious business. The others I don't care for much.'

'Those colours would suit you best,' I said. 'So I am music rather than serious business?' I put a smile into my voice.

'You saw me moonstoned in your visions. I wanted to be that when you first saw me in reality.'

I wondered then why Mossamber had not sent this light of his life to Immanion, for the Gelaming healers could surely have done far more for him than had been done here. They would at least have helped him hone his clearly powerful senses. Cost wouldn't have been an issue; the Gelaming would take on any case like this without asking for a fee. But then, hidden away in this corner of the world, the Whitemanes might have believed the Gelaming considered themselves above such matters.

'I couldn't leave here,' Peredur said nonchalantly, as if I'd spoken aloud, 'that's the reason. I wouldn't let Mossamber do anything. He'd had a reprieve: I lived. But if he wanted me to stay, then everything had to be on my terms.'

'Do you ever go beyond the domain?'

He shook his head. 'No, not in flesh. I rarely even go into the main house. I have my rooms, the attics, my roof terrace, my music, my cats, my loved ones. Nytethorne reads to me. Ember plays games with me. Mossamber strokes my skin to weave pictures for me. Others come to talk with me. We enjoy beautiful food, for my sense of taste is strong. That is almost like aruna to me... almost. All that's enough.'

'Well, fair enough, but perhaps it's time you *did* go out.'

Again a shake of the head. 'No.'

I took a breath. 'I think... now is the time for transparency. Too much has been hidden, or lied about, or left unsaid. I've been as guilty of that as anyhar. If we are to proceed from here, all the webs must be swept away. Those are *my* terms.'

Peredur gave me his hard moon stare.

'You don't know about your mother, do you?' I said.

He came back to sit beside me. 'What about her? They never found her. Over the years, I've hoped somehow she got away.'

'Not exactly. Like you, she tried to kill herself, after what was done to you. She felt a hideous end was all that was left for her too. She cut her wrists in my tower.'

His hands flew to his face. 'Christ!'

So strange to hear that anachronistic expletive. 'Like you, she wasn't successful, but in a different way. This is going to sound... well... I'll just tell you what's happened.'

He listened in an agitated silence, his hands moving constantly – wringing together, touching his hair, his face, picking at the shawls on the sofa. When I'd finished what I had to say, without pause or question he said, 'Bring her to me!'

I reached out to still his hands. His skin was warm and smooth, slightly furred, made to touch. A pang of pity shot through me and he snatched his hands away. 'I can't bring her,' I said. 'She can't leave the tower, Peredur. *You* must come to her.'

He put his hands to his face again, then stood up, walked in a circle behind the sofa, making soft sounds of distress. I twisted round to watch him, allowing him these moments without further words from me.

Then he stood still for a few seconds, before turning to me. 'White is too harsh for her,' he said abruptly, the fingers of one hand gesturing at his face. 'I think red, but would that be too much like blood?'

'What other colours have you got?'

He made an impatient gesture. 'Everything. Dozens.'

'What colour were your...?'

'Golden, after inception.'

'Then, topaz? Perhaps?'

He nodded. 'All right. You must tell me, though. Come.'

I confess I got to my feet with reluctance then, but perhaps this was the price, or a further test. He led me up the stairs to his other room, which again was barely furnished, containing a bed, a dressing table, a packed bookcase, a low table strewn with belongings, and several thick rugs on the floor. What seemed to be about half a dozen black and white cats were sleeping on the bed. Two more sat like matching porcelain ornaments on the window casement and turned their faces to me idly to see who I was. The room also contained a tall cabinet packed with shallow shelves. They were laden with Mossamber's gifts. Peredur ran his hands over them, removed a few trays, such as those in which gem collectors store stones. Some of them were like real eyes, staring up at me as if in shock to be disembodied. I swallowed. 'Maybe a pair of these ones that look... real?'

'No!' Peredur snapped. 'Why should I try to make others comfortable with what's been done to me.'

'Yes... I'm sorry.'

'These are yellowish,' Peredur said, grabbing one of my hands and making me touch a tray.

'I could do with light...'

He went to a lamp and turned it on. I carried the tray over. They were just beautiful stones, I told myself, not wanting to linger over the choice. But he would know if I didn't examine them carefully.

He laughed, 'You're squeamish for a magus.'

'Guilty,' I said, 'at least in this respect.' It was peculiar I felt that way, since I could operate surgically upon hara unflinchingly, and deal with all manner of medical situations that might turn most hara's stomachs. I think it was because I *knew* how these lovely stones had become necessary, the barbarity they could not help but symbolise. Eventually, I took his hand, pressed his fingers against two of the stones. 'These.'

'Give them to me.'

They were beautiful golden stones, not spheres but concave, almost warm to the touch, slippery. I put them into his hands. He smirked at me, hesitated for a moment, then turned his back on me. When he turned to me once more, he held back his moonshawl mane with both hands. 'Well?'

'Come into the light.'

He let me lead him.

'Yes, just right.' The warm glowing colour made him less spectral somehow.

'I need to do something with my hair. I must look like an old witch. Excuse me a moment.'

He took his moonstone eyes with him into another room, which I assumed was a bathroom, since I heard water running. He came back, drying the stones carefully on a soft cloth, before selecting a tray and placing them into an empty slot, nestled in silk. Then he went to a dressing table, picked up a hairbrush. I watched as he made a thin plait on either side of his face, then confined them at the back of his head with a jewelled, tarnished silver clasp. 'Will this do?' he asked me, knowing full well it was perfectly neat.

'Yes, it's fine.'

'Then...' He drew in his breath, steadied himself against the dressing table. 'Suddenly I'm afraid. I feel panicky.'

'It's all right. I'm with you.' I paused. 'Will Mossamber just... allow this?'

'You say that as if you assume he has any control over what I do,' Peredur said lightly. 'Do you think he's cruel or something?'

'No, but concerned for you... yes. You must tell him where you're going.'

He shook his head. 'No. He knows I can take care of myself, and besides I have you to protect me, don't I?'

I wasn't convinced what he said about Mossamber was true, but didn't argue. Before we left the tower room, Peredur turned back at the threshold, as if to absorb its familiar ambience, as if he'd never return to it. In a way, of course, he wouldn't, because he was shedding a part of himself that would leave that room forever.

The dawn was beginning to unfurl as we came out into the yard behind the house. Already, lights were coming on in high rooms and presently hara would be up and about. Did Mossamber lie awake in a room somewhere, knowing his chesnari was taking this brave step? What did he think about it? I'd never met the har; he seemed like a creature of myth to me. And Nytethorne, who'd known the secret all along, but had been too afraid to tell me, perhaps fearful of incurring Peredur's wrath rather than Mossamber's. Where was he now? What were his thoughts?

Peredur took my arm. 'He is glad,' he said.

We went to where Hercules was waiting, and I helped Peredur onto the horse's back before mounting up behind him. I put my arms about him and he leaned back against me. 'We'll be riding into the dawn,' he said. 'I can hear it rising.'

I urged Hercules forward and he walked across the lawn. Birds were waking, singing in the morning. Crows argued in the cedars. Once across the bridge, I urged Hercules into a canter. Peredur held out his arms to embrace the air and I held him tight. 'There's so much out here,' he murmured, 'so much...'

In the sky above us, I heard the call of a swan, and looked up, but I could not see it flying, not yet.

As we approached the tower hill, Mossamber's hounds began to yelp in the farmyard below. 'They know me,' Peredur said. 'Fox, Bramble, Cutter... I know all their names.'

'How many are there?' I asked. 'Sometimes it sounds like a dozen, sometimes hundreds.'

'Perhaps that is the truth,' Peredur said, laughing.

I helped him dismount at the field, where I released Hercules to graze.

'She used to bring me here,' Peredur said. 'When I was very small. Vivi didn't like that – she said it was too far from the house, dangerous. Mum didn't care. She liked to get away from Vivi. And Dŵr Alarch looks after its own.'

'It certainly tries to,' I said.

He climbed the steps ahead of us that led to the door, turned the immense old handle ring. The door creaked open. 'You don't lock it?'

'No. I'm sure the only threats around here won't be put off by a barrier of mere wood.'

Peredur was about to enter the tower, then he paused, turned back to direct his perception over the land. 'Feel it, Ysobi,' he murmured. He held out his hand to me, which I took. 'Close your eyes and feel it.'

I did so. Holding on to Peredur in the flesh, my own senses were heightened. From the moment I shut my eyes, I could see a dark purple mist creeping over the land. It was like fingers, or footsteps, not devouring or covering, merely moving around, retreating, advancing, *nosing*. 'Is that Vivi?' I whispered.

'She travels in it sometimes,' Peredur said softly. 'I have too... sometimes. Where it goes so a secret will open up, or a hole with a darkness in it, or a memory long forgotten.' He let go of me and I opened my eyes, for a moment still able to see that dark mist over the glorious summer landscape. 'The dead *will* rise,' Peredur said.

'Some already have, it seems.' I gestured at the doorway. 'Come, it's time.'

I could sense that Arianne was alone in the kitchen above us. She always rose very early. Was it cruel to spring this on her unannounced? I toyed with the idea of sending Peredur in without me, then realised this was somewhat cowardly. I had created storms of emotion in my past and fled them. Now I should simply weather them – even when they belonged to others.

I went into the kitchen first. Arianne had emptied all the cupboards and was cleaning them – I suppose she had to find things to do. She heard me and turned, 'Ari,' I said. 'You have a visitor.'

Peredur walked past me then. The expressions on Arianne's face changed quickly. Surprise, horror, fear, disbelief, joy. 'Peri?' she said.

'To me, you never died,' he said. 'I saw nothing. You saw

everything. This is less shocking for me than for you.' He went to her then and touched her arm.

She reached to his face hesitantly, her gaze flickering all over him. 'Ysobi went to see Medoc,' she said. 'We were told... But then, we weren't, were we? Medoc knew only what the Wyvachi knew.'

'Mum,' he said simply, a word that had not been uttered in affection in these lands for over a century. They embraced, wept, laughed, kissed – the stew of reactions that flavour the most intense moments of life.

'Don't leave me,' Arianne said, 'promise me, Peri. Don't.'

'Neither of us is leaving,' Peredur replied, 'not yet.'

Then *I* left them, went back outside, sat down on the stone terrace that surrounded Dŵr Alarch. The Swan Tower. Peredur's tower. Waiting for him all these years.

Around half an hour later, Peredur came out of the tower and sat down beside me. 'Thank you,' he said.

'My pleasure.'

He turned his face to me, observed me goldenly. 'Ysobi, I'm sure of something.'

'What?'

'I'll be staying here at Dŵr Alarch for some time... if you're agreeable.'

'Of course. Whatever you want to do.'

'Good. I'll let Mossamber know.' He dangled his hands between his raised knees. 'I can't opt out of the future. I know that now. For her sake, for yours, for the harling's, for stupid, lovesick Nytethorne's...'

'Peredur! Please don't say that.'

He uttered a derisive snort. 'Well, I'm just impatient with that sort of thing now.'

'Understandably, I suppose. But Nytethorne and I aren't "that sort of thing".'

Peredur said nothing, but he was smiling.

'So,' I said. 'What do you want to do?'

He leaned back on straight arms, the morning light falling over him, this *creature*, like a being from a fairy tale. I could still hardly believe he was real. 'I want you to let me be part of whatever *you* intend to do,' he said. He turned his face to me. 'I could demand that, but I won't. I'm asking.'

I reached out to touch his shoulder. 'You don't need to ask. This is your history, Peredur. If anything, I should be asking you! Thank you, anyway. Your help and knowledge will be an asset.'

He reached out in return and touched my face. So much easier between us to touch than between Nytethorne and I. 'That's settled then.' He paused. 'Aren't you afraid that part of me is *drwg* and will sabotage your plans?'

'No, not in the slightest.'

He smiled. 'I hope you're right.'

'I am. Things are proceeding as they're meant to be. Can't you see how the pieces are all fitting together?'

'Maybe.' He ran his hand up and down my right arm. 'So strong, aren't you? Yet weak as a kitten in some respects. True strength, maybe. Kittens are fast.'

I simply laughed, unable to comment on those observations.

'Now,' said Peredur, 'make me a sumptuous breakfast, because food's my main enjoyment. I'm hungry.'

'All right.'

We went back into the tower.

Later that day, as twilight fell, Peredur asked to walk with me amid the trees below the tower. At Ludda's farm the hounds were fretful, occasionally yelping discordantly but not singing together. I heard the distant faint tolling of a bell.

'Do you hear that?' I said. 'The bell...'

'All the time,' Peredur answered. He took one of my arms in his. 'You are the only other har to hear it. That is the ghost of Plenty, Gwyllion's bell, sounding an alarm too few can perceive.'

'We will raise it,' I said. 'The Silver Swan will return.'

Peredur laughed sadly. 'I can't feel the future yet. There are too many hidden variables.' He turned to me, put his hands upon my upper arms. 'Ysobi, there is something I must say to you.'

'Yes?'

'Don't tell anyhar else about Arianne, nohar.'

'But if she remains...'

'She won't,' Peredur said simply. 'That's one aspect I can see clearly. She's lent to us and has a task, but beyond that... whether we succeed or fail... her place is not here and now. We have our little group and we must be contained, closed. Trust me on this.' His voice was tight. How difficult it must be for him to find Arianne after all this time, only to know their reunion wouldn't last. Rinawne had also become very attached to Arianne. He wouldn't be happy to lose her either. 'You can trust me,' I said, 'but what about Rinawne and Myv? Might they not tell?'

'Afterwards, they might, and they also might be believed, but...' Peredur shrugged. 'Just for now. Say nothing.'

'She can't leave the tower, though,' I said. 'Are we supposed to deal with the *ysbryd drwg* from here?'

'No, she'll be able to leave it. Tomorrow, maybe. I'll see to it.'

I wasn't convinced Arianne would ever be able to do that, but Peredur seemed sure. His faith, like Kinnard's had once done, could perhaps change reality.

Chapter Twenty-Two

A message came from the Domain the following morning. Written in an elaborate script in black ink upon a thick piece of pinkish handmade paper, were the words: *Ysobi: Please call at the Domain today. I wish to speak with you. Mossamber har Whitemane.*

I was under no illusion that this was anything other than an order.

Mossamber had kept away from me completely, occasionally sending out relatives to befuddle and beguile me, but even when I'd stolen his chesnari away from his house, he'd not shown himself personally. I knew so little about the Whitemanes, not even who Ember's father was. There'd been no opportunity so far to discuss this. The previous day's conversations had focused solely upon Peredur and Arianne becoming reacquainted and, apart from my brief conversations with Peredur, I'd given them privacy for that. The Whitemanes had kept me out; now I was somewhat 'in'.

I rode Hercules to the Greyspan, intrigued about what was to happen. Was I to receive warnings about how I must conduct myself or would the Whitemane phylarch offer help for my task? I imagined Mossamber would meet me in some grand, gloomy room, distant across a vast desk. But as my horse set foot upon the bridge, a rider came cantering from the other side.

Like all of his kind, Mossamber was dark-skinned and sensual of feature, but he managed also to appear somewhat austere. I'd glimpsed him in the darkness of a Cuttingtide night, but now, in full sunlight I could see him clearly. I could tell he was first generation immediately, even if I hadn't been aware of the truth. He carried the years on his shoulders and within a certain expression in his eyes. He had come alone to meet me; Peredur had no doubt advised him of my approach. As he drew near, he gestured for me to halt.

'Thank you for coming, tiahaar,' he said, once he did not have to raise his voice for me to hear him.

'I'm pleased to meet you, tiahaar,' I responded, inclining my head.

The horse he rode today was pure white but with a dark nose and eyes. Its mane reminded me of Peredur's hair, spilling wantonly over Mossamber's hands as he rested them on the animal's neck. 'It's time we talked,' he said. 'Come. There's purpose to this meeting. Will you follow me?'

'Lead on.'

On the Wyvachi side of the river, we turned back roughly in the direction of my tower, keeping close to the water.

We kept to a walking pace, so that Mossamber could draw his horse alongside mine to talk. 'Peredur will have explained what we know,' he said. 'I never thought this day would come. I believed we controlled the environment. Now the opposite is true.'

'What would happen if nothing were done?' I asked.

He shrugged. 'The end,' he said. 'Oh, not immediately in some dramatic, crashing fashion, but this community would die, slowly, as the poison seeped through the soil, through hearts and minds.'

'You are sure of this?'

He glanced at me coldly. 'My swan convinced me you were sent to help us, like some deharan angel. Are you telling me now you propose we do nothing?'

'No. I was just asking the question.'

Mossamber nodded thoughtfully. 'I see what you're getting at – our own fear *feeds* what we fear, creates it. There is some element of this, of course, but the egregore has been allowed to gorge itself for too long. It does have independent existence. Of this I am sure. So in answer to your question. Yes.' He tilted his head back a little, flared his nostrils. 'You will see.'

For some moments we rode in silence, keeping pace with

the rolling river. Willows had come to crowd the banks, dipping their hair into the sparkling water.

'All those years ago, when the conflict was over,' Mossamber said at last, 'we heard a sound as of great horns being blown down through the valley, as if the dehara themselves had rallied to battle and were sounding the alarm. Every heart was for a moment stilled. Hair stood stiff from scalp and arm. Animals cowered. It was not the dehara, of course, for they had not yet come to these ancient hills. It was older gods, breaking free of the earth, coming once more to seep into the sap and water, the roots and stones. I knew then that we had woken something, and now it was awake it would never sleep again. I felt it flow over the land like a mist, absorbing everything in its path, so they became part of it; the corpses, the ruins, the laments still echoing in the air.' He paused, eyed me keenly. 'Do you know how Yvainte har Wyvachi died?'

'Poison,' I answered simply.

'From a nail that been driven into Peredur's flesh. Did you know that?'

I shook my head. 'Only that it happened in the stables.'

'Vivyen tried to bind him with iron, without really knowing what she was doing,' Mossamber murmured distantly, as if to himself.

I remembered the legend of the iron-bound witches Rinawne had told me, what seemed like a year ago.

'The nail fell when I freed him,' Mossamber continued, 'fell into the blood and dirt, was kicked aside, later swept up, lost, forgotten, lying beneath the hay in a far corner of the stalls. Then, years later, Yvainte came upon it, was pierced by it, and its enchantment killed him.'

'If bad things have happened, so have good,' I said tentatively. 'That Peredur survived is a miracle, pure and simple. This land *has* thrived, despite everything. It is a place of great beauty.'

'He is its swan, he cannot die,' Mossamber said. And I

wondered then if he wasn't a little crazed himself.

We had come to another bridge, this one hump-backed and of mossy stones. Mossamber led the way over it. Ahead of us ancient forest crowded to the river's edge. No willows here, but oak, beech, holly, blackthorn and birch. I saw only darkness before me, and unnatural stillness, a place where in legend no birds would sing.

'We are in the days of the Dog Star,' Mossamber said, almost in a whisper, 'in the build-up to the old festival of Lughnasadh, the hot, pulsing heart of high summer.'

'When ghosts walk in sunlight.'

'Yes. This is a treacherous time.' Mossamber smiled at me conspiratorially. 'Some believe that Shadetide is the most dangerous, or even Natalia when the Wild Hunt rides the gales, but no, they are wrong. At Reaptide, the entity we now call Verdiferel seeps out from the stones of the earth. He is freed from the round of the year, free to cause mischief. He is like a serpent you might encounter on the path. His tongue is forked.'

I had become used to the rather strange way most of the Whitemanes talked, but it seemed to me that Mossamber was like a peculiar old oracle, living in a body that appeared young. If an ancient hero or heroine had stepped forth from the mountainside to walk in flesh again, this is what they would be like.

We entered the shadow of the trees, and at first I could hear the creak of sun-warmed bark, the rustle of leaves overhead. But slowly these sounds died away, until all that could be heard in the silence was an occasional ominous crack as of a branch falling. One belief among hara, found commonly in Freyhella and other northern lands across the water to the east, is that alongside our familiar world there is another darker version, overlapping it all the time but unseen. Occasionally, a har might glimpse this strange world, and I felt I was doing so now. The forest we rode through was like a bleaker version of the woods around the Pwll Siôl Lleuad; more shadowy, dusty, with many dead trees, and those that lived had leaves that were almost black. Bracken was spiky and brittle and although I heard no birds, nor any other animal sounds, sometimes I saw tiny eyes glinting amid the undergrowth. How could this place be real? Or had Mossamber led me truly off the path?

'Where are we?' I asked, not wanting to raise my voice. We were riding in single file.

Mossamber turned to me and put a finger to his lips, then gestured ahead.

We emerged into a glade, where a black pool shone sullenly in the beams of meagre sunlight that came down through the blackened canopy. This clearing was larger than that around the Pwll Siôl Lleuad, and all around it were what appeared to be graves or monuments to the dead. There were offerings of red and white flowers, either wilting upon the bare soil, or planted, or cut stems in urns of water. The air was filled with their sickly decaying scent.

Mossamber dismounted from his horse and I did likewise. He gestured at the pool. 'This is the gateway to sorrow,' he said. 'This forest is not truly ancient. Its trees were planted only a hundred years ago.'

'It looks like a graveyard.'

'It is.'

'Why do you want me to see this?' I asked. 'What significance has it to what's happening now?'

'In this place we buried the dead,' Mossamber answered. 'Both human and hara. Tidied them away into the earth and covered them with trees. The pool was not black then.' He put a hand upon my shoulder. 'You want to feel what we're up against? Open yourself to it here, tiahaar, and know I am close so I might drag you away, if it becomes too much to bear.'

'Very well.' I glanced down at the ground, unwilling to compose myself upon it, yet that reluctance, of course, was part of my task. Mossamber stood over me, his arms folded, gazing around the glade, as if alert for intruders, although I was sure nothing living lurked nearby.

When I entered a meditative state, I was prepared for an

ugly onslaught upon my senses, gathering malevolent shadows, hideous shapes. Yet all I saw was a single har, with a brown woollen cloak wound around him, weeping at one of the graves. In that sound was the tragedy of the earth's history. If there is a dehar of grief, I met him that day. To be near to that entity was to be engulfed in a hopelessness and despair that is beyond mere words to convey. His tears ran onto the black earth and trickled in viscous streams to feed the pool.

As I watched, he became aware of me and lifted his head. He had a pointed, pinched little face, his white features striped with red where his tears had burned him. His eyes were entirely black. I could see he was angry in his grief. He wanted somehar to blame, somehar to punish. Suddenly, in a rush of fetid air, he was right in front of me, screaming into my face. His mouth was a yawning grave that went deep, deep into the earth. I could smell loam and rot. His hands were twisted sticks, grasping for me. I reached out to fend him off, and when I gripped his body it too felt like a bundle of twigs and thorny branches, wrapped in rags.

I realised then that the sticklike creature I had found – or imagined – in my bed weeks ago had not been a presentiment of Ember, but of *this*. I called upon Lunil to dispel the vision – to no avail. Then I prayed for aid to Agave, Miyacala, Aruhani, even the Aghama himself. But still that contorted bundle of grief and fury clawed at me. I tried to pull myself from the visualisation, but was unable even to do that. I tried to utter a cry but my mouth was sealed. The creature hauled me across the cold, dank ground towards the pool. He meant to drown me. The curse made flesh, if flesh can be made of sticks and thorns.

A crowd of arms, formed of congealed filthy fluid, lifted from the surface of the pool. Blindly, yet sensing my presence keenly, they reached for me with spidery fingers, pawed at my clothes, took hold. I fought against them, my feet scrabbling helplessly in the stinking dirt, but I'd never come across anything so powerful in my life before. The will and intention of these entities – this egregore – were like steel.

And then I saw her. Vivi, the woman I'd glimpsed at Meadow Mynd. Her face was severe, the skin grey, and she was dressed almost incongruously in work clothes of shirt, trousers and boots. Her dark hair hung in tight plaits over her shoulders. I could see there was no pity or mercy within her. This was the woman who could blind her own grandson, torture him, cripple him. This was the woman who wished all harish children dead. She was accompanied by two creatures that I can only describe as dog men, walking on all fours and with the limbs of a dog, but also hideously human or harish. These trembled beside her, naked with leathery hides and whiskered snouts, undoubtedly what I'd sensed around me at the Pwll Siôl Lleuad on the night I'd met Peredur. Vivi lifted a grey arm and hissed at me. 'Abomination,' she said, matter-of-factly, 'that which should not live, that which stole, murdered, killed the world.'

I could tell that to this shred of living hate the worst idea of all was that Wraeththu could live ordinary lives upon this land, that they could thrive and be the race that humanity had lost the chance to be. There was no point trying to reason with her; she simply wouldn't hear me.

She stalked closer to me, still pointing with a stiff arm, like some dire prophet. 'You can do nothing,' she said determinedly, then turned her back on me. 'Take him!'

The waters ahead of me began to churn and those disgusting rubbery limbs that held me helpless began to drag me down into the chill darkness. I was utterly powerless, like a newly-hatched harling, or a har tied to a stake, waiting for the worst of fates. The only thing I could do was shriek in my mind 'Mossamber!' hoping it would be heard.

Then I felt strong warm hands upon me, words in a strange language in my ears, his breath within my mouth, pulling me back to the waking world. I opened my eyes, gasping, coughing, hanging onto Mossamber like a terrified harling.

'You see?' he said.

Behind him, both horses were still with us, but their eyes were rolling. They trembled. Sweat had foamed upon their shoulders.

'Let's go,' I said, 'now.'

Mossamber led me to the Domain, and I did not – could not – speak upon that journey. I needed all my will to remain upright on Hercules' back. I realised now I could never have taken action against the *ysbryd drwg* alone, or even with only Arianne, Myv and Rinawne to help me. I'd been arrogant, proud, unaware of the extent of my capabilities or indeed the strength of my foe. If Peredur hadn't drawn me to him, I wince to think what might've happened. Disorientated and shaken though I was, I was grateful Mossamber had revealed that dreaded spot to me. Truly cursed land.

He did not take me into the cavernous office I'd imagined he'd have, but into a sunny conservatory at the back of the house, furnished with chairs of woven branches softened by embroidered cushions. The room overlooked a lawn leading down to the river, and just beyond the windows a fountain of stone nymphs sprayed glittering water into the air. I could see hara everywhere, going about their daily business. The house felt full and industrious. I'd hoped Nytethorne might be waiting for us, but he wasn't. Hara who looked like him, yet were to me nowhere near as desirable, greeted Mossamber as we passed them and gave me curious glances. The Wyvachi were right, it seemed – there were a lot of Whitemanes hidden away in the Domain.

In the conservatory, Mossamber gestured for me to sit down in one of the cushioned chairs beside a slate-topped table, and I did so. My mind couldn't focus, my temples ached, and I felt faintly sick. All I could do was press the fingers of one hand against my eyes and try to regain equilibrium. Mossamber allowed me these moments and did not speak. I heard somehar else enter the room and lowered my hand. Ember had come to us with a pitcher of cold elderflower cordial.

I drank greedily from the mug he handed to me. When I had slaked my thirst, I put down the mug on the table and said, 'Thank you, Mossamber, for what you showed me.'

Mossamber flicked his fingers at Ember, indicating he must leave the room. He didn't speak until the door was closed. 'You couldn't have gone further in your task without experiencing it,' he said. 'I'll not let Peredur near that spot now. He is drawn to it, but I prevent that.' He paused. 'A har died there this week, some poor soul who takes flowers to one he remembers. No more. He was taken, found white upon the grave, his eyes open.'

'One of your hara?'

'No. A har attached to the family har Brân – farmers. There have been several accidents, two fatal, over the past few weeks, of which you won't have heard. Peripheral players on the main stage, whose passing will go unnoticed except by those they leave behind.'

'The Wyvachi know of this?'

Mossamber made a low growling sound. 'Of course they do. Wyva is the self-appointed phylarch of this territory. Nothing escapes his ears.' He sighed through his nose contemptuously. 'This time of year is perilous, as I said. It's when the *ysbryd drwg* is at its strongest. There are often deaths, more accidents than is natural.'

'Surely the egregore must be dealt with at its peak, when it reveals itself fully?'

Mossamber nodded. 'Yes. I've come to this conclusion; it squirms away otherwise. Believe me, I've never stopped trying to destroy it. Your predecessor tried. Over the decades we've attempted many times to rid the land of this curse, but always at different seasons. To take it on at high summer seemed folly and yet, of course, it is the only time when, at its most powerful, it is also vulnerable.'

Mossamber sat down opposite me. 'It's not always this strong. It ebbs and flows like the tides. Myvyen har Wyvachi has drawn it out with his scent, that of a har at the cusp of adulthood. Ultimately, he will have to put away the shawl, stand before it naked.'

'Was it this way for Wyva and his brothers?'

Mossamber shook his head. 'No, because Kinnard was alive then, and the fire of his will was enough of a blaze to create a barrier around his sons.'

I put the fingers of one hand to my lips, briefly. 'You know I intend for Myv to be part of any action I... we... might take?'

He fixed me with a stare, but I saw no judgement in it. 'Yes, that's unavoidable. Peredur likes the harling, the first blood har of that tribe he has liked since...'

'I understand.' It occurred to me then that Mossamber did not know about Arianne – Peredur had kept that knowledge even from him. I wondered why, when in all ways they seemed so close.

'Peri is both strong and weak,' Mossamber said. 'Physically he is weakened, because of his past injuries. Psychically, he is a tidal wave, but both aspects are needed now. Myvyen is the lightning rod. You must be their strength and take the blows that will come.'

'Rinawne har Wyvachi will assist. I assume Peredur told you that.'

'Yes. He's a donkey but admittedly a sturdy one.'

I laughed at that.

'Well, he is,' Mossamber said amiably. 'Anyhar who can live with Wyva for this long must be.'

'He has a good heart,' I said.

'Let's hope so,' Mossamber replied. 'So, what are your plans?'

I outlined what I'd discussed with the others so far.

'Your ideas are good,' Mossamber said, 'but need refining. Peredur will assist you with that, and of course the Whitemanes will add their strength to yours from afar.'

I gazed him for some moments. 'I feel this alliance has come late in the day, but that it's come at all is a blessing. Yet... is it complete?'

Mossamber breathed in through his nose, then sighed. 'I know what you're implying, but the Wyvachi have always been weak. Kinnard was plain stupid and Medoc a coward. Wyva has inherited "aspect of mule" from his hostling. Gen is a fop and Cawr a dolt. I feel fairly certain you can complete your task without them.'

'Perhaps I can, but would it be right to do so?'

'You have Myvyen and the Erini,' Mossamber said abruptly. 'You have the Swan. You have enough.'

I stayed at the Domain all morning and took lunch with Mossamber at his invitation. He told me much of his life and how he'd built the Domain over the years – the spiritual Domain as opposed to its bricks and mortar. He told me how Peredur had transformed from little more than a corpse to this creature of mystery and power – or rather had reclaimed that part of himself. I still wondered whether if I'd gone with the harlings across the bridge, which seemed so long ago, whether this was the Mossamber I'd have met, rather than the surly antagonist I'd imagined, who'd have been set upon my humiliation and defeat. Had the *ysbryd drwg* created my fear that day, in order to prevent such a meeting?

Mossamber explained how difficult it had been – especially in the early years – to keep Peredur hidden. 'Right from the start I tried to build walls to protect him,' he said. 'I wanted private roads so he could go outside and meet nohar. That never happened, because how could I tell Kinnard *why* I wanted that privacy? Everyhar felt I was simply being awkward, chafing against the fact Kinnard outranked me. That wasn't the case. Any fool could see Kinnard was the obvious choice for leader.'

I could tell that Mossamber hated the Wyvachi because the arrow Kinnard had shot into Peredur had of course made his healing all the more gruelling. Mossamber didn't say so to me, but I knew he was still angry that Kinnard and Medoc hadn't even tried to save their brother. An arrow through the heart had been their answer to the problem, and in Mossamber's eyes, only because they were too selfish or stupid to deal with what Peredur had become. These sentiments smouldered through his words, but all I could think of was the tragic waste these decades of hatred had been. Nohar had needed to die. Kinnard and Yvainte would have lived to see their high-harling. No curse. No *ysbryd drwg*. Vivi's voice would have been too faint to hear if the Whitemanes and the Wyvachi had stood together, mourned Peredur's life-changing injuries together. If their scorching, damaging emotions had been exorcised early on, the future would have been entirely different for Gwyllion. I thought then: Malakess had left this mess behind. He hadn't been the kind of har to understand that growth had to come from more than rebuilding walls and replanting fields. Hearts had needed mending. Friendships. Hara had had to come to terms with a complete change of physical and mental being in the reeking flotsam that conflict and horror had left behind. The Gelaming, for all their faults, would never have countenanced walking away from that. Interfering meddlers as they'd been in those early days, (some will say, still are), their adepts would have picked up on the undercurrents, and their probable consequences, and made hara deal with them. I wouldn't even be here now if that had happened. But the Gelaming had virtually ignored Alba Sulh, concentrating their attention on Megalithica. And this was not the only land where that had happened.

I returned to the tower in the early afternoon to find that Rinawne and Myv were there. When I walked into the kitchen, where all of them were seated around the table, Rinawne gave me a look of unfathomable confusion and wonder. In mind touch he sent to me: *Are there any more risen dead up your sleeves?*

I think this is it, I sent back, although he didn't smile and turned away from me, as if Peredur's survival was entirely my fault and I'd kept it hidden from him.

Chapter Twenty-Three

Reaptide stole closer to us and while we planned and trained for it, we had to maintain the illusion our everyday patterns were the same as ever. While Rinawne and Myv came nearly every night to the tower, we made sure I still visited the Mynd twice a week to stay for dinner. Wyva was given the story that Rinawne and I were training Myv for a major role in the next festival, which required a lot of rehearsal. This was not, in fact, a lie, although Peredur had more of a hand in his high suri's education than Rinawne or I. Often, they worked alone. Rinawne sometimes questioned this, imagining I must be uncomfortable with it, but even though I knew that Peredur might take Myv into dark areas of his own mind, give him glimpses of what writhed over the land, I had no fear for his safety.

Rinawne didn't share this conviction. 'But *you're* his teacher,' he once insisted. 'Peredur is... well, he's *damaged*. I don't like him taking over like this.'

'Peredur is strange and somewhat damaged, yes,' I said, 'but I trust him with Myv.'

'That's my son you're trusting him with, not yours,' Rinawne said darkly.

How else to assuage his fears and doubts but through aruna? I'd not forgotten its power, how it can be used to manipulate a har, turn his mind. I'm not proud of that, but it was a tool I had at my disposal, and I needed to silence Rinawne's fears. Constantly trying to use words to reassure him was too exhausting. I remembered, with some shame, how I'd often used aruna to silence Jassenah too. That was my gift, blithely misused.

Much as in some ways I agreed with Mossamber's scathing opinions of the Wyvachi, it grated not to be honest and open

374

with Wyva. Mishaps and accidents were occurring with increasing frequency at Meadow Mynd, although thankfully no more deaths, at least not of hara. Some of the injuries, however, were life changing. One har lost an arm that was crushed completely when an old building fell upon him out in the fields. Others were maimed by falling trees that were centuries old yet seemed to fall dead on the spot, taking sacrifices with them. Part of Wyva's sheep flock ran down a mountainside into a turbulent part of the river and drowned. Animals gave birth to dead young. Crops developed peculiar blights nohar had seen before. In the house, crockery fell from shelves and dead birds were found upon the kitchen table three days in a row. And the air boiled around us, stifling, making us gasp for breath in the open air in the afternoons. Verdiferel stirred, the rags of his garments comprised of the strands of the egregore, the *ysbryd drwg*, shifting and coiling in dark purple light beneath the soil.

On Aloytsday, five days before Reaptide eve, my fighting company sat down to put the final touches to our strategy. Rinawne was due to join us but was late. I'd found that when Peredur made a plan, such as our conversation beginning at precisely midday, then he'd stick to it unwaveringly. Ever since he'd asked for my help, he'd assumed a mantle of leadership, as if my compliance somehow gave him permission or the ability to take action he should have taken decades ago. So we began our meeting without Rinawne, which I was content to do, since Rinawne's role in the proceedings was simply to do what we thought was appropriate for him. I didn't think we'd make any changes that might include him before he arrived.

We aimed to call the *ysbryd drwg* to us at the Pwll Siôl Lleuad and bind it into the waters. As the spirit of the pool had a close association with Peredur, this seemed even more appropriate than before. Peredur was interested in my initial festival ideas about containing Verdiferel in a pool. This part seemed fairly simple. We were the bait, Myv especially. There was no reason why the *ysbryd drwg* wouldn't heed us. The difficult part would be dismantling that entity, dispersing it, cleansing its energy.

When Rinawne did finally arrive, he appeared flustered. 'Wyva is getting suspicious,' he said as he sat down with us. 'He made a point of cornering me in the...' he flicked a nervous glance at Peredur, '...when I was tacking up Marie, my pony. He asked why I was spending so much time over here. All I could say that I was helping with Myv's training, learning from it even, and that we were planning the Reaptide rite.'

'Did he accept that?' I asked. Really, Wyva was foolish not have become suspicious before.

Rinawne shrugged. 'He seemed to, but it's clear he thinks we're up to something.' He sighed. 'Things are strange at home. The house is so haunted it's ridiculous. Most of the family are jumpy, and so are the staff, yet Wyva continues to waft through the day untouched.'

'That doesn't surprise me,' Peredur said. 'He's incapable of accepting reality.'

'Have you ever met Wyva?' I had to ask, knowing full well the answer.

Peredur raised his head to me. 'Not in person. I don't need to.'

'Clearly not, if you can make such assumptions.'

I felt Peredur studying me, which was like being patted by invisible hands. 'I'm sorry, Ysobi. I understand what you're getting at. My assumptions are based on hearsay. Is that what you want me to say?'

'It'll do,' I said, with the swift mind-touch, *Remember who's sitting here with us.*

He sent me a feeling of contrition and said aloud, 'Then I'll make more effort to set my prejudices aside.' I wondered whether he was being sarcastic, but he seemed genuine enough. 'Anyway, back to our business,' he said. 'We'll enact our own rite, ahead of the Wyvachi ceremony.' He grimaced. 'If we fail, maybe there'll be no Wyvachi ceremony.'

I saw Myv's mouth drop open, and Arianne reached out to muss his hair. 'Peri,' she said warningly.

Rinawne made an agitated sound, looked at me, wide-eyed.

'Don't worry, Myv,' I said. 'We won't fail.'

Peredur again poured the waters of gloom into the conversation. 'Simply trapping it won't be enough.'

'What must we do?' Myv asked, looking at Peredur.

Peredur was still grimacing. 'Something's missing... an important piece.' He shook his head. 'It'll come to me.'

'If I can somehow communicate with the part of this thing that's Vivi, I'm sure I can reach her,' Arianne said.

'You think so?' Peredur said icily. 'Like you influenced her so much in the past?'

Arianne winced at the implications. 'I want to try.'

'The entity must be dismantled,' I said, to steer the direction of the conversation away from Peredur's remark. 'We have the strength of our will, and we are united. We have more than Kinnard ever had. And I do think Arianne is right – and that is her part in it all.'

Peredur nodded, his expression introspective. 'Yes, I see what you mean. If we can separate Vivi from the *ysbryd drwg*, that's our chance. Then we rip it apart.'

But how do you dismantle many lifetimes of hurt, and blood, and crying in the night, and enmity, and cruelty and loss? We were a peculiar ensemble to tackle this seemingly impossible task. Arianne announced she was going to prepare lunch for us, and Rinawne went to help her. While Myv and Peredur discussed possibilities, their heads close together, I studied the group, removed from it. There was Peredur across the table from me, a kind of fairytale miracle, with golden stones for eyes and hair and skin like a creature of snow. His hands, however, were strong, a pianist's hands. It was clear that Myv adored him from the start, mainly because of his high hura's strangeness; Myv was intrigued by things that were different, uncanny. To him, Peredur was an elemental made flesh, brought to life from the waters of a magical pool, who saw with his skin, and through gemstones, and could taste the colour of the fields.

Myv himself was like a changeling child, and Arianne was a ghost made flesh. Rinawne and I were the roots, the grounding of this bizarre team, Rinawne more than me. He caught my eye at that moment as if catching my thought. He smiled at me sadly, and without even a mind touch, told me with his gaze that he knew our time together was all but over. If I'd feared jealous retribution I'd been wrong. All I saw was resigned sorrow. *But what you see will be brief,* he told me, again without any means of communication known to Wraeththukind, a simple sureness. *My grief will be temporary because I won't add to what's out there.*

Many times over the past couple of weeks I'd been tempted to ride to The Rooting Boar at lunchtime to see Nytethorne, but I'd stopped myself. What is desire but simple greed? *I want that. I have to taste it. Now.* I couldn't have such distractions when I needed to be clear-headed and focused. And yet, I was also aware that all it would take would be for Peredur to say something like 'Go to him' and I'd be hauling Hercules from his field and galloping to town before he'd finished chewing his latest mouthful of grass. Thankfully, the last thing on Peredur's mind was my relationship with his suri.

And yet, fate has its own say in such matters.

The following day, Peredur decided he needed to study the land through the medium of amethysts, which he'd not brought with him. 'Will you go to the Domain and fetch them for me?' he asked, apparently in all innocence.

'Will Mossamber mind me doing that?'

'I'll inform him you're coming,' Peredur said flatly, turning his attention back to Myv, who was writing some notes for him.

I stared at Peredur for some moments, thinking: *Why doesn't he just ask Mossamber to send them over here?*

Peredur raised his head to me. 'Well, go on. The message is already sent.' He smiled.

The Domain by day was – as before – overrun with hara, all of whom stopped whatever they were doing to stare as I passed them. There were feathers in the air, a faint smell of burning. Clouds above me looked like dogs racing across the sky. Ember, perhaps instructed by Mossamber, came sauntering out of the house as I approached the front door. He took hold of Hercules's bridle, by the bit. 'Go in,' he said, giving me an intrinsically Ember look of smirky secret amusement. 'You're expected.'

I felt strangely *funnelled*, first by Peredur, now by Ember. I didn't ask who I was to see or present myself to. Let what must happen, happen.

I went inside the house, and then there *he* was on those grand and beautiful stairs that were like a stage set, in the dim hallway, empty of sun. 'Mossamber says...' he began.

'Yes, the amethysts....'

Nytethorne beckoned me. 'Come upstairs. No idea which they are. Looked but there are many purple ones. Purple is right, yes?'

'Well yes, normally so, but won't Mossamber know?'

'He's not here now.'

'Oh.'

I went up those stairs for the second time. On this visit I passed several hara, who flicked brief glances at me, before carrying on with their business. I saw no ghosts, although there was a strange film to the air. Nytethorne and I climbed the house in silence.

We reached the upper parts and the corridor that led to Peredur's tower. 'You worked out between you what's to be done?' Nytethorne asked me.

'More or less.'

'Haven't much time now, have you?'

'No.'

We'd reached the tower staircase, and again silence fell between us as we climbed, until we came to the bedroom door, which Nytethorne opened. 'Wanted to tell you from the start,' he said.

'Yes, that might've been better.'

I stepped into the room, made for the cabinet. Nytethorne remained by the door. I took out the drawers, one by one, until I came to the tray containing purple stones. Some were pure transparent crystal, others milky.

'Ysobi, I had no choice,' Nytethorne said.

I turned to glance at him. He'd folded his arms defensively. Beautiful as the stars. 'It's fine.' I gestured at the stones. 'I'll take all these, since Peredur didn't say which ones exactly.'

'OK. Get more if he needs them.'

'I've been given the key to the Domain,' I said, smiling. 'I feel privileged.' I wrapped the stones in one of the pouches of soft leather that were stacked in a neat pile inside the cabinet.

Nytethorne took a step into the room, like a cautious cat. 'Mossamber told us to wait, so we did. Had to be sure.'

I put the stones in my satchel. 'It's all right, Nytethorne. I don't need your excuses. This is hardly an ordinary situation and I don't – and didn't – expect it in any way to be conventional and logical.'

He shrugged awkwardly. 'Still...'

'It's fine.' I'd crossed the room to him now, and my words made it acceptable for me to clutch his shoulder briefly. He rocked a little as if I'd punched him. 'I'd better get going. We've a lot to do.'

He followed me down the stairs and when we reached the hall again, he blurted out, 'Take me back with you. Can't stand this... doing nothing.'

'Well... I... It's not just up to me.'

'Who, then? Peri? He summoned you to help. You make the calls, I'd say.'

'He's quite emphatic about how things should be done,' I said. 'And he has far more experience of this matter than me.'

'You give him strength,' Nytethorne said, a tremor of anger in his voice. 'All these years, hidden away, now this. Out of his tower like a bird in flight.' He made a sweeping gesture with one arm. 'Take me with you.'

Still I hesitated, wanting dearly to say yes, but mindful of the distraction this would be and how I'd told myself to steer clear. Also, Peredur had been firm on the matter of nohar else knowing about Arianne.

'Don't mistake me,' Nytethorne said. 'It's for my hara and this land, not to sidle up to you.'

'It's not that...' I paused. 'There are things...' I sighed. 'Oh, maybe maybe. Peredur says there's a missing piece, but there are secrets also. One thing in particular he doesn't want others to know.'

'*You* can know but not me?' Nytethorne asked darkly.

I held his gaze. 'Peredur is your relative. You know him better than I do. If you think, truly, he wouldn't mind you coming over, then come.'

'If *you* truly don't want me there, I won't.'

I sighed. 'Let's not play games, Nytethorne. I have what you might call a rag-tag team to deal with this situation. To be honest, personal feelings aside, I'd welcome your... *immovability.*'

He laughed. 'My what?'

'Oh, never mind. Just come. But expect surprises.'

This was a har who'd willingly let himself by pierced by arrows for a Cuttingtide rite, as part of the complex web of rituals that Peredur believed kept the *ysbryd drwg* at bay. Nytethorne wasn't a coward. I didn't believe he'd crumple or run. We might need that strength. Perhaps, even, the distraction of him was part of it all.

On the ride over, I explained about Arianne, not sure how Nytethorne would take this information. I expected him to believe we were deluding ourselves about her, that she must be some maddened human who'd somehow survived unseen, from a family who'd survived unseen, even though that theory was even more unlikely than what I thought to be the truth.

Nytethorne listened to me without commenting. At the end of my story, all he said was: 'Clocks, you say?'

'Yes. I think that's what helped her... come through... the fact I put all the clocks in the room.'

He nodded. 'She know she's here for only one reason?'

I stared at him for some moments. 'If you mean to help us now, yes, she does. We've all faced the possibility she won't remain with us.'

'*Certainty*,' Nytethorne said. 'She's just part of what haunts.'

I hadn't considered that aspect exactly, but I suppose it made sense.

Walking into Dŵr Alarch with Nytethorne wasn't one of the most comfortable things I'd ever had to do. As usual, my four companions were sitting around the kitchen table. Peredur stood up when we entered the room. 'That's a very big amethyst,' he said, in a frosty tone.

'My choice, Peri,' Nytethorne said. 'Told him you'd not mind.'

Peredur shook his head, sighed, and sat down. 'I suppose not. Where are my amethysts?'

I gave them to him, and he spilled them from their pouch onto the table, causing Myv to exclaim and want to touch them. Rinawne fixed me with a stare that I met only briefly. There was an element of 'How could you?' in it, but I had no intention of doing anything Rinawne might find unsettling. I wouldn't have been surprised if he'd got to his feet and stormed out, but I could tell he was trying hard not to react in that way.

As the afternoon progressed, and we – or mainly Peredur and Myv – explained to Nytethorne what we hoped to achieve, I felt Rinawne settle down. There was no frisson between Nytethorne and I to upset him, only a polite distance between us. Before Nytethorne left the tower some hours later, he said to me at the kitchen door, 'I'll take care. No Wyvachi will see me come here. Don't fret about that.'

'I wasn't going to.'

He smiled uncertainly, nodded, closed the door behind him.

The following day, when Myv arrived at the tower, he had something he wanted to show us. Rinawne wasn't with him, and Nytethorne hadn't come over, so it was just the four of us. Myv had a satchel, from which he removed a wrapped object. Reverently, he revealed this to us: a swathe of iridescent cloth. 'This is the moonshawl,' he said softly, 'siôl lleuad that has protected my family for many years.'

This was far from the old rag Rinawne had implied it was.

'It gives off a powerful light,' Peredur said, reaching out to touch it, 'like starlight, somewhat cold, but pure.'

'It's beautiful,' Arianne said. 'You can see it's very old, and yet still so strong.'

The shawl was delicate, finer than I'd imagined. White as the moon, tender as moonbeams. Somehar had once taken great care to weave this. When Myv spread it out over the table, I could see the shape of owls within its lacy pattern. Its fringes were long, like hair. I asked Myv if he knew who'd made it. He shook his head. 'No... some har in Gwyllion. I don't think he's around anymore.'

I didn't think he was either. I did wonder then exactly who had made this magical shawl.

'I'll take this with me at Reaptide,' Myv said, stroking the fabric. 'It feels right to do so.'

'Yes,' Peredur agreed, running his hands beside Myv's. Occasionally, their fingers interlaced. 'This old shawl is as much a part of our task as you or I.'

Later that day, I asked Arianne if I might speak with her privately. She behaved as if she was simply a part of Myv's family, who'd always been with us and always would be. I was mindful of what both Peredur and Nytethorne had said about this, and knew Arianne must think the same. I suspected she and Peredur had discussed it. With the rest of us, she simply kept her fears hidden. Perhaps also she harboured the hope her kin were wrong and she'd walk from our task tonight free to remain among us. I knew in my heart that hope was futile, and if she held on to it, this was a weakness within our circle. She had to face reality, such as it was. I had to be sure about her.

I took her up to my nayati, where we generally held our meditations. She sat on the rug in front of me and said, 'What is it you want to say, Ysobi?' There was a challenge in her voice.

I reached out and took her hands, stroked the backs of them with my thumbs. 'Ari, you are a gift to us, and I believe you were sent to help right the wrongs of the past, but you being here, arriving the way you did... I think that is merely part of the strangeness we're living through now. I don't believe this will extend beyond Reaptide.'

She looked down at the carpet, nodded. 'I know that. I give thanks for every second I spend with my family.' She looked up at me. 'If I am a gift to you, then knowing that Peri lives, and is loved, that Medoc lives on and thrives, and that I've been allowed to meet Kinnard's grandson, are far greater gifts to me. If I am the sacrifice, then I'm prepared. I've been given this astounding second human life, however brief, and am willing to pay for it.'

I leaned forward to embrace her. She shuddered a little, but there were no tears. She pulled back from me, dry-eyed, although she kept hold of my hands. 'Thank you, Ysobi, for what you did, giving me this chance to see the future of my family. Wherever I go next, I'll move forward knowing they will carry on.' She drew in a breath. 'My task is to reach Vivi and convince her of this, too.'

I grimaced. 'I've met her – what remains of her. You'll have your work cut out. But yes, I think that is your task.'

She squeezed my fingers. 'We face a time of endings and beginnings, and this must include yours as well.'

I raised my eyebrows at her.

'Oh, come now, don't give me that look. I see the walls in you, with bricks of grief and cement of sorrow. You think you're tough, and you are, but perhaps it's time for you to start knocking down those walls.'

I laughed uncertainly. 'The walls are there for a reason, Ari.

I've made many mistakes in my life. As Vivi has had to be contained, so certain parts of me must be contained too.'

Arianne put her head to one side, smiled quizzically. 'Yet here we are, attempting to free her. Doesn't that say something to you?'

I shrugged.

'Just don't miss the opportunities when they come,' Arianne said. 'Promise me that.'

'OK.'

'And *mean* it.' She rolled her eyes. 'Oh well, I've said what I wanted to say.' She shook my hands a little. 'You will always be my beautiful friend, Ysobi, the woman I never had close to me in the past. I always wanted a friend like you, and to enjoy such a friendship, freely, experiencing all the good little things of life, but circumstances took that from us. I never knew a world free from turmoil and terror. You have that now. Please take all its bounties, if only for me.'

'I'll remember that.'

'You better!' She let go of me and stood up. 'I feel like making a cake, a very big one.'

She left the room ahead of me. I sat there for some minutes, thinking of nothing.

The day before Reaptide eve, I decided to give Wyva a last chance and went to visit him. We had plans to finalise for the Wyvachi festival, which really I couldn't concentrate upon. I was relieved I'd written it so swiftly after Cuttingtide, because my priorities were far from cheerful communal events at that time. Myv and Rinawne would not visit Dŵr Alarch again before tomorrow.

I found Wyva out in the stableyard – his favourite horse had gone lame inexplicably. At once, I offered my help and went into the relative cool of the stable to give the animal some healing. Wyva stood at my shoulder as I crouched with my hands on the horse's leg. I could feel he was tense, like a strand of wire pulled thin. 'Any more incidents?' I asked him

'No... not really. The weather will break after Reaptide, and so will this strange... atmosphere in the land.' He laughed unconvincingly. 'It's traditional in this place.'

I glanced over my shoulder at him. 'Is it?'

'When the weather's so hot and close, animals and crops get sick. Verdiferel plays his tricks.'

As if to punctuate this observation, several slates fell from the stable roof into the yard, where they smashed loudly. Wyva sighed. 'The heat,' he said.

A thin scream came from the kitchens.

'Wyva...' I wanted to tell him then, all that I knew, all that we must do, but he must've sensed this because he said, 'I'd better see what that was,' and hurried away. I smoothed the horse's leg, rested my forehead briefly against it. Tonight was the last night. Tomorrow at midnight, we would symbolically take up arms, such as we had. The Wyvachi festival seemed like a harling's dream. How could it be possible?

I didn't bother to stay and talk with Wyva further, because I knew it was pointless. To keep my mind from the challenge ahead, I rode into Gwyllion, visited The Boar for lunch, wondering if it was the last time I'd do so. After this, I rode round the sites that were now familiar to me, that I loved. I drank from the Pwll Siôl Lleuad. I sat by the riverside and dangled my feet in the cool water, then lay back on the grass. I felt melancholy, tired, fired up, hopeful...

Arianne had cooked us dinner again; she adored cooking. I was surprised and pleased to discover that she and Peredur had spent the afternoon in the forest around the foot of Dŵr Alarch. Peredur had been right. In his company, his mother could leave the tower.

'I saw a little of the land,' Arianne said to me. 'If anything, it's more beautiful than I remember but of course it's a new land really.'

'How did it happen... Peri taking you outside?' I wondered whether there had been any difficulty.

'He simply held out his hand to me and said "Come on, it's time", and the next thing I knew I was downstairs and the door was open and...' She clutched herself for a moment. 'The sky was white, the light like a trumpet. And the smells... Overwhelming. I can only say it was like stepping out of a spaceship onto a planet that wasn't Earth, but was very like it. A planet more intense to the senses.' She shrugged. 'More than that. Can't explain.'

'Were you afraid?' I asked gently, my own skin shivering at the image she'd conjured.

'Yes, because if I couldn't take that step over the threshold, what would we do? But there was Peri before me, my beautiful son, holding on to my hand, so I stepped into this new world, and I could walk in it.' She smiled wistfully. 'Perhaps that is what death will be like.'

I hugged her then, unable to speak. I thought of the terrible love between her and Peredur, the sky of sadness. And yet in this strange dream of summer heat and madness, they could meet and hold one another, if only for a short time.

Nytethorne showed up as we'd finished eating; this was not planned. He seemed odd, as if slightly drunk, being somewhat more demonstrative than I'd seen him before. He hugged Peredur, then Arianne, then stood behind me to run his hands swiftly through my hair. I felt distinctly uncomfortable. Why had he come here?

Peredur and Arianne retired early, before midnight. I sat with Nytethorne in the kitchen. 'So here we are, Ysobi,' he said, into the silence our companions had left.

'For the time being, yes.' I didn't want to talk about our task anymore, because we'd said everything. I wanted to be alone to prepare myself for tomorrow. There was nothing beyond that.

'So tonight I'll be staying here.'

I had been staring at my laced hands. My head jerked up. 'What?'

'You heard. Don't need to say why.'

'You do! Why? The boundaries are clear between us. The beds are all taken. Go home and sleep well so you're properly rested for...'

'I meant in your bed.'

My surprise was genuine. Nytethorne had said no to me in creative ways; he'd meant it. We'd said no to each other. 'This is an immense change of mind. Do I get a say in it?' Even as I spoke I was wondering whether in fact he meant simply he would sleep beside me for the night.

He smiled. 'No, you're limp as a cut reed. You need it.'

'But...'

'Don't know the outcome for tomorrow, do we? Ancient concept. Don't die with regrets for things undone.'

'I don't intend to die.'

He shrugged. 'There are different deaths. This is our moment. We must take it.' He stood up. 'Think, if you must, to remember who you are, then join me.' He left the room.

Whether I decided to go along with this or not, one thing was certain. He'd already claimed the remaining free bed. The worst aspect was that I couldn't drink alcohol to deal with this. My mind had to be absolutely clear tomorrow and no matter how good the harish body is at clearing up after its owner's worst lapses, traces remain. *I'll have a drink of water to fortify myself* doesn't work that well. Down at Ludda's farm, a single hound yelped, as if in pain.

When I stood up, a rush of images raced across my mind: Jassenah, Gesaril, all those who'd come before them. A series of impulses that hadn't been left undone and which I regretted bitterly. Yet what else was I to do? Any other har would have been upstairs already, seeking solace, comfort, strength. This was what we were *supposed* to do. Yet all I could see was a potential mess because I couldn't trust the feeling of really liking somehar. I was afraid I'd go back to that dark, fevered place where my love for Gesaril had sent me. Nytethorne was right; there were different deaths. Rinawne hadn't done as much to bring me back as he'd thought.

Just do it, I told myself, *just focus on the physical and do it.*

It was an insane notion I'd considered myself healed.

So I went upstairs like a har condemned and there was this new nemesis spread out over my bed in a tangle of hair and lean lithe limbs. 'Come here, but take off the noose and leave it by the door,' this vision said.

I wished I could be like him. He'd thought about us and had come to a decision and was now utterly sure about it. 'There are things you should know,' I said.

'Don't care,' he replied. 'Better leave your brain by the door too.'

I went to him and lay down, put my head on his breast. He held me close and stroked my hair. We didn't say anything. I surrendered myself; simply that. Let what must happen happen.

There came the moment before, after which everything must change, and it was a lifetime and yet a nanosecond. He moved in me slowly, so that trails of stars ignited throughout my body, until it seemed each cell must explode, and the tower would be punched open above us, and a new tower of light would reach towards the skies, which would be all that was left of us, straining to join the stars. But I didn't spontaneously combust and neither did he. The pulse of the arunic tide began to ebb and my body settled. I wasn't changed forever, only left with a burning thirst.

Nytethorne fetched us berry cordial from the kitchen. 'Wanted to give you something you'd not quickly forget,' he said.

I drank the juice. That was a game that more than one could play. I'd show him... soon.

He watched me as I finished my drink. 'You let nohar in. Has it always been like that? I heard aruna was your speciality, some kind of magic.'

'*Who* did you hear that from?'

He shrugged. 'Mossamber has friends. He asked.'

'Friends in Kyme? Where?'

'Not sure,' Nytethorne said, 'he has friends everywhere.'

I think I knew then: Malakess. Mossamber had contacted him about me.

'Well, whatever he think he knows, whatever he's heard I am or was, you don't have to be emotionally enlightened to tweak the nerves of the body. It's mechanical, and not hard to master.'

Nytethorne shook his head, smiled to himself. 'Somehar has much to answer for.'

'I *have* let hara in,' I said. 'All it ever brought was trouble. Some are made for it, but not me. I just ruin things. Somehar once said to me I wasn't supposed to have a cosy life with chesnari and harlings — and he was right.'

I didn't want to speak like this, hard and cold, but was unable to change it. I wanted to tell Nytethorne he was amazing, and I would like more than anything for it be different with us, for it to work. But no. I had to change the subject. 'Never mind that. Who's your father, Nytethorne?'

He studied me for a moment. 'You really want to know?'

'Yes.'

'All right. Know you like stories.' He lay back down beside me and drew me into his arms. Our bodies seemed to fit together like a timber joint. 'Mossamber and Peredur could have no sons, but they wanted them. Mossamber wanted nohar but Peri, didn't want to go to a blessed place with some other har, so they called upon the Gwerin Crwydrwyr, the roamer folk.'

'And who are they?'

He told me that in the early days of Wraeththu in this land, the Gwerin Crwydrwyr were hara unthrist, without tribe, drawn to the most shamanic of paths. They scorned physical conflict and all they deemed human in hara. Everyhar used them for various purposes – healing, teaching, and the creation of harlings. I'd not known this, but roamers were among the first to enable this function among the Sulh. For a price, they would give hara a son. Nytethorne thought they probably still would, although they weren't seen around so much nowadays, just occasionally at some of the fayres.

'Mossamber never knew his name,' Nytethorne said. 'Was with him only an hour. In that time, he grew older in mind and heart, and came away from it with me in him.'

Three years later, Mossamber again called upon the services of the Gwerin Crwydrwyr and the result of that was Emberflax, Nytethorne's brother who I'd not yet met.

'We call him Flax,' Nytethorne told me.

'Your son is named for him?'

Nytethorne shook his head. 'Partly. *His* full name is Emberstrife.'

'And Ember's father?'

Nytethorne was silent for a moment, stroking my back. Then he said, 'A roamer. After Porter – way I wanted it.'

'You are a fecund tribe, it seems! Why two sons?'

'We know the secret, that's all. Our custom is to have two sons. We are many at the Domain: hara who were Mossamber's human hura...' He wrinkled his nose. 'Had names for it, can't remember.'

'Nephews, uncles, I think you mean.'

He nodded. 'Mossamber's father took them in during the Devastation. Whitemanes survived better than the Wyverns.'

'Medoc isn't doing too badly.'

'He's sensible. He fled. No longer part of this.' With these words, Nytethorne silenced anything further I might say with a kiss. 'Enough of stories,' he said. 'Let me in, Ysobi. Think you can heal the world? Well, I can heal you.'

I put my hands on his beautiful face. 'You can't give Peredur new eyes. You can't give me a new heart.'

'If Peri only had *broken* eyes, they might be mended. You can't say you have no heart. Be brave enough to trust. Not yourself. Me. Won't fall. I'll catch you.' He kissed me again. 'Begin with the breath.'

I had never realised before how little I let go during aruna. Not even with those I thought I'd loved had I ever truly opened the doors to my inner self and allowed them to walk around looking at the things that were me, my history. I think some had seen me as a challenge because I was so closed and distant. Everyhar believes he can break down the doors of the ice tower, find the living warmth hidden within. I'd never let them, because I'd never faced how incomplete I was. Something old and dank lurked within me. Eyes across a fire, all I ever remembered. And yet, now, as I lay in Nytethorne's arms I realised this inability to truly connect was my greatest weakness, and if the *ysbryd drwg* was to find a chink in my armour, this was it. The missing piece. I opened myself to Nytethorne Whitemane.

I didn't find it easy. Even opening the breath was difficult, because so much can be revealed in that – the first sign of trust between two hara coming together. His breath was a storm, blowing through me, breaking barriers. My instinct was to resist, shutter all doors, batten down, but behind one of those doors, like those of an immense old barn, horror lurked. We could both feel it there, hear it yelping, biting its own limbs. Nytethorne pulled away from me. 'Are you ready?'

'Yes,' I said, 'but bear in mind tomorrow you might have no hienama to aid you.'

'Will take that risk.'

Having opened the portals of my mind and body through breath, all other sensations beyond that were symbolic, often bizarre. I could see Nytethorne as a warrior riding a chariot drawn by maddened horses with forked tongues. The chariot thundered through me, into my history, into battle.

There...

I couldn't pull his name from my memory, even though I could see his face so clearly. Laughing. In firelight. A camp of hara spread out all around us. We were young and new and full of blood and temper. We fought like cubs, ending up inside each other, licking each other's faces, making wounds with nails and teeth. That love, though feral, had been pure, beyond thought or analysis, mere instinct. First love, you'd call it. We'd kill side by side, full of joy, not caring who we killed or even why. We took aruna amid the carnage, blood on our skins. Animals. No, *less* than animals, for animals do not kill like that. But perhaps they love in that way. We weren't unique. Many of us had these fierce, intense relationships. We were new to ourselves, aghast at what we could do, the pleasure we could bring to one another, the damage we could wreak. We thought we were immortal. Him I loved. I let him *be* me. Gave everything.

When he died I was right next to him. One moment he was beside me, the next a mist of red as the detonation of a buried human explosive device took him. I was painted with him. Nothing was left, nothing to bury or kiss. I'd been so close, yet was untouched.

I went mad, as many of us did when we suffered these losses, which were common. Some managed better than others. Our leader beat me until I stopped shrieking, until I nearly stopped breathing. Then he took me, made me experience the terrible pleasure of aruna, terrible because it over-rides everything else, and I didn't want to do it. I fought him and he hurt me, but all the time that grim goddess of carnal delight took her due. 'This is all that matters,' my leader said. 'No weeping. Find another. It's done.'

But it never had been *done*. While senseless with grief, I'd been raped and beaten. Beaten, beaten, beaten. By my own body. By his. Until I didn't care. Until I learned.

As I'd lain there, breathing in the gulping way that is swallowed tears and grief, lying upon the hard ground, I'd vowed I would beat that goddess, bend her to my will, make her mine. She'd never possess me like that again. And I did tame aruna, made it feed from my hand, do tricks that made hara gasp in amazement, while they were all but dead in mind and body because of what I could do to them. The greatest revenge. Love me. See what happens.

This voice is who I used to be.

I came back into the present moment, sobbing like a harling, Nytethorne motionless upon me. He allowed me some moments, then murmured, 'Take what I give you. Like the waters that gave Peredur life.'

Pleasure seemed an abomination in the face of what I'd remembered, because of the associations, but I clung to him, wreckage in the storm, with the cold waves lashing over me, and then there was a warm wave that was the essence of compassion, and I could breathe it in and make it into light, a tower of light reaching to the stars. It was orgasm, but experienced as a universe-filling sheet of glass or crystal, mazed with cracks that sang like shattering ice, like a world-spanning frozen lake that is breaking. I exploded into a million pieces, each one shining like diamond, flying out. Unlocked.

When I opened my eyes, with Nytethorne panting upon me, as if half drowned himself, I saw motes of golden light in the room, floating around, not even sinking. I watched them for some minutes until they faded away, but then the room was still haunted by soft light, and I could hear voices singing. Nytethorne seemed to have fallen asleep, still joined to me. 'Get up. Get up!' I hissed.

He rolled off me, clawing hair from his face. 'What?'

I rose from the bed and instinctively hunched low to cross the room, fetching up between two of the windows. I looked out. Nytethorne had come up behind me. We saw a serpent of light around the tower, snaking round the winding path that led from the bottom of the hill to its summit. At first I thought it was hara with burning torches, but the light was too yellow. As I peered through the glass, I could make out nebulous forms within the light, vague outlines. Nytethorne breathed into my ear, '*Ysbryddon garedig*,' he said. 'The good ghosts.'

The light of this procession pooled around the base of Dŵr Alarch, perhaps drawn or conjured by what Nytethorne and I had experienced, or perhaps there simply because of what must happen the following day. I knew instinctively they had come to add their strength to ours for the coming fight.

We watched them and listened to their song for maybe three minutes, although it seemed longer. Then Dŵr Alarch absorbed their light and they were gone. Even in a landscape of sorrow, not all ghosts are bitter.

Chapter Twenty-Four

Despite what I know now, I still wonder exactly how Wyva felt that morning, what he did. He would of course have sat with his family to eat his breakfast, no doubt discussed in some small measure the Reaptide festival for the following day. Did he notice something in Rinawne and Myv? Did he sense their secrets? Or was he so immersed in and consumed by his own thoughts he didn't notice? We thought he didn't notice much at all, or that, if he did, he deliberately became blind to these things. On that, we were all wrong.

As for me, I woke that day from what I thought was a strange and wonderful dream, but I was in fact held in Nytethorne's warm arms. I had faced my most deeply buried demon and hauled it shrieking to the surface of my mind. I wasn't sure if this was enough to vanquish it, but now I knew its face, its story, and what it had made of me.

Nytethorne stirred as I woke, as if attuned to my state of being. He kissed my shoulder and said, 'You all right?'

I turned onto my back, reached to touch his face. 'I think I *am*.' This said in a tone of wonderment.

He laid his head on me. 'You see, it was meant. How could you go to the fight with that lot squashed into you?'

I frowned. 'But how could I not remember? Surely...' I closed my eyes, tried to think back, but even now all I remembered was the aruna vision and that it was true. I couldn't recall standing by him I loved; I could only see the moment after I'd been drenched in his blood. I couldn't remember the intricacies of taking aruna with him, but the details of what that other har, who we called our leader, did to me were there in sharp relief.

'Don't question,' Nytethorne said. 'We did what we had to.'

'Was that all it was?' I smiled somewhat sadly. 'My therapy?'

Nytethorne sighed and rolled his eyes. 'You want me to answer that? We don't need that crap.'

All those domineering words: *Do you love me? I love you. Don't leave me. Please don't leave me.* The minute something is loved it brings as its dark gift the fear it might be lost. Betrayal, abandonment, death. That is the true terror of allowing love to happen. This is what our wise hara were trying to tell us all along. Slaughter the need, embrace the love.

Reaptide is the second of the harvest festivals, when hara give thanks for all they have so far gathered and what they have yet to harvest. It is, as I have said, a strange in-between celebration, but one of its symbols is the burning of the fields. Therefore, its theme is that of new beginnings, making the landscape fit for next year's growth. The fires burn away dead plants, disease and weeds. Perfect imagery for our purposes. The field burning would start tomorrow in reality, but ours would start tonight.

Nytethorne and I dressed and went down to breakfast. The preliminary rituals we'd decided upon were due to begin at mid-day. We would work slowly. Rinawne and Myv hadn't yet arrived, but Arianne was already up, as usual taking charge of her kitchen. I liked being in charge of it too, but allowed her this because after tonight she would not come back to it. And anyway, this tower had been hers long before it was mine.

When Peredur entered the kitchen, some ten minutes later, he came to me at once and embraced me. 'I heard you last night,' he whispered to me.

'I apologise,' I murmured back.

He laughed softly. 'Not that... I heard what you *saw*.'

'We both have our stories,' I said. 'I doubt there are many who don't from those times.'

'I won't think any less of you if you let some of that joy my suri gave you peer out beyond the surface of your skin,' he said and kissed the top of my head.

Myv and Rinawne arrived at eleven. As planned, we spent half an hour or so in meditation, preparing ourselves for what was to come. I took great care not to betray any intimacy with Nytethorne for Rinawne's sake. First, I didn't want to hurt him and second, that kind of emotional fallout could jeopardise our work. I'd told Nytethorne about Rinawne, and he'd surprised me by saying I didn't have to end that relationship for his sake. 'Have no contract for you,' he'd said. 'Live and love as you please.' This was how different Nytethorne was to anyhar I'd been close to before. I noticed Rinawne didn't look at me directly, perhaps not wanting to see evidence within me that Nytethorne and I had become closer. I wasn't sure he'd react as calmly as Nytethorne had done when eventually I told him the truth. Still, that was for another day, which I hoped we'd live to see.

Our journey would begin in the baked mountains, where insects sizzled in the heat. We would take water with us, but not food. Other than a light breakfast, we must abstain from that. As we sat in my nayati, I extended my senses into the landscape. I could feel the *ysbryd drwg* prowling, gathering strength. Simultaneously, the form of Verdiferel took shape. This was the trickster dehar, who at midsummer had murdered his creator and lover to become the creator for the coming season. Already new life grew within him, but for now he was set free from his obligations, the magician on the path. But despite his less clement aspects, Verdiferel was still a dehar, the stuff of gods shaped into a harish form by harish hearts and minds. Into him we must lure the egregore of Gwyllion, then we must lead and ultimately trap him. After that... it was difficult to make precise plans. I had to trust we would know what to do. Mossamber had shown me some of what we faced. I was not so proud as to think our task would be easy, but I had to believe we could succeed, otherwise there was no point in trying.

At mid-day we left the tower, travelling on foot, carrying satchels containing the small amount of equipment we'd need and our water supply. We headed south down the valley, crossing the river at the mossy bridge Mossamber had shown me, but we did not go towards the haunted forest. Instead we turned our steps to the primordial sweep of the ancient mountains that were mostly covered in lichen, short grasses and heather. Peredur had told us of a granite boulder called Craig Drygioni, which had associations with a trickster spirit. He thought this a good place to invoke Verdiferel. To reach this site we must climb for over two miles. From the valley floor, the slope appeared gentle, yet was anything but that once we began to ascend it. A pair of red-billed choughs soared above us, uttering piercing cries, occasionally diving through the air with folded wings. They seemed to be keeping pace with us, perhaps curious. But other than these black birds, the landscape appeared weirdly empty, desolate. The air hummed with the heat.

Craig Drygioni looked out of place, as if it had fallen from the sky and been dumped in the wrong place, alone on a high mountainside. The height of a har, it was attended by broom bushes, still jewelled with a few yellow blooms, and ground-hugging white stonecrop; altar flowers for this sacred space. As we climbed, I could visualise Verdiferel sitting on top of the stone, observing our approach. His feet were bare, the toes long, gripping the lichened rock. He was chewing on a broom stem, his hair in coiling brown tendrils around him, his ragged clothes made of leaves and leather.

We sat against the rock and drank some water. Myv opened his satchel and withdrew that pale swatch of fabric, which glistened in the sunlight. 'This is the moonshawl,' he told Nytethorne, offering it for him to inspect. Myv's ritual robe.

'It's Gwerin Crwydrwyr work,' Nytethorne said, in a tone of wonderment.

'How do you know?' I asked.

Nytethorne shrugged. 'Seen similar, only once. Rare they give hara such things.'

'Who are Gwerin Crwydrwyr?' Arianne asked.

'Roamer folk,' Nytethorne said.

'Do you know of them, Myv?' I asked.

He shook his head. 'No. Are they sorcerers?'

'Yes,' Nytethorne answered.

Myv smiled.

We composed ourselves in a circle, me with my back to the Craig. Myv draped the moonshawl around his shoulders before joining hands with the rest of us. On my right side was Arianne, Myv on my left. Rinawne sat between Myv and Peredur, Nytethorne between Peredur and Arianne. I bid them close their eyes, regulate their breathing and then aloud I said, 'Astale, Verdiferel, you are welcome among us.'

I could see him again on the rock above us, now standing. This was no benign, gentle dehar. No flowers fell from his skin. His eyes were the green of the forest canopy, shining like light on water. When he smiled, his teeth were long and white, the canines, while not abnormally large, clearly more pointed than those found in a har. Above him, in the pulsing blue of the hot sky, a white owl flew by day. The choughs, who had remained with us, fled shrieking, for the owl preys upon them. Verdiferel crouched now on the rock, one hand slung across his knees, the other braced against the stone. He watched me intently, as wary as a dehar of his nature could be, but it was our will and intention that called this being into reality and shaped him, therefore it was up to us to banish any hint of suspicion within him.

Myv had draped the moonshawl around his shoulders. I told him to cast its net over the rock; not in reality, but in the inner world, that 'other summer' we inhabited. I saw the glistening white folds, light as feathers, settle around Verdiferel. 'Call the spirits of the land to you, both *drwg* and *da*,' I told the dehar. 'We will sing you to the sacred places.'

The moonshawl did not burn or constrict him – it was after all patterned with white owls, his own creature. Now was the time for us to open our eyes, but also to remain half in the inner summer, seeing both reality and the world of imagination at the same time. This would be easier for Peredur than for us.

I composed a song spontaneously that had no words, but even so the sounds meant *follow us, come with us, there are wonders at the journey's end.* I know that the entity we'd summoned and fashioned heeded these instructions. In his sly feral way he saw only the flight of owls by day. Around us, I could sense confused spirits walking through the sunlight, not knowing how or why they'd come to be there. If a har dies at Reaptide, his phyle takes extra precautions so he doesn't fall into Verdiferel's long cruel hands.

We went down the mountainside and the shadows grew longer over the land. I wouldn't take Verdiferel to the forest of the dead so he might conspire with the tumour of grief that lurked there. We led him along the river, through its shallows. The water was cool and quick. We led the dehar to Pwll Siôl Lleuad and here we laid out offerings of bread and wine for him on the rock next to the water, where I'd seen Nytethorne sit to dry himself what seemed like years ago. We composed ourselves to wait for nightfall, each taking a drink from the pool.

Slowly, the sun dipped redly down the sky, but it became twilight at Pwll Siôl Lleuad sooner than anywhere else nearby. Foliage rustled as if creeping paws stepped through it. The leaf canopy above us sighed and swayed. Slowly, all things that crept through darkness were drawn to us. I could feel this.

Verdiferel was almost dozing above the pool, the moonshawl shining around him like a caul. Midges gathered in balls above the water, dancing lightly on the air. I heard the clack of wing feathers; the white owl, heard but not yet seen.

'Call the spirits to you, Verdiferel,' I said. 'Bring all of them, throughout the ages, to this sacred spot.'

'Ysobi,' Myv said softly next to me. 'We must help him. We must put our blood into the water.'

I felt Arianne flinch. Briefly, her hand gripped mine harder.

'Yes,' Peredur said. I looked at him and his eye stones were black obsidian. Hadn't they been moonstones earlier?

Rinawne said nothing, but brought from his own satchel a small, sharp knife, which he handed to me. I let go of the hands holding mine and went to the water's edge, made a small, swift cut in my palm. 'For Verdiferel and the burning of the fields,' I said, then put my bleeding hand into the water, kept it there, until one by one all of my companions had done the same. Our pale and dark hands and the ribbons of red. This was our first sacrifice.

I told the group how I'd seen Verdiferel among us, then asked them how he appeared to them.

'A har in a red cloak,' said Myv. 'The hood covers his face except for his mouth, but I can see his eyes gleaming gold.'

Arianne frowned as she spoke with closed eyes. 'He is in a mist, so I can barely see him. Yes... in a cloak, as Myv saw, but it is brown or black.'

'I see him,' said Rinawne, 'as small, almost like a harling with a sharp, cruel little face. His fingers are like twigs and his eyebrows are made of leaves.'

'His smile is too wide,' Nytethorne said, 'teeth are sharp, but eyes dark and kind. He wears a garment of knotted cloths, twined with flowers and grasses, and a crown of owl feathers.'

There was a silence, then Peredur said: 'He is me.'

'He is all of these things,' I said. 'As you visualise him, try to incorporate all these details you've heard. Make him *our* egregore. He works for us.'

'I'll speak to the spirit of the *pwll*,' Peredur said, 'wake it up for us.'

Shadows extended their groping fingers into the glade as the night came down about us. The owl called, once, twice. And then I heard the bell, distantly. In the Domain, the Whitemanes would be gathering to send us their strength. Beyond the glade, I sensed the pale shimmer of the good ghosts, the *ysbryddon garedig*, distant yet close. And the *ysbryd drwg* smelled Myv's blood in the pool and was intoxicated by its scent.

I could see this clearly in my mind's eye and described it to my companions. The entity was sometimes like a serpent of smoke, close to the ground, at other times walking upright like a har, or on all fours like a dog. It filled the landscape with its presence, holding within its fabric the hurts of centuries. I could sense Peredur inside it, the part of him forever nailed and chained to a stake in the stableyard of Meadow Mynd. I could sense Vivi, a cold female presence, full of vengeance and righteousness, who saw herself as the righter of wrongs. But these were only two parts of an immense company, not simply those who had died terrible deaths during the Devastation, but humans from earlier times, killed by parents, lovers, siblings, strangers on the road, criminals, senseless justice, warfare and disease. All these despairing souls had been supped upon by the *ysbryd drwg*, for it believed they belonged with it.

And now as the Dog Star ruled the heavens, and the heat conjured ghosts in the day, it had come to take what had been promised to it; the son of the Wyvachi. I did not believe this entity would suddenly manifest before us and hurt Myv physically. Its influence was more insidious than that. But it would come to taste, and leave its mark, and later some accident might befall Myv, perhaps weeks afterwards, when hara might think that nothing bad would happen. A scythe in the fields, a poisoned nail in the straw, a bolt of lightning, a maddened horse. There are many ways to kill a har. We might be strong, but we are neither invulnerable nor immortal.

Verdiferel stirred upon the rock by the pool. I could see him at the edge of my vision even with my eyes open. He stood up, quivering, facing away from us. The *ysbryd drwg* was trickling through the trees, leaves blackening and falling dead as it touched them. Verdiferel stretched his body, his arms high, welcoming this diseased power.

'Embrace it, my lord, it is yours,' I whispered.

In mind touch, but 'audible' to my companions, I asked Peredur, *Is the water spirit with us and ready?*

Yes, he replied. *Here as it always has been*. There was no mistaking the affection in the flavour of his thoughts.

To all of them I sent the instructions: *When Verdiferel takes the ysbryd into himself, see the moonshawl tighten around him like bonds of unbreakable silk. Visualise that we get to our feet and push him into the water, that the spirit there takes hold of him and contains him. Try to visualise this without violence, that the spirit's embrace is unbreakable but not harmful.*

Then...? Rinawne asked.

I didn't have time to reply because, at that moment, the force of the *ysbryd drwg* collided with Verdiferel. The impact sent a blast of sound through my mind, like clashing rocks and the discordant howl of a war trumpet combined. It took all my effort not to open my eyes. 'Keep focused within the vision,' I told the group aloud. 'Don't falter.'

The force of the egregore pounded into the dehar, enlarging him. He stood as tall as the trees now and still that dark energy flowed into him. Peredur chanted softly words of the ancient language, that I could barely hear or understand, but we all caught the rhythm of it and joined our voices to his. Between us, our own power began to form and rise in a spiral of pale white light.

I had to choose the exact moment for us to bind Verdiferel. I was sure it was nearly time, just mere seconds away – silver ripples had begun to form upon the surface of the pool – when suddenly Verdiferel emitted a roar, which sounded like an immense bell shattering. Before we could react, he bounded away from us through the trees.

Our visualisation splintered like crystal, and the weave of our combined energy broke up and scattered.

'What the...?' Rinawne cried.

'No!' Myv cried.

'Follow him,' I ordered. 'Now!'

We had no choice but to open our eyes and pursue what in the waking world would most likely be invisible to us.

'Peredur, you guide us,' I snapped. 'Myv, take Peredur's hand so he doesn't have to concentrate on the physical world.

Lead him!'

Without further delay, I got to my feet and ran after the dehar, pushing through foliage and shrubs that seemed to bend towards me to hinder my passage. Peredur was at my side, barking directions at Myv. I could hear the others following. Verdiferel must not get away from us, not now we'd helped him engorge with the power of the *ysbryd drwg*. There was no sense of the gentle, benevolent *ysbryddon garedig* during that desperate pursuit, only the hectic rush of our chase, and dark vortexes of power spinning round us. Ropes of dark purple smoke, sibilant hissing, the yelp of unearthly predators.

'He's making for the fields beside the river,' Peredur said, 'probably the Maes Siôl, the river field.'

I could sense this too. As we ran, I glanced up and saw the white owl in the sky, its gigantic glowing wings spread against the night. 'The owl is our guide,' I yelled. 'Follow it, Myv, it'll lead us to its master.'

The end of the trees was in sight. I could see a strange ruddy glow ahead.

'Something's burning,' Arianne said.

I could smell it – the reek of burned grass, which became stronger as we ran. We emerged from the trees and kept running. We had to clamber over two hedges to reach the Maes Siôl. I could see that it was on fire. There was, in fact, a ring of flame. I could just perceive, within the black smoke that issued from it, a shadowy figure in its midst. Verdiferel was slowing down. I could feel the pulse of his movement within me. I realised he hadn't run away from us; somehar else had called him. Somehar, or a number of hara, were enacting their own rite in the Maes Siôl, and I felt sure this wasn't a simple Reaptide event.

I signalled for my companions to stop, spreading my arms to keep them behind me. 'What can you tell us?' I asked Peredur.

'Another har summoned the *ysbryd drwg*,' he said, as I'd known he would. 'It feels like a Wyvachi.'

'It's Wyva!' Rinawne cried. 'Dear Aru, it is! I know!'

'We must go to him,' Myv said, in a panicked tone, and made to run towards the fire, but I grabbed hold of him and kept him back.

'Not yet!'

'It'll kill him!' Myv wailed.

I shook him a little. 'Hush, we'll not help by blundering in. And it won't kill him immediately.' I looked at Peredur, then reached for his hand. 'Well?'

Peredur raised his other hand and pointed at the field, all the time his black stare on me. 'Can you all see that? With your living eyes, I mean?'

'Yes,' Nytethorne murmured.

'Dear God,' Arianne whispered.

Yes, they could see it. Ahead of us, the looming figure that was the transformed Verdiferel had stepped into the ring of fire. The flames cowered low before him. Our combined will, plus the potent mesh of energy contained within the *ysbryd drwg*, was strong enough to manifest the dehar in reality. I'd seen nothing like this before. Verdiferel was as tall as the greatest of oaks, with rags of clothing and hair whipping around him.

'Peredur, help Wyva,' Rinawne hissed. 'For Aru's sake, we must...'

'Hush,' Peredur said. 'Go closer, but slowly. Join hands. Don't let go of each other.'

We obeyed his words.

I saw Wyva har Wyvachi standing in his fragile temple of fire with the egregore looming over him. It was no longer merely our invoked dehar, but something far larger, far more distant, yet obscenely close. This creature turned to the side, so Wyva would not be able to see its face. Neither could we. Then it began to emit a roaring, booming sound that was the essence of fear, despair and hopelessness. This was a sound that nohar should hear; it made death seem benign. Everyhar in the county must be able to hear it.

'Beansidhe,' Rinawne murmured.

'What?' Arianne asked him.

'The cruellest spirit. If you see her, if you hear her, she takes somehar. We mustn't see...'

As Rinawne spoke, the egregore began to turn around to face Wyva, all the while emitting that foul noise.

'No!' Myv cried, fighting against my hold.

Unable to wait any longer, Rinawne released the hands he held and raced across the field, waving his arms in the air, shouting, 'Verdiferel! This way! Look this way!'

Myv struggled like a hysterical cat in my grasp and screamed, 'Let me go, Ysobi. Those are my hara there. Let me go!'

The edge of one of Peredur's hands slammed down on my wrist, numbing it. Myv broke free. 'Let him act,' Peredur said. 'It's his fight.'

Perhaps Verdiferel, deep within the egregore, this fully manifested *ysbryd drwg*, had heard Rinawne's cry. He'd paused, his body stooped. But then, slowly, he began to turn once more.

Arianne said softly, 'Vivi's in that thing. I can *feel* her. She's here.' She too ran after Rinawne and Peredur followed her.

I glanced at Nytethorne, who shrugged.

'Go after them?' he suggested.

We did so, but more cautiously. I needed to gauge what would happen. If the rest of them panicked, only Nytethorne and I could hold things together.

Everything seemed to move in slow motion: the running figures, the silhouette in the centre of the circle of fire, held motionless in shock. I saw Wyva's face through the smoke and flames, soot-streaked, wild, nothing like I'd ever seen him. I could see he had steeled himself to fight, perhaps die. Now he could see his chesnari and son running towards him, no doubt thinking this was an illusion and they weren't really there. A trick to lure him from his protective circle.

While all this was happening, Verdiferel turned to face us fully, but only Nytethorne and I, maybe Peredur, had our attention on him. He held to his features a white mask, expressionless, not fearsome at all. Behind him, it appeared Wyva had realised Myv and Rinawne were real and not deceiving phantoms. He was shouting at them, gesticulating, urging them to leave.

Of course, they took no notice. Once they reached Wyva, they flung themselves upon him, protecting him with their bodies. The moonshawl, spreading from Myv's body, seemed to cover them all, gleaming like mercury.

The white mask of Verdiferel stared at me, ignoring the drama behind him. Then, almost casually, he drew the mask from his face. I was ready for anything but... There was stillness between us. Seconds that extended for hours. Behind the mask... there was nothing. *Nothing at all.* I saw a black void extending away forever. The hideous sounds issued from it, as if from a great distance. And yet even within that nothingness I perceived a cruel smile. The *ysbryd drwg* had shown me its face. I remembered the fear Rinawne had spoken of, that gut deep, primal fear. I could feel it scrabbling within me like a trapped animal. But then I thought: *I've seen your face before. I've fallen into that void. Yet here I am. Let's see what happens.*

The *ysbryd drwg* appeared to study me for a moment, perhaps curious in its inconceivable way, then, almost shrugging, it removed its attention from me, and turned to confront those in the centre of the flames. Easier prey. They seemed pitiful, helpless, a bundle of writhing bodies. Wyva was trying to fight off Myv and Rinawne; they were determined to hold him down.

Arianne had paused at the edge of the circle. She had raised her arms, her head flung back.

Peredur stood motionless just ahead of Nytethorne and me. He appeared to be assessing what he perceived before him. When we caught up with him, I grabbed hold of his arm. 'What do we do?' I snapped. 'Peredur, ideas, something! Please, for Aru's sake.'

'We must...' Peredur began.

Then Arianne's voice rang out, 'No, Vivi, no! For the love of your children, hear me! Look at me!'

I thought at first her voice would have no effect. For a few agonising moments: nothing. And then the towering *ysbryd drwg* straightened up, became motionless. It was listening to her: the dead that walked it did not own.

You have its attention! I sent to her, hoping to all the dehara she heard me. *Reach Vivi, call her from it.*

'Vivi, you know me,' Arianne cried. 'It's Arianne. Look at me. Remember me!'

For a moment, an immense flickering image of Vivi's face appeared in the yawning maw of the *ysbryd drwg*. A wavering voice slithered from it. *All women are dead... There is no Arianne.* Then the image faded.

'That's not true,' Arianne said, her voice steady. 'Come forth, Vivi. Listen to me. Just listen.'

I could sense Arianne's compassion and calm, her determination to remain this way, not to falter. She had not been able to save her family from Wraeththu aggression, nor Peredur from mutilation. She had, once, not been able to save herself. But now... I was awed by her resolve, which was as hard as the ancient stone of the mountains. 'See me here,' she said in a low fierce voice. 'Try to touch me, *ysbryd drwg*. But you cannot kill the dead, can you? I'll take back what is mine.' She raised her voice. 'Vivi! Follow my words. See the shining rope of sound. Come to me. I'm waiting.'

For a moment, only stillness, but then the flickering image of Vivi appeared once more in void of the *ysbryd drwg*.

'The past is done, Vivi,' Arianne said firmly, 'yet our family lives on. Meadow Mynd still stands. The cows graze in the meadows. The crops grow. Our descendents thrive. There are still men and women, but just in a different way. And look how strong they are, how brave, how beautiful. A child would give her life for her parents. Would you destroy all this? Wasn't peace what you really wanted?'

Persuasiveness, and a simple, strong conviction of truth,

rang out from Arianne's voice. This was her task. Failing it was inconceivable to her; she gave over her entire being to victory. I admired the way she spoke of Myv as female, which of course, he half was. If Vivi could taste the essence of Myv, she'd find the feminine within him. But she wasn't yet ready to try.

Our family is gone... Vivi hissed. *Only lies and misshapen abominations remain. I must kill them.*

'No,' Arianne said. 'You mustn't. Our family isn't gone, it's simply changed, that's all.' She pointed at the group within the fire circle. 'That's your great grandson over there and his daughter too. And here...' She turned briefly to Peredur, who was like a white statue at my side. 'Here is your grandson, Peredur. After all you did to him, he survived, because it was meant.'

I did not survive, nor did your daughters... All our people died.

Arianne shook her head. 'No, not all. What happened was horrific, a foul fever that gripped the world. We were done, Vivi. Humanity's time was over. The world was dying, and so were we. We would have destroyed everything. Our ending was unspeakable – but did we not call this on ourselves? We had become a disease, an infection. The badness had to be let out, and it was. It exploded in a disgusting torrent. But then the wounds of the world could heal. *We* healed. Made new. Look into my heart and see this truth. See if you find any shred of anger or grief inside me.'

Traitor! Vivi hissed. *You joined them! You betrayed me!*

'No,' Arianne answered firmly. 'In fact, I died. I took my own life in Dŵr Alarch, because I could no longer bear to live, but my body was never found. You know why? Because the world, the universe, or God, or merely the simple pattern of life – whatever you want to call it – meant for me to come back and talk to you now. I was taken somewhere, stored like a prayer, a wish, a hope – then allowed back. Here I am.' She held out her hands. 'You can leave that painful nest, Vivi. You can be with me, and we can go somewhere else. Together. I'm here to free you. Break away from the darkness. Come to me!'

For a brief moment, the form of the *ysbryd drwg* wavered, and then I saw a small, twisting shadow fall from its face like a rag. This scrap fell slowly, coiling on the air, before landing softly on the burned ground. Here, it rested, fretted as if by a breeze. Then slowly it rose up, *inflated*, until it resolved into the wavering form of a woman, who stood upon the field, just ahead of Arianne. Vivi: a disorientated, confused woman, her hands to her face. She appeared unaware of where she was and how she'd got there.

The *ysbryd drwg* bellowed its rage at Vivi being pulled from its fabric. Its dire voice grew louder. I knew it was ready to pounce.

There was one perfect moment of complete stillness, then the world exploded into chaos.

The ring of flame flared up, its tongues of fire hungry and wild. Talons of flame scampered out across the field in strangely liquid trails. Verdiferel's body exploded into a multitude of owls, not white now but black, with blood-red feet and eyes. Feathers burst from them in a storm of darkness and the voice of the *ysbryd drwg* became a hellish choir. The owls swooped around us, snagging us with their claws and beaks, uttering hoarse screams no bird could possibly make. The owl is traditionally a symbol of wisdom; these owls were merely cruelty.

Arianne stood tall, heedless of the vicious strikes upon her. She was still calling Vivi's name, holding out her bloodied hands. 'Come to me, Vivi. I'm here. Take my hands.'

Slowly, Vivi did so, taking the stumbling steps of an invalid.

I saw Arianne grab hold of her, pull her close, protecting them both from the vicious claws.

'Come', Peredur said to me. In the weird light he appeared calm, sure, and gestured at the hara within the ring of flame. 'It is they who need us.'

I glanced back at Arianne and Vivi, who were at that moment taking on the full might of the attack. I couldn't just leave them to deal with that, but knew also I had to trust

Peredur now. All I could do was project to the women a blast of energy, a pitiful shield.

'Come!' Peredur commanded, and walked unfalteringly towards the group within the circle of flame. I followed him, Nytethorne at my side.

When I reached the centre, Wyva stared at me with wide, wild eyes: furious. I could hear him thinking: *You brought my son here! My chesnari! You! With a Whitemane and dehara know what other oddities!*

Myv saw me and tried to shout through the cacophony: 'It's time. We must turn the birds. Help me turn the birds.'

Peredur took his hand. 'Yes. Turn the birds.' His voice was only a whisper, yet I heard it. 'All of us,' he said, louder. 'Make the circle.'

'Arianne!' I called, but Peredur put a hand on my arm.

'No, I meant all *hara*. Not her.'

'But...?'

He closed his eyes briefly, for a moment unable to quell the pain he felt. Then he composed himself once more. 'It has to be this way. This is her moment too, but different. She's giving us time.'

Myv and Rinawne sat either side of Wyva, who refused to take their hands. 'This is madness,' he said, his voice breaking. 'Ysobi, take them away. You must go!'

'No!' Myv cried.

'If my hara die because of you,' Wyva spat at me, 'the curse I'll put upon you in death will be worse than any we face now.'

Peredur leaned down to Wyva and took his face in his hands. 'Shut up, you fool,' he said.

Wyva spat at him, tried to free himself, but Peredur did not release his grip. 'What are you?' Wyva cried hoarsely. 'What sick lie are you?'

'Me?' Peredur said, silkily. 'Look at me. Take a guess.'

Wyva became still, stared at Peredur for a moment in silence, while those mad birds wheeled above us, shrieking so hideously I felt sure my ears must bleed. Peredur was a blade of light in all that darkness.

Then Wyva managed to pull away, set his face into a sneer. 'I don't know who you are or what you're trying to do, but go! If anyhar can end this, it must be me.'

Peredur sighed. 'As I said: you're a fool. Look closer, Wyva. I am your hura. I am Peredur. Now shut up and do as I say.'

Wyva appeared about to throw himself violently at Peredur, but Rinawne pulled him back, held him tight. I saw him take two blows to the head from Wyva's flailing arms. 'Liar!' Wyva yelled. 'Peredur is dead. Dead! You think I'm that easily fooled?'

Peredur folded his arms. 'I'm no liar, but we've no time for arguments. You want to end this curse forever? Then be still and give your son your strength. You won't ever end this, Wyva. This is Myv's task.'

'It *is* him, Wyva, it *is!*' Myv wailed pitifully. 'Please believe me. Rin, tell him. Tell him!'

'It's Peredur,' Rinawne said, somewhat hopelessly.

I could tell Wyva didn't believe this, but he did stop fighting, probably because there wasn't really anything else he could do.

Peredur leaned down to touch Myv's head. 'This *ysbryd drwg* is yours,' he said gently. 'Own it, Myvyen. If you would rule the spirituality of your hara and this land – claim ownership.'

Myv nodded, his expression resigned. He squirmed away from his parents, taking the shawl with him, then sat beside his hostling. Peredur also sat down, took the harling's other hand. We closed our circle, with Arianne and Vivi still standing some distance away from us, almost hidden by the spiralling riot of feathers.

'This is your time,' Peredur said to Myv. 'End it.'

In response, Myv put back his head and howled: a battle cry. Then he got to his feet, releasing the hands to either side of him. He went to stand in the centre of our circle, which we closed again around him. He lifted his arms and the moonshawl billowed around him. Then he cast it off and it fell limply to the ground, a shining pool about his feet. Beyond our circle, the black owls and swirling feathers began to condense into a twisting dark ribbon like smoke. This swarmed towards the harling and, through his open mouth, slammed into him.

This was our second sacrifice.

The silence that came with this was so sudden, the impact so great, that for a moment I don't think any of us understood what had happened. Myv trembled, his pale skin mottled with threads of black like polluted blood. His eyes were reddened, staring wildly. What had we done? I saw in that moment, a hundred images: Wyva furious, physically attacking me in his grief, Rinawne distraught, then a funeral, a dozen goodbyes, Nytethorne disappointed, turning away from me, Peredur returning to his isolation in disgrace, and Arianne?

I saw her and Vivi standing side by side outside our circle. They held hands and were singing in the old tongue, their faces and arms scratched and bleeding, their clothing torn. They did not look wholly real, but glowing, almost transparent. Ghosts. I could not tell what the song was, whether a folk song or a hymn, or just some nonsense that meant nothing. The feeling within the tune was its magic. They *had* bought us time. Without Vivi, the *ysbryd drwg* was weaker, perhaps only slightly, but enough. The women sang to the ysbryd drwg that had slammed into Myv. Their song was the essence of the *ysbrydrion da*, all that was good in the land.

This moment of stillness, punctuated only by the soft, steady voices, ended. We were in *no time*, I'm convinced of that.

Myv's body contorted. He stood on tiptoe as if strings attached to him were being pulled towards the sky. His skin was mottled black, like that of a rotted corpse. His arms were stiff and twisted, as if broken. Then, he took in a deep, shuddering breath. So much power contained in such a tiny vessel. How could he survive it?

'Send him strength,' I managed to say, although my tongue was thick and dry in my mouth, barely able to shape sounds.

I'm not afraid, Myv said, although the words didn't come from his lips.

Peredur also rose to his feet, pulling us up with him. 'Gadael, ysbryd aflan!' he cried in strong, clear voice, repeating this phrase over and over. *Be gone, foul spirit!* We joined our voices with his.

Myv groaned, shuddered, his neck twisting unnaturally. I thought it must break, that he wouldn't be able to finish his task. And then, in a jet of disgusting vomit, the egregore erupted from Myv in a black, purple-veined torrent, not only spewing out of his mouth, but from his eyes, his skin. Black birds, black feathers, malign and eternal, twisting, turning, and then... then...

'Yn dod yn dda!' Myv cried.

Feathers turning white like a snowstorm, filling the air. And fragrance. Such a fragrance. The essence of summer, every sweet flower, every crushed blade of grass, the mown hay, the sap bleeding from the hot trunks of trees. And the feathers became petals, falling to earth, as I'd visualised the blood of Morterrius only weeks before.

'This is my land,' Myv said. 'And here we have only *ysbridion da.'*

I could feel them then, the good ghosts, absorbing the energy that Myv had expelled, taking it into themselves, spirits of the land. I saw them as a shining company, hanging in the sky – just for a moment. Then all was still, the night empty.

Smoke rolled lazily across the burned circle, although the flames were doused. I saw Arianne standing some distance from us, still holding Vivi's hand. It was as if she was far, far away, and would soon be farther still. Beside me, my companions were embracing, enacting each in their own way their utter relief, either through tears or laughter.

Peredur touched me gently and I turned to see him standing right behind me. *Go to her,* he told me in mind touch.

And you?

There is nothing more I can say. I can't embrace her now. She knows my heart.

So I went alone to Arianne. I felt Nytethorne's attention upon, but sent him a wordless message, and he didn't follow me. Peredur had said goodbye to his mother before this. For him, she had already faded away.

As I drew nearer to the women, they appeared more solid, the injuries inflicted by the birds clear upon their bodies, blood drying on their skin. Arianne smiled at me sadly, reached for my face with her free hand. I couldn't feel her touch. 'Thank you, Ysobi.'

'Thank *you*,' I said. 'It's done.'

She nodded. 'Yes.' At her side, Vivi was like a convincing image of a woman; mindless, unspeaking, more of a ghost than Arianne had ever been. I don't think she could see me. She didn't belong here now.

Arianne sighed. 'Well, time to move on.'

I nodded. 'Do you know how or where?'

Arianne turned her head. 'The sunrise,' she said. 'When it comes. Until then, we'll walk on the land. I hope she sees it, understands.'

I leaned forward to kiss her cheek, kissed sweet air, nothing more. *This,* I realised was what Peredur had meant about not being able to embrace her. Not the pain of it, just the simple physical inability. 'Care for Vivi,' I said. 'Be happy, wherever you go.'

'I will.' Arianne kissed me too, on the lips, and for a moment I felt a faint pressure. 'Goodbye, my friend.'

'Farewell, Arianne.'

She was our last sacrifice.

As Arianne and Vivi walked away across the field, into the night and beyond, I heard the bell tolling once more. This time, there was no note of melancholy within it.

When I returned to my companions, Myv jumped up and said, 'Where's Arianne? Where *is* she?'

'She's gone now,' I said.

Strong little Myv. He'd taken on so much, far more than most adult hara could withstand, without flinching. Now he simply sank to the ground and wept. 'She's dead,' he said. 'Really dead.'

I hunkered down beside him, stroked his hair. 'No, Myv, no. She's not *ended*. She's just somewhere else. She couldn't stay here. You know that.'

Peredur clasped Myv tightly, said nothing. His weeping was contained within.

Myv clung to his hura, still sobbing, and as I straightened up I caught Wyva's eye above the harling's head.

'I should hate you,' he said.

'Yes,' I replied. 'Somehar always has to be the scapegoat.'

Wyva shook his head slowly. 'The risk you took... with my son...'

'There was no other way. It wasn't your fight, and yet it was everyhar's fight – including the Whitemanes. Time for you to move on, Wyva. You can't deny this.'

Wyva sighed, glanced at Peredur. 'And *him*?'

'He spoke the truth,' Rinawne said. 'I've come to know this har. He's who he says he is.'

Wyva gave Rinawne a studied look and later there would be questions about what he'd said, but for now Wyva turned his attention back to Peredur and said bitterly: 'Why?'

Peredur remained silent, his face resting upon Myv's hair. I could sense he was seeking words within him, finding none that could convey his feelings.

'Just tell me *that*,' Wyva insisted. 'Why this silence, letting us believe...? You could've...' He shook his head.

'There's only one innocent in this,' Peredur said at last. 'Your son.' He kissed Myv's hair and guided him to his hostling's arms. Then he turned his face to me. 'I want to go home. Come with me.'

I was torn then. Shouldn't I return to the Mynd with Wyva and his family? Perhaps they didn't want me to. Suddenly, I was lost.

'Ysobi and me go back to Dŵr Alarch,' Nytethorne said decisively. 'Rest of you go where you please. We meet tomorrow. The Mynd, if you prefer, Wyva har Wyvachi.'

Wyva stared at him for some moments, then nodded, his mouth tight. Rinawne laid his head on Wyva's shoulder for a moment, then stood up. 'I'll take Peredur home,' he said. 'Go back with Myv, Wyva. I'll not be long.' He gave me a sad look, then smiled. I know it cost him to do that.

Mossamber would have known the battle was over, but he did not ride out to bring Peredur home, as I'm sure he wanted to, desperately. Allowing Rinawne to do this was a gesture of trust. Mossamber had laid the first brick in the foundation of a new temple.

Nytethorne and I remained in the field as the others left. We simply stood there, exhausted, looking out over the river. Nytethorne bent down and picked something up from the scorched ground. This was a ragged piece of cloth, full of holes, falling to bits. No shine to it. No pattern. The moonshawl.

He looked at me. I nodded.

Together we went to the river's edge, where Nytethorne crumpled the old fabric into a ball. This, he threw into the water, where it dissolved completely.

Epilogue

The end of one story is also the beginning of many others, and further stories did begin after that night. First, there had to be clarity, with Wyva sitting down with his family to discuss matters openly. I wasn't part of that. Then there was the matter of the bridge between the Whitemanes and the Wyvachi, which as well as being a structure of grey stone was also a har of flesh and blood: Peredur.

I went with him the first time he visited Meadow Mynd, which was the day after our battle with the *ysbryd drwg*. As Nytethorne had suggested, a meeting took place that day. Mossamber attended, but Peredur asked to go with me, before everyhar else. Nytethorne and Mossamber would arrive later.

Peredur rode before me on Hercules, as he had on the day I'd taken him out of the Domain. Wyvachi hara stopped to stare as he passed them, because Peredur will always be strange, somewhat unearthly, a faerie type of creature. He asked to go to the stableyard and there Wyva and his brothers were waiting for him, along with Myv and Rinawne. The silence was absolute as Peredur dismounted from Hercules. He stood motionless for some moments. His eyes that day were rubies. I half expected him to weep blood tears from them. But the stableyard, a hundred years on, was only a yard. Blood had long since washed from the cobbles. Horses had walked over that spot. Dung had been swept from it. Rain and snow and sun had weathered the stones. What had happened there was long ago. Nothing of it remained except the survivor, a har of remarkable strength and certainty, and the love that had made his survival possible. Mossamber loved Peredur, but so did the land and its spirits. He could not be the har he'd been destined to be – that job was now Myv's. But he could be there for Myv as friend and mentor for as long as he lived.

That day, before the meeting, I spoke with Wyva. I couldn't apologise to him, because I didn't feel I had anything to be sorry for. He knew that too, I think, but he's a proud har, had to remain somewhat surly for now to make a point. I trusted this would fade, as Wyva isn't naturally truculent. He did, though, tell me something of what had impelled him to act. Over the weeks building up to Reaptide, he'd witnessed death and destruction throughout his domain. He'd felt helpless to defend his family and the hara who looked up to him, and depended upon him to keep things running.

'Had you so little faith in me?' I asked

He smiled wanly. 'Ysobi, I felt only *I* could deal with the curse, end it as Kinnard had tried to do years before. I was sure I was Myv's last chance and I was prepared to give myself to the *ysbryd drwg* to protect him.'

So, alone, without even the comfort of words, let alone embraces, he had planned his sacrifice. He had walked around the Mynd, experiencing his home for what he believed would be the last time. All he could think of, he told me, was the burning of the fields and that only fire could cleanse the land. When he'd been born, and the curse had been born, the land had drowned. He'd intended to call the *ysbryd drwg* into himself and burn it. I could see the sense in this grim idea, and I'm now sure he was always supposed to be part of our small army. When he'd called Verdiferel to his circle of fire, it had been a necessary part of our purifying ritual.

I also spoke with Porter that day, when he came across me alone in the house, while preparations were being made for the meeting. Rinawne and Myv were showing Peredur around the Mynd, and I didn't feel my place was with them. I was in the library, clearing the table, and Porter passed the door, saw me. I had my back to him, but sensed a living presence and turned. He hesitated, no doubt considering whether to keep walking, but then came in. He didn't say anything, just stared at me inscrutably.

'It should be easier for you now, Porter,' I said. 'No divided loyalties.'

He offered me a grim smile. 'Well, you certainly shook them up.'

I opened a book I had in my hands, blinked at it blindly. 'And I learned the sounds, as you told me to.'

Porter shifted awkwardly. 'It was best you knew. Not just the sounds. About what haunted us. Fush was right.'

I realised this was the nearest I was going to get to an apology, but that incident seemed trivial now, in any case. 'Bridges are important,' I said, putting the book down on the table. 'There is a bridge of stone, and a bridge of hara. Peredur is part of that, but so are you.'

'And my hostling,' he said, somewhat defensively.

'Yes, him too.' I paused. 'Perhaps he should be told about what's happened.'

Porter nodded thoughtfully, then said, 'I'm off. Work to do.'

'Until later, then,' I replied, but he'd already left the room.

The meeting, later, in the library of Meadow Mynd, went as well as could be expected. Mossamber and Wyva were wary of one another, conversation was stilted. Gen and Cawr slunk like suspicious cats to the table. Wyva's stance of authority and disdain was undermined by the fact that Rinawne, Myv and Peredur already knew each other. Their friendship was deep because of what they'd jointly experienced, and they talked together freely. It was difficult for both Mossamber and Wyva to be stiff, formal and distrustful in the face of their obvious closeness. In fact, to be caustic and confrontational would merely have made them look stupid, like harlings spoiling for a fight.

The Whitemanes did not stay for the Wyvachi Reaptide rite, which would have been pushing things too far at this delicate stage. Wyva fought with wanting to forgive me and wanting to chastise and punish me. I could see he wavered between the desires to punch and hug me. Everyhar in Gwyllion knew that something momentous had happened, because the fallout from it had surged over them like the cloud of dust and smoke after an explosion. Everyhar had heard the bellow of the *ysbryd drwg*, whether in dreams or in reality.

The festival necessarily had to begin later than planned, because of the Wyvachi/Whitemane meeting, and by the time those of us from the Mynd reached The Crowned Stag, the crowd outside it was huge. I saw Yoslyn was present with his family, and noticed a clandestine kind of acknowledgement pass between him and Selyf, merely a gesture. The secret society of keephara, perhaps!

Wyva stood before the crowd and told them the truth, much as it must've galled him to do so. He explained that the Wyvachi and the Whitemanes had worked together to banish the *ysbryd drwg*. What hara might have heard last night was the roar of the entity as it perished. There was no longer a curse on Gwyllion. Myv, as its hienama, had been most instrumental in ending it. 'Was this curse real?' Wyva said, his voice clear and strong. He shrugged, gestured. 'Did we unwittingly create it ourselves, fear it, feed it, make it real? This we shall never truly know. But what we do know – and certainly – is that the strength of our combined will was enough to *unmake* it. This is a new era for us, and what more fitting time of year to celebrate this rebirth?' He raised a tankard. 'Astale, Verdiferel! Come to us now in your true form, a dehar of the season.' He drank.

Hara cheered. That was enough of the story for now, although later, no doubt after the Maes Siôl had been investigated, and hara had interpreted what remained of our fight, tales would begin to take root and grow. Such is the way of small communities, and it is also how legends are born. That day, most were simply amazed, and keen to discuss, the unexpected truce between the Wyvachi and the Whitemanes. But mainly they were united in praising Myv, which he withstood without showing too much embarrassment. From now on, they would believe him capable of anything.

There is a story to tell about the raising of the Gwyllion bell, but that does not belong here and is part of another story. There is a story to tell of Porter, and how the changes affected his life and allowed him openly to acknowledge Nytethorne as his father, and to become a har of note himself. There is a story to tell of Rey and how he came down from the mountains. But then, stories are ongoing, never-ending. There is never a point at which the tales just stop.

Wyva – some days after the festival when he decided I'd been punished enough and ceased being frosty with me – told me I'd achieved the impossible. Not in that I had single-handedly freed Gwyllion from its curse, because that wasn't the case: many of us had had a part to play. But Wyva insisted I was the true bridge between the feuding clans, and had smashed, with unwavering determination, that particular part of the affliction. I wasn't shy of taking credit for that, because from the start that had been my aim. The suspicion between the Whitemanes and the Wyvachi wouldn't end overnight, with everyhar becoming best friends, but the first approaches had been made, and I strongly believed the harlings of both families would be the ones to build upon the foundations. Wyva agreed with this, then laughed to himself. 'Will there come a day when we all celebrate the festivals together here in Gwyllion? Will Mossamber ever sit at my table as a friend?'

I reached out to squeeze Wyva's shoulder. 'Perhaps, if you are content to sit at his.'

Wyva grinned, shook his head. 'Well, I think we can safely say that stranger things have happened!'

As for Nytethorne and me, we made what might seem a strange choice. We didn't trust in convenient happy ever afters and didn't want to goad fate, so we decided to travel. Kyme would have other jobs for me, far shorter than the commission I'd taken and in fact had failed to complete. Before I left, I would give Myv as much assistance as he needed to finish the task I'd begun, but really the inventions for the wheel of the year should be his, as he was hienama now. Peredur and he would enjoy working together on that, weaving spectacular festivals for the hara of Gwyllion. I made arrangements with my good friend Huriel in Kyme – who I trusted – to give Myv distance instruction and visit him in person to perform caste ascensions. Until I returned.

Nytethorne and I wouldn't be gone forever; we knew that. But we needed to roam, to expand ourselves, not simply settle into a daily routine in Gwyllion. We had our own stories to explore.

Before we began our travels, I would return to Jesith to finish off my business there and hopefully create a new kind of relationship with my son. After that, we planned to meet up again in Kyme, see about work. Nytethorne was keen for us to seek out others who still suffered blights that derived from the dawn of our kind, whom we could help. The idea appealed to me too. We could discuss this with Huriel in Kyme. But we didn't want to leave Gwyllion immediately. We'd stay till Smoketide.

As this festival approached, a meeting of great importance was held. Not in the Domain, nor at Meadow Mynd, but at Harrow's End.

One bright yet cool Harvestmoon day, representatives of the Whitemanes and the Wyvachi crossed the county boundary and rode to Medoc's hall. Nytethorne and I were with them, as were all the hara of significance I'd met during my time in Gwyllion, even Peredur. I can recall the feeling of that day so well, the smell of the air, the sense of the season turning, Nytethorne riding at my side. In some moments, we truly understand what it is to be alive, and how we turn as the seasons turn, in cycles.

The spirits of the land are strong in Alba Sulh, but so are the spirits of its hara. I had made a new home in Gwyllion, had found myself there, and while I might be gone for some time I knew this: I would return. At the cusp of Natalia, when snow silvers the land, or at Feybraihatide when the land renews, I would ride once more along the ancient avenues to Meadow Mynd. There would be no wards on every door and lintel, no fear, no darkness, no secrets. Just the mystery of the natural world, which is the greatest mystery of all.

Weaving the Moonshawl

Author's Afterword

This book can be seen as the third in a trilogy about the hara of Alba Sulh, which began in 'The Hienama' and continued in 'Student of Kyme', both of which though are very different novels to the one now in your hands. 'The Moonshawl' is completely separate from the events in Jesith and Kyme, found in the first two books. In this story, the hienama Ysobi accepts a commission from Gwyllion – a town in what was formerly Wales – and travels there alone from Lyonis (formerly Cornwall). He's there to do a job, but finds a mystery to solve. There are ghosts – both out in the landscape and within him. He has a lot of exorcising to do.

At the end of 'Student of Kyme', Ysobi didn't come out of events – one of which nearly killed him – looking particularly good. Having left a trail of ruined lives in his wake, he appeared not to realise – or care – about the consequences of his emotional experiments. In the past, some of his students had been broken by his training, or perhaps even simple proximity to him. Yet he's not an incarnation of evil, or even someone who wants to hurt others. He himself is damaged. Yet unlike 'Student of Kyme', 'The Moonshawl' is not an agonising examination of emotional misery. This book is at its core a mystery, a ghost story. Ysobi's self-learning is a by-product.

How these Alba Sulh novels came about involves rather a story. Back in the early 2000's, before social media like Facebook existed, I belonged to several online groups that had been formed by fans of my work, Wraeththu in particular. I used to visit their chat room once a month or so, to answer questions and join in with discussions. During one of these chats, someone asked me what aruna – Wraeththu sex – was really like. Yes, I might describe it poetically in the books, and allude to reshaped genitalia, but somehow the *details* just weren't clear. Those nitty-gritty details. 'Do you want Wraeththu porn from me?' I asked jokingly. Perhaps inevitably, there was a clamouring cry of 'Yes!' So 'The Hienama' novella was written with this in mind – especially for the fans, and brought out as a Wraeththu curio by Immanion Press when the company was fairly new. I never intended 'The Hienama' to evolve into a trilogy.

Even though 'The Hienama' had initially been conceived to be pure erotica, darker elements and plot ideas inevitably crept in and made it a fully-rounded story. At the end of it, I wanted to know what happened next. This is what led me to write the much gloomier 'Student of Kyme', which is a story of the tragic consequences of obsession. In this novella, I also first began exploring the gulf between incepted Wraeththu and the second generation 'pureborns' and beyond. This was more than a simple age gap. While I was writing 'Student', I began to think about how the horror of the Devastation, as it was called – the first days of Wraeththu when humanity fell and the world burned – must have had catastrophic effects on hara. In most cases, inception itself had been harrowing and brutal, spawning little more than monsters, albeit beautiful ones. First generation hara, while now approaching what in human life-spans would have meant the certain approach of death, often carry within them legacies of their savage creation. They might try to hide this and live up to ideals promoted by advanced tribes like the Gelaming, but at heart many of them are still raw inceptees, dancing around a fire in the dark, with bloodied skin and feral eyes. For some, the past has thorns embedded so deeply in their psyches they can't be pulled.

'Student of Kyme' is a bitter story – the protagonist Gesaril's diary of events. I didn't find it pleasant to write, but that was the voice – and the tale – that needed to come out. Wraeththu's shadow self. Yet once it was done, I felt that the story was incomplete without Ysobi's narrative. All readers had seen so far were acrimonious accounts of what Ysobi had done to others. But I *knew* he wasn't bad. If anything, he was just plain unlucky and rather stupid. He was first generation: scarred.

'Student of Kyme' was published in 2011, but it wasn't until the start of 2013 that I began work on Ysobi's story. His voice simply didn't come to me until then. But once I started writing, I found I didn't want to immerse myself in Ysobi's past but in his future, his redemption. And then I saw Gwyllion in my mind, and knew the hara who lived there, and the legends of the landscape. And there was a ghost and a buried mystery. And more to tell about the early days of Wraeththu and their legacy. In relief – Ysobi's as much as mine – I could remove my main character from Jesith, away from his mistakes and the hara who judged him for them. He could start anew in the magical landscape of what humanity had called Wales, itself steeped in ancient mysteries and tales.

Apart from having wanted to write a ghost story of novel length for some time, I was also keen to explore the consequences of Wraeththu's beginnings, especially now that nearly a hundred years had passed. As Ysobi puts it in the story:

'I felt a hundred years old and then realised, with some amusement, I actually nearly was. I'd lost track of the years, because time is different for hara than it had been for humans; it is less of an enemy. Humans had experienced each day as a step nearer to the grave, in what had seemed like a fraction of time that flashed past in an instant. In contrast, Wraeththu have been given the gift of longevity, a friendship with time.'

In 'The Moonshawl' being referred to as 'first generation' is now considered somewhat impolite. Some hara even go so far as to disguise their origins. Again, using a quote from the book:

Gen took a breath. 'Rey is... Rey. He was never at home in a community, although he did his best. I'm sure he's happier now. He's first generation.'

'Oh.' I let the word hang darkly, with all its implications
of instability, weakness and perhaps madness.

Lacking Wraeththu longevity – more's the pity! – I'm now well
into middle age, the years flashing past in what seems like
weeks, and naturally the ageing process isn't something I can
ignore. There are so many benefits to being older – from a self
knowledge and acceptance point of view, as well as the
wisdom gained from accumulated experiences – but these gifts
are viciously countered by the failing of the body. Humans
never get *really* old. We begin to disintegrate and die before we
ever find out what having the wisdom of a hundred or two
hundred years, in a fit and healthy body, could be like. Hara
have this gift from time. When I first wrote about Wraeththu,
way back when I was still in my 20s, I didn't think about this
aspect of my created race. Now, it's of prime interest and
importance to me. And consequently, it's of interest and
importance to Ysobi.

But this isn't the main thrust of the novel, which is truly a
mystery, and I hope a riveting one. Ysobi's knowledge and
experience help him deal with that mystery and give him
strength.

'The Moonshawl' is also about story-telling and the potency
of legends. Nowadays, figures from Welsh myth, who were
kings, queens and sorcerers, are often regarded as gods and
goddesses, especially in Pagan beliefs. Humanity has shaped
them that way, and for some those figures are very real. The
human mind can shape reality to some degree, but how far
could that go if it was shaped by the minds of more powerful
beings? Could not the raw shout of thousands of years of war,
grief and treachery not be dragged from the very earth and
given form? And then, equally powerful artefacts must be
created to counter such entities. The moonshawl is such an
artefact, fragile and shimmering against the roar of the dark,
with only fragile beings of flesh and blood to vitalise its
symbolism.

'The Moonshawl' is three times the size of its predecessors and I enjoyed writing it immensely. While the places described in the story don't actually exist, the tower Dŵr Alarch, where Ysobi lives while in Gwyllion, was inspired by Brynkir Tower in Gwynedd, where I once stayed for a few days with some friends over a decade ago. We had some very peculiar experiences there! The tower is still available for hire, so if you should want to immerse yourself in the landscape of 'The Moonshawl' that is the place to go. There are a lot of pictures of it online, and it's easy to find the booking page. When I inspected the images, I was rather sad to see that the tiled floor has gone from the bathroom now and has been replaced by wood laminate. The whole place looks a lot smarter than it was when we stayed there, but I'm sure the atmosphere is unchanged. The houses Meadow Mynd, Deerlip Hall and Harrow's End are all made up, although they incorporate aspects of various old piles I've visited over the years. I have a fascination with big old houses, and this novel enabled me to indulge that interest completely.

Wraeththu have been with me since my teens, even if I didn't start writing about them seriously until I was 25, and they have evolved and changed as I have. There are now new aspects of them to explore, relevant to our human experience. Ysobi realises that what he goes through in Gwyllion might be found in similar situations elsewhere, where hara are tortured by the past, if not chained by it. He has a desire to seek out those tragedies, unearth their mysteries and restore balance. I already have an idea where he might be headed next!

Storm Constantine
November 2014

Appendix 1: Harish Names and Family Relationships

A Comparison with Human Terms

Hostling - mother
Father - sire
Harling – child
Brother – sibling
Hura – uncle/aunt
Hurakin – any hara who are siblings of the father or hostling, but sometimes used to denote all manner of family relationships within a group, i.e. 'relatives'.
Harakin – members of a family, sometimes including those not related by blood or chesna-bonds, but who nevertheless are close to the family.
Hura-brothers – an uncommon term for cousins
Surakin – other extended family relationships, used in the same way as hurakin sometimes is, but most often to denote a younger generation.
Sori or *Sura* - cousin, nephew, niece and all derivatives thereof (second cousin, etc.)
High-Father - grandfather
High-Hostling - grandmother
High-harling -grandchild
Grand High-Father/Hostling/Harling – great grand-father/mother/child. (Further generational distinctions simply add another 'grand' to the term.)

Harish Names

As Wraeththu became more established and a second generation of hara began to appear, many hara took on family names. Previously, a har would take for his surname, as identification, the name of his tribe, i.e. Ysobi har Sulh. But as communities and families formed and expanded, and relationships between phyles became more complicated, innovations came to names and titles.

To use hara in 'The Moonshawl' as examples of how names and epithets are formed, Wyva's full family name would be Wyva har Wyvachi har Gwyllion har Sulh – even though he is generally simply known locally as Wyva har Wyvachi. Sulh is the overarching tribal name of most hara living in the country of Alba Sulh; Gwyllion is the area in which Wyva lives; Wyvachi is the family or phyle name. Some hara, however, might elect only to take regional names, so if Wyva wished to keep his family/phyle identity private, he could offer his name to strangers as Wyva har Gwyllion, with or without the qualifying 'har Sulh', depending on how much he wished to reveal. Abroad, and still seeking a degree of anonymity, he might use the name Wyva har Sulh.

Hara of Ysobi's community in Jesith simply use the town name as a phyle name, so Ysobi might employ the title Ysobi har Jesith. His family of Jassenah, Zeph and himself have not taken on a private family name.

Some hara might use even more complicated tribal names, for there may be mini-phyles within a phyle or regional preferences. Ultimately, the purpose of surnames is to offer information to others – a har may reveal as much or as little of this as he prefers.

When hara become chesna, one of them will generally change

his name to match his partner's, depending on where they decide to settle and with which tribe and/or region they ally. Hara sometimes move from phyle to phyle, (or even swap tribes), and in these cases full names, giving all information about a har's heritage, would obviously be too cumbersome. In general, a har uses only the name of the tribe/phyle/family he currently lives among or identifies with most strongly, unless he has a good reason to make his lineage known.

Appendix 2
The Wheel of the Year – Arotohar

(Adapted from 'Grimoire Dehara: Kaimana)

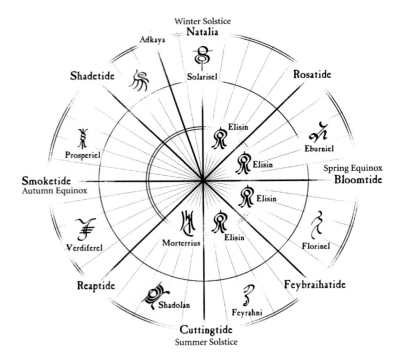

The harish spiritual wheel of the year follows the traditional pagan festivals, incorporating androgynous reinterpretations of the myths. The cycle is known as Arotohar, and the festivals associated with each significant date are Arojhahns (ah-roh-zharns). There is one extra min-festival (or majhahn – mah-zharn) of Adkaya two weeks before the winter solstice, when

the pearl of the dehar Elisin is delivered from his hostling.
Deities are referred to as dehara. The principle elemental dehara of Wraeththu are Aruhani (earth), Lunil (water), Agave (fire) and Miyacala (air). The Aghama represents the fifth element of Spirit. Separate dehara, with their own mythology, populate the wheel of Arotohar.

Natalia - December 21st

This is the arojhahn of the Winter Solstice, the longest night of the year. At this time, the dehar Elisin emerges from the pearl that nurtured him. The pearl was dropped two weeks previously, and now the deharling comes forth from it. He represents the reawakening of nature and the return of the sun. This is the new year of Dehara.

Solarisel, the deharling's hostling, is a benevolent dehar of great beauty, dressed in gold and white, with a mane of golden hair. He grants the gift of a light heart, of fortune, promise and opportunity. He is the dehar of abundance, whose cauldron of creation offers up the ultimate potential. His is the arojhahn of the new sun. His plants are the holly, the ivy and the pine. He is accompanied by sleek white hounds, who at the moment of the deharling's emergence, fly through the sky yelping out the news. To hear the hounds of Solarisel on the solstice night is a fortuitous omen for the coming year.

The deharling is named Elisin, the child of light. He retains this name until the moment of his hostling/lover's death at Cuttingtide.

Rosatide - February 1st

This arojhahn is named for the fact that the trees become rosy with new growth at this time. The last grey white days of winter are marked by the colour of blood as life begins to rise and surge from the earth.

Elisin is now beginning to grow and his hostling has transformed from his soume or female aspect into Eburniel, the white dehar of the snow-covered earth. All early spring flowers, especially those with white petals, are sacred to him. He has nurtured Elisin, borne him from his body and now devotes himself to teaching the deharling the lessons necessary to maturity and eventual solitude. Eburniel teaches Elisin how to imbue the earth with his life-giving energy to encourage new growth.

Traditionally, this is the Arojhahn of Torches, when hara seek to bring the growing light of the sun into their life. Eburniel is also the light of the candle flame. On Rosatide eve, candles and lamps are lit in every window. The shadowy figure of Eburniel, dressed in a cloak of snow white fur, walks across the fields. His animal is the white wolf, whose breath is freezing mist.

The wistfulness sometimes associated with this arojhahn derives from the fact that, in assuming a more masculine aspect, Eburniel faces the prospect of his own death at Cuttingtide. If the early spring flowers are found sprouting from snow, they are Eburniel's tears. Despite this aspect, Rosatide is a time of hope and promise. As light fills hara's homes, so they banish the bleakness of the short days and cold weather.

Bloomtide - March 21st

This arojhahn marks the Spring Equinox. The ascetic Eburniel transforms into the dashing Florinel, who begins to woo the maturing Elisin. Elisin's hostling has now transformed into his potential lover and is no longer regarded as a blood relative, but rather a separate dehar that has grown from the substance of Solarisel. Eburniel is seen as a lissom young dehar, dressed in green with nut-brown hair. Florinel conjures flowers to open with the sound of his voice, which is the music heard in the wind, in spring rains and in the surge of swollen streams as the snow melts. His animal is the white hare. Florinel is a trickster who can sometimes deceive. He leads the unwary into dangerous territory, but can also bestow a change of luck for the better.

Florinel is far too full of life to contemplate such dreary concepts as his own demise. He presides over planting and the reproduction of animals. Elisin is coy and rejects his advances. The only contact Florinel can have with Elisin at this time is to cover his sleeping body with white blossom.

While Florinel's thoughts begin to turn to aruna, Elisin is entranced by the wonder of being alive. His is the unbounded joy of youth, as yet untarnished by adult cares. Bloomtide is the celebration of life for its own sake. On the arojhahn night, hara put aside fears and uncertainties and focus on hopes for the future. The light hangs in equal balance, but only for a short time. From this night on, the days lengthen and the air becomes warmer.

Feybraihatide - April 30th/May 1st

This arojhahn is named for the rite of passage harlings undergo as they enter maturity. It is the feast of aruna, of first love and the deep, spiritual passion that enables harlings to be conceived.

Elisin now is full grown, a vision of beauty, like a radiant form of his Shadetide hostling, with fiery red hair. His consort is Feyrahni, but this is properly Elisin's arojhahn, as he is regarded as the presiding dehar. He and Florinel have barely seen one another since Bloomtide, and now – transformed – it is Feyrahni not Florinel who steps from the forest, dark of skin and hair, dressed in clothes made of leather and leaves. His sacred animal is the stag. On Feybraihatide eve, Feyrahni initiates Elisin into the mysteries of aruna and together they create a pearl.

Cuttingtide - 21st June

This is the Summer Solstice, the moment when the sun begins to decline in strength as it moves away from the earth. Feyrahni becomes the lord of the corn, the sacrificed one, Morterrius. He is at the height of his potency, and therefore in surrendering his life force at this time, the strongest energy enters the earth.

Elisin, now with pearl, sheds his youthful name and becomes Shadolan, the hunter, the executioner. Gone are the cares of youth. The sacred animal of the dehara is the hawk.

Morterrius appears as the golden dehar of the corn, with yellow hair. He wears a crown of barley and poppies and is dressed in red and yellow, symbolising the crop and his own blood. Shadolan has a darker aspect, dressed as an archetypal hunter. His beauty is fearsome, his gaze compelling.

On the arojhahn eve, Morterrius walks the fields as a willing sacrifice. In sorrow, Shadolan must take his consort's life. In a grim repetition of Feybraihatide, the lovers meet in a wild place and take aruna together. But its conclusion this time is death. Shadolan's fingernails have become blades that make a thousand cuts in Morterrius' flesh. The dehar stumbles from their trysting place and as he staggers through the fields, so his blood flows down to fertilise the earth. He eventually falls to the ground, which swallows him up, dragging the dehar's body down into itself, so he begins his long journey to the Eternal Plains, the World Beyond, from where he will eventually be reborn as his own son.

Reaptide - August 1st

Like Shadetide, this is a time when unusual events are likely to occur. Apparitions can be seen in the fields at mid-day. The landscape holds its breath and the hills become haunted. Shadolan becomes the Field Walker, Verdiferel, wandering in solitude through the ripening crops. His hair is dark and he wears garments of earthen colours, decorated with leaves, flowers and heads of wheat. His sacred creature is the white owl, which sweeps through the spectral night and even appears during the day at this time.

Verdiferel, like some of the other seasonal dehara, has a trickster aspect.

One story concerns a har who came upon Verdiferel in a cornfield, apparently making a crop circle. As the har concealed himself and observed, he noticed that the dehar appeared strange, and somewhat unhinged. Verdiferel made decorative talismans from the crop, which he hid around the landscape, in trees and beneath rocks. The observing har knew that these talismans were hidden for hara to find, and that an audience with Verdiferel could be sought this way. He considered himself fortunate to have witnessed where Verdiferel had concealed the talismans. He took a talisman to a sacred site, which comprised two upright stones supporting a vast slab. Verdiferel was already present in this place, and said he knew the har had come to enquire about his future. He told the har to lie down on the slab. Verdiferel then produced a sickle blade and sliced the har open. He read the future from the entrails. With somewhat dark humour, he said, 'I see you're about to go on a long journey into the otherworld'. He then collected the blood and made a libation in the crop fields. This story suggests that the rehuna should employ caution when asking boons of Verdiferel.

Another story concerning this dehar relates that Verdiferel might appear to a har as emerging from the trunk of a tree. He has very long brown hair that comes out of the bark as peculiar strands, and while not as dangerous as other forms of Verdiferel, is extremely haughty. He carries a green orb of light, which is called ozaril. It is said that if the invocation 'Astale ozaril' is chanted, then the light of the dehar goes into a har, enabling him to see the ghosts that walk at noon.

Smoketide - September 21st

This is the autumn equinox and the major harvest arojhahn. The dehar transforms into Prosperiel. He is already a hostling, and in that way fecund. At this time, he appears dressed in garments adorned with autumnal leaves and fruits, and he smells of smoke. He also wears a cloak of fox fur. His sacred animal now is the red fox.

Prosperiel, of all the dehara of this half of the year, is the least tricky. Gone are the shadowy aspects of Cuttingtide and Reaptide. He is the expression of fruitfulness, and this is the time of year for hara to make plans for the future, to plant their own seeds of intention that will come to fruit in the New Year.

Shadetide - October 31st

This is the last of the harvest arojhahns, and traditionally a time when the portals between different levels of reality become unstable. It is the time when the veil is thin and discarnate entities can make contact with the living.

At this stage, the dehar transforms into Lachrymide (La-CRIM-ee-day) the Keener. Heavy with pearl and alone, Lachrymide stalks the bare earth. In nature, he can be unpredictable. His tears bring floods and the coldness of his heart brings snow. Only at his arojhahn time does he really show any lighter side, and that is when, compassionate with his own sense of loss, he leads lost souls to the light. It is a night of trickery and feasting, of carnival and costume. Lachrymide is one of the most intimidating and fearsome of the seasonal dehara, but he is appeased by merriment and feasting.

Lachrymide can be petitioned to give glimpses of the future or news of lost loved ones. After being invoked, he appears at the threshold as a tall har dressed in black with long red hair. Often, his face is veiled.

As Lachrymide presides over the dark weeks between Shadetide and the solstice, he is asked to provide warmth, food and shelter, to keep animals healthy through the cold months and to preserve the stored grain. His animal is the black cat, cats being invaluable in guarding grain stores from rats and other vermin. Often, during his reign, tall dark figures are spotted in the fields or at crossroads, or beside lonely tracks. If a har comes across Lachrymide in the dark, they should offer him a gift. If he is pleased with it, he will grant them fortune.

Adkaya - December 7th

This majhahn, (a minor festival), two weeks before Natalia, is not one of the major arojhahns, but still an important part of the seasonal calendar. Adkaya observes the time when the dehar

Lachrymide drops the pearl of the deharling and transforms into Solarisel, who will be the presiding dehar of Natalia. The pearl of the deharling takes two weeks to mature before opening, so hara use this time to perform majhahns associated with planning and preparation.

Characters

Hara of Jesith
Jassenah – Ysobi's chesnari
Ysobi – a hienama of the town, who is sent to Gwyllion to work for Wyva har Wyvachi
Zephyrus – Ysobi and Jassenah's son

The Wyvachi
Barly – a househar of the Wyvachi
Briar – head stablehar of the Wyvachi family
Cawr – brother to Wyva
Dillory – the Wyvachi family's cook
Fush – a member of the Wyvachi's househara staff
Gen – brother to Wyva
Modryn – chesnari of Cawr
Myvyen – son of Wyva and Rinawne
Porter har Goudy – son of Rey, the Wyvachi's departed hienama
Rey har Goudy – hienama of the Wyvachi who left the community before Ysobi's arrival
Rinawne – chesnari of Wyva, originally from Erini, father of Myvyen
Wyva – phylarch of the Wyvachi in Gwyllion, hostling of Myvyen, chesnari of Rinawne

Historical Wyvachi
Arynne – hienama of the original Wyvachi family
Kinnard – Wyva's hostling
Peredur – Hura to Wyva
Yvainte – Wyva's father

The Wyverns
Beiryan – a cousin of Medoc, who left Meadow Mynd with him
Caerwyn – a cousin of Medoc, who left Meadow Mynd with him
Edryd – a cousin of Medoc, who left Meadow Mynd with him
Medoc – Hura to Wyva, phylarch of the Wyverns
Meilyr – a cousin of Medoc, who left Meadow Mynd with him
Persys – son of Wenyf
Thraine – chesnari of Medoc
Wenyf – son of Medoc and Thraine, hienama of the Wyverns
Ysgaw – son of Medoc and Thraine

The Whitemanes
Mossamber – phylarch, hostling of Nytethorne and Emberflax
Nytethorne – son of Mossamber, hostling of Ember
Emberstrife (or Ember) – son of Nytethorne
Emberflax – son of Mossamber

Hara of Gwyllion
Ludda – a farmer, who keeps the farm below Dŵr Alarch where Mossamber's hunting hounds are kennelled.
Selyf – Member of the Gwyllion Assembly and keephar of The Crowned Stag
Tryskyr – a farmer/landowner, member of the Gwyllion Assembly
Yoslyn – keephar of The Rooting Boar

Other Hara Mentioned in the Story
Bronna – phylarch of Rinawne's phyle when he lived in Erini
Flick har Roselane – a har who first created the harish version of the spiritual Wheel of the Year
Gadda – a friend of Rinawne from his harlinghood in Erini
Gesaril – a former lover of Ysobi, now living in Immanion
Huriel – a friend of Ysobi's living in Kyme
Malakess – an early commander in Alba Sulh, who became High Codexia of Kyme

Pellaz – Tigron of Immanion
Thiede – the first har

Human Ancestors
The Wyverns
Vivyen or Vivi, matriarch of the family
Arianne, wife of Tobias, born of the Mantel family
Erling – son of Vivi
Gwyven – son of Arianne
Peredur – son of Arianne
Kinnard – son of Arianne
Medoc – son of Arianne
Tobias – son of Vivi, husband of Arianne
Vere - son of Vivi

The Mantels
Thorne – patriarch of the Mantels
Bryce – son of Thorne (who became Mossamber post inception)

Places

Alba Sulh – the country that was formerly England
Almagabra – equating to Greece in the old human world, the country that is home to the Gelaming, most influential of Wraeththu tribes
Deerlip Hall – original name of the Whitemane domain
The Domain – home of the Whitemanes in Gwyllion
Dôl Cartref – the Home Meadow, close to Meadow Mynd
Dŵr Alarch – the Swan Tower, where Ysobi lives while in Gwyllion
Erini – Island to the west of Alba Sulh, formerly Ireland
Gwyllion – a town in what was formerly North Wales, owned by the Wyvachi
Harrow's End – domain of the Wyverns
Hiyenton – the nearest large market town to Gwyllion
Immanion – capital of Almagabra, principle town of the Gelaming tribe, who are the most influential among Wraeththu. Corresponds to the old country of Greece.
Kyme – a town in northern Alba Sulh, famed seat of learning
Llwybr Llwynog – The Fox Run (or Path), a wooded hill on Wyvachi land
Maes Siôl – the Shawl Field
Meadow Mynd – domain of the Wyvachi in Gwyllion
Afon Siôl Lleuad – The River Moonshawl
Pwll Siôl Lleuad – the Moonshawl Pool
Yorvik – a town in northern Alba Sulh, formerly York

Glossary of Terms

Althaia – the process and period of change from human to har following inception

Arojhahn – a season festival, the ritual to celebrate it.

Arotohar – the name give to the Wheel of the Year, the annual cycle of eight seasonal festivals.

Aruna – sexual union between hara that is both spiritual and physical.

Astale – (ass-tar-lay) a ritual word of invitation and welcome, also a term of respect, most often used to greet invoked dehara.

Carehar – a har designated to care for a harling who is not a parent

Chesna – (chez-nah) a close relationship, a chesna-bond can be equated to marriage

Chesnari – a partner in a chesna-bond

Daghda – In Erini, 'the good god', he is seen as the father and protector of a tribe in that country.

Dehar – a Wraeththu deity (pl. Dehara)

Devastation, the – one of many terms used to describe the final days of humanity, when the world was in turmoil, and there was catastrophic conflict between hara and humans. The days of change.

Egregore – an occult concept representing a 'thoughtform' or 'collective group mind', an autonomous psychic entity made up of, and influencing, the thoughts of a group of people.

Erinish – a har of Erini, formerly Ireland.

Feybraiha – a period of time equating to puberty in humans when a har matures sexually. The term also refers to a day of celebration for this. At the end of his feybraiha, when he is physically ready, a har will take aruna with another for the first time. This is regarded as an important rite of passage.

First Generation – hara who were became Wraeththu by being

446

incepted as humans

Gelaming – the most influential tribe of Wraeththu, whose tribal home is Almagabra

Har – a Wraeththu individual

Harakin – a term used by a har to describe members of his family

Harling – a young har not yet at feybraiha

Hienama – equivalent of a priest/teacher/healer

Househar – a member of the household staff

Hurakin - relatives

Inception – the process by which a human becomes har, involving a transfusion of blood.

Keephar – an innkeeper/landlord

Majhahn – a ritual

Nayati – a temple or sacred space for spiritual work

Ouana – the masculine aspect of Wraeththu

Phylarch – leader of a phyle

Phyle – a distinct community within a tribe, a sub tribe

Pothar – har employed in an inn

Pureborn – a har who has been born to harish parents rather than inception from human. A second-generation har and beyond.

Nahir Nuri – a har of high spiritual rank, who has undergone all caste training.

Soume – the feminine aspect of Wraeththu

Tiahaar – a polite form of address (as in Sir, Madam)

Tigron – ruler of Wraeththu in Immanion

Wraeththu – (ray-thoo) androgynous race that came to replace humanity

Glossary of Welsh Terms and Phrases

Dôl Cartref – Home Meadow
Dŵr Alarch – Swan Tower
Gadael, ysbryd aflan! – Be gone, foul spirit!
Craig Drygioni – Mischief Rock
Gwerin Crwydrwyr - Roamer Folk
Llwybr Llwynog – Fox Run (the fox path)
Maes Siôl – Shawl Field
Pwll Siôl Lleuad – Moonshawl Pool
Siôl lleuad – Moonshawl
Afon Siôl Lleuad – River Moonshawl
Yn dod yn dda! – become well or good
Ysbryd garedig – a good spirit (pl. *Ysbryddon garedig*)
Ysbryd drwg – an evil spirit

About the Author

Storm is the creator of the Wraeththu Mythos, the first trilogy of which was published in the 1980s. However, the influences and inspirations for the Wraeththu world go much further back than that, and continue into the future as she plans more stories for it.

Her other full length works cross genres from science fiction, to dark fantasy, to epic fantasy, to slipstream. She has written over thirty books, including full length novels, novellas, short story collections and non-fiction titles.

Storm is the founder of Immanion Press, created initially to publish her out-of-print back catalogue, but which evolved into the thriving venture it is today. Her interests include magic and spirituality, Reiki, movies, music and MMOs. Among her many occupations, most of which are unpaid, she runs a Reiki school and a guild called Equilibrium on the EU servers of World of Warcraft. She lives in the Midlands of the UK.

Other Stories of Alba Sulh from Storm Constantine

The Hienama

£9.99 $19.99; ISBN: 9781904853626

When Jassenah arrives in Jesith to train magically with the famous hienama Ysobi, he's unprepared for the effect this har will have on him. Ysobi opens Jassenah's mind to the potential that hara can reach for and, in doing so, also opens his heart. Just as it seems Jassenah has achieved his heart's desire, a new student arrives, in the form of Gesaril, a damaged young creature with mysteries lurking in his past. The magic of both the unseen world and that of harish emotions conspire to destroy Jassenah's idyllic life, until he feels he's forced to stoop to equally cruel methods to salvage his happiness. But at what cost?

The Hienama is a rich and deeply erotic tale of the Wraeththu, set in the magical land of Alba Sulh

Student of Kyme

A Sequel to 'The Hienama'.

£10.99, $20.99; ISBN: 9781904853411

In a powerful story of obsession, betrayal and doomed love, Gesaril has been shamed and cast out of Jesith, after an inappropriate affair with his hienama, Ysobi. Ysobi's reputation was at stake, so Gesaril was made the scapegoat. Taken in by Huriel Har Kyme, a codexia of the famed Alba Sulh academy, Gesaril vows to begin his life anew in the Wraeththu city of learning. He is determined to put the past and its ghosts behind him, to restore his name and prove to hara he is not what Ysobi painted him to be. But sometimes the past will not lie quietly in its grave, and Gesaril soon learns he must confront the restless ghosts and fight them. If he is to retain his sanity and his hard won new life, Gesaril must win this bitter war alone, with magic dark and light.

NewCon Press

http://newconpress.co.uk/

The very best in fantasy, science fiction, and horror

Colder Greyer Stones by Tanith Lee

Released to commemorate the author being honoured with a Lifetime Achievement Award at the 2013 World Fantasy Convention, this stunning collection of stories provides further evidence of why Tanith Lee is held in such high regard by fans and contemporaries alike. The book features twelve wonderful, rich-textured tales including the brand new novelette "The Frost Watcher" and five stories previously available only in the (sold out) signed limited edition "Cold Grey Stones".

Paperback: ISBN 978-1-907069-60-4   £9.99

The Moon King by Neil Williamson

"Beautifully written and thoughtful… one of the best debuts of this or any other year." – *Jeff Vandermeer*

"The Moon King is literary fantasy at its best." – *The Guardian*

Life under the moon has always been predictable: day follows night, wax phases to wane and, after the despair of every Darkday, a person's mood soars to euphoria at Full. So it has been for the five hundred years since Glassholm was founded, but now all that has changed. Amidst rumours of unsettling dreams and strange whispering children, society is disintegrating into unrest and violence. Three people find themselves at the eye of the storm: a former policeman investigating a series of macabre murders, an artist embroiled in the intrigues of revolution, and a renegade engineer tasked with fixing the ancient machine at the city's heart…

Paperback: ISBN 978-1-907069-62-8   £12.99

Immanion Press Titles by Tanith Lee
The Colouring Book Series

Greyglass 9781907737046 £10.99

The house... always growing, adding to itself, blooming, decaying, becoming reborn... But Susan doesn't live in the house of Catherine, her grandmother. When Catherine dies, no one mourns. The house is always changing. As if at last it must achieve some irresistible transformation. Frankly, there is something *uncanny* about the house. Isn't there.

To Indigo 9781907737213 £11.99

Don't talk to strangers. Don't even look at them. Novelist Roy Phipps leads an uneventful existence in the house inherited from his parents. His only aberration is the story he's been secretively writing for years of the mad poet Vilmos, a study of murder, angst and alchemic magic. Then one evening Roy meets Vilmos, face to face. As shadows close in on him, Roy understands he's now fighting for his own sanity. And probably his life.

L'Amber 9781907737251 £11.99

Jay has very little. Jilaine Best has everything. But even Jilane's perfect life is flawed, longing for the baby she's unable to conceive. She's willing to let another woman give birth for her. And so Jay confesses she is already pregnant with an unwanted child. Lies are so easy to tell, if you've had enough practice. Harder to change into truth. Spin your web. Watch it tangle. Now see what you've caught.

Killing Violets 9781907737367 £10.99

1934... Starving to death somewhere in Europe, Anna meets Raoul, who takes her to England and the dubious mansion of his arrogant and unsavoury relatives, the Basultes. Anna is a survivor. Both the aristocratic malignities, and the Hogarthian orgies of the servants, can be accommodated, if they must. Anna has a past as savage and explicit as anything seen in the Basulte house.

Ivoria 9781907737404 £11.99

Nick Lewis certainly has no liking for his TV historian brother, Laurence. Aside from anything else Nick blames him for the death of their mother, the beautiful actress Claudia Martin. And so, is it possible the off-handedly childish trick played by Nick on Laurence really does cast some kind of curse? This is probably *not* a supernatural story. It might be less unsettling if it was.

Cruel Pink 9781907737497 £11.99

Emenie, a serial killer, lives alone. She can read omens and knows exactly her legitimate prey. Rod has a dreary life, working at an unrewarding job with something uneasy hanging over him. Is it the wardrobe? Klova is young, beautiful, living on benign handouts, in a Science Fantasy existence of sprints and liquid-silver...Until she meets the challenging Coal. Here, at the outskirts of this City they all call London, what the Hell is going on?

Turquoiselle 9781907737596 £11.99

Not much is what it seems. The job can be dull, but quite demanding. The work is lucrative, however. He can easily afford the costly wants of Donna, his partner. It's just that suddenly things are running less smoothly. This stuff with Donna... Various unusual tensions at work... the bizarre and threatening business over Silvia... In the end, maybe all you can rely on is yourself.

Lightning Source UK Ltd.
Milton Keynes UK
UKOW02f0840300115

245393UK00002B/29/P